NOT WET YET

(I GOTTA GO V. 2.00)

AN ANTHOLOGY OF COMMENTARY (1982–1996)

IAN SHOALES

DESIGN: **ENDLESS** ∞

2.13.61
P.O. BOX 1910 · LOS ANGELES ·
CALIFORNIA · 90078 · USA

ISBN 1-880985-45-4

2.13.61 Publications, Inc.
P.O. Box 1910
Los Angeles, CA 90078

Printed in the United States of America

Other books from 2.13.61:

HENRY ROLLINS / The First Five
HENRY ROLLINS / Black Coffee Blues
HENRY ROLLINS / Get In The Van
HENRY ROLLINS / See A Grown Man Cry & Now Watch Him Die
HENRY ROLLINS / Eye Scream
HENRY ROLLINS / Do I Come Here Often?
JOE COLE / Planet Joe
DON BAJEMA / Reach
DON BAJEMA / Boy In The Air
BILL SHIELDS / Human Shrapnel
BILL SHIELDS / The Southeast Asian Book Of The Dead
BILL SHIELDS / Lifetaker
EXENE CERVENKA / Virtual Unreality
EXENE CERVENKA & KEN JARECKE / Just Another War
IGGY POP / I Need More
TRICIA WARDEN / Brainlift
TRICIA WARDEN / Attack God Inside
MICHAEL GIRA / The Consumer
ROB OVERTON / Letters To Rollins
NICK CAVE / King Ink
NICK CAVE / King Ink II
NICK CAVE & THE BAD SEEDS / Fish In A Barrel
ALAN VEGA / Cripple Nation
ROSS HALFIN / Fragile: Human Organs
ROSS HALFIN / Metallica: The Photographs of Ross Halfin
STEPHANIE CHERNIKOWSKI / Dream Baby Dream
THE PHOTOGRAPHER'S LED ZEPPELIN
GLEN E. FRIEDMAN / Fuck You Heroes
ROKY ERICKSON / Openers II
JOE CARDUCCI / Rock & the Pop Narcotic
NICK ZEDD / Totem Of The Depraved
HENRY MILLER / Dear Dear Brenda
NATALIE JACOBSON / No Forwarding Address

INTRODUCTION

This book represents fifteen-plus years of cultural sniping, and a career so checkered it can cause hallucinations if glimpsed too closely. I'd like to thank Henry Rollins *et al* for the opportunity to gather a bundle of diatribes between two covers and on a compact disc. Major thanks also to Deirdre O'Donoghue for putting us together.

Some of these pieces, or variations thereof, have aired on National Public Radio's MORNING EDITION and ALL THINGS CONSIDERED; regionally, I have been heard performing a fast-paced but largely comprehensible oral interpretation of some of these on public radio stations KCRW-FM (Santa Monica, California) and KQED-FM (San Francisco). I can still be heard on those stations by the way; even though they don't pay me anything, the cheap bastards, I'm grateful for the attention.

Some of these pieces were captured on video for ABC's NIGHTLINE and WORLD NEWS NOW. I'm also on the world wide web, of course: Check out *salon1999.com* with your powerful search engine.

Printwise they've appeared in the SAN FRANCISCO EXAMINER, both on its op/ed page and in IMAGE, the EXAMINER's now-defunct Sunday Magazine. They've also appeared in CALIFORNIA Magazine, where my editor once told me that the staff didn't hate my stuff as much as other stuff that appeared there. Then the magazine folded. (Connection? Think about it.)

Some have also appeared in the pages of the NEW YORK TIMES, the LA TIMES, the MINNEAPOLIS TRIBUNE, USA TODAY, the late beloved (or behated?) NOSE Magazine, and through United Features Syndicate (thank you!), once a week in a newspaper near you, if it felt like printing it.

In random order, thanks also to FUNNY TIMES, Steve Baker, Mary Kessler for years of love, Susan Pedrick and her salamanders, Robert Levy (and the tech support folks at United Features Syndicate), Dad & Mom, David Talbot, Gary Kamiya, J. Raoul Brody, Jack Boulware, Stephanie Weisman and the MARSH, the Balogna Boys (princes!), Tammy Angelique Rydell (*cara mia!*), The Movie Channel, Dave & Mimi & Ellen, the Whole Sick Crew in fact (you know who you are), Big

Chico Creek and all it represents, Duck's Breath Mystery Theatre, Monte Carlos and Howard Gelman, KQED, KCRW, Sedge Thomson and the whole WEST COAST ensemble, the former Ruth Hirschmann, Jon Winokur, Harry Shearer, the very fine folks at Sega of America (especially Dave Albert and Barry Blum, who saved my sorry ass from the poorhouse) and my readers and listeners.

So go ahead, open this sucker up, have a few laffs.

A disclaimer:

Some of you may complain that this is just a repackaging of material that appeared in my first collection, I GOTTA GO, spiced up with more outmoded commentary on people and events that have come and gone.

To which I reply, "Okay, what's your point?" Lighten up! Go easy on yourself: think of this collection as a *time capsule,* a bold portrait of an era!

As a sop to your sensibilities, I have included what we in the commentary game call *evergreens* (Madonna, movies, politics, you know)—each essay a deeply-felt, thoughtful exploration of our deepest eternal desires.

For your convenience and protection, and in *lieu* of an actual structure, the contents have been entirely alphabetized.

— Ian Shoales

A

ACCESS

This noun, like the noun, "impact," is now a verb. I want to access my feelings on this, but I can't, except to say, "It impacts my emotional area," and let it go at that.

ACCORD

Use only with "reach." A tentative agreement between nations. Some accords used to become pacts, but this was before the fall of Marxism.

ACCORDINGLY

When writing an editorial, always use "accordingly" instead of "so."

ACCOUNTING, CREATIVE

Underrated art form.

ACCULTURATION

What new immigrants must achieve in order to gain approval from old ones.

ACLU | 1985

In a moment of weakness several years ago I signed a petition demanding that somebody stop doing something or other. Ever since then I've received solicitations from every political stripe there is.

I usually throw the things away as soon as they cross the mail slot, but I got one from the American Civil Liberties Union this summer which began, "Dear friend, it is late at night. I'm tired and my burning eyes are telling me it's time to quit.... But before going home, I wanted to write to you and ask for your help. Frankly, I'm feeling a bit scared right now..."

Then he spent three pages on his sales pitch, urging me to give money to the ACLU so it can continue to defend the Bill of Rights.

Well, I'm worried about the Bill of Rights, sure, but I'm more worried about you, Ira. (Can I call you Ira, since you called me "friend?") I'd say you've got bigger problems than our rights, if I can be as frank with you as you were with me.

The first thing you tell me is it's late at night and you're tired. Well, listen, if this letter to me is so important, why didn't you wait until morning to write it, when you're refreshed and thinking clearly?

Why did you want to share your exhaustion with me? I was tired when I read your letter too, but I don't see what that's got to do with anything.

Not only are you overtired, you're "scared" of an "ominous new mood in America."

You shouldn't be scared of Republicans, Ira, you should take a tip from them. They go to bed at night. They don't stay up till the wee hours writing desperate letters to strangers.

You're so tired and scared you're punchy, or you wouldn't have written to me in the first place. I only have twenty bucks in my checking account. Even if I did have large sums of money, why should I send it to a frightened man who doesn't know when to call it quits for the night?

Before you collapse from nervous exhaustion, take what reserve of energy you have left, and send a letter to the Fortune 500. They have bucks. But don't blow it by telling them how tired you are. They don't want to hear it. Write, "Dear friend, it's six a.m. and I'm raring to go. The early bird gets the worm! Please send money."

You have to use basic sales techniques. Think positive.

I'm sending you a check for five bucks (please don't cash it until September) and a bag of herbal tea. Make yourself a nice cup and then take a nap. The Bill of Rights will probably still be there when you wake up. You can't keep burning the defender's candle at both ends. Go lie down. I don't want you falling asleep in the courtroom while some well-rested right-wing yahoo rides roughshod over my freedom of speech. Say good night Ira.

ACTING OUT

What the New Age says you're really doing when you get pissed off.

ACTION FIGURE

Term coined by advertisers to get boys to buy dolls.

AD HOC

Committee which issues a report repressing the truth it was assembled to reveal.

ADULTERY 1992

In response to the rumors of Bill Clinton's dalliance with Gennifer Flowers, Belgian legislator Jean-Pierre Detremerie was quoted in NEWSWEEK: "In Europe, extramarital affairs are considered a sign of good health, a feat." Mme Detremerie's views on Jean-Pierre were not recorded.

Even so, the difference between Old World and New World attitudes is obvious. Adultery in the USA leads to divorce, therapy, and Woody Allen movies. On the Continent, adultery is just a Gallic romp. I suppose if you're a social liberal trying to work up a sweat, adultery beats jogging, but it just goes to show what a couple world wars on your soil will do to your priorities.

Still, we must be honest. Americans have mixed feelings about adultery. The Judeo-Christian tradition frowns on it (see Ten Commandments for details), yet operas thrive on it. It can ruin a political career, yet provide plot ingredients for Joan Crawford movies. In pop culture, adultery is ubiquitous. As a kid I formed the impression, based on what I saw on television, that Los Angeles was an infinity of sleazy apartment buildings and dingy motels, populated by blackmailing babes, extortionist gigolos, and bigamist smoothies.

No wonder Perry Mason never married Della. What chance would a serious relationship have had in that environment? And vacations?

Forget about it. Whenever poor Perry tried to go fishing, there was always some two-timing embezzler spoiling his fun by framing an amnesiac. Stoic Perry would pack his lures, and return to the City of Angels, where swindlers are thick as trout.

But it still looked pretty good to me. Throw in Disneyland, and you really had a package with appeal for a chaste North Dakota lad. Compare the LA of yesteryear to the picture we get on television today—roving armed gangs, brutal cops, mountains of mud, and torrents of raw sewage pouring into the Pacific—a sundappled haven for adulterers doesn't sound bad, does it?

Personally, I've always hankered for adultery in Los Angeles: a torrid guilt-ridden affair with an outwardly staunch inwardly lithe Republican woman, married to a banker. We'd meet in a Beverly Hills suite, noonish, throw our sunglasses on the chaise, and heave ourselves at each other, genuine pearls flying around the room, the only sound her whispered, "We've got to stop meeting like this."

Or I could be a lawyer too smart for his own good, taking up with the bitter beauty married to my client, the real estate mogul. Oooh, I can just hear her growl, "Come kiss me, counselor." Sometimes I wish I'd gone to law school, just so attractive women could call me "counselor." I love it when a woman growls, "counselor."

Among more morbid erotic options: I could take up with a frightened bride, and snatch her away from her cruel mobster spouse. We'd have three months of bliss before unsmiling gunmen found us in Mexico. Worth it? You bet!

Or I'd get seduced by some femme fatale, who either wants me to kill her husband for the insurance money, or the money from the armored car job. Wow! Cheap sex, duplicity, and a stab in the back. Glamorous!

If I don't want to die after my fling, there's always the languid affair with the world-weary countess option. She'll cut me loose the moment I start to show enthusiasm, causing me to become a brooding presence in small cafes, a Byronic figure of enormous appeal to young American debutantes, none of whom can melt the icicle that is my heart, though I let them all try.

So many adultery options! Dozens of neglected wives, kept women, and Madame Bovaries to choose from. And thousands of attitudes, from anomie to hopeless yearning, perhaps even all the way to zeal.

And yet, adulterers in real life are hard to find. Real-life adultery is bad sex and bitter separations, while the predatory media scan the horizon for scandals. Who needs that kind of scrutiny? That's why so many modern marrieds would rather rent DANGEROUS LIAISONS, than have one. Singles too. Americans everywhere are taking a closer look at the sex life of Perry Mason. What a role model! Perry Mason won that case too. He proved that abstention can be hip.

ALPHABET

Just because a bunch of Phoenician bean-counters wanted to scratch their thoughts onto papyrus thousands of years ago, must we cling to their outmoded symbol system?

AMERICAN PSYCHO | 1991

The novel AMERICAN PSYCHO (about an American psycho, coincidentally) sounds about as subtle as a chainsaw. The book, by former author-for-our-times Bret Easton Ellis, was dealt a series of body blows a few months back, mugged by a ragged mob of the outraged politically correct, fainthearted capitalists, and the plain old-fashioned grossed-out.

While I've never written a yuppie slasher novel, I did feel a desperate envy of his success with his LESS THAN ZERO, and wrote dozens of nihilistic youth-oriented novels with titles from Elvis Costello songs, all of which (alas!) gather dust in my sock drawer. Today's readers just aren't interested in the ennui of affluent teenagers.

Well, the brat pack/splatter pack author has changed with the times, and may be on to something. The original publisher passed on AMERICAN PSYCHO, but Ellis got to keep the advance, and another publisher is shipping it to your local mall even as I write. Yes, this serial killer yuppie thing could really take off, even become a totally new genre. This means Mr. Ellis could sell his book to the movies, and kiss the literary game good-bye. Perhaps his psycho could join the ranks of Michael, Jason, and Freddie, providing employment in the entertainment industry for thousands, well into the 21st Century.

What can we look forward to? AMERICAN PSYCHO, with James Spader in an earth-shattering performance! Then AMERICAN PSYCHO II, with James Spader reprising the role in exchange for a great deal of money, which will lead in turn to AN AMERICAN PSYCHO IN PARIS, AN AMERICAN PSYCHO IN LONDON, and AMERICAN PSYCHO GOES HAWAIIAN, in which our hero does things to Gidget that would make Jack the Ripper blush.

This will lead to the kiss-off of the first part of this series, The Americanization of AN AMERICAN PSYCHO IN PARIS, with an Americanization novelization by Ellis himself, which will leap to the top of the bestseller lists, and catapult Ellis into the superstar ranks, at which point he will throw his word processor out the window, retire to a villa in Aspen, and devote all of his creative energies to aggressive party attendance and the development of a personal fragrance system available exclusively at Macy's.* It will also be at this point, probably, that no amount of money will induce James Spader to return to the series, even with an executive producer credit, even if they let him direct. This will throw the producers into a tizzy, the likes of which have not been seen since Johnny Weissmuller kissed Tarzan good-bye, or Sean Connery threw James Bond over.

They'll persuade Julia Roberts to do PRETTY WOMAN PSYCHO, but the disastrous box office will force them to get back on track with Kiefer Sutherland, who will promptly get the money ball rolling with AMERICAN GIGOLO PSYCHO and AMERICAN GRAFITTI PSYCHO, a sensitive exploration of the psycho's empty teenage years in an Northern California town. This will prove so successful they'll make MORE AMERICAN GRAFITTI PSYCHOS, followed by AMERICAN PSYCHO PREDATORS, in which the psycho goes to other planets to murder alien life forms. Then Disney will take a shot at the series, making THE SHAGGY AMERICAN PSYCHO.

The series will degenerate into lame comedy vehicles, like AMERICAN PSYCHO MEETS THE WOLFMAN, AMERICAN PSYCHO IN THE HAUNTED HOUSE, and ABBOTT AND COSTELLO MEET AMERICAN PSYCHO, with Chevy Chase and Dan Aykroyd.**

The final picture will be an action/adventure movie shot in the Philippines, AMERICAN NINJA MEETS AMERICAN PSYCHO with Jean-Claude Van Damme and Steven Seagal. That'll be it: a long profitable run from one simple idea. But lest we forget, it was the book industry that got that psycho rolling, taking its post-literate cue from the self-styled rebel of the fast food game, Burger King: "Sometimes you gotta break the rules." What rules? Beats the hell out of me. ***

*Macy's was a popular department store for many years.
** Chevy Chase and Dan Aykroyd used to be funny.
***My predictions for the success of American Psycho, alas, were totally off-base. And whatever happened to James Spader anyway?*

ANCHORS | 1983

Nightline.

Ted Koppel's mildly amused face floats before us as he states the theme of the show (unemployment, terrorism—the subject varies night to night, but the format stays the same). We move to the news clips, the updates, then back to Ted and the interviews with the experts and pundits of the world, and Ted isn't even in the same room with them. The video images of the people being talked to hang in the rear like talking portraits, disembodied heads. It's surreal, but Ted Koppel moves the talk along. Ted Koppel is a tiny god. He has the power. Ted Koppel is the news anchor.

The news anchor anchors down the images we see. The anchor is the soothing presence we can always return to, like Mommy after a nightmare, the friendly cop after a mugging. The anchor keeps us from drowning in the airwaves, keeps us from crashing on the rocks of bad news. As the sails fill with the winds of war, as we drift from war-torn port to port in the distressed Global Village, we know that the anchor is at the helm, as amused as Ted Koppel, bemused as David Brinkley, stern as Dan Rather, avuncular as Walter Cronkite. The anchor is our eyes, our roots, our anchor in the deep, still waters of the news.

And we need a human face in the face of all that suffering. Sure the advertisements offer us portholes on a more attractive artificial world, but we always return to Beirut, Salvador, Nicaragua, and we must have that familiar face to steer us, an undamaged face, someone the news can't touch. Even MTV has a TV DJ we return to between the smash hits, so we won't think the images are random.*

Because television is random. Video is a hungry. mouth devouring information and images, it doesn't matter what—Falklands crisis or LOVE BOAT episode, cop or killer, Fantasy Islander, Fidel's Island, the reporters are sailors in their drip-dry suits, the actors are sailors in their blow-dried hair. Quincy, Johnny, Alice, Ted are faces bobbing in the waves. Television is just a window on a piece of furniture, a window on a cruel world, where people are killed for no apparent reason, where unseen audiences laugh at unfunny jokes. The world may sleep, but television never sleeps. I watch it till my eyes grow heavy. I watch it till I drown, anchored on the couch. Television is a daily dark vicarious voyage on the waves both old and new. It never stops, it just fades away. I turn it off at midnight, the screen grows dark, a pale pinpoint of light diminishes slowly in the center of the tube, an artificial sun going down in a dark and nameless sea.

*As far as I know, MTV no longer features VJ's.

ANDROGYNES | 1985

The conspiracy seekers among us, both Falwellian and Orwellian, have been exercising their tongue muscles clucking at the concept of androgyny, which is supposed to be a problem for somebody.

Androgynes are objects of terror, I guess, for those who seek to be terrified by pop-culture icons. Boy George, Prince, and Michael Jackson are usually held up as the quintessence of androgyny.* But George was thoughtful enough to put "Boy" in front of his name; it's "Prince" not "Princess," and as for Michael Jackson, well, maybe there is such a thing as an androgynous Jehovah's Witness, but if there is, none has ever come to my door. So what's everybody so worried about? You gonna take a shower with these guys or listen to their music?

It seems to me the only problem an androgyne faces is what to do on a date. There's supposed to be something vaguely sensual about an androgyne, though frankly I don't know what you'd do with one if you had one—go to an Andy Warhol party, I guess, or start a band. If Prince and Nastassia Kinski start dating, for example, what would they do? Shop for clothes? What people mean when they say androgynous is really "rich" or "French" or "skinny."

On the meat of pop culture unisex is just another tenderizer, a preservative to increase the shelf life of stars. It really doesn't mean anything. Male and female characteristics just aren't that easy to define. As a matter of fact, I'm not even sure that male and female exist anymore, except in perfume commercials.

Clint Eastwood, for example, is held up as a manly man. In his last Dirty Harry movie, he decked a lesbian with one punch. Well sure, she hit him first, but what a woman (or a man for that matter) would find sexually attractive about this behavior is anybody's guess. And who am I, as an American man, supposed to find sexually appealing? Loni Anderson? Not for Ian. A man could fall into her coiffure and never be seen again.

If there is a moral to be gleaned from the sordid aftermath of the sexual revolution, it might be from Prince's movie PURPLE RAIN. If you stop hitting your girlfriend, you'll become a star. That is truly a message for our times. And here's my message: if you're over the age of, roughly, seventeen and feel a lack in your life of what is commonly called a "sexual role model," I recommend putting on side one of Prince's 1999 album. Bop till you drop, then take a brief nap. You'll feel a lot better, believe me.

Prince is no longer Prince. George is still Boy George, occasionally. Michael Jackson remains Michael Jackson (I think).

ANITA HILL | 1990

In the sunny hazy depths of show business, where I live and work, relentless flirting, bitter outbursts, and blue humor are more than sexual harassment, they're a way of life. During the festering final days of Clarence Thomas' confirmation process, I spent my time in a cosmetic process, sitting in a make-up chair, having my face manipulated and coated by large bawdy Lucille (not her real name) who started Day One of the Anita Hill testimony by shouting, "Whose pubic hair is this on your cheekbone?" and ended, when Judge Thomas was confirmed, by shrouding my head in a cloud of powder, as she whacked my face with a puff, and belted out, "I'd better get pregnant so I can get an abortion while I still can."

There we were, employed by a Major Network—I as an on-camera humor professional, she saddled with the hopeless task of making me appear youthful. Between takes and rehearsals we would all rush to available televisions (the cast to watch the hearings, the technicians to watch playoffs). When Clarence Thomas compared the hearing to a lynching, I found myself thinking, "Now wait a minute." I'm no legal expert, but being lynched and being asked embarrassing questions by a bunch of boring self-serving white guys struck me as two entirely different things. When I wrote a humorous observation to this effect for my segment of the program, word trickled down to delete it.

"Just cut it, okay!" was the way it was put to me, between clenched teeth.

Too sensitive, I was told.

Too sensitive for a program whose comedy treated women as man-hungry ditzes whose breasts are always good for a laugh, and men as above-it-all know-it-alls whose penises are also pretty darn funny. Still, I complied. As always on network television, the unspoken subtext of "Please don't fire me," overshadows personal comedy principles.

In the context of show business, then, Anita Hill's testimony seemed unreal. Your boss talked dirty to you? You were shocked? What part of town you from, babe?

While talking dirty in Hollywood is just spice on the schmooze, in DC talking dirty is an aberration so horrifying that only closed doors can contain its shame. When those doors are opened (always by left-wing special interest groups), the hardball of dirty words leaves in its wake a revulsion so thick that only dirty pool and gutter politics can clear the air. In the wake of that, smooth-talking women swarm onto talk shows across the nation to inform us cheerfully that women in the workplace frequently experience intimidation and fear. (Yes! Right here in America! Can you believe it?) Such feminist insights are a predictable ingredient in what has come to be called the healing process.

Now, I believe that Clarence Thomas was lying. The Republican symptoms of being caught in a lie certainly seemed to be in place: stonewalling, absolute denial, and aggressive attacking of the process. I also believe that most Americans thought he was lying, and just didn't care. If he picked up his social skills from the Travis Bickle School of Etiquette, well jeeze, he was still that innocent kid from

Georgia who washed his face from the pump and grew up to sneer at his sister for being a welfare victim. If that doesn't make him Supreme Court material, I don't know what does.

On October 15, an Oklahoma State Representative wrote to the University of Oklahoma wishing that someone would "...remove Professor Hill from the campus and hopefully our state." The letter went on, "We must get this left-wing extremist influence off the campus before it spreads further." Anita Hill, formerly a black conservative, has become a sinister comsymp highly delusional compulsive liar. I guess this too is part of the healing process. Judging by the way things turned out, one can almost believe that the master of feigned outrage Orrin Hatch leaked Ms. Hill's accusations to the press himself.

Yet, even before Anita Hill reared her coifed head, Clarence Thomas avoided the appearance of anything. To every query he insisted that what he once said, he didn't mean. When asked what he means now, he declined to say. Only when confirmed would what he says again have meaning. What does it all mean?

Obviously, in order to form a legal opinion today, you must have no opinions. Supposedly, America once admired an open mind; now we only want the empty one.

APOCALYPSE NOW | 1991

When will we put the nightmare of Viet Nam movies behind us? Every few years, it seems, a studio with money to burn gives some hunk a whirly-bird, shiny weapons, and pyrotechnicians, then ships them off to the Philippines to act out another fantasy of airlifting captive MIAs to freedom.

Then there's Oliver Stone who won't stop throwing his footage into combat, like a mad president ordering troops down the jungle trail to see if anybody shoots at them: "We've lost too much to stop now! It's got to mean something." Even his non-Viet Nam movies are Viet Nam movies. Wasn't JFK killed because he planned to pull out of Viet Nam? Weren't The Doors a grunt's favorite post-firefight audio companion?

The Doors, of course, were also a prime factor in the Dien Bien Phu of Viet Nam movies, APOCALYPSE NOW. All you Viet Nam movie veterans out there will recall its famous opening sequence: the jungle going up in flames, the hazy helicopters slowly hovering into view, as Jim Morrison mutters and screams on the soundtrack, that awful blue bus song (you know, the one with the lyric, "Father I want to kill you/Mother I want to—ARG!").

Even though they were strictly black and white, World War II movies at least gave us "As Time Goes By." When's the last time you and your friends crooned "This is the end, my beautiful friend," at the piano bar?*

Yes, APOCALYPSE NOW'S heady mix of napalm, megalomania, Wagner, and overacting, was for many viewers best appreciated under the influence of mild hallucinogens. Back in the Golden Age of Drug Abuse, this marijuana consumer preferred gaping at FANTASIA'S hippos in tutus, but then I was always a maverick. I'll take the mindless over the grandiose any day.

The movie tried to answer the big brain teaser of my youth, "Why are we in Viet Nam?" but by the time it actually got made we'd left the field, and the question became instead, "How do we make the movie equivalent of Viet Nam?" They pulled out all stops. The motion picture, like the late benighted conflict, became upstaged by sinister backstage doings. The War had secret bombings, assassination programs, fraggings, low morale, and rampant drug use; APOCALPYSE NOW had Martin Sheen's heart attack, Brando's weight problem, Francis Ford Coppola's emotional instability, low morale, and rampant drug use.

There was lots of hot grist for the gossip mill while the movie was being made, then the grist was baked a golden brown with NOTES, Eleanor Coppola's best-selling journal of the making of the movie. Now the grist returns to haunt us once more with HEARTS OF DARKNESS, a new documentary compiled from footage Eleanor Coppola originally shot for a "behind the scenes" promotional film. All the familiar motifs are back—a leader gone out of control makes a movie about a leader gone out of control! Dennis Hopper was stoned all the time, just like the character he played in the movie! It's a movie about a movie that captures the spirit of that movie better than the original movie did. What is reality? Well, it ain't hippos in tutus, that's all I know.

* Piano bars have since been replaced by karaoke machines.

17

ARISTIDE

Whenever news occurs, we are offered spokespersons, who do a "spin" on events we never quite understood in the first place. When a CIA representative called exiled Haitian President Aristide "unstable," I just couldn't see the relevance of this information. Wasn't Aristide elected with 67.5% of the vote? If Haitians want an insane president, isn't that one of the perks of democracy? Why is it any of our business? I never thought that President Reagan's oars were touching water, yet the CIA never issued dark warnings about him, did they?

AWESOME

Cute. See cute.

BABY'S FIRST ROBOT | 1987

Grocery stores can be frustrating places.

For instance, I always wind up buying Manhattan Clam Chowder, when what I really want to buy was New England Clam Chowder. I was halfway through checkout just the other day when I realized I'd done it again—I had Manhattan instead of New England.

I had to stomp back to the canned goods aisle, sending housewives sprawling in my wake. I was about to make my substitution when my eye stopped on something.

Now every grocery chain features bizarre specialty items—Yugoslavian crackers, African table wines, *etc.* At the end of the canned goods aisle, my eye was stopped by a vertical row of alligator clips, each clamping a plastic bag stapled shut and sealed with a strip of red cardboard. Emblazoned on the strip, in bright yellow letters, were the words, "Baby's First Robot." And, by golly, the package did contain a little red plastic robot, reasonably priced at a dollar fifty-nine.

What a world! Where do these things come from? What do they mean?

Somewhere in Hong Kong, this tiny grinning thing was first conceived, an object based on half-remembered dreams, and bad movies. It is an icon without ideology, the mutant byproduct of the alchemy of the marketplace. Some intrepid entrepreneur thought, "In America, babies need robots! We will make the first!"

Baby's First Robot is the idiot child of foreign gossip: In America, everybody has a robot. In America, robots make robots. In America, robots *own* robots. Find a need and fill it! Baby needs a robot!

Here is a vague commercial impulse, as insubstantial as a rumor, that finds a manifestation halfway round the world. The underpaid girl on the assembly line, the girl who stapled the bag to the cardboard, what does she think? Does she weep as she staples? "My baby will never have a robot." Does she consider America a land of terrifying and wonderful variety, where robots stroll babies through the parks, while the parents toil in the highrises above, making money hand over fist? Does she dream of moving to America, where money moves like a prairie fire, and Mickey Mouse is as tall as a man?

Probably not. She's probably just grateful she has a job.

Anyway, I put the robot back, went back through checkout, and was home before I realized I'd forgotten to swap Manhattan for New England again. It just goes to show that curiosity may not kill a cat, but it can sure effect your lunch hour. If they ever start selling robots for pets, man, I'm emigrating to New Zealand.

BAD HAIR DAY

Never a problem for the homeless.

BARBIE 1992

As the infrastructure of our decaying society slowly disintegrates, a seemingly trivial issue has once again filled the hollow kernel we call the national attention span.

The latest controversy involves "Teen Talk" Barbie which has among its many preprogrammed expressions, "Math class is tough!" Math teachers everywhere have become alarmed by this inflammatory phrase, according to the Washington Post. "It's a subtle form of brainwashing," cried one. "Oh my God no, no, no, no," despaired another.

This outburst of hysteria from a once-reasonable profession prompted panic at Mattel. A spokeswoman was sent to the press to point out that the doll also makes many positive statements: "I'm studying to be a doctor," "We should start a business," and "Computers make homework fun," among them.

This didn't placate the Association of University Women however. These educators, who must have a pretty light class load, have demanded that Mattel recall the talking Barbies. In a transparent attempt at spin, the desperate toymakers have offered a swap: unhappy doll-owners may exchange their talking superslim for the traditional mute model. So far, no takers.

Yes, once again, the strident forces of political correctness lock horns with the craven profiteers of the free marketplace, to create cultural gridlock. And our presidential candidates remain oddly silent!

When America was young, we made our own dolls out of mud, old sticks, and—if we were lucky—a scrap of gingham left over after Maw had stitched herself a dress (using only her teeth) with thread made from mouse hairs tied together by hand. After a long hot day of milking the pigs, Maw and Sis would hunker in the root cellar with their makeshift action figures, role-playing a better life for themselves, while Paw and Brother seethed on the prairies, screaming in rage at the tumbling tumbleweeds. Those were the days! We'd entertain ourselves the old-fashioned way, through dysfunction, denial, and hard work. None of this talking Barbie stuff for us back then, no sir. Even if we'd had one, you can bet we would've walked thirty miles for batteries, and borne the inconvenience with stoic endurance.

Times have changed. In the prosperous years after WWII, parents began indulging a mysterious urge to buy their daughters a smiling speechless sylph made out of cheap plastic. Some little girls would play "dress-up" with the diminutive fashion plate, but others, apparently confused by a tiny anatomically incorrect victim of anorexia, would comb Barbie's hair until it fell out, deface its torso with crayons, and/or tear off its limbs to see how they were attached.

Since the late fifties, a shocking number of Barbies have also ended up as chew toys for frisky puppies. As if in self-defense, Barbie has since diversified: today the sinister shapeshifter can go from career woman to poolside lounger, college student to club crawler at the drop of an outfit. She has more incarnations than an ancient deity, each at twenty bucks a pop. So, I would say that Barbie is less a manifestation of rampant sexism than a metaphor for the limits of capitalism—even of experience itself! The outfits of Barbie are not, after all, as numberless as stars. The Barbie well must someday run dry.

How much longer can toymakers reconcile America's doll needs with its incoherent social demands? Is Tenured Barbie in the works? "Trigonometry is way def!" Will MultiCulti Barbie groove to World Music before the year is out?: "Columbus was an imperialist!" Will Fed-Up Barbie wipe the smile from her lips at the flip of a switch, to mutter through clenched teeth: "Scrub the toilet, Ken, or get the hell out?"

One thing is certain. Whether he's in briefs or tuxedo, poor Ken will continue to be a problem. Barbie sure doesn't need him. Everybody knows that. That's got to be a blow to any toy's self-esteem. So before the bottom falls out of the whole chatty statuette industry, I suggest giving Ken equal time, with some useful male phrases like, "How 'bout a month from Friday? You busy then?" "What do you mean you have to wash your hair?" "I'm a Scorpio!" "She's just a friend!" "Have you seen my socks, honey?" "Sure, in a minute." "You get the house over my dead body." "I may not be as popular, but I'll bet I earn more than you do."

BARGAINING CHIP

Missile.

BARNABY JONES

A Quinn Martin production.

BASICALLY

Useless word.

BEANY AND CECIL

Random television cartoon characters from my television-cartoon-character-crammed childhood.

BEAVIS AND BUTTHEAD | 1993

Japanese monster movies and poorly-dubbed Italian muscle movies are nothing new to late night television. Godawful movies from other lands have always been part of the global village's bad part of town. Godzilla and Steve Reeves have done more for multiculturalism than Zora Neale Hurston and John Woo combined.

The Comedy Channel's MYSTERY SCIENCE THEATRE 2000, however, adds post-modern spice to the Z-movie stew: In the future, in a distant corner of the universe, a mad scientists has exiled the series host, forever condemned to watch bad movies with only robots for companions. They sit in a row of theatre seats, shown in silhouette. We watch the lousy movies over their shoulders as they crack wise. Their comments are the hook upon which the show's popularity hangs.

Their cracks are funny, sure, but wasn't mockery of laughable movies something we used to provide for ourselves? Do we really need robots to be our sarcasm surrogates?

Now sarcasm surrogacy has reached a new level: MTV's BEAVIS AND BUTTHEAD. Imagine two Bart Simpsons. Make them sniff airplane glue for six months. Bake them in a closet in a heavy sauce of dysfunction and boredom, then release them to unleash their addled scorn on music videos. On the bright side, they're not robots. In fact, they're icons for today's youth. Unlike previous avatars Bill and Ted and Wayne and Garth, they don't want to be in a band, or have their own show. Beavis and Butthead don't seem to want (or even expect) anything.

Again, bonehead nihilism is always good for a laugh, but what kind of corner is MTV painting itself into? "Here are our viewers," the network proudly proclaims, "brain-damaged social misfits who despise our programming!" This display of contempt for its audience and its own output is daring, certainly, but as a ratings strategy, I just don't see the long-term pay off.

On the other hand, who am I to question the wisdom of the marketplace? Adolescent boys, apparently, remain today's demographic of choice. To reach them, advertisers present alarming media images: turn on the television and you see weaselly Legomaniacs everywhere, swaggering little snots who call each other "dude" relentlessly, their long dank hair moussed into a life of its own, playing Game Boy while skateboarding, firing Nerf pump-action shotguns, wolfing down sugar-laced junk food with arrogant gluttony, wearing running shoes the size of dogs.

How does this media feedback affect real boys? Well, here's an anecdote. I wandered into my local corner store the other night for a cold one, to discover two twelve year old boys leaving. Carrying skateboards, they both had hair blessed by modern fixatives, large floppy tee-shirts, shorts, and (of course) enormous shoes. One of them shouted curses at the middle-aged Korean proprietor, ending with, "Okay man, see what happens if you ever need thirty-five cents," as they stalked off into the foggy night.

Buying my beer, I observed to the proprietor, "Polite young men."

He shrugged and said, "They say they want thirty five cents for bus. I say no. They say 'How we going to get home?' I say, 'Walk.' They say they going to kill me. I say, 'Kill me, go ahead. You still walking home.'"

That's the cruel truth, isn't it? If target marketing continues, MTV may eventually find itself with just one ideal viewer: a surly twelve year old boy who only leaves his basement bedroom to buy game cartridges, and doesn't enjoy anything except gory revenge fantasies over half-imagined wrongs.

Even if the trick to reaching today's youth is to hate yourself prominently before he hates you, it seems to me that advertisers are still trying to make kids believe they're God's gift to culture. Call me reactionary, but I think this is a mistake. The last time America sucked up to its spoiled offspring (The Sixties, Boomers), all we got to show for it were the sexual revolution and Screaming Yellow Zonkers. In other words, kids, kill me if you want but believe me, in the long run you will end up walking home.

BICOASTAL 1984

The advent of jet travel has caused a lot of changes in America, but the main effect has been to make every major city in the US look like an airport. Since most places already look the same, I don't really know why we fly anywhere. Maybe it's a mysterious addiction to jet lag, I don't know, but the difference between one coast and the other is more a matter of personality than of architecture.

If you're flying to LA, for example, once you touch down, that's the last time your feet will touch the ground. Walking is considered a criminal action in LA. Most people in California come from somewhere else. They moved to California so they could name their kids Rainbow or Mailbox, and purchase tubular Swedish furniture without getting laughed at. It's a tenet also in California that the fiber of your clothing is equivalent to your moral fiber. Your "lifestyle" (as they say) is your ethic. This means that in California you don't really have to do anything, except look healthy, think good thoughts and pat yourself on the back about what a good person you are. And waiters in California want to be called by their first name. I don't know why.

In New York, on the other hand, you're lucky if you get a waiter. People on the East Coast regard people west of, say, Philadelphia as either slightly cute or slightly repugnant, alien life forms. Any show that comes from out of town to New York invariably gets a review which says in effect, "They might like this stuff in Hicksville, but this is the Apple, kids. This is the eye of God."

Californians don't have that kind of arrogance, luckily, because they can't pay attention long enough to finish anything. That's why so many Californians are consultants or producers, and so many people in the East are writers or directors. The two coasts are still the cultural power centers of America: books, theater and art in the East; movies, music and TV in the West. Those who wheel and deal in the commodity of entertainment in America are, by necessity, bicoastal, which is a nonconcept really, a feeble attempt to attach glamour to jet lag.

The airplane is just a big bus between airports. Once you're on board you're in Flyover Country, legally nowhere, flying over the vast in-between of the nation, where people live and work as the objects of scorn from both coasts, the poor suckers that soak up the nonsense of the bicoastals. And until they get limos in Omaha, and gossip columns in Denver, the power will stay where it is: among a handful of East and West Coast jerks who spend most of their time trying to keep track of time zones.*

*The Internet, of course, has changed everything.

THE BIG CHILL | 1983

I have a lawyer girlfriend who leaps into masochistic moods with both feet. When in Suffer mode she usually drags me to an Ingmar Bergman movie, where I endure endless healthy Swedish faces, filling the screen with ruddy self-pity; or she takes me to coffeehouses where morose feminists read monotonous odes to joy. These little doses of bland avant-garde seem to make her feel better for some reason.

In one of those moods last week she dragged me to see THE BIG CHILL. The title suggests Raymond Chandler, but the dialogue isn't hard-bitten, just hard to swallow—the kind of writing we're told is good, but isn't, the kind of self-conscious dialogue that tells us more than we want to know.

And THE BIG CHILL has no Bogart, just good-looking Hollywood people pretending to be people just like us, only more successful: sipping fine white wines, smoking incredibly well-rolled sticks of the finest marijuana, and reeling off semi-witty phrases about where their lives have gone since the '60s. THE BIG CHILL just sits on the screen because these people aren't going anywhere. They've arrived. They're in the full blossom of self-pity. They're in their middle thirties and acting like their lives are over. THE BIG CHILL is a movie about and made by all the people I hated in high school. They were hipper and smarter than I was then, and they make more money than I do now. Not only that, they feel guiltier than I do.

An article in ESQUIRE a few issues back said: "Years after the war, the relief many of the Vietnam generation felt at having evaded the military has been supplanted by shame. These non-veterans must suddenly heal wounds they never knew they had."

Not only is this insulting to veterans who are healing wounds they know damn well they had, it's insulting to people like me who squeezed out of the draft and still feel lucky.

What, are we dead already? Did our lives end in 1970? Is everything we've done since then just one long betrayal of half-thought-out youthful ideals? Are we just slim attractive cattle sitting around our ARCHITECTURAL DIGEST homes chewing the cud of the poisoned past? I say no, ladies and gentlemen, and leave you with a warning:

Pals and gals, our generation is fast on its way to becoming the most insubstantial group of human beings who ever trod the face of the planet. Don't we have anything better to do than sit around and feel sorry for ourselves over things that did or didn't happen fifteen, twenty years ago? What do you say, kids. Time to grow up?

BIG HAIR

Not a problem for the homeless.

BIKINI

Test site, swimwear.

BIMBO, YEAR OF THE

Obsolete technique of time measurement.

BIOFEEDBACK

Pre-Prozac relaxation technique.

BIOTECHNOLOGY | 1985

I can't get excited about the brave new genetic world promised by biotechnology. Okay, so we've got self-fertilizing corn, a milk cow that grows like a hothouse tomato, a frostproof strawberry. So what? Isn't a tendency towards frostbite a natural characteristic of strawberries?

How far can you take a berry and still call it a berry? Will we need legal definitions of food groups? In the future, when we say, "A rose is a rose is a rose," will it only be true under certain laboratory conditions? When nature itself becomes a product, home gardening could be in direct violation of copyright law.

Gene splicing will give us Strawberry Plus and Strawberry Lite. We'll have MooBerry, providing its own milk, and Stra-Berri II, the only berry that slices itself. This will be followed by Berry Wars, like last summer's Cola Wars, which will lead to complicated lawsuits among berry makers: plagiarism suits in which genetic maps will be entered as evidence. When we have berries as big as basketballs (and twice as tasty!) only lawyers will get fat. The rest of us will get fed up with being overfed and go back to Strawberry Classic, even though picking this berry could be a federal offense under the Endangered Species Act.

And who will grow the FDA-approved strawberry? It won't be farmers, that's for sure; what the banks started science will finish. There's no room for a tractor in the lab. No, the strawberry of the future will harvest itself, then wrap itself in plastic and drive itself to the grocery store.

Farming is just too iffy. Why gamble if you can load the dice? It's the job of science to eliminate chance from our lives. We already spot many genetic defects in human unborn, we can even choose gender. In the future, human birth will come with a 70 year warranty (parts and labor), and pre-natal career counseling.

Okay, a frostproof strawberry will increase the growing season (and profit margin) for agriculture, but it's not a product we really need, unless we have a burning desire to eat fresh fruit in a blizzard. It just goes to show you, genetic engineering is as much a marketing technique as a science.

In the future, the one-stop lifestyle offered by biotechnology will still allow us to eat, make love, and give birth. But those activities will all have one name: shopping. If this seems to smack of eugenics, don't worry. We're not going to make a Master Race, we're going to make People Lite. If we could make a truly perfect world, we humans probably wouldn't be here at all. It would all just be endless strawberry fields, forever.

BIPARTISAN

Use only with "effort."

BITESIZED

Use only with "nugget."

B MOVIES 1995

Senator Phil Gramm has been forced to engage in some Q&A recently involving a T&A flick called TRUCK STOP WOMEN (the 1974 movie that made Claudia Jennings a star). When Gramm's then-brother-in-law George Caton, showed him the movie in the early seventies, Caton claims the senator was "titillated." (As if being titillated by Claudia Jennings is a bad thing.)

Whatever his testosterone level was at the time, Gramm admits that he later invested $7500 in a project by TRUCK STOP WOMEN'S director, a movie called BEAUTY QUEENS, which never got made. Instead the director took the money and made a spoof of the Nixon administration, which wound up getting released the day Nixon resigned, and stiffed big-time. Poor Phil.

But that's show business. Does this make him a failed porno merchant, as some anti-Grammites have gleefully claimed, or just a fool from Texas with money to throw away?

I tend to lean towards the latter, not because I have any sympathy for Gramm, but because I too have seen TRUCK STOP WOMEN (at a drive-in, where the Good Lord meant us to see Claudia Jennings movies), as well as her later GATOR BAIT (1976, same drive-in). I don't remember anything about either movie now, but at the time if I'd had 7500 bucks I'd have laid it at Claudia Jennings' feet.

So maybe Phil Gramm and I have something in common.

In fact, I'd urge Senator Gramm to join me (and his fellow Texan Joe Bob Briggs) in supporting B-movies everywhere. I realize this is hard.

It might be too late, now that Claudia Jennings and drive-in movies are no longer with us, but we can sure make a stab at reviving a wonderful art form. A women-in-prison picture is still a good bet if you're looking for a return on your investment. I'd like to see a movie featuring bikini-clad women riding Harleys. I'd pay a buck to see a movie about bikini-clad anti-terrorists. I suspect Senator Gramm would too, in his heart anyway.

Sure, most major motion pictures these days are already B-movies with a budget of a quarter billion dollars, but I for one would have enjoyed JURASSIC PARK twice as much if the makers had left out the computer animation, and represented dinosaurs the old-fashioned way: iguanas with spikes glued to their backs. Sure, the producers wouldn't have made as much money, but if they'd spent a hundred dollars on the movie instead of a kazillion, their profit margin would have remained the same.

We keep seeing audioanimatronic aliens in 70 mm and Dolby Sound; what's wrong with using a stuntman in a monster suit? I don't even mind if the zipper is showing. Whatever happened to gorilla suits? What was wrong with showing the wires on flying rocket ships? And why do we have this compulsion to blow up buildings every time we make a new action picture? Haven't we ever heard of stock footage?

And who would be the new Queen of the B's? Who's worthy to step into the shoes of the glorious Claudia Jennings, Yvonne Craig, and Faith Domergue? Who in the 90's can compare? Actresses today: they can't two-time, they can't scream, they can't shoot, they can't faint. Put a modern actress in a room with a stuntman in a gorilla suit, she'd probably just yawn.

But if we do succeed in breaking the back of the sleek Hollywood fat cats, and bring back the producers of my youth, a cigar in one corner of their mouth, a "More cleavage!" snarled from the other, I believe America would be better off. A revival of B-movies isn't part of the Contract With America, but it should be. So get in that gorilla suit, Phil. Please. Put your mouth where your money was.

BOBBITTS | 1993

Lorena Bobbitt gained her fifteen minutes of notoriety by inflicting on her husband what VANITY FAIR called "every man's worst nightmare." As I understand it, this nightmare included having (or not having, he doesn't remember) sex with your wife in a drunken stupor, having her cut off your "body part" with a carving knife, and being so loaded, you don't even wake up when it happens.

Was it bludgeoning or a wake-up call to America when 20/20 tackled this story? Its correspondent showed what he solemnly called a "grassy knoll" (shades of Dallas and Kennedy!) where paramedics found the "severed organ." And the WALL STREET JOURNAL? More sobersided (except when writing about capital gains), it profiled the urologist whose know-how put Mr. Bobbitt together again. (If only someone would do the same for America!) The last I heard, Mr. Bobbitt was urinating without difficulty, and still trying to put his reattached self in places where it's not welcome. (Is this a metaphor for American foreign policy?)

The Bobbitts would make an excellent diorama in the Buttafuoco Hall of Infamy, if the Smithsonian ever builds one.

BODY | 1984

It used to be easy to dress casually. Ward wore a cardigan when he relaxed, and June wore a frock, even in the kitchen. Mr. Rogers is still a cardigan holdover, but the line between casual and sophisticated has somehow been erased. America used to adore a swell tuxedo, but the only men who wear tuxedoes these days are either British spies, or waiters, or some guy hanging around to make Joan Collins look good.

This holds true for women too. Grace Kelly has been replaced by Jennifer Beals, and Diane Keaton has been replaced by Boy George. You can buy your clothes pretorn a la FLASHDANCE; you can dress for success; you can dress to please the opposite sex, to please the same sex, to dress like the opposite sex—nobody cares anymore.

The playboy philosophy is on the wane, the barber pole has been replaced by the hair stylist's neon, and jogging clothes can be worn into the fanciest restaurant without putting the slightest dent in a waiter's sneer. Now that designer clothes come off the assembly line, high fashion is within reach of most pocketbooks, but beauty today is more than skin deep, and it's more than beauty. Personal hygiene in the '80s has been elevated into high art.

Take hair. Hair used to be just hair. You could tame it into submission with little dabs of goo and a comb. But today hair has to bounce; it has to fluff; it has to have a life of its own; it has to look like it wants to escape from the head altogether. Look at Tina Turner. Look at David Lee Roth.

Hair can't be hair anymore. Disguising hair is achieved by a bizarre process called feathering. Feathering demands special scissors, combs, brushes, and a blowdrier—a small torture device that blows scalding air streams at your damp hair. Towels are outmoded, my friends, and shampoo gets its own aisle in the supermarket.

You can buy shampoo that is "self-regulating," whatever that means. There are shampoos for dry, oily, or normal hair. Shampoo with lemon, wheat germ, coconuts, apples, shampoo you can almost eat. Shampoo is more than just soap. It has secret ingredients. It's designed to transform your hair, the way alchemy turns lead into gold. We turn hair into something else by eliminating all the things that make hair. Like dandruff, for example.

Dandruff today is more than just a mild inconvenience; it is an embarrassment so total it can kill you. Even the suggestion of dandruff can be socially lethal, as in, "She's scratching her head. That could be dandruff." Dandruff today is a virus, a mysterious toxic presence in the body. To get at the source of dread-dandruff leakage, shampoo goes deep, all the way to the roots, as deep as a razor blade, to enter all the secret places of the body where dandruff dwells, to root out and destroy dandruff, bad breath, sweat, dirt, grease—everything, in short, that makes a body a body.

This cosmetic strip-mining is designed to make our hair the hair of angels, to make a body that's truly worthy of the clothes we buy. And now we have perfect bodies in perfect clothes, a body without lust and without desire, content with itself, content in self-admiration.

We can admire these new bodies anywhere. Our tables are so clean we can see ourselves in them. Our glasses are so clean we can see ourselves in them. Everything in the house is a mirror. There's no reason to go outside. We've got our clothes, we've got our perfect bodies. And that's America in a nutshell—all dressed up and no place to go.

BOND, JAMES BOND | 1983

President Kennedy, my hero when I was twelve years old, turned me on to James Bond. When I read in TIME that Kennedy read him I had to read him too. Whenever a new Bond arrived at the library I would beg Miss Larson to let me check it out. She would tell me sorry, that was adult reading and smile her gold-and-silver smile, her reading glasses bouncing on the shelf of her bosom like a strange necklace. Let me clue you, I've read 'em all, pals and gals: 007 is not adult reading.

I remember the paperback of DR. NO. The Signet edition had a fiat-black cover with a tiny picture in the center: Bond protecting a cowering woman from Dr. No's flame-throwing death machine. On the back cover was a picture of the aging imperialist himself, Ian Fleming, the last of the "Old Boy" Britishers (looking like he had stepped from the pages of a Le Carre novel), smoking a cigarette in a holder, and nonchalantly holding a large pistol. There you have it, kids, the British smoothie with a license to kill was written *by* a stunted adolescent *for* stunted adolescents. A martini, shaken not stirred, a fast Bentley, a Walther P-38—this insane catalogue of detail appeals to twelve year old boys and readers of men's magazines, not adults.

President Kennedy is gone, Fleming is gone, but Bond lives on, getting bigger with every movie, and the *outré* villains, the women with one name like Solitaire or Domino—they get bigger too. Through cold war, assassinations, upheaval, Vietnam, the Falklands, Bond has strolled through his overblown adventures with arched eyebrows: the ultimate fantasy figure of a dying empire.

Women and gadgets are both drawn to him—in GOLDFINGER (the novel) even a lesbian is drawn back by Bond into the heterosexual fold. Q gives him gadgets; he saves the world with them and throws them away, smashes them, drives them over cliffs. When the world is safe the women disappear too. Bond is the ultimate consumer, saving the world from major destruction so he can enjoy the pleasure of his minor destructions. That world will never end. No buttons will be pushed as long as Bond is around. Arrogant and modest at the same time, he saves the world with a shrug.

As long as boys need heroes, we'll have James Bond. As an aging American boy I look back at Bond with mixed feelings. Or maybe my feelings aren't mixed. After twenty-five years of James Bond, maybe my feelings are the same as his martinis—shaken, not stirred.*

*After a few disastrous outings with morose Timothy Dalton replacing the thick Roger Moore as Bond, Pierce Brosnan is trying to restore luster to the tarnished spy. Good luck.

BOOMERVILLE | 1993

Let's take a little trip to Boomerville.

On Main Street you'll find at least two ice cream shops, a store selling giant flannel elves, clothing kiosks, a New Age bookstore, crystal and glass emporia, overpriced restaurants. You've passed through Boomerville before, another former small town that has, for mysterious economic reasons, become its own replica, a resort town without the slopes, an empty station, a decorated dead end.

The streets are still brick, but the smithy is now a Swedish sweater shop, the depot an upscale mini-mall. Stuffed animals fill the windows of the hotel where presidents slept, and a draft beer costs three bucks. Truffles are everywhere, but it's twenty miles to the nearest candy bar. There are coffee table books, no problem, but try to find a magazine. Buy a thirty dollar snow globe diorama depicting the town as it once was. The town as it once was is gone forever.

Through every pretty Boomerville walk morose groups of teenagers in black. Pretend they have disposable income. What do they spend it on? A framed photograph of Yosemite Valley? A sweatshirt containing the likenesses of all forty-two presidents? A fifty dollar cheese basket? No wonder kids get tattoos and pierce themselves. It's the cultural equivalent of pinching themselves, to prove they're not dreaming.

The December issue of ATLANTIC MAGAZINE'S cover story, called "The New Generation Gap" (by Neil Howe and William Strauss), posited a millennial conflict between what the editors cutely called "fortysomethings and twentysomethings." (That a word like "twentysomething" even exists is an argument for the death penalty. They could have at least capitalized the damn thing. But don't get me started.) The article itself chronicled an appalling litany of condescensions by our generation upon the one to come. For example, having stoned and sexed ourselves into oblivion in our youth, we now command today's young: "Just say no."

We treat them as if they were brain-dead (Because they prefer Clive Barker to Herman Hesse? Red Hot Chili Peppers to The Doors?). We hector them about "core values" and "emotional literacy." Worst of all, boomer editors keep trying to invent (or co-opt) little phrases to encapsulate them the way we were ourselves: "Tweeners," "Slackers," "Generation X."

Well, 1993 (the 25th anniversary of 1968, by the way) marks the swearing-in of Bill Clinton as the first boomer president, the first time, I believe, that my generation has actually done anything.

Sure, that's an exaggeration. Many cultural innovations can be laid at the feet of my self-satisfied peers. Automatic bank tellers,

Robert Bly, cocaine, recovery programs, Murphy Brown, acid rock, CD's, consultancy firms, happy talk news formats, and the digital domain, if not created by my ilk, were certainly fully geared for its maximum infotainment.

For some in my bratty age group, Elvis lives, all day care centers are Satanic. Others enjoy the self-help book, in which one can find a set of symptoms on which one's own personality can be overlaid. (If you have no memory of being an incest victim, it is scientific proof that you were one.) We even need books by Germaine Greer and Gail Sheehy to help us get through menopause. How did our foremothers ever do it? How did they ever survive mid-life without a damn book?

Indifference? Denial. Street people? Homeless. Admiration of beauty? Objectification. My generation dearly loves a meaningless euphemism. We have fuzzy little names for everything. Every time a smiling teevee face calls rain "the wet stuff," I shudder, personally, but I'm afraid most people my age give a little sigh of satisfaction, and reach for the Italian umbrella.

Beatle boots gave way to platform shoes which segued gracefully into Birkenstocks. Marijuana became cocaine and led us to the rampant misuse of Sudafeds today. Grief over the deaths of Kennedys and Martin Luther King gave way to Jim Morrison, Jimi Hendrix, Janis Joplin, and today's anguished posing over Woody/Mia, and Princess Diana's marital difficulties.

Our children will mature to be more than usually embarrassed by their parents. Let's hope they have the good grace to shut up about it. Still, even if they do, you know white-haired boomers will come out with another self-help book—THE SILENCE OF OUR CHILDREN: WHAT HAPPENED? Then we'll fade away in nice little overpriced Boomerville. It's a great place to visit, sure, but I'm afraid there's nobody home.

BOSNIA 1993

(Warning: the following contains references to polls and/or surveys. Reader discretion advised.)

Earlier this year I read a headline, "Sex is a casualty of war in the Bosnian capital," amazed that some intrepid reporter had actually found a light side to the twisted tangle of Bosnian atrocities. Skimming the accompanying story, I found this, "No substantive survey on disturbed sex lives has been made because of the sheer difficulty in moving about a city under constant gunfire," revealing what may be the only advantage of living in a wartorn country: you don't get pestered with idiotic personal questions from glib strangers.

The image of pollsters being felled by snipers has its appeal, but I'll bet most Americans picking a sex-free vacation spot still choose Disneyland over Bosnia. A Disney holiday isn't as thrilling, of course, but you don't have to dodge mortar fire while waiting in line for PIRATES OF THE CARIBBEAN.

That's probably why Susan Sontag, deep thinker that she is, when she visited Bosnia recently, made a point of saying she "...didn't want to be a tourist here. I wanted to give something, to contribute." Appropriately, she brought with her not food, but food for thought, directing Samuel Beckett's WAITING FOR GODOT, which opened in Sarajevo to a full house last month.

A play about two displaced persons waiting for a guy who never shows up would have a lot of resonance, I'd think, for people weary of waiting for ethnic cleansing to reach spin cycle. In America, where we adamantly refuse to wait for anything but theme park attractions, WAITING FOR GODOT doesn't have the same appeal. I've been to Disneyland dozens of times, and I've yet to see a glittery production with Mickey and Goofy waiting in vain for Walt to come back. That'd be worth two E tickets to me (if they still had them). I admit I'm not typical of my demographic.

Speaking of war-torn Bosnian cities, despair, and copyright-protected talking animals, despite a warning from Disney's legal staff, a Belgrade teevee station has refused to stop showing Mickey Mouse cartoons. (Apparently, Slavs worry more about stray bullets than stray lawyers.) Said a spokesperson, "[N]ot even the Walt Disney Company has the right to deprive children of this entertainment.... particularly not in an environment where most of what they see on TV are the horrors of Sarajevo and war, war, war."

Before Disney assembles a SWAT team to fly over there and take Mickey off the air by force, couldn't President Clinton use his Hollywood connections to persuade the megacorporation to resolve the entire Bosnian crisis? Disneyland and Disney World are, after all, models of management. We could subvert the whole conflict and turn Bosnia into YugoDisney, glittering above the ashes of the Cold War, even as EuroDisney gathers dust in France.

Earlier this year, Disneyland unveiled Toon Town (where Mickey allegedly lives when not providing cold comfort to Bosnians). A commercial for it featured interviews with "real people," including a woman who said she liked Toon Town because its buildings were "puffy." Around that same time, by a bizarre coincidence, the aggressively anti-puffy Holocaust Museum opened in Washington DC. There, among other grim gimmicks, museumgoers are issued gray identity cards, matched by age and sex, of actual Holocaust victims, which holders can insert at various computer stations to learn more about their massacred proxies. After each tour, I've read, the mall outside is littered with these baseball cards from hell.

Whom is the macabre learning experience supposed to teach? Those Americans who remain convinced that the Holocaust never occurred—in their leisure time do they squint at replicas of killing ovens in Washington, or poke puffy buildings in Anaheim?

Despite every effort, it seems, symbols often come to mean something other than what they were intended. If, to shell-shocked kids, Mickey offers hope itself, to Disney, Mickey's a unique logo to be protected fiercely. If, to a French neo-Marxist, he's the swastika of the New World Order, to me he'll always be Bugs Bunny after a lobotomy. WAITING FOR GODOT runs through September. If you plan to see it, better call ahead, and remember to pack your bullet-proof vest. It's a weird world, after all.

BOWERY BOYS

The Crips and Bloods of the thirties.

BRAINSTORMING

Discussion.

BRAINWASHING

End of discussion.

BREAKDANCING 1985

A cigarette commercial years ago showed a happy defiant smoker with a black eye and the caption, "Us Tareyton smokers would rather fight than switch." A strange message—"If you smoke these cigarettes someone will punch you in the face," but I guess it sold a lot of tobacco, because when they brought out their low-tar cigarettes, the ad showed a happy smoker, white-out painted under the eye, and the caption, "Us Tareyton smokers would rather light than fight," which made absolutely no sense at all, except as a comment on the first ad, and if you never saw the first ad, you'd have no idea what was being said. That's okay; it's as good a way as any to discourage smoking, but it just goes to show—making sense is overrated and will never sell a product.

Our advertising industry is always on the lookout for that elusive quality called the lowest common denominator, and they're not choosy where they find it. If it's not nailed down, anything unique will get turned into a selling point, and breakdancing is no exception. Breakdancing is genuine folk art and, as such, anonymous. Nobody took out a patent on breakdancing. The black kids on the street who invented the moonwalk were involved in a collaboration that will never be recognized with royalties or awards. Instead, it moved up in the culture. And the end result is clean-cut white kids breakdancing for clothing chains.

Any special regional or racial character trait which creates or exhibits genuine personality gets melted down into a comfortable image designed for the sole purpose of selling something. Thus, we see a Vermont accent used in maple syrup commercials, we see farm folks and Gramps pushing orange juice or cereal. If we need a testimonial from "real people," we go to Indiana or Ohio, where everybody talks like an astronaut, to lend credence to claims for headache remedies or bleach.

If there is such a thing as "trickle-down" economics, this is my "trickle-up" theory of pop culture. It's not really thievery, since accents and natural exuberance are not copyrightable. Until human grace gets a lawyer, kids on the street and the normal joe will continue to be victims of a nameless exploitation. Any real relish for life will be transformed into gusto. Any manifestation of joy will turn up next month as a beer commercial.*

*Among the biggest fans of gangsta rap are suburban white boys.

BREATH 1993

According to a recent story in the NEW YORK TIMES, airlines are circulating less fresh air among passengers than they used to. This is a cost-cutting measure of course, one of those bold capitalist leaps to the bottom line at which conservatives point with pride: "Ah! The marketplace in action!" Gasping passengers and wheezing flight attendants may hold a different opinion about this frugality, but they're probably socialists anyway, unless they're in first class. The times I've flown first class (on someone else's nickel), I noticed that I was surrounded mainly by suspendered men cutting costs on costly PowerBooks. I didn't notice if they were breathing or not. Maybe if you have a laptop, breathing is optional.

What can be done?

Children, being smaller, use less air than adults. Why not have cheap, kids-only flights? If they do pass out at the end of a long journey, this might even be an incentive for harried parents to pay more!

Passengers already pay cash for headphones, why not initiate a "You breathe, you pay" policy, making passengers rent their oxygen masks. Let the marketplace go to work. Stop serving free food. Don't strike a deal with fast food chains though (that'll cost money in the long run); throw the planes open to small businesses: gyros, pizza and hot dog stands, pretzel vendors. Cut fares, but charge passengers for the perks—magazines, playing cards, or those little wings you stick in your lapels.

Either fire those winded whining flight attendants, or make them pay their own way. Let them live on tips, like waitresses. There are many ways they could supplement their off-the-ground income (video rentals, notarizing documents, making keys—these come immediately to mind). Airlines should stop shipping passengers altogether, and get into livestock: lab rats, horses, cows, pigs, etc. After all, if they land at the slaughterhouse brain-damaged from oxygen deprivation, who's going to notice?

Speaking of pork, pundits say helium production is one of those government subsidized areas where feds could slash mercilessly. I disagree. I think we should bring back blimps. What a leisurely way to travel! Imagine! Sitting on a verandah, coasting nearly soundlessly across a checkerboard landscape, on which dogs look up and howl at the moving moon!

I realize this is unrealistic. Today's world moves way too fast. But we could fire the pilots, and replace them (at a quarter the salary) with disgruntled Greyhound drivers, guys named Slim with greased back hair and a half pint of Jack in the hip pocket. In fact, if we issued half pints of Jack to everybody in America, we might get the buzz we need to deal with the millennium. Remember, airlines stick passengers on a rusty flying bus, then ask them to believe that the experience is glamorous. Air quality aside, that's enough to make anybody gasp.

BUG GUTS 1996

"The june bug Jackson Pollocked my windshield."

What a sentence! It flatters the reader, presupposing that he or she is familiar with both the rudiments of entomology and modern art. At the same time, it paints a picture in the mind that the reader may not want there. (Cool!) Mildly annoying, vaguely elitist, self-important, Raymond Chandler-ish in a pretentious kind of way, and cute as a bug's ear, it's one hell of a sentence. I wish I'd written it.

But it's the lead sentence of a print ad I saw in MOTHER JONES. Unfortunately, the ad continued—

"And as I looked at its (i.e. the june bug's) innards, I saw substance. Which made me think. Is there still room in a society of disposable razors, disposable cars, and disposable marriages for anything with substance?"

(Disposable cars? Last time I went to the airport, I didn't notice any Bic four-wheelers littering the short-term parking garage. Have I missed something? Has Hertz been replaced by vending machines?)

By the end of the ad, I learned that there's room for substance in our disposable society after all— National Public Radio! That's right. NPR's programming contents were compared (favorably!) with insect guts. Is this an advertising first?

I don't remember june bugs having much substance at all. As I recall them from youthful summers in Minnesota, june bugs were large stupid beetles who, for unknown reasons, would fly into the screen door, fall on their backs, then flop around on the porch until someone flipped them over, and they'd fly away to repeat the process.

Sometimes a june bug would fly into the dog's ear. Oh, how we'd laugh! But I don't recall ever cracking one open to see what substance it contained. We weren't that stoned.

So as far as the ad goes, other metaphors might serve as well. The substance of NPR could be compared to the pus in a boil, the maggots in a cow carcass, or the coded language in a Pat Buchanan speech. But would any of these zesty tropes really induce more listeners to tune in? I wonder.

We seem to have lost the simple art of marketing. Not only that, maybe because our country is no longer as substance-jammed as your hypothetical june bug, we seem to have lost sight of what we're selling.

The April issue of PLAYBOY, for example, promised a peek at "Women of the Internet."

But did PLAYBOY include a modem? No. So where did that leave us? We were once briefly satisfied by the sight of an airbrushed airhead with a paper crease in her otherwise perfect little tummy, now we're supposed to get excited about a naked series of zeroes and ones we can't even access? I say forget it. Even if she does look like the algorithm next door.

What'll PLAYBOY do next? Women of Public Radio? Would the issue include a CD of Linda Wertheimer describing what she looks like naked?

Well, it beats bug guts, I guess. And at least you can read the articles (still the main reason men buy PLAYBOY, of course). But PLAYBOY too is rapidly becoming a dinosaur. There's no room for readable magazines in our disposable society.

Take graphic artist David Carson, winner of many designer awards. When he worked for the music magazine RAY GUN, he ran a cover upside down. He once continued a story from inside a magazine onto the front. When he put Liz Phair on a cover, he only showed her in the middle distance, from the waist down. (He also has his very own book called THE END OF PRINT— now in its third printing. What a paradox.)

He may be the antithesis of the bug guts school of marketing. Instead of Pollocking substance all over the windshield, savvy artist Carson removed the windshield itself, and anything else that might remind you that you're sitting in a car. But what are you left with? A little greasy spot on the datapike.

I'm a text-based kind of bug myself. I don't get the logic behind making a magazine indecipherable. I don't see the thrill in download-ing a naked woman, even if she's Cokie Roberts. I just can't make the connection between insect innards and information.

What's happening to us? Is this the end of history, the graying of post-modernism, the Pollocking of narrative, the slomo riot of deconstruction, the splintering of society, the downsizing of demo-graphics? I don't know. But we're staring at the clothes drier long after we've run out of quarters. We're gaping at bug guts on the windshield long after we've rolled to a stop.

In our frantic desire for efficiency in a buggy world, we suddenly have sub-species that didn't exist ten years ago. We have "sexperts," "eco-tourists," "technopagans," "bio-medical ethicists," "tech sup-port," "spin doctors," "cyberpunks," Ariana Huffington....

But are they june bugs, or helping hands?

Maybe we're all Gregor Samsas with rudimentary wings, flying senselessly into the void, smacking into the screen door of reality, and flopping around on our backs, hoping that some amused substance abuser will pick us up, and set us on our bumbling flight once more.

Or at least buy us a disposable car.

BUILDUP

Use with "arms," "waxy."

BUMPERSTICKERS | 1985

I'm not one of those tongue-clucking grammarians who leap on split infinitives or misplaced modifiers like a mongoose on a cobra. I'm not even much of a reader—I skim magazines, stopping now and then to sneer at some scorn-worthy nugget. I've leafed through the NEW YORK REVIEW OF BOOKS from time to time to see what new twelve volume biography of Vita Sackville-West has been unleashed on an eager reading public.

I used to think that bleeding-heart mourners of literacy were beneath my contempt, and believe me, my contempt will stoop to anything. Those who complain that nobody reads anymore usually mean nobody reads me, boo hoo. And what's there to read anyway? One more self-conscious novel about a novelist trying to write a novel? One more NEW YORKER short story packed with brand names about brooding divorcees in New England? A novelization? Any jerk who reads a paperback version of a movie deserves professional help, not our pity.

I can handle reading T-shirts, the Kiss-Me-I'm-Polish T-shirt, the My-folks-went-to-Disneyland-and-all-they-bought-me-was-this-lousy-T-shirt T-shirt, the obscene-message-to-the-Ayatollah-that-the-Ayatollah-will-never-see-but-the-jerk's-wearing-the-T-shirt-any-way T-shirt.

I can handle bumper stickers: I brake for animals, honk if you love Jesus, honk if you are Jesus, if you don't like the way I drive stay off the sidewalk—I can handle all this. If you want to advertise your half-baked beliefs on your body, or plaster unfunny used jokes on a moving vehicle, that's your business, and after all, bumper stickers and T-shirts are the prose form of the '80s, but I gotta draw the line, folks.

This heart business has me in a cold sweat. You know what I'm talking about: I heart NY. I heart SF. I heart LA. I heart my dog head.

It's got me buffaloed. What is being said? You love New York? So what? Who cares? You love your dog? Are you afraid people would think you didn't love your dog if you didn't have the bumper sticker? Why do you want people driving behind you to know you have a dog? Why is this important to you? Are you sure you love your dog? Do you in actual fact hate your dog? Did you hate your dog before you got the heart-your-dog-head bumper sticker, but now you love the mangy fleabag? Do you even have a damn dog? Maybe it's just wishful thinking. If you do have a dog and you do love it, why don't you just stick your head out the car window and yell, "I love my dog!" At least there'd be some passion, not this dimwitted graphic equivalent of baby talk, this so-cute-it's-creepy shorthand designed for not very bright three year olds, or Neanderthals. Write it out, shout it out, but throw those damn hearts away. Burn 'em. Get your heart off your bumper and back on your sleeve.

BUMPERSTICKERS 2 | 1995

Driving home from work the other day, I saw a pickup truck with a bumper sticker, "Friends don't let friends eat meat." Well now, I thought, that's a bizarre qualification for friendship: "Put down that cheeseburger, Bob, or we're through."

There was something vaguely hostile about the phrase as well: that verb "let" seemed to indicate that a true friend would simply not permit meat-eating to occur. A true friend would go so far as to wrestle the meat to the ground, or wrestle the friend to the ground as his confederates (true friends all!) spirited the meat away to a place of safety.

Behavior like this would make a mighty interesting barbecue, but I'd hate to think a true friendship of the future might have to have a "Don't ask, don't tell" proviso attached to it, regarding the cooking and devouring of animal flesh. Good grief, after all, food? One more thing we mustn't talk about?

Anyway, I was stuck in traffic, driving home, amusing myself by rewriting the bumpersticker. I had arrived at "Meat don't let friends eat friends," "Friends eat friends. Don't let meat," and had graduated to "Meat friends don't let friends eat," when I noticed another pickup with another bumper sticker, "Russia Sucks."

Hello? Isn't the Cold War over? Sure, Russia is running its formerly-known-as-mighty armies through Chechen villages like a rusted broken knife through sharp cheese, the Mafia has taken over its economy, and all right, President Yeltsin looks like he might possibly have, well, an alcohol problem, but to say an entire country "sucks" when it no longer has the power to harm us is pointless and extremely rude.

Did this pickup have some kind of personal stake in Russia, that it should be so venomous towards the homeland of Nabokov, Dostoyevsky, Tchaikovsky, and Spassky? Was the venom random? If so, why not "Bulgaria sucks," or "Madagascar sucks," or "Fargo, North Dakota, sucks?"

(Fargo is just an example. I have no animus for Fargo.* I admit that, as a boy, I once opened a door in a Fargo motel and three frogs hopped into the room, but that should indicate that I consider Fargo a place of mystery and enchantment, and not a place that would, by its very existence, suck.)

Russia sucking. The very idea is ridiculous. It's a meaningless verb anyway. "That sucks." Sucks what? Wind? Empty straws? And where would Russia get the energy to suck anything?

Not to sound elitist or anything, but why can't we get a little more creative in our rancor? If you don't like a movie, go upstairs and strangle the projectionist. Sure, that's blaming the messenger (who's probably a computer anyway), but at least you're not muttering "This sucks" just to impress your meat-eating false friends.

On the other hand, we might ask, does Aleksandr I. Solzhenitsyn suck? According to the NEW YORK TIMES, the Nobel Prize-winning author is now a television talk show host in Moscow. He might not match the ratings of rival Vladimir ("Hey, call me Vlad") Posner on another network but he's doing all right. He's become the Lawrence Welk of Russia, politically speaking. Is that such a bad thing?

Apparently Mr. Solzhenitsyn's technique for interviewing guests— haranguing them with his own opinions until his time is up—has proved successful enough that he is going to dispense with guests altogether in the future. His wife told the NEW YORK TIMES, "The phase of the program in which he gave an opportunity to someone else to speak is over."

I knew just how he felt, stuck there in traffic as I was, surrounded by pickups bearing mysterious and aggressive opinions. "Pickups suck," I thought. "Friends don't let friends drive pick ups," I thought. "Have I ever met someone who's actually read THE GULAG ARCHI-PELAGO?" I wondered. "THE GULAG ARCHIPELAGO sucks," I thought. "Do friends who let friends eat meat suck?" I wondered, stuck there in traffic, smack dab in the middle of the end of history. Oh, how I wish we could dispense with this phase of the program.

FARGO is a movie I reccommend highly, even as a former resident of MInnesota.

BUNCHES | 1995

Under the influence of some strange compulsion, I went to see THE BRADY BUNCH MOVIE last week. I must admit that the filmmakers were very clever. Rather than set the movie in the seventies, when the Bradys were just more banal tidbits in a cultural sea of tidbittery, they set the movie in the vicious nineties, making the Bradys seem like strange apparitions from another planet.

The urban landscape of the Brady Bunch Movie is less sitcom and more FALLING DOWN, TO LIVE AND DIE IN LA, or BLADE RUNNER. The streets are gridlocked; smog rules. Kids are sullen, tattooed, insolent, and dangerous. The adults are out of it, cruel, venal. Everyone snarls but the Bradys. Only the Bradys shine in their glowing polyesters and relentlessly cheerful groupthink.

People around the Bradys are appalled and puzzled by them. And yet the alcoholic housewife next door, Marcia's best friend, and the high school jock all want to have sex with some Brady or other. Sex with a Brady sounds like tickling a Barbie to me. It could be accomplished, in other words, but why? Anyway, everything ends happily, with chipper Bradyness infecting even their blighted urban milieu.

Coincidentally, last week also saw the re-release of Sam Peckinpah's masterpiece, THE WILD BUNCH, about this middle-aged guy, facing unemployment, who decides to shoot up the workspace.

Though this movie does not end happily, there are a number of similarities between Bunches Wild and Brady.

• Both bunches are stuck in a world that is passing them by (Mexico, suburbia).

• Both bunches are surrounded by people who are appalled and puzzled by them, yet want things from them (guns, sex).

• Both bunches have a patriarch keeping the group together (Pike Bishop, Dad Brady).

• Both bunches have implacable enemies (Mapache's army,
the next-door neighbors)

• Both bunches are held together only by a cheerful, can-
do, let's stick together attitude.

If I were still in college, I could probably make a post-modern
thesis out of this, chock full of words like "hegemony" and "heuristic."
I could earn both tenure and the wrath of anti-p.c. conservatives
everywhere. But with everybody toting guns these days, I'd better
watch my step.

The alarming truth is, wild bunches of roving train and bank
robbers may be a thing of the past, but the Brady bunches of the real
world have become more wild. All across America, Moms and Dads
are hacking each other with serrated utensils, shooting each other
over child custody disputes, and leaping with their offspring from tall
hard places.

It's the Wild West all over again! This time around, however, the
west has been conquered. I think therapists would agree, today's
domestic gunslingers are slapping leather in a Boot Hill of the mind.

Why are we becoming more lawless and violent? Well, for one
thing, we don't have much of a social structure any more. I understand
that even prosecutor Marcia Clark asked to delay the O.J. proceedings
last week because she couldn't find a sitter for her kids. Despite being
a world-class lawyer herself, she apparently is involved in some kind
of awful custody struggle with her ex; now she has to prove that she
can convict a celebrity, be a celebrity, and raise her offspring at the
same time. Sounds like simultaneous walking, chewing gum, juggling, and whining to me, but what do I know?

All I know is this: psychoBradyism is creeping in everywhere.
Rosa Lopez is Ann B. Davis' evil twin.* It wouldn't surprise me to learn
that Marcia Clark has a younger sister, Jan, who prowls the hallways,
muttering, "Marcia, Marcia, it's always Marcia." She may have a semi-
automatic concealed under her orange miniskirt.

Hoping to nip a domestic apocalypse in the bud, I called Marcia
Clark to tell her, "Look, don't freak out. I'll watch the kids for you.

Relax. Prepare a tort. Go buy some outfits."

I couldn't get through. Probably just as well: one of my all time favorite lines from the movies is William Holden's "If they move—kill 'em." Especially in today's moral climate, this won't inspire much confidence in my day care abilities.

Rosa Lopez was a defense witness in the O.J.Simpson trial.

CD-ROM 1993

A George Will recently column chided the Clinton administration for having too many Harvard people in it. (Republicans don't surround themselves with adult preppies unless they're from Yale and Princeton.) In the course of his column, ironically, he quoted a Harvard professor, Michael Sandel: "The risk is that he (Clinton) knows too much. Reagan did not have that problem. For Reagan, a thematic presidency was easy because he did not know very much. All he had were broad themes on three-by-five cards. Clinton has a CD-ROM in his head."

I took Will's argument to be that, in our post-literate society, a man with vision, even dumb as dirt, will make a more effective leader than a vision-free know-it-all who swoons when he sees a flow chart.

But Mr. Will went on to explain, parenthetically: "(A CD-ROM is a computer thing. I didn't know that but have noted it on a three-by-five card.)" He seemed to imply that he himself is as stupid as Reagan, ignorant of things newfangled. (Maybe it's true. I often get the feeling that Mr. Will writes his columns by gaslight with a quill pen. And more power to him. If you can afford that coveted Enlightenment lifestyle, I say go for it.)

But the point of Mr. Will's column, ultimately, was the expected one: "So why let free markets make decisions when there is a government run by people with CD-ROMs in their heads? That is the clear theme of Clinton's presidency, and protectionism is one of its implications."

I won't jump to the defense of Mr. Clinton, a man who tolerates concepts like "stimulus package", but for George Will, free market defender, not to know what a CD-ROM is—! Well, it's just shameful. After all, as far I know, a CD-ROM is an actual product of the free market.

What is it? CD, of course, means Compact Disc. ROM (short for Read Only Memory) is a nerdy way of saying, "Look, but don't touch." What good is that? For one thing, you can put an entire encyclopedia on a CD-ROM, if that's your idea of a good time. You can replace an entire wall of dusty books that you never open with a little shiny disc that you'll never view. Now that's the free market in action.

There are other applications as well (such as atlases, maps, games, music instruction), most of them interactive: you can enter the database at points of your choosing, by theme, word, subject—wander around, figuratively, for hours, exploring all the subjects that bored you in high school!

It shocks me that Mr. Will is not familiar with this technology. His own columns would make a worthy CD-ROM. You could enter Will's World on any level: references to baseball, quotations from dull Roman philosophers, aphorisms from wise Greeks, lunches with Nancy Reagan, free market's decision-making processes....

On the other hand, from a pure marketing standpoint, even on the INFORMATION HIGHWAY*, George Will three-by-five cards might be even more profitable. Sell them separately, with sticks of stale bubble gum. This is just off the top of my head, understand, but we could have cards with a Will quote on one side, and a portion of his face on the other (like those featuring Ninja Turtles or Marky Mark), which, when assembled would reveal our pundit asking a hard-hitting question of Bob Dole.

How about a contest? If you're the first to assemble George Will, you get an autographed copy of his book (on CD-ROM, of course), and a trip to Hawaii!

On the other hand, if President Clinton does have a computer thing in his head, that makes him an android, which could be an even bigger marketing breakthrough! We could make warehouses full of Clindroids, and sell them through the post office, like the Elvis stamp! That'd reduce the deficit.

Or perhaps Clindroids should be privatized, as *bionic stimuli packages.* Let an unfettered free market make its own decisions. I recommend more 900 numbers, more infomercials. We could even install a CD-ROM directly in the free market's head. Great idea! (Nothing programmable software, though. That would be interference, and could lead to socialism.)

The INFORMATION HIGHWAY is the road we ride.

CIA MURDER MANUAL 1984

The so-called CIA assassination manual probably won't make the bestseller lists, but it wouldn't surprise me if it did. We've already got how-to books about sex, eating, and making it in the business world, why not a how-to book on murder? And the CIA is the ideal author. Lying and murder (or to put it bureaucratically, disinformation and termination) in the national interest are part of the CIA tradition: the Bay of Pigs, Chile, Guatemala, even a bizarre plot to smoke Fidel with a poison cigar—all are part of the proud accomplishments (or in CIA lingo, disaccomplishments) of the CIA.

That's okay, that's their job. I'll concede that we have the right to enter any Latin American country we please and tell them exactly who their leaders should be and what kind of government they should have. I mean, after all, we're neighbors. We've got the nicest house on the block. We have to make sure the neighbor's lawns are well-tended so the property values don't go down. But fair is fair. If we can send agents to our Latin American neighbors, why can't they send agents here?

Let's say we got a little American town called Smallville, and they don't like their mayor. The rumor around the barber shop is Mayor Brown gave kickbacks to the City Council to change the zoning laws so the mayor's construction company can build the new mall. Smallville isn't pleased, but the election doesn't come around for a couple years. Okay. Enter the Latin American country: let's call it El Dorado.

The El Dorado armed propaganda team is cruising around America in large used station wagons, sort of like traveling salesmen, going door to door with their message of peace, fairness, and bullets.

First stop: the Smallville barber shop. The agents of El Dorado assure the barber that the submachine guns and C-4 plastique aren't meant for the barber shop, but the mayor's house. If the barber doesn't become persuaded that shooting Mayor Brown full of holes is the proper solution to civic corruption, they'll go ahead and shoot the barber as an example to others, then surround Smallville and broadcast messages of cheer and solidarity, alternating with bursts of submachinegun fire.

Soon the town will be behind them 100 percent. They shoot the mayor, the city council, blow up the mall, the hardware store, the Piggly Wiggly, install the barber shop survivors in key positions and drive on to the next town. They're sort of like the Lone Ranger. The survivors will realize, after they've rebuilt their homes, that the goals of El Dorado are the goals of Smallville: God, homeland and democracy.

This is an idea whose time has come: a swap meet of spies. It'll put some spice in American life and give us a firsthand taste of disinformation and termination. It's just a scenario, understand. Smallville needn't worry. RED DAWN aside, it can't happen over here. It will always happen over there. And I'm keeping my eyes open at Waldenbooks for the CIA Assassination Manual. It ought to sell like hotcakes.

CIGARETTES | 1994

I find it sad to see the dwindling crowd of nicotine fiends huddled in doorways outside their homes and workplaces, puffing sadly on their once-glamorous slim cylinders of death.

The last smokers in America are being rounded up, and slowly put to the lingering virtual death of mass culture disapproval. We're going to shoot them at dawn, and make them chew gum in lieu of that one last cigarette. They don't even have the breath left to run away. The only thing they can do is grumble about their "rights," but who's paying attention to their pathetic wheezes? They're like old swayback horses one step away from the glue factory. Nobody's in their corner but the Marlboro Man and Joe Camel.

Certainly there's nothing to recommend a smoker. He stinks, his teeth are yellow, he gets all kinds of disgusting and/or fatal diseases. Still, I find something hysterical and self-righteous in our sudden zeal to persecute those who indulge in what is, after all, an entirely legal addiction.

It wasn't that long ago that everybody smoked. Newscasters and teevee experts would light up at the drop of a hat. If news was especially bad, they'd chain-smoke furiously. On game shows, hosts would swap cigarettes with their guests. Stars not only appeared in cigarette commercials, they smoked like chimneys in their movies. In the forties, cigarettes were a kind of stand-in for sex, or at least heavy petting. Lucky Strike Green went to war, generously donating millions of dollars worth of its product. Sure, they created a post-war consumer base with the addicts that survived, but at the time it was a stirring gesture.

Think of the fierce warrior of WWII, tommy-gun blazing, a smoldering butt dangling from his blistered lips. Look at the Gulf War. Instead of huddling in foxholes puffing unfiltered cigarettes, our fighting force guzzled Evian like it was water. What kind of battle-scarred veteran drinks designer bottled water, from France yet? No wonder we're having trouble adjusting to the post-Cold War world.

Don't get me wrong. I think it's great that we have nifty little Spandex outfits, sports bottles, and Prozac. The rest of the world can smoke away, developing nuclear weapons in hidden bases, slaughtering each other over ancient slights, and staging bloody coups with the weapons we thoughtfully provided. We have professional counseling, and can afford to spend our free time slapping Generation X around for being too depressed. This is okay by me. It keeps our hands busy, and it's a lot cheaper than those nicotine patches.

But, in its zeal to jog into the millennium, America has taken its global twelve-step program a step too far. Let me ask you this. If you're going to issue a stamp of FDR, is it proper to airbrush his cigarette and holder out of the photograph? That's what the post office did. But FDR did smoke. It's an historical fact. Isn't removing the cigarette the basest form of propaganda, akin to removing Trotsky from photographs of Bolshevik leaders? Isn't it, in fact, a lie?*

And what about all these commercials for trousers that are saturating our magazines? You've seen them. They feature glamorous stars of yesteryear wearing pants. Supposedly, this provides the inspiration for you to buy some too.

The ad campaign certainly seems to have caught fire, but where's the smoke? Bette Davis and Bogart wore khakis, but where are their cigarettes? Did marketing people believe, that by doctoring some old publicity shots, they could play doctor to the reputation of the dead? I hate to break it the advertising world, but drinking and smoking too much were as much a part of the old glamour as yachts, divorces, and jodhpurs.

It's one thing to convince young people to give up a filthy habit, but to impose health-consciousness on ghosts just strikes me as bizarre. We ought to be more careful. The old adage has it, "Where there's smoke there's fire." If we root out smoke wherever it rears its ugly head, we won't even notice fire until it's too late.

*FDR update! Some disability rights activists have recently objected to certain proposed statues of FDR which depict him standing unaided. They want to show the famed president in a wheelchair. In his lifetime, FDR (a polio victim) would never have allowed himself to be photographed thus. So: do we adhere to the shrill demands of a minority with a self-serving agenda, or perpetuate the self-aggrandizing propaganda of a deceased president? In 1995, this is what passed for a moral dilemma.

CIRCUS 1990

I can't tell you how many times my arm has been clutched by an awestruck girlfriend, as we stood before a museum wall full of Monet—water lilies as far as the eye can see! She would emit these little art appreciation noises: "Mm," and "Wow," and "My God, his use of color has never been equaled."

I would cock my head to one side, like an eager dog trying to obey an unfamiliar command, but I'd be thinking, "What this thing could really use is a couple of Flemish peasants being devoured by demons." Unfortunately, despite brave efforts by all my former girlfriends, a sense of childlike wonder has never been installed in the hard drive* of my shriveled soul. I wouldn't know exquisite if it up and bit me.

The latest valiant attempt to tap me with the winsome wand of wonder brought my latest former girlfriend and me under the Big Top in Santa Monica, for the nouvelle experience of CIRQUE DU SOLEIL. As I looked around at the crowd I noticed that only a tiny fraction were kids (half of them were asleep), and half the adults were dressed in their Sunday finest! Three-piece suits! At a circus! I found myself thinking, "What is this? A circus you don't bring your kids to? A circus that bores kids? A circus you gotta dress up for, like the damn ballet?"

Plus, CIRQUE DU SOLEIL cost more to see than a lot of us make in a week (that didn't bother me of course; my girlfriend had paid for it). When the well-fed audience applauded the "No smoking under the Big Top" announcement with a solemn vigor usually reserved for heads of state, I realized the cruel truth: this was a circus for yuppies! Where was the hoarse-voiced, pot-bellied fierce guy trying to lure me into the Midway? He wasn't there! There was no grease on the costumes; not one tattoo was in evidence. No sullen snake girl smoked unfiltered cigarettes in the shadows, no skinny gypsy swallowed swords, nobody ate fire, not one creepy clown was shot from a cannon, no ducktailed Okie tried to rip me off at the ring toss, no girl Zambura turned into a gorilla, and no tamer named Lefty stuck his head in a lion's mouth. No sawdust, no tinsel—the clowns were actually funny. A circus with funny clowns? What has the world come to?

CIRQUE DU SOLEIL wasn't terrifying or seedy. The aroma of large animals and amused cynicism was nowhere to be found. This wasn't a circus, it was a phys ed demonstration. Not only were the performers in alarmingly good physical condition—they were Canadian. There's no such thing as a sleazy Canadian. These kids don't hang out after the show smoking big cigars and drinking rotgut from pint bottles, no, they do aerobics and down fiber-enhanced yogurt smoothies. If you ever dreamed of running away with the circus for a mad season of French-kissing with Natasha the cat girl of the high wire, this is not the circus for you. Running away with this crowd would be like running away with a gym class full of Mormons.

Yuppies apparently never had a childhood, and keep trying to get popular culture to create an artificial one for them, a childhood full of wonder and devoid of terror. Now, I don't know about you, but even as a child, I was a little short in the wonder department. Even as a child, I wanted to see sideshow fat guys stick sharp nails in their forearms, I wanted to see the geeks, I wanted to see things blow up. I always looked for the interface between precious and sleazy.

I tried to explain all this to my girlfriend, over a decaf cappuccino after the show, but she just shook her head sadly, realizing, like so many women before her, that "the child in me" just does not reside in the me the world calls Ian Shoales. She did ask me to go to a Robert Bly lecture with her, but I knew her heart wasn't in it. So I stiffed her for the decaf, and made my farewell. Oh Natasha, cat girl of the high wire! I hope you're reading this. If I must get in touch with my primitive side, frankly, I'd rather touch it with you than with Robert Bly. I'm between girlfriends right now. How about it?

*"Hard drive" is a computer reference, an important ingredient in any modern essay.

COCAINE 1982

Cocaine. As a drug it compares favorably to Novocain, or any local anesthetic. It numbs the nose and the back of the throat, destroys the sinuses; increased usage leads to psychological dependence, wild mood swings, paranoia, delusions of grandeur, and even worse, delusions of intelligence. It's expensive, and it spills all over everything. So why do people use it?

Because cocaine is a tiny emblem of power held over another person. When someone gives you cocaine at a party, it means you have to stand and listen to him jabber for ten minutes. Coke users talk intensely about the most trivial things in the world, like brand names of audio equipment and video playback systems, and where they got their coke and how pure it is, and how hard it is to fly the stuff out of Bolivia. They go into a list of all the phone calls they've made that day, and all the projects they've got in the works. A little tiny bit of coke offered to me in the dark corner of a party tells me, "Wow, this relatively useless person is giving me a little bit of this absolutely useless highly expensive thing." If someone set a hundred dollar bill on fire in front of me, I would get the same thrill minus the boring coked-out conversation.

Cocaine culture: synthesizers, movies like CAT PEOPLE, TV shows like FRIDAYS, very shiny clothing, REAL MEN DON'T EAT QUICHE—the cute disguised as the cynical. Real men do eat quiche. Real money and real lives do go down the drain from cocaine, which isn't to say I wouldn't take some if it was offered to me. It keeps you awake at those boring parties, and gives you the illusion your opinions are worth something, as you beam and spew out intense and detailed critiques of E.T. or any other nonsense that pops into your teeming head.

By the time I actually saw E.T. at the drive-in I'd heard it recapped so many times at parties, the actual viewing experience seemed redundant. That's cocaine in a nutshell. Drive-ins used to mean something. Movies used to mean something.

I remember once when I was a kid we went to the drive-in. There was a shower of falling stars, and all of us got out of our cars to stand in the grass and watch the stars fall down. The movie was ignored behind us. When I saw E.T. at the drive-in, the sky was filled with roaring jets and the real estate around the drive-in was so developed that I spent half my time squinting from the bright headlights of cars blinding me as they hustled busily on their way to somewhere. It is a cocaine world, fast and smug, and self-conscious—like putting your face in the photocopy machine, then making a copy of that, a copy of that, copies inside copies, echoes inside echoes, until we've lost the original. We just hear a voice droning on and on. The only thing we see is our own face, nodding, reflecting in those French import mirror wraparound shades. Sunglasses in the dark. That's cocaine.

COFFEE 1994

Last week I went into a coffee house to get, you know, a cup of coffee, only to be told that actual coffee was unavailable. Would I like a tasty cappuccino, cafe au lait, or espresso? A double decaf latte with one of those little Italian biscuits that tastes like chalk? They had those, but a steaming java, a plain ordinary cup of joe? No way.

This mutant coffee thing is getting out of hand. It's even hard to get a cuppa mud at the local convenience store. It used to be simple: get large paper container, put under urn tap, pour, attach appropriate lid, pay, and go. Today, convenience stores all have an Isle Du Cawfay or some damn thing: it offers cinnamon coffee, vanilla coffee, and decaf Viennese, from beans fresh-squeezed by formerly Soviet virgins. I'm not against this stuff, but it's not what I look for in liquefied caffeine: I want a blister on my lips and a knot on my stomach. I want my coffee black, bitter, and scalding. Give me that little pleasure, America. I promise I won't sue you.

Alas, we're well on the road to tepid exoticism. Have you tried to find vanilla ice cream at the grocery store lately? You could get frostbite from rummaging. You have to claw your way past Wally Walnut Peanut Brittle Supreme, or Cherry Brownie Fudge Syrup Surprise, ice cream with so much extra junk crammed into its mass it looks like a tub of frozen glue with chunks of bark floating in it. If you find vanilla ice cream at all, it's usually Milli Vanilla Whole Bean Rain Forest Saver, with vanilla beans suspended in its depths like boulders in a glacier.

While we're on the subject, isn't it time to declare a moratorium on microbreweries? Walk into an upscale tavern these days, and there's a twelve foot wall of bottles behind the bar, floor to ceiling. If you ask the bartender what kind of beers they serve, you'll die of thirst before he reaches the end of the list. And all the names have the same annoying, vaguely macho ring to them: Ugly Alligator Ale, or One-Eyed Pete's Pale Porter. I'll go mad, I tell you! Mad!

We've got to nip this thing in the bud, my friends. We're on the road to a world where we'll be able to flavor our foods with cumin, curry, or cilantro, but not salt. We used to drink water from the tap, remember that? Then we switched to bubbly water from foreign lands; now it has to be cherry-flavored bubbly water, or we won't touch it.

We have special shampoos for our individual hair needs. We need special outfits to ride a damn bicycle. We have call waiting, call forwarding, caller I.D.—but when's the last time you actually talked to a human being on the telephone?

Our new culture is all quarters, no pennies, prayer in school but no education, all croissants, and no doughnuts. We're not smoking! Tomatoes will stay ripe for centuries.

We welcome space aliens, but not illegal ones. (As though Martians carry work visas.) We used to shoot tin cans from stumps with .22s. Today we shoot each other with .357s (the devil's caliber!). We used to drive gas-guzzlers, guilt-free; today we drive little tiny cars with strange names not found in nature. Do we really feel better about ourselves? Of course we don't.

We're just trying to prove that we can control our appetites. "I don't have a sugar jones," we say to the world, "I just have a sudden craving for Huggy-Buggy Sweet 'N' Sticky Health Bars. That's all."

I don't want to alarm you (well, okay, I do), but it seems like we're ripe for an invasion. Lean and hungry barbarians from the East, take note. You won't even need weapons. All you need are basic goods: sugar, salt, coffee, tea, whole milk, alcohol, red meat, tobacco. I don't want to sound like a traitor, but we're a pushover.

COLONIC IRRIGATION

Enema with an ideology.

COLORIZE

New verb, replacing the old "to color."

COLUMBUS.

Zealous phallocentric intruder, jolly navigator.

COMEDY 1981

There are two kinds of comedy: sophomoric and sophisticated. In sophomoric comedy, two fraternity guys swap one-liners about breast sizes and then pour beer on each other's head. In sophisticated comedy, two guys in tuxedoes swap one-liners about the theater and then pour champagne on each other's head. It's all a question of environment. This is the basic dichotomy Bergson didn't see when he wrote his famous essay on the mechanics of laughter.

Alright, I've never read that essay, but I know we don't laugh at a joke because it's funny, we laugh at a joke because that's what we're supposed to do. Look at the past—Chaplin, Keaton, the anarchy of the Marx Brothers, so much admired by psychotic French aesthetes. Then we moved into chimpanzee jokes, funny dogs, Doris Day, bedroom humor, Little Willy jokes, Mommy Mommy jokes; finally we moved into cartoons of outhouses and desert islands. We had jokes about hunters and traveling salesmen. We saw cartoons of men reeling down the street at 3 a.m. with little X's over their eyes, spilling their martinis when their battle-ax wives hit them over the heads with rolling pins. And then came the '60s. Nothing was funny in the '60s. We thought LAUGH-IN was funny in the '60s.

Then the '70s brought a Comedy Renaissance: anorexic women and hyperactive men; silly pointless jokes on Saturday Night by smug leering emotional basket cases whose only claim to a sense of humor was their audacity, boldness, and willingness to see how much they could sneak by the censors without getting thrown into FCC Prison. I'm sorry, gentle reader, but humor is a one-way ticket to Palookaville. You want to make money, get into cocaine dealing.

I saw a "performance piece" the other night. We sat in a warehouse listening to tapes of laundromats and trucks, as seven naked women on bicycles wheeled slowly around the performance space.

Halfway through the piece, one of the twelve people in the audience began howling with laughter and ran out of the space, his laughter echoing behind him. I don't know if the laughter was part of the artist's concept, or whether it was nervous laughter of some poor sap who can't get behind the new aesthetics, but I do know this: some people laugh at conceptual art, some people laugh at jokes, some people laugh at car accidents.

COMPACT DISC

Overrated format.

COMPUTER

Has changed our lives for the better.

COMPUTER SEX

Recreation option.

CONGRESSIONAL HAIRCUTS 1991

As you may have heard, the bank of the House of Representatives will no longer cover the bounced checks of US congresspeople. Yes, writing bad checks was once one of the prime perks of holding elected office, and it wasn't the only one. Other perks available to congress included and may still include: dismissal of parking tickets, free airport parking, free medical checkups, free lodging at national parks, free assistance from the IRS, and most interesting to me, anyway, cheap haircuts—only five bucks a pop.

Concerning this last item, sure, the idea of a duly elected fatcat official wallowing in a barber chair at the taxpayer's expense could make the blood boil. But there is a tradeoff. As citizens, we are granted the God-given right to laugh at the bad haircuts of elected representatives. It's a time-honored entertainment that's not only pleasurable, but free. That's why I watch C-Span.

See, it always mystified me where that special tonsorial senatorial look came from. Now we know: from some underpaid Beltway barber who takes his revenge on his penny-pinching plutocrat customers by making them all look like professional bowlers.

As a media package, it seems to work! Mr. and Ms. American voter cast their ballots enthusiastically for these middle-aged men who comb their hair over bald spots, men with wispy little sideburns, gray fuzz sprouting on the backs of their necks. The mainstream vote always favors the aging beardless wonder whose very demeanor says "I'm a sensible guy," from the boatlike presence of his sturdy Florsheims to the top of a pasty head sporting genuine hair that somehow manages to look like an ill-fitting toupee. Isn't that what America is all about?

But when the congressional privilege of the five dollar haircut is truly history, what then? Are we going to see congressmen striding resolutely to the shopping malls, to get their hair styled at fashionable salons, by sullen young people all dressed in black—mop-topped kids named Andre, and Chantal—at fifty bucks a pop!

Once you step on that road of follicle fashion, folks, it's hard to get off. What are the taxpayers back home going to think when the junior senator from Kansas shows up on the Hill with a pierced ear and buzz cut that spells out his name on the nape of his neck? And what about congressmen wearing mousse! Styling gel! Dreadlocks! The wet look! We may even see United States Congressmen wearing the careful three day stubble previously seen only on the cheeks of saxophone players from the housebands of late night syndicated talkshows. Is that the America we want?

The Beltway will throw away their power ties, and start to wear open-necked shirts from Benetton, cowboy boots, and pre-faded Levis. They'll start to wear sunglasses indoors, play air guitar on the senate floor, even memorize the words to Michael Bolton ballads and insist that they be read into the record. Who knows? Michael Bolton may even become my next senator. C-Span will merge with MTV, and the ability to program a drum machine will be a deciding factor in the confirmation process.

But it's not too late. We can nip this in the bud. I say, let them have the cheap haircuts. Sure it sets the taxpayer back a couple grand a year, but as I have clearly shown—when bad haircuts are outlawed, only outlaws will have bad haircuts.

CONTROVERSIAL

Boring.

CRITICS 1993

The Los Angeles Film Critics Association, recently voted Steven Spielberg's SCHINDLER'S LIST best picture. At the same time, however, they voted THE PIANO's Jane Campion best director.

Faced with the paradox of a best picture not being directed by the best director, most of us would be satisfied with pondering the value of critics at all. Critic Martin Grove, however, is made of sterner stuff. He wrote in THE HOLLYWOOD REPORTER that Steven Spielberg had been "snubbed" and "ignored" by this voting.

Not to be outdone, Michael Medved was so annoyed that he wrote in his NEW YORK POST column: "...this feverish hunger to honor a woman—at all costs—helps explain why critics on both coasts picked Jane Campion as best director despite the fact that their votes indicated they clearly liked Steven Spielberg's movie better than hers."

I don't know what this all means, exactly. It seems like Medved's and Grove's outraged rancor is their way of saying they liked SCHINDLER'S LIST more than they liked THE PIANO. But why did they have to victimize Steven Spielberg or insult Jane Campion on the way to this opinion? A simple "Wow! Look out, Oscar! Here comes SCHINDLER'S LIST!" would have done the trick. That's the way a normal flack does it.

Still I'm so exhilarated to see people with nothing important to worry about working themselves into a dither, I feel compelled to point out some rudiments of criticism to my angry colleagues.

First, calling a film "best" doesn't always mean anything. In 1990, WILD AT HEART won the *Palme d'Or* at Cannes, and DANCES WITH WOLVES won the Oscar for best picture. Did those honors really coat the movies with excellence? A mere three years later, are they even remembered?

Second, when a bunch of people take it upon themselves to bestow an honor like "best director," only one person can win it. If Jane Campion is "best director," it doesn't mean that Steven Spielberg has been "snubbed." It only means that after the vote, Jane Campion was named "best director." What's the problem? The process seems simple enough.

If this morning, I chose Cream of Wheat over oatmeal, does it mean I "ignored" the oatmeal? Certainly not. It just means that after careful and anguished consideration of both oatmeal and cream of wheat, I opted for the latter. If I "go Nabisco," moreover, it's not an insult to Quaker Oats. I may even consider Quaker "best breakfast maker," and still vote Cream of Wheat "best breakfast." Only after careful consultation with my personal feverish hunger would I ever vote Cream of Wheat breakfast of the day.

Oh, I can hear the angry voices now. "What of fiber?" you're shouting between clenched teeth. "What's wrong with breaking one's fast utilizing a simple repast of shredded wheat, sugar substitute, and skim milk?"

Well, there you go again. If I choose gruel to start my day, shredded wheat need not feel humiliated, abashed, or humbled. Shredded Wheat has not been shorn of glory, stripped of titles, cast out of the garden, or sent to hide its face in the locker room. Shredded wheat has not been repulsed, dealt a death blow, boycotted, overcome, vanquished, or even out-generalled. It is not as dust, it has not floundered, been drubbed, fallen, or whupped. I have not stemmed shredded wheat's tide, nor have I crowned gruel with victory.

Of course, if my mother were still cooking for me, all votes would be off. It'd be bacon and eggs every morning, and the only loser would be my cholesterol levels. If Michael Medved wants to call that honoring a woman at all costs, I'll be happy to clean his clock for him, any time after my morning porridge. Hey pal, this is my mother we're talking about!

So I hope I've set the record straight. If I have, I certainly don't mean to snub Michael Medved and Martin Grove. But, as my mother used to suggest to me over breakfast, maybe they should try to find a real job.

CUTE

Ugly.

CUTE (EXPANDED) 1983

Before I got kicked out of graduate school, I had a job teaching rhetoric. One of my students was a "cute" freshman (she dressed in orange pants suits, with frosted hair and a nose she considered pug, but wasn't). She brought a "War Is Harmful For Children And Other Living Things" poster to class. She brought John Denver records to class, and Harry Chapin. I wasn't as mean to her as I should have been—partly from fear, partly from pity, partly from my need to find out what makes America tick. I did wind up flunking her from my course, but that's not the point.

The point is: when I saw ANNIE (at a date's insistence) I had to hit myself on the head afterward with a small hammer to get that stupid "Tomorrow" song out of my head.

We use up cute fads in this country the way we use up Kleenex, and it's a phenomenon I've never quite understood. Maybe when we buy a little fuzzy stuffed puppy with a tag, "I Wuv Oo," it's a kind of psychic sneeze, a way to rid the collective unconscious of consciousness-blocking mucus. I don't know. I do know there's a constant flow of cute in America: troll dolls. Repulsive aliens from outer space. Little two-dimensional dot gobblers. I can understand the fertility rites of certain South American tribes, but the American concept of cute is as slippery as Mississippi mud and as elusive as the butterfly of love. The neighborhood shopping mall—the twentieth-century equivalent of the medieval village unit—has entire stores that sell nothing but E.T. dolls, Snoopy-dog dolls, Garfields, Smurfs, Strawberry Shortcakes, and proud unicorns flying over rainbows.

Within our lifetimes—mark our words—plastic surgeons will have the ability to make human beings fuzzy and adorable. With a few strokes of the scalpel we'll all be cute as a bug's ear and cuddly as the day is long.

That day may be drawing near. I received an anonymous Valentine in the mail this year, a card with an idiotic picture of a simpering bear frolicking in a field of daisies and signed simply, "A Secret Admirer." Now I don't know if my secret admirer was being sarcastic, ironic or sincere—who can tell these days?—but I do know I spent a long time comparing the signature to other letters I've received, and frantically examining the postmark for clues to my correspondent's identity before I gave up and threw the damn thing away.

I don't know who you are or what your game is, Secret Admirer, but next Valentine's Day, if you're still around and still admiring, eighty-six the cuddly ursine, give the bum's rush to the cute bear. If you must send me something, send me a postcard of a cowboy riding a giant grasshopper with the caption, "We grow 'em big out here," or send me a "Dig those crazy freeways," or even a postcard of a jackrabbit with antelope horns. You know, send me something I can use. Because I white out the message, write my own, then send these cards on to my friends. Saves me a bundle at the Hallmark store.

And if you must admire me (something I don't recommend; admiration puts me in a rather sordid and embarrassing position), sign your card. Don't worry if I find out your name. I won't remember it anyway, to be quite honest with you. You can go ahead and give me a heartfelt message: "Yours till the end of time," or "I've never loved anybody the way I love you," but type it. Forget calligraphy—that kind of fancy handwriting went out of fashion with the Book of Kells. I don't even mind dot matrix.

But please: don't send me bears. This may not seem like a big deal to you, gentle readers, but this American fascination with bears has always bothered me. It's schizophrenic. The bear is used as a symbol of renewed friendship between Mainland China and the US (in the form of those two pandas who have trouble mating, probably because they've been shuttled from zoo to zoo so much they're too jetlagged to remember which gender is which), and we use the bear as a symbol of dread (representing Soviet Russia in Reagan commercials).

Somewhere in the fast in-between of the Panda and murderous Soviet Hulk is the vast cute wasteland of American beardom: the teddy bear, Smoky the Bear, Qantas koalas, Care Bears, jelly bears, Yogi Bear, and all those cute greeting cards that say, "I can't bear to be without you," or "My love for you is unbearable."

I hate to break it to you, America, but a bear is a lumbering half ton of musk, claw and tooth. A bear is smart, unafraid and definitely not cute. Why isn't the bear afraid of us? Because we persist in thinking that a bear is cute.

I've heard about tourist families who place small children on the backs of bears so they can snap a Polaroid, who handfeed bears table scraps, who poke them with sticks so they'll stand up on their hind legs and beg.

The consumer market on cute is bullish, but cute is what puts animals on the endangered species list in the first place. Wild animals are not cute; they're wild animals, and they belong in the woods, not stuck on your refrigerator with a magnetic piece of fruit.

CUTE NAMES FOR KILLERS 1984

I don't believe in taping TV shows. If God had meant me to remember old TV shows, He would have given me a photographic memory. But I wish I had a tape of the old TOMORROW show in which Tom Snyder interviewed Charles Manson. As revelations go, there weren't many, but it was still quite a spectacle, if you like bear-baiting, and the bear is a whitetrash acid head with more brains than the baiter. In America, we'll put a beast in the cage of public scrutiny and poke it with sticks. We call this a public service. We call this psychology.

One of the dearest liberal beliefs in this country is that understanding a problem and solving it are the same thing. And mad-dog killers have problems like everybody else. I guess we want to know what makes them tick. And I guess they're willing to tell us.

The killer usually has a nickname—Hillside Strangler, Zodiac Killer, Jack the Ripper, Green River Slayer, Son of Sam. Even the killer of the universe has a cute nickname—the Quark. A killer has a nickname, or no name at all.

But does a nickname really help us understand a killer? Once a killer is located on the grid of pathology—a paranoid schizophrenic, a disappointed office seeker, a man in love with Jodie Foster—once the killer is pinned to the map of medical opinion like a moth, is the killer rendered harmless? No. The only thing that happens is the nameless killer has a name, and once the beast has a name, we hope that it, like a dog, will come at our command.

But the beast usually chooses these names himself to transform himself into something he is not: not a dog, but a man who matters, a man who alters the course of events by acts of destruction. A random killing isn't a crime of passion, but an act of criticism. Life is a book to these monsters, and they rip out human lives like pages from a novel they wish they could have written.

Cold-blooded is as close to a description as we'll get. A random killing is the dark side of a miracle, a lightning bolt of human nature, an accident of passion and missed opportunities. A killer caught in this scheme of things is a killer rewarded; a killer found guilty is a killer made a movie star, a nickname screaming from the headlines. Then America moves on to the next sensation, a few citizens fewer, with a few more unsolved disappearances, a few more cute names for killers in our heads, more useless information only good for Trivial Pursuit, and a few more nagging questions:

What happened to Halloween? What happened to the unlocked door? Why must we teach children to run from the smile of a stranger? Now the sweet world has a bitter core—a razor in the chocolate, a knife behind an open grin, an invitation from a darkened car. Farewell, Hershey's Kisses. The kiss is poison. Only adults eat chocolate now—Swedish chocolates, exclusive chocolates, chocolates with tight security.

A tiny minority of insane people has altered America's social history. This is a world with mean tricks and no treats now, a world where all pleasures contain their own pain, all crimes their own punishment, and punishment is its own reward. It's a world where the bogeymen are real.

At my job, I recently overheard a co-worker say, "You're not gonna go postal on me, are ya?"

CZAR

Mysterious authority figure in charge of drugs or energy.

DATES | 1983

There's a new magazine called ONE WOMAN, and the entire ninety-six pages of its first issue will be devoted to the wit, wisdom and figure of Morgan Fairchild. If it sells, ONE WOMAN will appear quarterly with a different woman per issue. ONE WOMAN is the logical extension of monogamy, computer mania, and the lingering death of the printed word. A picture used to be worth a thousand words, and now a thousand words are worth one picture. You need ninety-six pages to examine someone you wish you forgot. Morgan Fairchild isn't a woman, she's a corporate merger, a public-relations stroke. And she wouldn't date you in a million years.

All right I admit it. I have trouble with women. They don't go out with me, and if they do go out with me they don't do it twice. And I'll admit that my idea of a good time is hitchhiking to a Ramones concert, followed by a malt-liquor nightcap and a chili dog at 4 a.m. Many women don't appreciate the fun of this.

But I've got something to offer a woman—a unique world view and a genuine, if stunted, sensuality—and I'm sure there's a woman out there with something to offer me. So let me give you guys advice about women:

Don't date a woman news anchor. She'll have that Dear Abby hair that will snap off her head when you touch it.

Don't date a woman who writes articles for COSMOPOLITAN. She's looking for a husband and career to juggle. If you're only after one thing, which I frankly am, you're barking up the wrong tree.

Avoid all women writers, as a matter of fact. They're probably smarter and have more problems than you. And women writers, like male writers, don't know how to have fun.

Never date a woman with only one name, like Alana, or Sunrise, or Cherri, or Rainbow. Don't do it pal, you're only asking for trouble.

Never date a woman with three names. Women with three names are almost always poets, and when the relationship breaks up (as it inevitably will), these women will write nasty poems about you that will be anthologized for years to come, poems that will haunt you in public libraries from coast to coast. Never write a poem for a woman. Women remember things like that and will hold it against you when you eventually betray them.

Never date a woman who won't fit in your car: women with spiked heels; women with high hairdos; Cher; Scarlett O'Hara; Cleopatra; Las Vegas showgirls; a six foot tall all-girl rock band drummer with a Mohawk haircut. You know the type.

If you luck out and do get a date, swallow your pride. Take her to see FLASHDANCE or STAYIN' ALIVE. Go see that French movie. And if she comes to your apartment for that Amaretto nightcap, keep a copy of MS. or MOTHER JONES on your coffee table. If you don't have a coffee table, rent one. Women love a man with a coffee table.

Finally, if a woman seems interested in you, for whatever reason, ignore my previous advice. Go out with her for God's sake. If you're anything like me, and I hope you're not, you gotta take what you get.

DEATH | 1992

When today's anxiety-ridden and up-to-date citizens muster the introspection to ask, "What's wrong with me?" they don't spend brooding hours curled up like Tammy at a big picture window, squeezing out tears, as the hard rain of a cold world pours down on the empty streets. No, they grab their plastic and head for Waldenbooks, to buy tons of paperbacks authored by Top Experts, with print so large you have to move your head to get through a word. There is an entire paper universe at the mall, where undependable co-dependents enable Iron Johns to oxidize and Cinderellas to miss the ball. Somewhere, among these large words and thin volumes, you will find the syndrome that's right for you.

The E-Z-To-Read and relentlessly functional nature of self-help tomes may have found ultimate expression in FINAL EXIT, by Derek Humphry, director of the Hemlock Society. This is a how-to book for would-be suicides, examining suffocation, over-medication, and many other techniques for making one's quietus. Its appearance on bestseller lists proves that America finally does have something for everyone; now you can even find the death that's right for you. Everything from bare bodkins to exhaust fumes can be yours, with your good credit.

If readers believe that suicide can be a form of painless self-improvement, it's disturbing, sure, but I'm not going to bluster and wring my hands in the TIME-honored "What does this tell us about America?" mode. Instead I'll treat America like the savvy shopper I always thought it was, and ask: if this suicide manual really does the job, why spend money on it? Isn't it like buying a cookbook for one recipe, or a round-trip ticket to your own funeral? What's the point? This handyman's manual doesn't tell you how to do home wiring, it tells you how to make yourself dead. Dead people don't read! Why shell out hard-earned money on a book you'll only use once? Why do you need a book at all? In pre-Waldenbook days, ancient Romans would go off quietly and open a vein in the bath; samurais would impale themselves on swords. They didn't need instructions. What happened to our pioneer pluck? Has even our despair become wussy?

Okay, you're depressed. You can still be budget conscious. Can't you at least summon the inner resources to wait for the paperback? If you can't wait, borrow it from a dead friend. Check it out of the library. Granted, if you follow instructions, you won't be around to return it, but what's an overdue library book to a dead person?

And if you ask me, the publishers don't seem very market conscious. When you urge your readers to leave this mortal coil, you're not really building a consumer base, now are you? If they're going to kiss off their readership in this cynical fashion, they could at least build up to it, with a preliminary series of volumes, learner's permits, you might say, training wheels for the bicycle of suicide, with titles like "Hurt Yourself With Pointy Sticks!" or "Who Cleans Up The Mess?"

If you're looking for creative means of self-slaughter, I can give you a couple for nothing: dress up like a Crip and diss a Blood, act like a Croat among Serbs. Personally, I've always thought it might be fun to buy a mastiff, get a huge bone, hide inside it, and command the dog to bury it in the back yard. Beats hemlock, anyway. That stuff'll kill you.

DEMON

Always use with "personal."

DIE HARD 2 | 1990

Warning! The following contains references to databases.
Reader discretion advised.

Let me take the edge off some alarmed opinions thrown at you about the movie DIE HARD 2.

First fire came from the LA TIMES on July 9, in an article by NBC newsman Fred Francis, who called the movie's ruthless newsman character "unbelievable," and accused the flick itself of lacking "plausible mayhem."

"I dunno," America said to its movie-going friends when asked to see this movie, "Does its mayhem achieve plausibility? It doesn't insult TV newsmen, does it? You know how I hate that."

Next, as if some media effort was conspiring to keep us from this fine film, Vincent Canby of the NEW YORK TIMES weighed in on July 16 with a history-of-movies-as-body-count, starting with PUBLIC ENEMY (1932, 8 bodies), and ending with DIE HARD 2 (1990, 264 bodies).

Canby's cautionary overview included a chart, which used a little gun to represent (roughly) 52 corpses. So PUBLIC ENEMY had a cute little sliver of a gun next to it, and DIE HARD 2 had a whopping five guns with a sliver of a sixth.

This chart, of course, is a perfect example of the trivial uses to which a database can be put. Still, I paid close attention to a disclaimer by the TIMES telling me that the bodies were indeed, "...counted by Vincent Canby." What a relief! You wouldn't want to entrust a job that big to a subordinate.

Unfortunately, this disclaimer also informed me that "because ... of camera angles, the counts are approximations." I can't help feeling sorry for Mr. Canby, sitting bleary-eyed through every movie ever made in the action/adventure genre, stopping every few minutes to wonder, "Was that guy dead, or just wounded?" Then he had to punch in pistol increments for his little charts, not knowing if his body count is accurate or not. Science isn't easy.

Well, to make a long story short, I saw the movie. Somebody had to do it. First of all, the jerk reporter was totally believable. Okay, his lines were all variations on, "I'll get the story and crush anybody in my way," snarled between thin lips, but as a hard-bitten journalist wannabe myself, I've uttered lines like these many times to the mirror in my bathroom.

I think Mr. Francis was just mad because the best lines in the movie were given to the air traffic controllers. If the sullen newsman had even one line as good as, "Stack 'em, pack 'em, and rack 'em," growled from the corner of the mouth, I believe Mr. Francis would have walked out of the movie theatre a happy guy.

But I don't know. I didn't walk away from DIE HARD 2 at all. I drove away blissfully, with the windows wide open. I never even got out of the car. To save on parking, I'd seen the movie at a drive-in that (it's rumored) will be torn down after Labor Day. I'm glad I seized the opportunity to recapture the unique drive-in experience of my youth. As jets drifted slowly by, high overhead, jets exploded on the screen below. (Three of them. Big suckers too. In one movie! Where's your chart for that, Mr. Canby?) That special SoCal aroma of jasmine and high octane filled the air.

Because of the kids running happily around, the crunch of heels on gravel, the constant glare of headlights on the screen, and the poor quality of sound emanating from the worst speaker in the world, frankly, I missed at least half the deaths abhorred by Mr. Canby, but I got the gist of DIE HARD 2. It's like this: when terrorists shut down an airport, you gotta do something about it. It doesn't matter what you thought about the airport, you gotta do something about it.

I really don't see why Mr. Canby has a problem with this.

If they'd had jets and mercenaries and ideologues in Jimmy Cagney's day, he'd have stuffed a few villains into the thrusters of a 747 himself. I have a hunch he'd have pulled down Bruce Willis' salary too.

Bottom line? When airplanes and drive-in movies are in danger, folks, plausibility goes out the window, and mayhem walks through the door.

Isn't that what popular entertainment is all about?

DYSFUNCTIONAL

Normal.

ELVITUDE | 1990

In a recent NEW YORK TIMES MAGAZINE, Stephen J. Thibeault, the assistant public affairs officer at the American Embassy in Iraq, was quoted as saying, "This is the Ted Bundy of countries." There's a soundbite after my own heart. This man is the Ian Shoales of diplomats, and his quote is the Elvis of soundbites, head and shoulders above the Pat Boone soundbites thrust upon us by the news media hit parade. I've always felt that Ted Bundy is the one true Elvis of serial killers—he had that extra little something that set him apart from the other serial-killer-hopefuls out there.

Saddam Hussein, in the Tin Pan Alley of shorthand media quips, has often been compared to Adolf Hitler (who was, of course, the Elvis of dictators), but really, Hussein is more the Mick Jagger of dictators—darkness lite (as in Bud Lite, the Elvis of light beers). Hussein might have had a shot at being the Elvis of religious despots, but he preferred military uniforms to the flowing robes of religious fundamentalism, thus leaving total Elvishood (in the religious sense) to the late great Ayatollah Khomeini, the man who Ted Bundy'ed Salman Rushdie into his present position—the Elvis of persecuted writers.

So who, you might ask, was the Elvis of presidents? Kennedy, definitely. Lincoln was the Roy Orbison of presidents, Franklin Roosevelt the Beatles of presidents, and Ronald Reagan was the Reagan of presidents—one of a kind really, they broke the mold when they made him. I hope they broke that mold. It's my personal Elvis of hopes. George Bush, again, is the Pat Boone of presidents, making Dan Quayle a kind of Pat Boone impersonator, I guess, or more precisely, a Pat Boone wannabe. I'd like to believe the preceding remark was the Elvis of gratuitous Dan Quayle jokes, but we both know the truth, don't we? It was just another Elvis wannabe, topical humorwise.

Like Madonna. Everybody knows that Marilyn Monroe is the Elvis of blondes. Madonna might hold claim to the title of Elvis of Jayne Mansfields, but what kind of title is that? It's like calling Lassie the Elvis of dogs. It's true, but where does it get you? Before you know it, you're calling Star Trek the Elvis of bad teevee series from the sixties, or Jeanne Kirkpatrick the Elvis of Republican women, or the Bible the Elvis of documents.

All of this might be true, but if all of the above is true—applying a little logic to this situation—that Lassie is the Elvis of dogs, then Benji is Pat Boone, and Cujo is Jerry Lee Lewis. This makes LOST IN SPACE the Fabian of bad teevee shows from the sixties, Pat Buchanan the Howlin' Wolf of Republican commentators, and The Koran the Jerry Lee Lewis of documents. Whither then Rin Tin Tin, William F. Buckley, and The Talmud? Are they just so many Sinatras in the forced metaphors of soundbite world? I think not, America.

Because we all know that America is still the Elvis of nations, and that we revere the Elvises among us—Hugh Hefner, for example, the Elvis of bachelors (retired), the man who built an American empire devoted to the relentless exposure of this or that co-ed's mammary gland, the Elvis of breasts. Walt Disney, truly an Elvis for our times, parlayed an obsession with the butts of fuzzy animals into a multi-trillion dollar empire which may yet overtake the world. I don't pretend to understand this empire, but it's definitely the Elvis of something. America understands the tragedy of Donald Trump, who wanted to be the Elvis of tycoons, but ended up the Monkees, the Elvis to which the New Kids on the Block aspire.

As we reel from the S&L crisis (the Elvis of scandals), we're still reeling from Viet Nam (the Elvis of foreign entanglements). Now we seem to be preparing to battle Iraq (Elvis of nothing special), either for the sake of oil, the Elvis of fuels, or to curtail the antics of the tinhorn Ted Bundy the world calls Saddam Hussein. Either way it's bound to be a new chapter in the chronicles of Elvitude. Stay tuned. As Elvis said, "Only fools walk in." I guess we just can't help it.

EMPOWERMENT* 1993

I always thought "empowerment" was a trendy left-wing term, like "hegemony," "intertextual," and "healing process." How wrong I was. Starting Dec. 6, National Empowerment Television will go on the air, funded by the Free Congress Foundation. A C-SPAN with attitude, NET will be the first all-conservative television channel.

Here's a partial lineup: "The Progress Report," with the omnipresent Newt Gingrich, "Youngbloods," a call-in show aimed at "challenging the cynicism" of MTV, and "Scoop!" featuring home video exposes of local government. Burton Pines will host Capitol Watch, which will expose the "real agenda of a White House action."

I don't know how much mileage conservatives will get from this channel. After all, thanks to Rush Limbaugh, most Americans must know the conservative tenets by heart by now. Less government! Stop Anita Hill! Public education is run by a cabal of left-leaning secular humanists! The marketplace rules! The rich ideological stew is thickened with the line item veto, term limits, family values, and the death penalty. Conservatives are also obsessed with "capital gains," whatever that means. I suspect they're mainly of interest to those with capital to burn.

For all the conservative blustering about activists and useful idiots sneakily committed to perverse and loony causes, I don't see much evidence. If public schools are being destroyed by self-serving bureaucrats, does that make self-serving bureaucrats liberals?

What radicals remain in public schools are a pathetic lot. I just read an essay by an anarchist teacher who just couldn't get his students to pay attention to him. "How," he wrote in anguish, "can I get them to accept that I might possess cultural tools they can use to overthrow the culture I represent?" He just didn't get it. By not listening to him, his students had already overthrown the culture he represented. But that's the trouble with the left. They're not happy if you just blow things up. You have to use their dynamite too.

On the other hand, I don't feel personally threatened by Anita Hill. I'm not sure, but I think that makes me a liberal. The fairness doctrine may be history, but I still think some left-leaning foundation (is there such a thing?) should give me the money for my own network, Demographically Dysfunctional Television, or DDT.

Here's my line-up:

SINGLE MOMS STRIKE BACK!

Single mothers, tired of being blamed for everything from rampant drug use to low SAT scores, drag deadbeat dads through a gauntlet of broken toys. If no deadbeat dad can be found, studio audience males will be selected at random.

GOVERNMENT AT WORK!

Conservatives often run for public office on the platform that we have too much government. Why should I vote for somebody who wants to make less work for himself? With this show, we'll put representatives of every stripe to work, fixing potholes, patrolling a beat, notarizing documents, duplicating keys, and baby-sitting for single mothers as they work two jobs to try to keep off the welfare rolls.

THE HOMELESS EMPLOYMENT HOUR

To build their self-esteem and willpower, homeless people are introduced to prospective employers. Many of them are crackhead winos, have no shoes, hear voices in their head, and haven't bathed in thirteen years, but this show will still get them off the street by "empowering" them. I guarantee it!

THE UNEMPLOYED HAPPY HOUR

Experts discuss world events before an unemployed studio audience. Every time the panel uses words like "retrofitting," "retraining," "global economy," or "fair market value," the unemployed will pelt the pundits with pink slips, thoughtfully provided.

FREE-FOR-ALL MARKET

In the pilot, cocaine dealers and children's television producers discuss ways to move product in a regulation-free environment.

NAME THAT IDEOLOGY!

Contestants will have thirty seconds to name the ideologies of various middle-aged men wearing blue neckties. Good luck!

I'd have a tough time with that one myself. Beware of charts, however. Whether they're liberal or conservative, when politicians start displaying charts, start clutching your pocketbook. That's an empowerment tip you can really use.

Let me clear up a common point of confusion. "Empowering" means to help in a good way. "Enabling," on the other hand, means to help in a bad way. I hope this helps.

END OF HISTORY

History ended briefly at the end of the eighties, then abruptly started up again. Authorities are baffled.

ENTRY LEVEL

Synonym for "shitty job."

EPIPHANIES | 1993

I've got nothing against epiphanies. I've had a few myself, (not that they've made me any money), but should epiphanies be accessed weekly in the pages of Sunday newspapers? The burden of insights into the human condition once fell exclusively on the shoulders of poets, novelists, or the occasional playwright—now any feature writer with a prose style can express the ineffable every seven days.

We are in the clutches of a disturbing phenomenon, the Pensive Essay Syndrome. It threatens to destroy curling up with the Sunday paper as we know it. The introspective pieces engendered by the Syndrome, by and large, are written firmly but gently from a gender-driven point of view. They often get their own site in the Sunday paper, called "About Men," "About Women," "His," or "Hers," from which the authors enter the realm of memory as if it were an empty church. Their prose style is the only thing that keeps them from fainting: "Watching my son/daughter play baseball/try on a bra I think of my father/mother and the first time we wrestled/went shopping...." The authors loosen ties, kick off shoes, and suddenly they're children again, touching and feeling their way blindly to a new tomorrow.

And they offer one darn epiphany after another: how Dad's den smelled after the divorce, how lost that first love seemed at the train station, how small the author's hand was in Mommy's vast gloved paw, how tall Pa seemed the day they laid him off. The writers project upon their children lessons from their bland pasts like slides on a living room wall. "Change, baby," the prose style whispers wistfully, "Learn."

These writers approach the stages of their children's lives as reverently as stations of the cross: Baby's first step, Baby's first nanny, Baby gets a day care, Baby finds a private school, Mommy/Daddy wipes the tears of baby, questions of Baby and anguish/concern of Mommy/Daddy in answering them, Baby meets bullies, Baby develops certain learning disabilities, Baby gets a wardrobe,

Baby meets puberty, Baby's prom, Baby's attitude problems, Baby becomes a man/woman, Baby leaves home...

I bet Baby can't wait to leave home, free at last of Mommy/Daddy's constant observation. Maybe it's the insidious influence of camcorders, or the growing sophistication of photography, but there's a sense of voyeurism to this lyricism. Family moments used to pop up, then disappear. We'd say simply "Hey you know what my kid did last night?" and go on with our work. We'd show the slides, "And there's my old man, drunk at the reunion," as our guests checked their watches and edged for the door. Today, thousands of boring moments are recollected in tranquillity, painstakingly and poetically recaptured, relentlessly examined by men and women who have found, against all odds, the leisure time to write about them.

Though seemingly wispy creatures, Sunday writers possess a rigid prose style developed over years of workshops: READER'S DIGEST meets THE NEW YORKER meets personal counseling. Reading their language nuggets, one can visualize (or see, I suppose) the writers curled up in window seats or sitting at antique desks with very nice notebooks. More likely these things are written on laptops, but they seem to emanate from a Mont Blanc pen: autumn leaves are always and definitely falling, triggering memories of a misty childhood, from which lessons, like beacons, summon.

They might have divorces, they may move to unfamiliar places, but these sensitive, thoughtful children have grown into endlessly responsible adults, worried about day care, worried about education, worried about yesterday, tomorrow, and today, yet still finding time to create a world where drinking problems and moonlight achieve equivalence, where everything's just a point on a learning curve.

They jog, they own their own homes, they can afford therapists and trainers—they dare to presume that their problems are important. I have no problem with that, but there's no neon in their world, no Tenderloin dives, the only homeless are their unsuccessful relatives. They all seem to be lawyers, or consultants, or slumming successful writers graciously offering a chunk of prose at the invitation of an editor. It's all Insights R Us, and it all seems to come down to this family moment: "We gathered our children around us, and drove to Grandma's house. Weeping softly, we put her in the home."

ESQUIRE | 1991

Warning! The following contains references to polls and/or surveys. Reader discretion advised.

It called itself "A Special Issue!," but the October ESQUIRE Magazine released its usual thick cloud of Obsession, and revealed a familiar theme dear to its readers: "What is a man?" The answer always turns out to be, "A guy who reads Esquire," but it never stops editors from popping the question. Like Sisyphus pushing the rock up the hill, men's magazines always end where they begin. Real men don't have a fire in the belly. Are you kidding? Real men have a Tommy Hilfiger wool crewneck sweater.

We were given profiles of Jeff Bridges (nice guy, good dresser) and Robert Bly (interesting guy, bad dresser), an inside look at a men's retreat (weird guys, really bad dressers), and the results of an ESQUIRE poll: "1001 American Men on Their Hopes, Dreams, Fears, and Betty Rubble-Lust." Now, I'm a humor professional (and reasonably swell dresser), and even I couldn't tell if this poll was a joke or not. A deadpan preface by Top Expert Dr. Herbert Rappaport assured me that the survey "...addresses the very subjects—masculinity, self-image, sexuality—that normally defy honesty and openness in men.... At the very least, the answers show what men think is expected of them. And from those expectations we can infer how men see the abstraction we call masculinity." This is probably as much scientific rigor as we can expect from a breezy men's magazine.

So what inferences can one draw about the abstract masculine from question 9 on the poll, "Would you rather read a good novel or get a peek inside a well-built woman's blouse?" According to the survey, peeking beat reading by a whopping 6%. But how can you even compare the two? Browsing and leering are incompatible social activities. You can read a book on a public bus, where sneaking a peek at a woman's decolletage is discouraged. In the privacy of the boudoir, a woman may permit you to tear away flimsies for a visual confirmation of her pleasure orbs, but believe me, she'll insist that you tear yourself away from your book first.

What are the rules of etiquette? If a man is alone with a well-built woman and a hefty novel, how does he sneak that peek? Does he say, "Hey, look how thick my book is!" and peer quickly while she's distracted? Or does he ask permission, like a gentleman: "Pardon me, ma'am, do you mind if I have a little glance inside there?"

Is the American male a drooling illiterate who'd rather get socked in the eye by Dolly Parton than pick up PALE FIRE? Does even the rare and endangered booklover try to picture Madame Bovary's alabaster bosom whenever he rereads Flaubert? Surely, there must be test-osterone-bearers somewhere who enjoy reading a well-built novel in the company of a good woman, or a good novel by a woman. Feminism and literacy must have made some inroads in that gaudy cocktail lounge we call male sexuality.

The survey, unfortunately, indicated otherwise. There weren't any topless babes or female mudwrestlers displayed as sexual choices in the survey, but in other respects, the poll seemed to show the median male, once again, as a 12 year old in a 40 year old body. There was question 19: "Who would you rather marry? Jane Pauley or Mariah Carey?" Well, really! Jane Pauley is already married, and Mariah Carey is a pop singer. Any nitwit can tell you that you never get involved with pop singers; when the relationship falls apart, they'll do a glib double album about the breakup—in all three formats. Ask Sean Penn! Or check out question 31, "Who would be wilder in bed? Connie Chung or Diane Sawyer?" I can't say this strongly enough: *the orgasmic states of anchorwomen should never be visualized.* It can cause irreparable damage to the male psyche. And question 47! "Who would you rather make love to? Wilma Flintstone or Betty Rubble?" Does ESQUIRE really want us to commit adultery with a poorly animated cartoon character?

I admit: I am the new American man, post-modern, ironic to a fault—just last week I arched an eyebrow so hard I sprained it. I'd rather reek of Egoiste than the honest musk of manly labor. But is the price of this manhood a quick grab-and-tickle with Betty Rubble? If that's safe sex, I'd rather read a book.

EUROTRASH

The mainstay of discos.

EVANGELISM

Insistent social movement.

"EVIL EMPIRE"

Dead as vaudeville.

EXCELLENCE

What is supposed to be rewarded, but never is.

EXERCISE | 1991

David "Kung Fu" Carradine, perhaps the last hippie in America, has been plugging an exercise video on late night television: a Tai Chi workout, based on Taoist principles, for the whole being, physical, mental, and spiritual.

I don't see much of a future for the David Carradine video though, even with his ample credentials ("Hi. I'm not a spiritually evolved martial artist, but I play one on television..."). I just can't visualize (as we say in California) a customer. For Jane Fonda's video, I can picture some desperate, recently divorced housewife, deep in the bowels of a suburban rumpus room. I can see our consumer bravely don Capris pants, pop Jane into the VCR, and follow along in a toddler-smudged mirror. There Jane is, taped forever in the faded glory of the last dregs of Hollywood youth. "And there I am," thinks our gasping housewife, "Jell-o woman! It looks like two small dogs are wrestling in my Spandex." In despair, she puts her fist through the television, goes upstairs to guzzle two bottles of chilled Chablis, and pass out on the couch. Nothing in this appalling scenario smacks of the way of Tao, now does it?

No, humility and inner peace are just not found in a personal fitness program. Americans exercise for the same reasons they do anything else, to be objects of envy and desire, achieve power, make money, and live forever. But if jogging does extend your life, I'll bet the time added is exactly equivalent to the time spent jogging. I won't even dwell on the time wasted shopping for running outfits, or the time loss suffered when pumps go flat. I must include professional sports in this indictment: there is no Socrates in sports medicine, no Buddhist boxer, no lama in the end zone.

While truth in exercise is as rare as a football player with functioning kneecaps, I suspect most self-improvers, if they'll just admit it, give up before they begin, staring sadly at the pastel Spandex outfits, at the dusty Abdomenizer™ in the closet, unable even to summon the energy to drag weights to a dumpster. Surely, there are millions of unfit Americans out there, neither pacifist nor ambitious, who are willing to surrender to their own misery, and whine proudly, "That's too hard!"

Cheer up. I am one of you. It is for you that I've developed the Ian Shoales Exercise Program.

What is it?

Not much, I'll tell you that. I take the minimalist approach to self-improvement—no jumping jacks in ATM lines, or squeezing balls during business meetings. My simple suggestions are untinged by even a hint of enthusiasm. Here are some lurid highlights.

Hide all remotes. Getting out of the Barca-lounger every time you have to change the channel can really firm up that tummy! Make a series of important phone calls, then pace nervously while waiting for the powerful to call you back—yes, you can use your own ineffectuality to build strong calves. The compulsive chewing of nails can do wonders for your jawline. Stop payment on all checks, and watch pounds disappear as you elude your creditors.

Next time Congress holds a hearing on whatever scandal is waiting in the wings to be revealed, turn to C-Span for gavel-to-gavel coverage. Stand loosely before your television. Shake out. Now, hyperventilate, and scream, "Liar! Lies!" If you perform this exercise properly, the tendons on your neck should be stiff as a pencil and vibrating slightly. Throw pennies at your throat. If the coins bounce, you're on the right track.

Gosh, I'm getting a spasm in my pecs just thinking about it. So give up with me! As gasping joggers run grimly to the sea, you can sleep the satisfied sleep of the fat. Gals, dream of that dream date with

Ted Turner, and guys—gain the strength at last to throw those barbells in the trash.

That's the Ian Shoales Workout, available soon (as soon as I find a friend to loan me a camcorder), Barca-lounger not included. Remember: no Taoist has ever been, or dated, Ted Turner. Order now!

EXIT POLL

A survey designed to let people know what they just did.

F

FACTOID

"Timothy Busfield won an Emmy," for example, or "Michael Jackson is a reclusive superstar."

FACTOR

Increments of factors are involved in any decision, especially *major decisions*. Many factors are themselves *tough choices*.

FAMILY CEO | 1995

Thumbing through the NEW YORK TIMES last Sunday, I found a full-page ad in the Book Review section for a book called EVERY FAMILY NEEDS A CEO.

We used to have a Dad and/or a Mom; then we learned to settle for an authority figure, a role model, or even someone who has simple "socialization skills" and the confidence to "parent (to use the latest psychoverb for an activity most warm-blooded animals can accomplish without the aid of books at all)." Now, apparently, the family needs an overpaid corporate executive to oversee the process whereby human offspring are taught to fend for themselves in a vicious world.

Well, why not? Why not EVERY FAMILY NEEDS A WARDEN, EVERY FAMILY NEEDS A DRILL SERGEANT, or EVERY FAMILY NEEDS A MUSSOLINI?

I suppose the concept of having a CEO run family matters is meant to be a tad more humanizing. A CEO generally wears a white collar, not a brown shirt. In other words, it's permitted to pal around with a CEO at certain special times (office parties, conventions, etc.). But you never toss a nerf ball to a warden. You never play Parcheesi with a drill sergeant. If Mussolini started reading "Good Night Moon" to you, prior to tucking you in, I'd be more alarmed than comforted.

In the past, however, "Chief Executive Officer" has meant "head of a company" to me. Will families have to sell stock in themselves?

And if the bottom falls out of the market? Will we have to sell off Mom or (more likely) poor old Uncle Charley, to pay off our debt?

What if the family gets taken over by some lean and hungry family down the block? The Johnsons have a high overhead because they maxed out their plastic on a big-screen teevee. The Nelsons, meanwhile, like bees with their pollen, have shrewdly amassed credit cards and never used them. When their credit rating is high enough, they strike, buying Johnsons' debt with their debt, paying Dad off, and putting the rest of the Johnsons to work at sub-wages in the rec room polishing old bowling trophies, while the Nelsons upstairs enjoy the full-screen fruit of the Johnson's hard-earned bankruptcy. I can see this happening.

If families are run by CEOs, then, all the kids will have to hunker down and pull their weight for the good of the company. But this means they'll have to cover their behinds as well. This means e-mail.

When the CEO barks a command, "Someone wash the dishes!" say, it will result in a flurry of inter-family memos, as members argue furiously about who is responsible for what ("I'll wash if you dry." "I'll wash everything but the greasy pans."), down to the most minute of details ("I'll put away the forks, if you do the knives."). Hopefully, by the time this has been straightened out, the family crisis will have passed (Ever the thankless admin, Mom will have put everything in the dishwasher, and pressed "On"), and the actual need to obey the CEO's command will not be necessary. This is how corporations work.

Other issues such as bedtimes, proper workspace attire, the piercing of a member's ears, would all be handled through interminable meetings, featuring ring binders, flow charts, and multimedia presentations. After which, each family member would deluge the CEO with faxes trashing every one else's positions. This will go on, again, until a decision becomes moot. The ears will be pierced, the kids will stay up all night, the formalwear will be traded for a power app; productivity will flourish, and the CEO will take credit for everything. So where's the problem?

Well, the CEO has the ability to downsize. What if he decides that little baby Johnny isn't pulling his weight? What if he's given a pink slip, and replaced with some eager beaver replacement toddler from Sumatra, who's willing to drool on his Legos for twice as long at half the wage?

I'm not saying families should unionize, mind you, but members should have some protection from their CEO's. Where's the golden parachute for little baby Johnny? That's all I wonder.

FAST FOOD 1983

Every time I go to McDonald's, and I go there about once a week, I try to imagine America without fast food. Fast food has become a necessity, like cars and telephones. I sip my tepid shake, chew my cold fries and double cheeseburger, and try to understand what I'm doing—am I eating or shopping? The commercials make McDonald's seem like a place where lovers meet, where families gather, where memories leap into being like the magical appearance of a ghost or an old friend. We're supposed to remember going to McDonald's the same way we remember going to the prom or the occasion of our firstborn.

But these are just Hollywood images, not real. The memories blur into one large pleasant, fuzzy image. Those endless bags of fries merge into one archetypal bag.

No matter where you are in the country, the food will be the same. That's the comfort and that's the terror. But that's not really what McDonald's is trying to sell us.

There is no McDonald anymore, it's just a pleasant name that conjures the pleasant image of Old MacDonald and his harmless farm. What McDonald's is is a doorway to another dimension, another world—a different global village with its own citizens: Ronald McDonald and Mayor McCheese, happy families and lovers in love.

But who guards the gates to this other world? Polite teenagers in uniform. What you're buying when you pass under the golden arches is a tiny unit of politeness frozen in time—fast food in friendly bags, bright colors, friendly teens who serve you with a smile, friendly cartoon faces that tell us "we do it all for you." It's all for me. It's reassuring. It's a temporary utopia that only lasts as long as your lunch hour.

The signs tell us politely there's a twenty minute time limit to the booths, the signs in the parking lot give us a half hour. This is the wave of the future. Twenty years from now they won't even serve food, they'll just be politeness centers scattered across the nation, little golden islands in the face of The New Rudeness, islands where you can rest up for the onslaught of a vicious world.

You can bask in the friendly faces of strangers, but only for a little while. Twenty minutes of affection, that's all you need and that's all you get. Well dressed men and women will greet you attentively and listen politely for twenty minutes, and then the bad teenagers will come and take you away.

Fast food for the soul. That's McDonald's.

FEAR | 1985

Somewhere in the fifties, William Powell and Myrna Loy stopped dancing the rumba till dawn, and Manhattan became the Naked City. The Concrete Jungle buried The Thin Man. And somewhere in the seventies, the Concrete Jungle became a Charles Bronson movie. The clash between civil liberties and "traditional values" (whatever that means) has created what TIME likes to call "a climate of fear."

All that this means is: the movies changed. The climate of fear ain't the weather I live in. The gun isn't my umbrella.

And isn't fear one of the reasons we move to the Big City in the first place?

As a hick with urban pretensions I know I moved to the city for the romance—writing hard-edged prose in a garret, having a painfully thin girlfriend, and friends who wear berets and only shave every three days. As a younger man I welcomed my fears, which were mundane enough—Where is the rent coming from? How will I eat? Is anybody paying attention to me? What if people start to take me seriously, what will I do? Will I ever publish that 1,500 page rock and roll novel that doesn't quite fit in the sock drawer?

As far as real fear goes, yes, the streets are unsafe, full of intense confrontations, the ravings of street people, the desperate poor, and hardened criminals, but I don't see how subway showdowns will solve anything. Juvenile delinquents and vigilantes would love to live in a city where they can take pot shots at one another as they dodge down the mean streets. But they shoot straighter in the movies. In real life, innocent people get in the way.

How can the government help? Is it really the job of government to second-guess the actions of potential psychopaths? What do we want? A personal armed guard? A SWAT team at every stop? These things cost money, you know. Most Americans would rather live in mortal terror than pay more taxes.

Nowadays if you see a couple in a tux and mink you don't say "Hiya Nick and Nora," you mutter "rich jerks" under your breath and move along. I miss The Thin Man as much as anybody, but if you can't stand the heat, go live in a Jimmy Stewart movie. New York ain't Smallville, folks. Archie and Veronica don't live in the Big City. If The City was a nice place to live, nobody would live there.

FLIPFLOP

What the media call it when a politician changes his mind.

FOCUS GROUP

If it likes a teevee show, the theory goes, so will you.

FORMAT

A box in which to place virtual realities.

FRANKLIN MINT

Purveyors of fine art.

FRANKLY

Word thrown into conversation to give credence to a lie.

FUTURE 1993

I was spinning the dial late-ish a while back and stumbled upon a STAR TREK episode I'd never seen before. As usual when catching STAR TREK, I only caught part of it and I wasn't paying much attention, but I did notice that the episode featured that familiar orange sky, Abraham Lincoln, and cruel, unfeeling aliens (who looked like sacks of potatoes) putting Kirk and Spock's humanism to a test. During the course of the grueling exam, if I recall correctly, Kirk got the little tear in his uniform and tiny ribbon of blood on his cheek that are the official Star Trek indicators of intergalactic hardship. Anyway, they passed the test, Kirk scolded the potatoes for being manipulative and uncaring, everybody but Lincoln beamed up, McCoy said something cranky yet endearing, and they were off to the next star cluster.

Now, I've been catching snippets of STAR TREK for close to twenty-five years now. After all this time, shouldn't coming across an episode I haven't seen before be considered a miracle of sorts? As miracles go, this is pretty bland, admittedly, and I don't discount the possibility that I had seen it before, and forgotten. After all, I've viewed most Star Trek snippets in less than ideal circumstances, at two o'clock in the morning, for example, or while suffering from jet lag and/or the lingering effects of mild substance abuse. Still, you'd think the sight of Abe Lincoln juxtaposed with potatoes from Mars would be an image with long term staying power, even in my battered synapses.

Nowadays, I forget television shows all the time, even those I've actually watched. I caught SEINFELD once, for example, because I'd read that it was hip and post-modern. Seinfeld himself is funny enough, I guess, though his brand of humor doesn't do much for me: "Ball point pens, I dunno, is it just me? Shoes are weird!" Well, all I can remember about SEINFELD the show was some annoying bald guy whining about something, intercut with a bunch of anxious people ordering Chinese food.

If having absolutely nothing happen is stretching the limits of the sitcom, I'd say SEINFELD is definitely on the cutting edge, but is a sitcom without a sit a good idea? If they'd thrown in a dead president and a smattering of potatoheads from other worlds, we might have had something. I felt the same way about THE COSBY SHOW. Every time I watched it, it seemed like Dr. Huxtable was trying to get a blender to work. Is that entertainment? If he'd thrown a Tribble or two into the food processor, maybe.

But the face of television is changing. In our modern television sea of infomercials, plotless comedies, and Canadian cop shows ("Stop or I'll shoot, eh!"), I believe the fine hidden hand of a secret network of Trekkies is computer-generating "new" episodes of the old STAR TREK. I can't think of any other explanation for what I've seen, can you? The question is, should we be alarmed or comforted?

If STAR TREK is invading the airwaves, both covertly (DEEP SPACE NINE, STAR TREK: THE NEXT GENERATION) and overtly (generation of "new" old episodes by all-powerful Trekkie hackers), mightn't they join forces? We've already seen Scotty, Spock, and McCoy show up on STAR TREK: THE NEXT GENERATION, and Picard show up on Deep Space Nine. Could these inter-series invasions be a rehearsal for a takeover of existing syndicated series?

If Data ever shows up on JEOPARDY, the game show bank would soon be broken. A small Romulan invasion could wipe out the entire cast of BABYLON FIVE. If Romulans and Klingons ever debate on each other on Maury Povich, it could lead to a confrontation that would make World War III look like a picnic. Smarmy and ruthless Ferengi merchants could take over infomercials: "Here's your five point success program, earthlings: Surrender or die!" If it's true that Federation reps are standing on a starship bridge in their silly pocketless uniforms, even as I speak, dreaming up ways to infiltrate the airwaves, what happened to the Federation's logo, "Leave people alone," the so-called Prime Directive? Has the Prime Directive been replaced by Prime Time?

But the system's running at full warp now! She canna handle any more! She'll fall apart! For God's sake, turn it off before it's too late.*

Since I wrote this, Star Trek: VOYAGER has gone on the air. Consider it a warning.

FUZZY LOGIC | 1990

When I was kid, I'd pretend that grapes were eyeballs, which somehow had the effect of making me want to eat them. In this spirit, here in the nineties, a Berkeley professor has steered a brave new concept into the digital domain: FUZZY LOGIC.

A computer using fuzzy logic isn't like a bicycle with square tires though. Fuzzy logic *expands* a computer's reasoning capacity, allowing not only "Yes/No" responses but "Maybe/Holy Cow," "Higher/Lower," "I dunno/I forget," "a skosh more/less," and even "Come again?/Perhaps you'd care to talk to my supervisor."

California, of course, has been on a first-name basis with fuzzy logic for years, but we've never used it to make trains run on time. Instead we use it to formulate statements like "Think globally, act locally." As if we could act anywhere else!

In Japan, however, they've used fuzzy logic for years—to shift transmissions, condition air, focus cameras, maybe even turn grapes into eyeballs, I don't know.

All I know is, while we're frittering away the hours visualizing world peace, networking, and timeshifting, Japan is pulling into the station on time, and ready to go to work.

If fuzzy logic is ever going to have a practical application in America, we're got to give up any vain pretense of rationalism. Fuzzy logic must become a way of life.

Let's measure your *Fuzzy Logic Potential.*

1. COMPLETE THE FOLLOWING.
If shampoo is a hair-care system, and screaming at employees indicates a hands-on management style, then screaming at your hair is _____.

2. WHICH STATEMENT DOES NOT BELONG?
A pay raise is an ethics package. A missile is a message. Tom Cruise is a great actor. Taxation is revenue enhancement. A smoking gun is a memo. A grape is an eyeball.

3. WHICH DOES NOT BELONG?
Demonize. Womanize. Simonize. Moralize. Plagiarize. Agonize. Ostracize. Bette Davis Eyes. Grapes.

4. CONSTRUCT A PROPOSITION FOR THE FOLLOWING CONCLUSION:
"Therefore: D."

5. (T/F)
Dan Quayle joke.

6. WHICH PHRASE DOES NOT BELONG?
*Hidden agenda. Cautious optimism. Deplorable incident.
Senseless tragedy. Papal nuncio. Panamanian strongman.
Seedless grapes.*

7. CHOOSE THE TAUTOLOGY THAT'S RIGHT FOR YOU:
*(1) Let Reagan be Reagan. (2) A rose is a rose. (3)
Reeboks let U.B.U.*

8. IF WORLD PEACE CAN BE VISUALIZED, AND
BATMAN CAN BE VISUALIZED, IS WORLD PEACE
BATMAN?

ANSWERS:
(1). A hands-on management style-care system. **(2).** A grape is *not* an eyeball. **(3).** Grapes. **(4).** "If A—what did I do with that A? Oh here it is—damn! I'm out of B's! We don't have the budget for C. Well, we'll use D and hope nobody notices. **(5).** True. **(6).** Papal nuncio. **(7).** [3] **(8).** *Some* world peace is BATMAN.

GANGSTA MOM | 1996

The New York Times Sunday Magazine ran a profile a few weeks back of Suge Knight, CEO of Death Row Records, for whom Tupac Shakur and Snoop Doggy Dogg record their state-of-the-art gangsta rap. Tha Dogg Pound and Dr. Dre (formerly of N.W.A.) are also part of Death Row, with whom Time Warner lately had a distribution deal.

(This deal, you'll recall, was the bane of Bob Dole and William Bennett. Thanks in part to their efforts, Death Row was dropped by Time Warner. And the nation probably sleeps better tonight, knowing that these rappers' CDSs are now being placed in record stores by an entirely different corporation. Thank God for free market Republicans!)

Mr. Knight, bearlike and known as Suge to his friends, comes across in the article as every inch the Scary Black Person we've come to know and love from white media. He neither confirmed nor denied having threatened rivals with baseball bats, but didn't seem displeased by the accusation. One of his employees was shot to death last year, allegedly by a rival East Coast producer. Like the mobsters of yore, Mr. Knight travels everywhere (even by charter jet to Vegas) with a vast crowd of bodyguards, who have names like Neckbone, Trey, Rock, Hen Dogg, and Bountry.

Bountry, when first encountered in the profile, was removing lint from his black fedora with masking tape. Bountry described this as "an old ghetto trick."

Well, this gave me pause.

She never had a posse, never traveled anywhere by stretch limo, and never bludgeoned anyone to death at a music awards ceremony, but my mother did in fact teach me how to remove lint from clothing with masking tape. Did she have a secret past I knew nothing about? Among her friends was she known as Soup Mommy Momm?

Thinking back on my boyhood in the Dakotas, I've been trying to remember: was our neighborhood a 'hood? When Mom put a penny in the fuse box was she employing a Norwegian-American version of street smarts? When she darned socks, or tore up old tee-shirts for rags was she promoting a gangsta lifestyle or just being frugal?

On the other end of the spectrum, as a media-obsessed so-called adult, I find myself wondering: in all the interviews with rappers I've read in free weekly newspapers and 'zines, have I ever seen evidence of an interface between rapper and mom cultures?

I vaguely recall Ice-T in an interview somewhere reminding his fans that "Yogurt is a healthy substitute for sour cream— try it on mashed potatoes!" But I could be wrong. Didn't Ice Cube once close his live performances by telling his audiences to dress warmly and rotate their tires? Or maybe it was something about removing ketchup stains with baking soda and vinegar.

I don't know if many gangstas try to fool their children by putting generic frosted flakes in a Kellogg's box, or how many offset the high cost of limo champagne with the exclusive use of lower priced spreads back at the crib, or if they've discovered the incredible variety of interesting things you can do with leftover turkey after the holidays (Tried croquettes, by the way?), but even without this information, I think we can make some pretty solid comparisons.

Let's go to the chart:

GANGSTA	MOM
surrounded by posse	surrounded by bridge club
raps at the drop of a hat	bursts into "I've Been Working On The Railroad" at the drop of a hat
likes hats	likes hats
calls home a "crib"	has baby crib in attic
weears baggy sweats	weears baggy sweats
affects large gold jewelery	affects large gold jewelery
often makes complicated hand gestures	often clutches purse tightly
hates police	obeys speed limit
removes lint from clothing with masking tape	removes lint from clothing with masking tape
wears dark glasses	wears tinted glasses
often complains about being disrespected	often complains about being disrespected
knows all about life on the street	knows what every family on the street is up to
has nickname in the 'hood	is called "Mrs. Shoales" in the 'hood
is dangerous when crossed	is dangerous when crossed
doesn't take crap from anybody	will brook no nonsense
busts rhymes	uses dustbuster
uses the word "fly" to mean "great"	hates flies, doesn't care who knows it
calls friends "homes"	calls friends daily
cellular phone is constant companion	constantly gets caught in the phone cord when talking with her homies
is a cause of conservative alarm	is an alarmed conservative
is fiercely loyal to friends and family	is fiercely loyal to friends and family
is very macho	thinks men are childish idiots

There are several conclusions to be drawn here. I'm no sociologist, so I'll be damned if I'll draw them.

It is obvious however that a cellular phone would make an excellent Mother's Day gift. And if you're looking for a present to give to that gangsta in your life, we can recommend either a Glock 9 mm semiautomatic or HINTS FROM HELOISE— in paperback, now, not hardcover, and preferably used. After all, as our homeboy Ben Franklin put it, "Yo, a penny saved is a penny earned. Word up."

GENEX 1994

In a spot from a recent series of beer commercials, long-haired young slackers played golf and waxed nostalgic about pop music. One of the songs mentioned was the Knack's "My Sharona," also featured prominently in previews for REALITY BITES, the new Generation X movie with Winona Ryder. The Knack must have really been a seminal influence on GenExers.

To us Boomers, though, the Knack are only remembered for briefly threatening to become "the next Beatles." Unfortunately for them, around that time Fleetwood Mac *did* briefly become the next Beatles. Not that GenEx cared. To them, the Beatles are just the group Paul was in before Wings, if they remember Wings.

Not only that, GenExers don't even care about who's going to be the next Dylan! When I was their age, the woods were *full* of next Dylans. When it finally looked like Springsteen was, in fact, going to be the next Dylan, and became Springsteen instead, something broke inside the Boomers.

If today there's some loose talk about "the next Springsteen," nobody's heart is in it. Even Springsteen doesn't seem interested in being the next Springsteen. Dylan himself has become a bit of a joke. And what happened to the Knack anyway?

Yes, pop culture can really break your heart.

Another commercial from the series displayed a group of young men playing pool and discussing the relative merits of Mary Ann and Ginger from GILLIGAN'S ISLAND. (These ads all had a strange semi-documentary quality. They pretended to be little slices of life: what young bucks today *really* like to do is indulge in mild physical activity, and rattle off random semi-famous names while drinking name brand beer in moderation.)

But also in the spot, hunched over and sullen on the sidelines, were a couple of women. At one point, one muttered bitterly to the other: "Ginger was a bimbo." She was jealous of a character from a stupid sitcom made thirty years ago! And, in fact, the pool-players did seem more interested in old teevee babes than the *actual* teevee babes in the room.

In that regard, speaking from experience, the ad was true to life. Boys of my generation also ignored actual girls in favor of virtual trivia. The only difference was we weren't "on beer," but marijuana (in moderation, of course). Triviawise, therefore, today's young men may have a tactical advantage—they can actually remember the names of old television programs. On the other hand, a short attention span allowed my generation to spend entire evenings exploring a single topic: the names of the seven dwarves, say, or even something as simple as the name of Howdy Doody's clown. (Tinkerbell? Caramel?)

On the downside of today's information highway, there's a lot more useless data for GenEx to assimilate: the names of rap stars, for one. GenExers are probably wise to leave marijuana alone, and stick to cold brews, unless they want to spend a week trying to remember the name of Snoop Doggy Dog.

And, alas, they will try to remember the name of Snoop Doggy Dog, or someone like him. Kids today have succumbed to the same fatal obsession that destroyed my generation, the compulsion to remember trivia we should never have paid attention to in the first place.

Take the Beatles. We made them so famous that after they broke up they couldn't compete with their own past. Even as they bought it, boomer consumers subjected everything they did to little sniffs of minor disappointment. We *still* can't get enough Beatles! A pending album of outtakes is being previewed in the media as if it were a Dead Sea Scroll. The recent rumor that the remaining Beatles might regroup forced Paul, George, and Ringo to barricade themselves and issue surly press releases denying everything. There's a new movie about Stu Sutcliffe, for God's sake! What's next? Judd Nelson as Pete Best?

Today's object of cultlike devotion might be the Brady Bunch, not the Beatles, but the end result will probably be the same: BRADY BUNCH: THE MOVIE, with Judd Nelson as Mike Brady. Some young Judd Nelson is dreaming *even now* of playing Kurt Cobain in NIRVANA, a film by Oliver Stone, Jr.

I don't see any real cultural difference between generational obsessions. STAR TREK'S in its next generation, but it's still STAR TREK. Zoning out on aimless guitar solos and on *sampled* aimless guitar solos are still the same activity. If you take away the martinis and cigarettes, is there any difference between the Rat Pack and the Brat Pack? When it comes to our media martyrs, River Phoenix and James Dean were both (dare I say it?) mediocre actors. The ceaseless nattering about who was sexier, Annette or Hayley Mills, Wilma or Betty, Mary Ann or Jeannie, will not help boys of any age find true love, now will it?

Let's nip this behavior in the bud! Otherwise, we'll see today's tensomethings wistfully hefting cold ones in tomorrow's virtual reality, trying to remember the names of the babes from Baywatch: Snoopy? Clarabelle? Sharona? Tonya? Lorena? Heidi?*

*Kurt Cobain has since committed suicide. Bob Dylan is an obscure songwriter. The Beatles are once again popular than Jesus.
** Brady Bunch: The Movie was actually made. There was even a sequel.

GRAFFITI | 1994

Many Americans have responded with favorable fervor to the imminent caning of Michael Peter Fay in Singapore. "He spraypainted some cars!" says this self-righteous crowd. "Whip the little creep 'til he bleeds!" I wonder what these law and order types will make of this:

In Rohnert Park, north of San Francisco, a zealous policeman recently detained a six year old girl for writing in chalk on the side of a building. This being California, instead of being arrested, she was issued a "youth services citation," which requires child and parents to attend counseling. When the girl's mother complained, however, authorities dropped the charges.

The wusses. In Singapore, she'd have been dragged down Main Street by her nose, as highly sanitary observers shouted, "Flay her. Please." They're nothing if not polite in Singapore.

Personally, I can't believe they let that little vandal walk. For all we know, she could be the leader of a vicious hopscotch ring, a swaggering gang of first graders drawing squares on public property. She'll grow up to be a jaywalker with no respect for authority. What chance will this miscreant have if she ever moves to Singapore? She'll tool along in her rental car, turn left without using her directionals, and the cops will have her in a guillotine so fast it'll make her head spin.

Michael Peter Fay's life of crime didn't just begin with spraypainting cars, you know. Some stolen traffic signs, flags, and a sheet of glass from a phone booth were found in his room by the incredibly alert Singapore cops. It turns out that these were given to him by the Swedish ambassador's son, who can't be arrested because of his diplomatic immunity, but still—even possession of a stolen flag is a serious crime. It's right up there with stealing post office pens and removing the "Do Not Remove" tag from a mattress. Flog the jerk!

In the time honored tradition of career criminals everywhere, Fay now denies everything. He says the police held him in detention for over a week, denying him access to his parents and the US embassy, beating him until he confessed.

Why would the Singapore government go to the trouble of framing an American teenager for minor vandalism?

Remember—in Singapore, possession of chewing gum is a misdemeanor. Spitting in public and smoking in a no smoking zone are capital offenses. Roving bands of cleanliness monitors roam the streets sniffing armpits at random. If you're not sufficiently deodorized, it's off to the hoosegow with you, pal.

Maybe it was a slow crime day in Singapore. Officers had issued a few citations for inappropriate frowning, sure, but the perpetrator responsible for those spraypainted cars remained at large. The chief was chewing them out royally. They wanted a bust, and they wanted it fast. The kid was in the wrong place at the wrong time. These things happen.

Even if he is innocent, some might say he should be caned anyway, to atone for the bland crimes of an entire generation. Somebody should pay for the indecipherable scrawls sprayed across the faces of urban centers everywhere, like the markings of wild beasts in a pitiful attempt at territoriality. Somebody should be punished for this, I guess.

But if this kid was framed, what about that little girl in Rohnert Park? Did somebody set her up? Did a corrupt cop, aching to make his quota, place the pastel chalk in that little girl's hand? What if he's getting kickbacks from the suspicious-sounding "youth services." What if a cabal of counselors are deliberately lowering the self-esteem of America's youth in order to create jobs for themselves? And if an entire generation is off on a vandalism spree, what good are these counselors anyway?

Maybe we should be grateful that police and young people everywhere are learning to express themselves. Or maybe we should join that growing chorus that's shouting, "Cane them all and let God sort them out." This is fine, so long as you don't cane me. I swear, the graffiti was dry when I got there.

GRAFFITI 2 | 1994

Graffiti used to get respect. When I was in college, the creation of graffiti was even considered art, more socially acceptable than going to class. I once owned an actual graffiti anthology, containing the famous "God is dead—Nietzsche. Nietzsche is dead—God." graffito, among many others. Coffee houses set entire walls aside for scrawled witticisms. The men's rooms of America held more words than the Library of Congress. Putting a post-modern spin on the "For a good time, call..." genre may have been the crowning achievement of my generation, and the finest legacy of the sixties.

Like everything else in the sixties, this purity of expression soon became degraded. Message tee-shirts and cute bumperstickers supplanted the arch remarks scrawled in public places. Impromptu drolleries turned into strident calls for "Revolution," written on warehouse buildings in blood red letters six feet tall.

It's hard to find decent men's room graffiti any more. The ancient couplet which begins, "Here I sit, all broken hearted," is even beginning to show up in public men's rooms again. Can anybody still think this is original? It's depressing.

Everything is debased, devolved. The "Kiss me, I'm Polish" tee-shirt hasn't been seen in years, but just the other day I saw a ten year old boy wearing a tee shirt that said, "Shut up, bitch." I was shocked!

Where was this little psycho's mother? When I was ten, if I'd dared to wear a tee-shirt like that in public, and my folks had found out about it, I would have been grounded so hard I'd probably just now be allowed to leave the house.

Moms and Dads just aren't up to the job any more. I guess that's why the state of California is taking it upon itself to turn things around. There's a law in the works here that "taggers," as graffiti makers are called, if caught and convicted, will have their behinds paddled in public, by their parents (if they choose to exercise the option), or by officers of the law.

I recognize the impulse, but it's a bad idea. First of all, we're all laboring under a misapprehension. America seems to believe there are roving gangs of swaggering youths out there, waiting for night to fall so they can don camouflage. put spray cans in special holsters, and disperse through every urban center, whispering commands over headsets, as they deface garage doors and store fronts.

The only time I've ever seen a tagger at work was in broad daylight. A nerdy black kid was standing at a bus stop, all alone. He wasn't cold, hip, or dangerous. He was just a frumpy boy. He pulled a spray can out of his back pack, sprayed something on the bus shelter, then walked quickly away. I went across the street to examine his handi-work. It was a square with some kind of squiggle going through it.

Was this a private name he had? A coded message? Was this kid in a gang? In his dreams, maybe. Was he just marking territory, like a dog? Does he deserve to be whipped like a dog in front of the television cameras you know will be there when the first paddling occurs? For what? For spraypainting something incomprehensible on public property?

I have a theory. When graffiti was witty, we didn't mind it. It was when the graffiti became closed to the public at large, we began to be outraged. It's all just demographics. Ratings.

And what about the imposition on the public of large ugly sculptures? We not only don't paddle the artists responsible for these garish intrusions, we give them grants. What about public buildings themselves? If you were shown a photograph of a modern building, could you say with certainty whether it was a school, hospital, or prison?

Maybe if public space actually became hospitable to the public, kids wouldn't feel compelled to scrawl symbols that look like the name of the guy-that-used-to-be-Prince all over it. Paddling these kids is just more incomprehensible ugliness. Don't we have enough of that? Enough of unavoidable public expressions, the meaning of which is both obscure and grim?"

GRAFFITI 3 | 1995

Here in San Francisco, sports fans are wailing and gnashing their teeth because, in exchange for a generous renovation donation from a Silicon Valley company named 3Com, their beloved Candlestick Park is now 3Com Park.

Well okay, Candlestick isn't really beloved; it's closer to tolerated (an acceptable substitute for beloved in the nineties). Sports fans complain constantly that attending games at "the 'Stick" is like sitting in a freezer in a forty mile an hour wind. Sports fans have been trying to get a new stadium here for years.

But never mind that. Tradition dictates that Candlestick retain the name it was given when it was first built by corrupt contractors, just like Wrigley Field in Chicago. Oh sure, that's a corporate name too, but at least Wrigley makes gum. What does 3Com make? Computer networks? Right. Try chewing that a thousand times and sticking it under your seat in the bottom of the ninth.

The main objection to the name change seems to be that 3Com is not a cool name. It's as if Sean Connery suddenly changed his name to "Merle." It's dorky. It sounds rather cold, in fact, rather corporate, in even more cold fact. Even more disturbing to this disinterested observer, 3Com sounds like a corporation from the eighties. Remember the eighties? Every airport was surrounded by dozens of gleaming stainless steel buildings sporting names like GelTid, Prolapsys, BlorTech, or Xephus? What were these companies? What did they make? Where did they go? Why didn't their buildings ever have windows?

Speaking of windows, if these were truly the nineties wouldn't Candlestick now be Microsoft Park? Cripes, Microsoft has enough money to buy out baseball and football altogether, upgrade them, and make them impossible to watch without massive tech support. This may yet happen. Before you know it, residents could soon be living "Microsoft's San Francisco."

No, I haven't become "Walt Disney's Ian Shoales" yet, but there are other surefire signs that these are the nineties. Even as Deion Sanders kept representatives from major football leagues hanging by their thumbs, adding skillful juggling to his already well known baseball and football skills, Cal Ripken got the awestruck gratitude of a nation just because he went to work every day for a really long time. Yes, the work ethic is now a museum relic. Most of today's laborers won't show up at all unless their agent okays it.

And those of us without agents just don't want to pay taxes any more. This means that any corporation with money to burn can burn its name on any public entity any time entity and corporate lawyers can agree to mutter, "Done deal." What pays for parks, museums, streets, libraries, schools, and stadia these days? Power lunches, that culminate in public and private partnerships, CEOs rolling up their sleeves, lawyers in hog heaven, bureaucrats in ecstasy.

Every day in San Francisco I see public buses whiz by, behind schedule. Any indication that they are a public conveyance has been erased, replaced by tire-to-tire commercials, airbrushed ads for everything from local radio stations and soft drinks to sports teams. Municipal buses now look like billboards as seen by a psychotic on hallucinogens. What power lunch led to the appalling display? It would be more like a power snack, I'd think.

I've grown used to living in a country in which pretty near everything is up for grabs, a country where every available surface is available, after negotiations, for the purpose of thrusting products into our sour faces. I have accepted that.

What I don't understand, in this context, is our attitude towards graffiti. Why do we despise and fear the pathetic attempts of the underclass to announce themselves to the world, and welcome the pathetic attempts of the overclass? Is it only because the overclass paid for the privilege?

That must be it. Corporations have paid for the right to spraypaint ugly self-promoting images on public property. They've paid for the right to plaster their senseless names anywhere they desire. Those who do this without going through the proper channels are fiends who should be horsewhipped publicly. I understand it clearly now. I'm sorry I brought it up.

GREEN WEENIE | 1992

I've spent most of the election year so far brooding quietly in my gloomy flat. Every once in a while I rush to the window and shriek, "You fools, don't you realize what you're doing!" The window is painted shut, so I'm not really bugging anybody. How many presidential candidates can make that claim? None. Their windows are open, advisers crouched behind them, and they're leaning over the sills, gabbing away.

If I find Bill Clinton the most annoying of the irritants, well, I'm prejudiced. He's a dead ringer for Chuck, this kid I knew in high school. Everybody called him "The Green Weenie." (I was called "Sunshine Superman," so you can see that the system by which nicknames were bestowed was not infallible.) We shared study hall, and I'd often spend the entire period just staring at him, amazed, as he sat hunched over Robert's Rules of Order, brow knitted, lips moving. What an unbelievable dweeb! I couldn't take my eyes off him! I neglected my studies, got a D in Psych, *all because of Chuck*. He ran for senior class president on the Hall Monitor ticket, as I recall, but lost to a guy named Bud or Spud, who ran on the promise that he'd throw a party at his house the next time his parents were out of town. As it turned out, Chuck did become class president by default, when Bud/Spud's party got busted, and his father sent him off to military school. Chuck did have a way with a phrase though. Every time he said, "I move the previous question," little shudders would ripple through the entire student body. As for Bill Clinton himself, I've come to think he spread the Gennifer Flowers rumor himself, to convince voters he's capable of passion.

H. Ross Perot doesn't have *that* problem anyway, oh no, not Mr. Guts 'n' Glory. He's setting fire to his own money at a million dollars a whack, just to prove a point. What that point is, I'm not sure. In this wonderful country, even a Texas billionaire can run for president? Maybe. He does have some weird notion of updating the old time "town meetin'," using interactive video to get immediate responses from touch-tone America on issues of the day. I don't know, though. It sounds like Family Feud to me, and H. Ross Perot is no Richard Dawson.

At least he and Bill Clinton seem to have watched television at some point, perhaps even read a book, for all I know. President Bush has people who do all that for him. He himself can't really spare the attention span. He's too busy stepping off the links into limousines or charter jets, trying to get people on the phone. Does he ever sit still? Kennebunkport! Texas! D.C.! Japan! When *realpolitik* got jet lag, we got George Bush.

Candidates aside, politics has become very strange. The right wing seems to be having a nervous breakdown. Bereft of Communism, its nemesis, it has to make gays, poor black people, and mediocre subsidized artists be its stunt double. "They don't wear neckties!" is the conservative subtext. Even Commies wore neckties, for crying out loud! They've ridden that horse about as far as it'll go; that horse is dead, yet they still kick it. Now and then they pause for breath and denounce Ross Perot as a demagogue.

As for Democrats, they don't even have the pretense of an issue. They've got their fingers up to see which way the wind is blowing, but they're just not finding those breezes any more. And we have no left left. I think they've all been replaced by condescending mental health professionals on public television, nattering ceaselessly about "denial." Who *are* those people? Denial-mongers are becoming as ubiquitous as mimes were back in the seventies. or stand-up comics on A&E.

What's my point? Simple. *Don't panic*. The right has attained its dream. Big government is dead. Government itself is dead, and both right and left may soon be out of work. Go ahead! Let the situation strike you as slightly surreal. Don't deny it, flow with it. Yell "Theatre!" at the crowded fire. Quit whining! Don't give up on parties just because you can't find a caterer. BYOB, for goodness' sake! That's what we did at Bud/Spud's! We had a *great* time. Well, okay. Until the cops showed up.

GULF 1990-1991

NEW WORLD ORDER (1990)

Now that the Cold War is just a bitter memory, President Bush and his people are busily thinking up chapter heads for the history books of tomorrow. By far, the catchiest catchphrase they've come up with has been "New World Order." Its mildly fascistic tone aside, I don't have any problem with it. After all, in the absence of forethought, presidents have to fill the vacuum with something. A bully pulpit for empty sloganeering has always been a choice perk of the executive branch.

Our president, however, seems a little unclear as to what, exactly, this New World Order will be; so I thought I'd provide some models—paradigms, if you will. These options come to you hot from the fevered brow of the Ian Shoales New Brain Foundation, a private sector think tank located in a windowless office building somewhere deep inside the Beltway.

First off, we have the GLOBAL VILLAGE option. In this New World Order scenario, everything is televised (I mean that in a good way). Families compete for airtime, with each household assigned its own reporter, video crew, and publicity unit. Family night is devoted to the creation of on-air promotions—"Tonight at the Andersons: Can't make mortgage payments, kids on drugs, fired from job! The Andersons! Tension '91! Join us!" Families with poor ratings will, of course, be canceled.

A more upbeat sub-option might be to expand AMERICA'S FUNNIEST HOME VIDEOS to the WORLD'S, encouraging family members around the globe to push one another into swimming pools, smash one another in the groin with footballs, and give each other snuggies in public situations. Fun!

Speaking of fun, try the DISNEY WORLD ORDER—a reasonably priced vacation-paradise-on-earth, chock full of little fuzzy animals and roller coasters, protected by a vast team of corporate lawyers, and overseen by anxious men in Italian suits. Just remember where you parked your car, and leave the rest to us.

Don't make up your mind yet. We also have NEW WORLD MONEY ORDER. Under this system, we don't destroy military targets with smart bombs, no, we buy them with smart money. It's a system that replaces bombs with more of what we got. And it gives us more of what we got, a world where we can keep on spending like there's no tomorrow! Every man, woman, and child on the planet is issued a credit card! Democracies are replaced by lotteries, with leaders chosen by random selection! Whether this is a punishment or reward, however, remains to be seen..

Try ORDER YOUR NEW WORLD NOW! Imagine a brave new world filled with Amazing Television Offers, a world where phone sex, dating services, and shopping by phone create a fiber-optic utopia, full of ceramic Hummels, bone china plates embossed with Elvis and scenes from GONE WITH THE WIND, a world full of disco anthologies in all three formats, where every home possesses the complete John Wayne video collection. The demand for operators creates 100% employment in a world where phone ownership is compulsory, and discarding junk mail is a capital offense.

If all else fails, why not give TOM CLANCY WORLD a shot? Citizens of this New World Order option are urged to dress like fighter pilots, and chew gum slowly when speaking. Spandex flight suits and wraparound shades are distributed free of charge. We spend our free time developing acronyms for weapons systems and lawn furniture. We even speak a new language called ClancySpeak. How does it work? Well, the English phrase, "Okay, we'll see you tomorrow then," would become, in ClancySpeak, "Debriefing engagement mode Z-14—stroke—time-cluster seven. Over." It's that simple. Even our homes would be described purely in ClancySpeak—the living room is ComSitFac 4. Children are Microunits, and parents are MacroSub(s) A1 and A2.

Still and all I'm going with the final option: A DIFFERENT WORLD ORDER. It's so easy. You just stand in your backyard screaming to the stars, "Get me out of here!" Sure you'll annoy your neighbors, but what have you got to lose?

RHETORIC GAP (1990)

Our former playmate in the Mideast, Saddam Hussein, is a lot more than a once moderate Arab. An unnamed Iraqi poet (not Omar Khayyam, I assume) calls him, according to last Sunday's NEW YORK

TIMES, "the perfume of Iraq, its dates, its estuary of two rivers, its coast and waters, its sword, its shield, the eagle whose grandeur...*etc.*"

To your typical house-proud poetry-reading Iraqi, then, it would appear that this Hussein guy is some kind of perfume/fruit/water/large bird combo previously unencountered in nature. Beneath his stern gaze, moreover, the Iraq government newspaper, AL JUMHIRIYA, has become a beautiful tower ablaze with fiery rhetoric, a flaming tower in which armies become Swords of Vengeance, enemies are made to drink the Bitter Chalice of Defeat, and the Iraqi people are as lofty as the day is long—with equally lofty "ambitions of freedom" which must be accepted by the forces off the west "no matter how bitter it tastes inside the stinking mouths of their masters."

Want to know what I think?

I think we'll have to import a lot more than foreign oil if we're going to remain a superpower. I've got a hunch that we'd better import some of those strong words and install them immediately in our stinking mouths. It doesn't do us any good to lug briefcases bulging with cautious options into the cloakrooms of the Beltway, when our oil-rich adversaries are lugging tanks and tough talk into the bleak plains of the Partitioned Zone, now does it?

Before it's too late, public sector spin doctors should insist that President Bush be called, oh, "the cologne of Columbia, its used cars of manifest destiny, its pointed finger of rugged ABS plastic, America's pigeon whose droppings confound the wicked passerby." Of course that's off the top of my head, but put something *like* that in the smelly mouth of a Dan Rather, or a Patrick Buchanan, and I bet we'd have OPEC quaking in its estuaries.

We're already calling Barbara Bush "The Silver Fox" at every opportunity, let's just expand the whole concept. Call the Secretary of Defense, "Our Mighty Saber of Retribution!" Call the Secretary of Labor, "The Wiry Sinews of Commerce!" Come on, America, let's show the world that we can hyperbolize with the best of 'em. Let's get out there and bluster. Let us mangle our metaphors together, if not for ourselves, then for our children, and our children's children.

I'm talking about bringing pride back to America, folks. Pride in the workspace—stop calling your boss a backstabbing slimeball behind his back. That won't get us anywhere. No, face your boss with a reverent, almost sickly grin and call him, "Great Father-Leader! He-

Who-Leaves-His-Closest-Competitors-Whining-In-The-Boardroom!
He-Who-Wears-The-Golden-Parachute! Artist-of-the-Deal!" I know
that's what I'd do, if I had a job. It might bring new life to today's
service oriented economy.

Think of it. Fierce corporations with fierce names staring fiercely
eastwards. CBS could take a cue from its own logo and call itself "The
All-Seeing Gaze of the Unfettered Airwaves." Disney could call itself
"The Roaring Mouse of Litigation and Family Fun." If the S&Ls had
had names like "The Pitiless Money Movers of Partial Deregulation,"
well, we might not be in the unfixable fix we face today.

And curses! America needs curses!

> "Accept the fax of inconvenience, O dog of another time
> zone!"
>
> "Heed this memo of death, drone of a different floor!"
>
> "Face the Fed Ex of fate, Wall Street lackey!"
>
> "Strangle on your power tie, mealy-mouthed
> macromanager!"
>
> "May your system fail, drudge. Face the database of
> doom!"

We must act now, and close the rhetoric gap. And we must all
heed the wise words of John Philip Law in THE GOLDEN VOYAGE
OF SINDBAD: "Trust in Allah, but tie up your camel."

LEGLESS JOURNALISTS (1990)

When I was in eighth grade, I tried to get out of a geography final by
faking a nosebleed, using a cup or so of Hershey's chocolate syrup,
and forging a letter to my teacher from our family physician, which
said, if memory serves, "My patient, young Ian Shoales, is suffering
from extreme nasal fatigue. Any form of written examination in his
present state would probably kill him."

Well, it didn't work. If I hadn't peeked at my neighbor's answers,
I might have flunked! Once again, Mom was right: if I'd spent half the
effort studying that I spent avoiding it, why, I could have used that
chocolate syrup on some ice cream, and I might have been a famous
geography expert today.

It looks like Iraq is facing a similar pickle. Abdul Amir Anbar, the
Iraqi delegate to the UN, has been forced to miss several UN sessions

because of, he says, a chronic nosebleed. I'm not saying that Mr. Anbar forged a letter from the family physician, or that he threatened the family of a physician with the death of a thousand cuts unless such a letter was provided, but the fact remains, one way or another, Iraq seems to be avoiding that geography final. And they've got tricks an eighth grader never dreamed of. I never threatened my geography teacher with supercannons, poison gas, or megabombs that mimic nuclear weapons. Or this one: just last week, Iraqi spokesman Taha Yasmin Ramadan responded to journalists' desire to investigate charges of alleged human rights abuses in Kuwait, "Kuwait is none of your affair. And we will cut off the leg of anybody who should enter Kuwait illegally."

Well, sure, if I was asked the question, "Are there human rights abuses in Kuwait?" on a geography final, faced with potential leglessness, I'd leave that one blank. Still, you don't need to be a despot or rabid right-winger to feel the occasional urge to cut the limb off a journalist. The insufferable Diane Sawyer, for example, or the humorless Sam Donaldson—wouldn't the airwaves be a far better place if they walked with a slight limp? It wouldn't matter that much for them, career-wise—how often do you see journalists below the waist?—but wouldn't it make the rank and file of America turn on their televisions with a lighter heart, knowing that some overpaid network functionaries had been taken down a peg by a concerned viewer with a chainsaw?

But I guess that's the difference between an informed citizenry and the fearful inhabitants of a police state. To typical Americans, chopping the legs off people who annoy them is only a foolish dream. Saddam Hussein can make those dreams come true. If I had Saddam Hussein's power, who knows how many limping Americans would be struggling down the street?

But then again, I might be one leg shorter in your fantasies. Where do you draw the line, and who draws it? Take Sinead O'Connor the brooding yet winsome bald pop singer who refused to allow the national anthem sung at a recent concert. Last week at Mrs. Gooch's of Beverly Hills, described by the LA TIMES, as a "trendy food store," an employee retaliated by singing the "Star Spangled Banner" at Sinead O'Connor, who happened to be in the store at the time, perhaps to purchase some organic chocolate syrup, I really don't know. Ms. O'Connor's publicist said he sang it loudly, the employee said he sang it softly, but Mrs. Gooch's of Beverly Hills fired the guy, saying they have a policy prohibiting employees from harassing customers. (I guess, by the way, this policy must set them apart from those other trendy food stores, that *encourage* employees to harass customers.)

Minimum wage drones are probably fired every day for annoying politically correct pop stars. That's America in the nineties. That's neither here nor there. The real question is: whose leg do we cut off here? Sinead O'Connor? Her publicist? The employee? Roseanne Barr? Mrs. Gooch? Francis Scott Key? I'd like to say I have the answer, but I'm not as up on the Constitution as the whiners on your local op-ed page. I just don't have a legal leg to stand on. Besides, I think I feel a nosebleed coming on.

PUNCHLINES IN THE SAND (1991)

January 15, 1991: high noon lite for George Bush. By the time this reaches you, perhaps the whole world will know whether we've shot ourselves in the foot again or we're swaggering up to the bar after a desert duel to the death with the Sammy Hansen gang. I suspect we'll spend the next twenty years limping through the new world order with a bullet in our Florsheims, but hey, what do I know?

I know that things don't look good. Just last week, at the fiasco in Geneva, Iraqi Foreign Minister Tarik Aziz refused to accept George Bush's letter to Saddam Hussein, saying it didn't contain "polite language." Aziz should talk! He opens and reads a letter addressed to another guy? That's not only rude, it's a federal offense. If President Bush had placed postal authorities in Switzerland, the way a far-thinking global leader would have, we could've busted the guy and ended our Mexican standoff right there. But you can't really accuse George Bush of thinking ahead. He can't even pronounce "Saddam" properly. You'd think if you were angling to obliterate a guy, you'd at least get his name right.

Even our ever-alert and highly responsible media seem to have given up. I offer as evidence this worried exchange between a reporter and Secretary Baker at the post-Geneva press conference:

REPORTER: Mr. Secretary, your mood, if I may say, seems pretty somber at this point. Can you kind of describe your state of mind and your mood after what has occurred today?
BAKER: Somber.
REPORTER: Somber.
BAKER: You got it.

If Secretary Baker is our foreign policy mood ring, I'm glad the press took the time to disclose just how gray his aura has become. This is fast-breaking news the world has been holding its breath to hear, and I for one think we need to do something to cheer our leaders up.

This somber mood is trickling down to the rest of us, even in sunny California. For example, our new governor Pete Wilson's catchphrase is "preventive government." This doesn't sound like a coherent policy, does it? No, it sounds like a dental plan.

Listen to talk radio—it's all Persian Gulf, Iraq, Kuwait—nobody's bracing for the Super Bowl, we're all holing up with CNN, and squinting at our representatives to see if they're really as somber as they say they are.

That neo-conservative smirk of self-satisfaction is gone, wiped from our faces. All the smug boneheads of the eighties, except for Rush Limbaugh, now proceed with caution. Poor Rush is out there all by himself, like the sidekick of some long gone cowboy hero who's hightailed it back to the ranch to scrape enough cash together to buy a bigger gun. Rush stands alone on the prairies ready, willing, and able to put a slug into his wingtips, but nobody's there to feed him that ideological ammo he so desperately needs.

Look, we've got this worldwide wild west show—roving youth gangs shooting up the streets with semi-automatic weapons, the National Rifle Association clutching their MAC-10's like toddlers with a teddy, Soviet armies gunning down Lithuanians with a smile, Israel acting like a sheepman in cattle country, and America girding its loins like The Wild Bunch, but trying to pretend it's Kevin Costner.

Who we trying to kid with this somber politeness? Look, we've got the posse together, we've got the rustlers trapped in the arroyo, so what if we have to pass the hat to pay for the bullets, we've still got the biggest hat in the west, and we know how to handle a gun. Let's drop the glum outlook and face the music with the laconic humor of a Gary Cooper. Better enjoy it now. I predict we'll be laughing out of the other side of our faces soon enough. Right after we deliver our grim punchline in the sand, I predict we'll be hopping around on one foot, howling like Yosemite Sam in a wilderness of rabbits.

POSTWAR ANALYSIS (1991)

Now that Saddam Hussein is demonized to the max and a fear of Shiites blossoms once again, a giddy euphoria spreads, flu-like, across the land. But you know what, America? I think you should call a timeout on those hoarse shouts of victory. Stop mothballing those yellow ribbons a sec, and join me for a quick squint back at those elements of the Gulf War which annoyed me personally.

Peaceniks

Talk show America wouldn't stop griping about "peaceniks." Apparently, the fear was that "peaceniks" would sap our ground forces' resolve: "Agh! I'm haunted by hippies! I can't pull the trigger!" Why won't talk show America just accept that peaceniks come in twenty year cycles, like locusts? They're a magical part of nature's rich tapestry!

Post-Post Viet Nam

Experts said the Viet Nam nightmare is finally behind us. It's over. Got it? For stray vets or peaceniks who haven't received the news, will celebrity volunteers go caroling "Voices That Care" to surly shut-ins, so they, like our ground forces, can sob in gratitude, "Chevy Chase loves me?" God, I hope not.

Retired Generals

These guys were swarming all over the airwaves, with their opinions on possible military tactics. And for what? I'm as military as a fashion model, but I had our strategy sussed from the get go: (1) Detonate high explosives among Iraqis. (2) Scrape Iraqis from desert floor.

Sure, it worked like a charm. But what do the old soldiers do now? Hang out on street corners with their maps and arrows? Do we sic the "Voices That Care" singers on them? As the Democrats say, we're facing some tough choices.

Peter Arnett

Alan Simpson, the very senator who once told Saddam Hussein that the American press was his enemy, told America that CNN's man in Bagdad was our enemy.

Huh? If you show America something it doesn't want to see, does it mean you're a traitor? By that logic, the BONFIRE OF THE VANITIES producers would be lined up and shot. This may in fact be happening, but the point is, senators shouldn't interfere with a free market economy. The media will kill their own. Remember Jimmy the Greek?

Saddam Hussein

Halfway through the air war, experts discovered that his eyeblinks per minute had doubled since June. They concluded that this was a mental stress indicator. Oh duh! What about *counting* eyeblinks? Sounds compulsive to me.

Maybe this data was vital for national security ("Update me on Saddam's EPM's mister! I need those figures yesterday!"). Still, why give consultants the job? The homeless would monitor the tics of world leaders for minimum wage. Give them a clipboard, a stopwatch, and videotapes of Gorbachev and Bush! Blink counting could become a real job for the nineties!

The Coming Sarcasm Shortage

I wish we'd skipped the war and made Saddam Hussein a straight cash offer—a trillion dollars, say, for Kuwait, Iraq, and the oily cormorants. We'd probably still be money ahead! If he'd accepted, of course, we couldn't have hurled smart bombs at air vents. Pete "I can't discuss that" Williams, among others, would have been out of a job. On the other hand, we'd have seen Saddam Hussein trot out of a bunker, blinking furiously, and shouting, "I'm going to Disneyland." Is this such a bad scenario?

Next to Vanilla Ice, Saddam Hussein might be the most despised man in the media today, but I feel sorry for him. He could have had a condo in Hawaii or cell space with Noriega—he could have written his memoirs, IRAQ AND A HARD PLACE. He could have had a TV job as color man at minor global conflicts—"Ouch! That's gotta hurt, Bernie!"

But he threw it away. Leaving me stumped in the New Elation. Gloating is not my strong point. And what's the point of my pointless negativity in the face of a national outbreak of perky enthusiasm?

Michael Novak, a director at the conservative American Enterprise Institute, stated the problem best: "This is the end of the decline. This is the decline of the declinists. The mother of all battles turned into the daughter of disasters for the declinists—" Yeah, yeah, okay, Mr. dutch uncle of defense, but tell me this—what's the daughter of disasters doing Saturday? Dates are tough in the New World Order and she sounds like my kind of gal.

GUN CONTROL | 1984

I believe you only need a gun for two things: to kill rattlesnakes and stop cattle stampedes. If you live in the city, you need a telephone, not a gun. If you're robbed, wait till the thief goes away, then call the police. There's no messy moral issue, no blood on the floor, just a brisk touch of the touch-tone, and it's out of your hands. And the telephone's cheaper than a gun. Also consider the lawsuits and legal fees incurred by killing an intruder in today's society. And a thief, after all, is just trying to make a buck like anybody else. Call the cops. Cops may be rude, they may be slow, but they know how to use a gun, and that's a lot more than you can say about most gun owners. Gun owners make a habit of keeping a gun in a night table by the bed, where it's found by curious youngsters, or used by couples to kill each other in arguments about who loves each other the most. Sometimes gun owners keep handguns locked in a safe place, where they don't do much good against a burglar, and are probably in fact stolen by burglars while the gun owner sleeps the well-protected sleep. Then these guns find their way into the hands of professional criminals who either kill each other in gambling arguments or in what our journalists cutely call "gangland" slayings. It's obvious that we don't need gun control; all our gun owners are killing each other off.

Movies and television somehow get blamed for the morality of their viewers. Blaming a movie like Deer Hunter for the gullibility of its audience is like blaming the Beatles for Charles Manson or Jodie Foster for John Hinckley. There's no way we can stop psychopaths from owning a television set, or from making a movie, for that matter. Or from owning a gun. I think this is healthy. A nation on a hair trigger is a well-protected nation. A well-protected nation doesn't need Valium, just more emergency rooms. And a nation without people doesn't need protection at all.

In Celtic mythology, satire was used as a weapon: words actually had the power to kill. Today's libel laws have made that impossible, of course, but my main weapon will continue to be pure unapologetic unconstructive sarcasm. Sarcasm doesn't really change anything, or hurt anybody for that matter, but it sure makes me feel better.

HALOGEN

Trendy light source.

HAYLEY MILLS | 1984

A while back I was watching Saturday morning cartoons when a McDonald's commercial came on. Mayor McCheese was talking in a cute voice to what looked like a big purple rug with legs. My jaw dropped and I found myself screaming at the television, "What the hell is that thing?"

I'm sure many American kids are screaming that same question. When we turn on the tube we're asked to accept some pretty bizarre characters and relationships. A talking car? A bionic man? A dog who hunts ghosts? You didn't have to make these great leaps of faith when I was a kid. Characters were obvious. You were in love with either Hayley Mills or Annette Funicello.

Now, I'm a Hayley man from way back. I've still got my Davy Crockett coonskin cap, and let me tell you, if they ever revive the Mickey Mouse Club and they need a replacement for Jimmy, I might be persuaded to set aside my bad attitude long enough to introduce Spin and Marty one more time. Why not? I'm a sap like everybody else. I've been to Disneyland fifteen times. When you pass through the gates, you enter a world where pirates are cute, gophers can sing, and President Lincoln can actually stand up and talk at the same time. It's always 1955, and the older I get, the more I appreciate that. If the underpaid teenagers who pick up the litter seem a little bored and the friendly smiles sometimes seem a little fixed, well, even paradise has a price. And the price for paradise gets higher all the time.

One of our great grotesque rumors is the rumor that Walt Disney had himself fast-frozen, cryogenically stopped in time, so he'll be ready to thaw in the twenty-first century, when they will have the cure for everything. Then Uncle Walt will come back to life, like a vampire or a Rip Van Winkle, to create more miracles in a future better prepared to deal with them.

These are confusing times, and the lines around our lives are often drawn by a shaky hand. Disney's hand was firm, and the world he drew is clear. Like the Playboy Empire, Disneyland is a kingdom based on one man's vision. The death of Walt Disney is like the death of God.

Without Uncle Walt behind the scenes we can't accept Disney World, or Epcot Center. We can't make the mental leaps demanded by amusement parks. We sit in the moving car, taped voices singing in our ears, watching the artificial world go by. It's like being inside a video game. When we ride that ride, we're expressing a human desire to disappear or be manipulated by God, to be coin-operated by a benign and wise game player.

But without Walt we can't believe in the artificial world, the rides, the video games, the space movies. It's hard to vanish inside them. Sure, we're amazed that the funny gopher can sing, but it's the same amazement we occasionally feel when we turn on a light. It's a miracle, but one you get used to. And a light bulb at least gives us light. A talking bear just gives us a bizarre image that only lasts as long as the ride—then we join the throng of tourists once again. If talking bears aren't a figment of Walt Disney's imagination, then they're just more random corporate images unconnected to anything.

We only need these cute images to justify our technology. Going to the moon isn't enough. Computers and heatseeking missiles aren't enough. The electronics aren't real to America until a billion pre-teenagers have dropped their quarters into Donkey Kong.

It's empty fun. The old cartoons gave us Bugs and Fudd and Mickey and Donald in an awesome mythological world of cruelty and reincarnation. Even if Bugs dropped an A-bomb on Fudd, he'd come back together for the chase. It's a perfect parallel to certain versions of the Isis-Osiris myth. But so what?

The amusement park without an uncle is a spectacle that doesn't want us. It's predigested food. Pac Man wilts, comes back, devours, and is devoured. As long as we've got quarters, television, or the price of admission, these creatures will live, and the cold spectacle will continue.

But listen, maybe Walt Disney will come back. And until that time, if Hayley Mills is still available, somebody tell her I'm available too. I'll wait for her at the Matterhorn, she'll recognize me right away. I'll be the pale skinny guy in the threadbare coonskin cap.

HERPES | 1982

Herpes. The Love Bug. The Time-Life empire* says it's an epidemic. I could have told you that. We didn't need that picture on the cover of TIME: anxiety-ridden young people standing in front of a hopeless wall, with the word Herpes scrawled in bright-red letters, letters as bright as Jayne Mansfield's mouth and twice as scary, sort of helter-skelter lettering, doomsday lettering. And what does TIME call herpes? "The New Scarlet Letter," a reference to the famous novel by Nathaniel Hawthorne, a better writer than the staff of TIME and a man who, I'm sure, did not have herpes. Who does have herpes? We know who has herpes.

Respectable young people, people on the go, guys and gals who jog, who ride ten-speed bicycles, upwardly mobile, tanned and healthy people. The sexual rebels of the '60s, slim and trim, they drink Lo-Cal beer, diet wine; they wear those little alligators on the left side of the shirt. Herpes is the lie of that perfect society: graffiti on a clean white wall, the mark of Cain, the blot on the escutcheon (whatever that means), a mistake.

That's right, guys and gals, a six pack and a date on a country road won't get you babies anymore, and no shotgun wedding, just occasional blisters. That's why I don't jog. What's the sense in meeting people? And what's the sense in eating vitamins and starch blockers and kelp and spirulina, any of that dried-out green stuff sold by forty year old hippies with gnats flying around their dreamy eyes. Herpes is the worm in the high-tech apple, you Cosmo gals and Playboys. But who's eating the apple? Who's minding the store? TIME Magazine.

Herpes is the synthesis of some bizarre dialectic, proof that the Russians are right. Do Russians have herpes? Does the PLO have herpes? Or Americans who have been faithfully married for fifteen years and live in a three bedroom split-level in Larchmont, or some exurbia that was nice in the '50s before the bad elements moved in? Now the shattered families are lonely in their ranch-style homes. The family's breaking down. The only decent thing on television is HILL

STREET BLUES, and that's boring. Television is boring. The family is boring. The family is afraid. But the family doesn't have herpes. The kids who left home have herpes. The typical Time-Life reader is the one with herpes.

TIME Magazine gives you its version of the world and puts you there, but it's not the world I live in. The Time-Life world is this strange alternative universe, a looking-glass world where everything has the same fiat look—murder and movies, people and politics all get the same slightly snide evenhanded style. To the average reader, the threat of nuclear annihilation, the "situation" in the Mideast, the flights to outer space—all get the same weight in the Luce empire prose as photo captions of Marilyn Monroe, who seems to pop up in LIFE Magazine every five years or so, like some kind of periodic half-clad goddess. Marilyn Monroe's image seems to have the same kind of significance to the people at Life as images of the Virgin in small south-of-the-border villages. All right, I'm bitter. I applied for a job at TIME reviewing records, and they wouldn't hire me. But history has shown me the world is full of tragedy, revenge, larger-than-life events; how does that tragedy compare with the embarrassment and inconvenience of herpes? Herpes might be irritating, but people aren't going to start bringing wet suits and gloves to intimate contact with other human beings.

They might stop reading TIME Magazine though. I would. Look where you buy that thing—at newsstands. Thousands of people have thumbed through those magazines. Who knows what diseases those readers have. You don't know where TIME has been, you only know where it's coming from, because I just told you.

FYI, the TIME/LIFE empire is now the TIME/LIFE/WARNER empire. And herpes has taken a back seat. Now AIDS is driving the car.

HOBBIES | 1983

Thirty years ago everyone had a hobby. Boys had the baseball cards, Sis had a thousand dolls from other lands, Mom had her yarn, Dad had his hi-fi kit, his woofers and tweeters. We'd assemble the jigsaw puzzle in the blond living room, listening to a freight train moan from speaker to speaker. Hobbies were the empire of the middle class, a strong nation taking its leisure, a strong family seeking temporary joy from solitary pleasures.

I'm not here to defend hobbies. I haven't had one since I was ten. I got a model Flying Fortress after seeing some John Garfield movie. I got the airplane glue, the decals, the small bottles of eye-damaging phosphorescent paint. I was trying to put Tab D into Slot Double Z when I spilled glue on the tailgunner turret, at the exact point where John Garfield had shot down two Zeroes at twelve o'clock high. So I threw the damn thing across the garage, and blew it to smithereens on the Fourth of July with one well placed cherry bomb. It was really cool, and I did it myself.

Hobbies today are a way to let the neighbors know how we fit in culturally. You're on top of the new, you've got the bucks to be hip. When Dad collected coins he didn't interface with anything, and when Mom made a quilt she didn't think she was experiencing a New Age Alternative Lifestyle. Hobbies used to be silly. Now there aren't any harmless ways to spend time. Video games gird our reflexes for war, prepare the young for Star Wars in the thin interface between blue sky and black space. We don't do anything for the hell of it. We have the hobby because the experts say we need to counter on-the-job stress, to counter executive burnout (a real *maladie moderne*, the perfect disease for the '80s). We jog because we want to live longer, but the amount of time added to our lives is exactly equivalent to the time we spent jogging. We're big on choice but the choice is always twelve different episodes of Three's Company. We're a lonely nation of consumers, choosing our tired evenings away.

And the HO trains that used to fill entire basements, all the miniature trees and park benches, the cute villages and villagers tiny as ants and bright as a promise of utopia. Those trains are gone; now we ride those trains. We take our tiny lives to our 9-to-5's, scanning the paper for computer bargains as we stand and rock, hemmed in by strangers. Now it's just a straight unbroken line from suburb to skyscraper, and everything is work.

HOLIDAYS 1984

I spent the holidays trying to visit a girlfriend who didn't want to see me. I could understand that. I wouldn't want to see me either, but my holiday plans went out the window in her large Midwestern town, and instead of spending time in her nice warm apartment, I spent a week in a cheap motel in the dead of winter. The motel had everything you need in a cheap motel room: HBO and a hideous abstract painting bolted to the wall. Every cheap motel room in the country has a hideous abstract painting bolted to the wall. Why is it bolted to the wall? Is the motel afraid I will steal the painting? I don't want the damn painting, I just want to stuff it under the bed until checkout. I thought abstract expressionism was another fad like the hula hoop, so why do these things keep showing up on bank and motel room walls? Who makes these things? Who buys them?

All you can do is throw a sheet over these paintings, which helped me to concentrate on HBO showing Steve Martin in PENNIES FROM HEAVEN. What's a great movie like that doing on cable? If PENNIES FROM HEAVEN had been a foreign movie it would have made a million bucks. It makes me furious that a genuinely funny man like Steve Martin is falling by the public wayside just because he's too popular. Too many frat guys put arrows through their heads, too many fat teenage boys said, "I am a wild and crazy guy." We heard a thousand Excu-u-u-use me's, but only ten of them were Steve Martin's. There are people who were sick of Steve Martin before they'd even seen him. Is that his fault?

Why are his movies on cable and a movie like SCARFACE still in the theaters? All right, I haven't seen SCARFACE, but why should that stop me from having an opinion on it? Everybody else does. I read a column by George Will saying that SCARFACE should have been rated "X" because parents were taking their children to see it. So what? Why should the motion-picture industry be responsible for our morality?

Dad says to Mom, "SCARFACE is in town."

"What's it about?"

"Human scum who kill each other over cocaine deals."

"Sounds great! Let's take the kids!"

There are so many things in America I wish would die a natural death, so many things worthy of sarcasm it's hard to find time for them all. And what of the frightening possibility that there's only a finite amount of contempt possible in one's lifetime? If that's true, should I squander my sneers on my old girlfriends, cat food commercials and

Joan Rivers? Should I save it all up for monumentally stupid events like the invasion of Grenada or FLASHDANCE?

And with a person universally accepted as laughable, like William Buckley, Kissinger, or this new guy my girlfriend's going out with, is a sneer worth my time? Is my opinion but one more bitter drop in an ocean of words? And timing is so important.

I believe that Cabbage Patch Dolls are stupid, and if you buy one you probably have severe emotional problems, but the dolls are all sold, Christmas is over. I missed the sarcasm boat.

So the next time you're in a cheap motel room, trying to unbolt some garish purple and green monstrosity, and there's nothing on the tube but THE BRADY BUNCH, and your girlfriend would rather keep company with a Cabbage Patch Doll than with you, think of me and the hard job I have to do. Then give a sneer. Remember: a sneer is a terrible thing to waste.

HOLIDAYS 2 | 1993

Our national holidays get lamer by the year.

The growing American subculture of sniffy disapprovers can be blamed for most of it. Before the 4th of July, they creep from their shuttered houses to whine about crowds and loud noises, or mutter darkly about Extreme Fire Danger. Then, after suggesting that America celebrate the Fourth with a silent display of patriotism, accompanied by a simple meal of grains and water, they crawl back into their holes to start drafting letters to the editor about the Satanic origins of Halloween.

You can't buy a decent cherry bomb any more, much less a lowly ladyfinger. To get a firework, you have to apply for a special permit from the Bureau of Alcohol, Tobacco and Firearms, who'll send armed marshals with mounds of paperwork to make sure you set off your puny squibs in a fireproof location that complies fully with the Noise Abatement Emergency Act.

On Labor Day, lusty working people used to barbecue beef slabs the size of a mattress, and play softball while downing beer a keg at a swallow. This year I didn't see one working person, just scattered morose families clutching pink slips and pinching pennies around a cold grill.

Halloween celebrations are now tempered with caution. Many parents have mini-metal detectors, to examine toddlers' plunder piece by piece. This year I heard a father cry hoarsely, "The telltale odor of bitter almonds!" and try to wrestle a candy bar from his son, who kept shouting, "It's an almond bar, Daddy, let go!" (Spectral analysis revealed that the candy was harmless, but the whole incident sure put a damper on that pre-teen's sugar rush.)

I even fear for Thanksgiving. Even as I put the old groaning board to sleep for the winter, and breathe a sigh of relief that I won't have to dust off a can of cranberry sauce until next year, I wonder how long this tradition can last? The sniffy say that the holiday wrongly celebrates colonial exploitation of Native Americans.

To which I say, "Okay. So what? Pass the mashed potatoes or get out!"

In our glum health conscious nineties, I read articles about how fatty the food is. I hear radical vegetarians protesting the devouring of turkeys—as if turkeys were sentient beings! If the national health plan pays for itself by making smokers and the obese pay more for benefits, will the police break in the door if we take a second plate of stuffing, and arrest us for being health criminals? It could happen.

Now Christmas is coming. We'll discover that every single toy our children have seen advertised on television, that they've been screaming for at the tops of their spoiled little lungs for months is sold out. Thanks for nothing, Santa. An even crueler truth: batteries will never be included again. We must learn to accept this.

Even as our traditional holidays decay, a chilling new holiday grows in popularity. The anniversary of the assassination of President Kennedy is slowly becoming a festive occasion. Every year, it seems, more reporters pop up to ask, "Do you remember where you were when President Kennedy was shot?" Of course we do! The same place we were the last twenty-four times we were asked! Good grief, it's been twenty-five years. If we can't give it a rest, can we at least give it a little dignity? A moment of silence would be good.

Instead, we've become a nation of yapping Zapruders, taping senseless violence at the drop of a shutter, and examining the videos inch by bloody inch until they've lost all shock value, until nothing remains but legal niceties. All these niceties are adding up to a new nasty holiday, celebrated with nonstop natter about Camelot, stupid teevee movies, poorly written paranoid books, and fatuous editorials about the day our dreams died. I believe I've had enough now. Whether our tarnished president was shot by a psycho, or a mysterious cabal, can we please get over it now? Let's get a life. Oh, and have ourselves a merry little Christmas.

HOLOGRAM

Boring scientific breakthrough, used mainly to make three-dimensional images of scorpions and unicorns.

HORROR 1994

Wes Craven's new movie, WES CRAVEN'S NEW NIGHTMARE, is being touted as the first post-modern horror movie. Boy, that ought to bring in the crowds! It's scary. It's hip. It's—self-conscious!

I'm still deciding whether to catch it in the theatres or not. After all, waiting-for-the-video is fast becoming a time-honored American tradition, and I'm nothing if not American.

But I'm also as post-modern at the next galoot. I'm ready to bust a genre at the drop of a hat. And experiencing the post-modern, as with 3-D and Dolby Sound, may best be done in a large darkened room with a bunch of strangers. It may even require special glasses. I'm not sure.

What does post-modern mean? It means a lot of things. If you make up a story, for instance, in which the Lone Ranger has a gunfight with Tonto, that would be very post-modern. If you make up a story in which you find out that Superman is merely the delusion of a psychotic Clark Kent, that would be extremely post-modern. Another post-modern idea might be to do the Snow White story from the point of view of a dwarf, or the wicked stepmother. Or tell the Snow White story from the point of view of the prince, ten years later; he's grown a little bit tired of stumbling over dwarfs and cuddly forest creatures day in and day out. What if Prince Charming has an affair with Rapunzel and Sleeping Beauty finds out about it? That's post-modern too.

And if you make up a story in which the characters in the story are aware that they're characters in a story? Last year's LAST ACTION HERO told the story of a movie hero, played by Arnold Schwarzenegger, who has to escape the movie he's in to stop the movie villain from killing "real life" Arnold Schwarzenegger as he attends the world premiere of the movie we are watching. That's about as post-modern as you get.

But WES CRAVEN'S NEW NIGHTMARE may give a new spin to the genre. Plot? To get out of Hell (to which he was consigned in the previous NIGHTMARE), insane yet lovable dead serial killer Freddie Kruger has to kill the woman who destroyed the fictional Freddie in the original film: Heather Langenkamp. In a daring bit of double casting, Robert Englund plays himself and Freddie. Heather Langenkamp stars as Heather Langenkamp. (Couldn't they get Jamie Lee Curtis?)

Oh, it's even more post-modernized than that. The director in the movie has dreams of a movie called WES CRAVEN'S NEW NIGHTMARE. As he writes it, his visions come true. And since the movie, Wes Craven's WES CRAVEN'S NEW NIGHTMARE, is an actual movie, directed by Wes Craven (co-starring Wes Craven as Wes Craven), playing in actual theatres, it could rip an actual hole in the fabric of a viewer's reality.

On the other hand, if we go to the movie, maybe we wouldn't be an audience at all, but an audience playing an audience for the benefit of another audience in another dimension, watching a movie called Wes Craven's WES CRAVEN'S WES CRAVEN'S NEW NIGHTMARE.

Or maybe this movie doesn't even exist. What if I made it up: Ian Shoales' IAN SHOALES' WES CRAVEN'S NEW NIGHTMARE? Maybe Freddie Kruger made me write the screenplay so he could get out of Hell. Or maybe I made Freddie Kruger do it so he could get out of Hell, and I could get out of debt.

But if that's true, where's my check? The horror! The horror!

What is reality? Either Freddie Kruger has disguised himself as Ian Shoales to write a column seducing you into the theatres to see his new movie, or this is just another column by Ian Shoales about a guy writing a column. You're either reading it, or I'm dreaming that you're reading it. Either way, you're probably better off waiting for the video. That's not very post-modern, I know, but there are some traditions you probably shouldn't mess with.

HYDROELECTRIC

What "bionic" was to the seventies, "entrepreneurial" to the eighties, and "virtual" the nineties, "hydroelectric" was to the thirties.

INSTRUCTIONAL VIDEO 1992

Those of you still paying attention to the Rodney King case must be amazed by recent developments. The LA TIMES recently published police officers' testimony, which revealed that the cops in question were terrified of Rodney King, mainly because the guy wouldn't cooperate with their efforts; he just wouldn't lapse into unconsciousness. Because of their fear that Mr. King was under the influence of some mind-altering drug (after all, to take the punishment they were dishing out just wasn't normal), the police were forced to use all the resources at their disposal—superior numbers, nightsticks, and tasers—to get this guy before he got the two dozen of them.

In deference to the sensitive souls of the LAPD, to improve civilian/police relations and to guard against future misunderstandings, Chief Daryl Gates has suggested that some kind of instructional video be made, that would teach the layperson how to respond properly when arrested. This seems as good a way to throw tax dollars out the window as any, but I'm not sure exactly what Chief Gates has in mind.

First of all, who is the video for? I'm sure that Mr. and Ms. Law-abiding Public would be proud to pop a cautionary cassette into the VCR, gather the kids around the set, and say, "See? That's where the suspect went wrong. He should never have ingested crack, PCP, and eight malt liquor tallboys, so he could do ninety down the freeway the wrong way with the lights out, number one. Number two, when the police caught up with him, he shouldn't have come running at them with a tire iron, shrieking, 'You all must die!'"

But this video is wasted on Mr. and Ms. Law-abiding Public. This information is already second nature.

If this cassette is designed to raise the consciousness, *re* arrest etiquette, of the common criminal, where is he going to get a VCR to view it? Obviously, being a criminal, he's going to steal it. So this cassette is already encouraging crime, not stopping it. And once the video is set up, the mental state of the alleged perpetrator must be taken into account. If the suspect is watching the tape while high on crack, PCP, and eight malt liquor tallboys, he's probably just going to smash the VCR with a tire iron halfway through, while shrieking "You all must die!" Again, nothing has been solved.

Maybe the thing to do is provide a VCR and cassette to the suspect at the scene of the crime, wait fifteen minutes, and ask politely through a bullhorn, "Have you had a chance to view the videotape?" If the answer is yes, the police officer then asks, "Do you have any questions?" If the answer is no, the arrest can then proceed smoothly, with minimal damage to both suspect and participating nightsticks.

And what will be the content of the "Busted Made E-Z" video itself? The obvious course, when pulled over by the LAPD, is to scream, "Please God don't hurt me," and hit yourself on the head until you pass out. That'd make a good, if short tape; the rest could be filled up with courtesy tips: "That's a nice uniform you have there, officer," "Love your shades," or a sure-fire ice-breaker like, "Come on, funny face, how 'bout a smile!"

A different angle might be to reenact wrong ways to get busted. Hire a trustworthy narrator, like Robert Stack, and have him say, over appropriate visuals, "When arrested by the Los Angeles Police Department, do not brandish your automatic weapon, and shout, 'You'll never take me alive, copper!' A good rule of thumb is to leave the automatic weapon in the back seat for the duration of your arrest."

I know from personal experience that when police pull you over, they really don't appreciate it when you say things like, "Don't you know who I am?" Or "What's the matter, pig, too fast for you?" Or, "You're a brave man with that gun on your hip, aren't you?"

Still, the best approach might be to show the Rodney King video itself, with a big red "X" flashing over the image, and Charlton Heston chanting over it, "Wrong. Mistake. Major blooper. Wrong wrong wrong." I know that's what I'd like to see.

JAGGER | 1992

My pathetic generation gets more like an old dog every year, sniffing the air for the scent of a kind master who knows the old tricks. Unfortunately, the kennel called culture is now run by mysterious masters whose commands we cannot fathom. Ears pricked, eyes wide, we cock our heads one way, the other, watching for clues. What do they want us to do? Rap? (What is that, is that like *black power*?) Dance to an *acid house dance mix*? (Huh? Whine.) Send a dollar to Jerry Brown? (Whimper.) Vote against quotas? Is that the same thing as "Roll over?" If I vote for you, or buy your CD, or pay attention to your soundbite on CNN, will I get a treat? (Woof.) Please, we *want* to learn a new trick, but our heads are stuffed with the useless consumer training of our demographic youth: Boogie! Paint it black! Fetch! Wag tail! Sit! Play dead!

Of those willing to walk the dog there are few left, but we can always count on good old Mick Jagger. Each interview with "Jagger" or "Mick" (to employ the overly familiar style of my generation's music critics) was once called "rare." Thirty years and thousands of features later, his words are no longer precious, merely sporadic. We turn to the semi-annual interview, not to discover new information, but to snuggle up to the old. True, he's found only in the finer stores (VANITY FAIR, not NATIONAL ENQUIRER), but he's just another item on the shelf. If Mick were ice cream, he'd be Haagen-Daaz. If he were chocolate, he'd be a truffle. He's more than a snack, less than a meal: a slightly overpriced treat.

One of the reasons for his continued popularity is the irresistible impulse by boomer editors to quote old Rolling Stones lyrics; his most recent (and only slightly fawning) VANITY FAIR profile is promoted in the table of contents with, "It's only rock 'n' roll, but no wonder he likes it," and the tease at the top of the article asks, "Is Mick Jagger a man of wealth and taste, or is he the Midnight Rambler?" These are variations of the same question pop chroniclers have been asking now for half a lifetime: "Is Mick Jagger a surly androgyne, or what?" Throw in a couple Annie Leibovitz photographs, and you've got yourself a cover story. It practically writes itself.

Still, in today's troubled times, it's good to know that Mick Jagger, erstwhile bad boy, now *eminence grise,* of rock, remains slippery as an eel, imagewise. He's cornered *exactly* as much ambiguity as the market will bear. In the pages of VANITY FAIR, he discusses Peter Ackroyd's Dickens biography, hosts a cross-dressing dinner party in the south of France, and buys paintings from Sotheby's while dancing to James Brown. Asked about his elusive quality, Mick replies,"...I don't find life quite so simple, that everyone's got these tiny personalities and that they can only behave in one kind of way..."

Well, who *doesn't* resist being pigeonholed? Even the famous, who are usually famous for *something* (Richard Simmons excepted) will, sooner or later, try to weasel out of the something that brought them fame in the first place. Garbo laughs! Vanna White does Lady MacBeth! Dylan goes electric!

Not cagey Mick Jagger: he pigeonholed himself as the guy who dances around the pigeonhole. I am consumed with envy, frankly. If, in the bleak corner of my relative notoriety, I am often perceived as a barely ambulatory attitude problem, am I not more than that? Don't I have dreams, aspirations? Don't I want to be Ellen Barkin's *love slave*? Don't I want to be photographed by contest winners? Don't I want to *carry a feature*? Don't I really want to direct? Don't I want my youth back? What about Ian Shoales, *the person?* Whine. Whimper.

Let me grudgingly yield to the generational impulse, and say, okay, you can't always get what you want—but *Mick Jagger can.* Who's that wiry old dude in the black chiffon? Why, that's *Jagger,* children, receiving his *lifetime achievement award.* Where you going after the ceremony, Mick? Taking the grandkids to Bermuda? The Senior Citizens' Transvestite Ball? The studio, to *cut some new tracks*? *A really nice hotel*? Going for a walk, Mick? Can we come with? Reach for the leash, Mick. Woof. Woof.

JAVA JIVE | 1996

I don't drink colas. I don't do decaf. I like my coffee so hot I have to sign a release form to buy it. I'm a large-black-to-go kind of guy. My morning goal is to drink just enough coffee to set my back teeth grinding, form beads of sweat on my forehead the size of marbles, and cause my hands to shake uncontrollably.

How do I know when my caffeine needs have been met? Simple. When the slightest noise makes me jump four feet in the air, and when I can no longer hold small objects, I use both hands to turn the cup over. It's a good system. It works for me.

But I'm no snob. I realize that everybody has his or her own favored method of caffeine ingestion. Some chew tablets. Some sprinkle instant coffee on their corn flakes. Some enjoy a frosty malted laced with ground beans. Some make a thin paste of sugar, cream, and Italian Roast and smear it on their gums. These are all viable ways to stay awake.

And more are being launched every day.

According to the New York Times, a new "caffeine delivery system" is doing quite well in the 12 midwestern states where it is being marketed. It's called Water Joe— a 16 ounce bottle of artesian well water with a 70 milligram dollop of caffeine. It's intended it to be a healthier alternative to coffee and cola.

Who's buying it? "[T]ruckers and traveling salesmen whose stomachs rebel at the day's fifth or sixth cup of coffee or can of cola, bartenders and students trying to stay alert in the wee hours, coffee fanatics looking for ways to brew their java with an extra kick and folks who want their breakfast orange juice to be a real eye-opener." Also guzzling the hyperwater are futures traders at the Chicago Board of Trade, where, "to avoid messes, bottled water is the only beverage allowed on the trading floor."

Apparently the market for caffeine is endless. There must be a way for an entrepreneur like me to cash in on it. Here are some ideas. Any marketing types out there, give me a call. We can make a deal, I just know it.

How about a Prozac and coffee capsule? Easily dissolved in water, it picks you up then puts you down! (My last product along these lines, ZAC 'N' JACK— a mixture of Prozac and bourbon— did very well, especially among college students.)

We could make a caffeinated lipstick, balms and nail polish. My research lab is currently working on a sun screen lotion that will block harmful ultra-violet radiation, and deliver a 100 milligram dose of java right through your skin.

My development team experimented with a coffee styling mousse. Unfortunately, it just wouldn't keep you awake. All it did was curl your hair.

A portable caffeine i.v. drip (for use in the car or home) is now in the testing stages.

We're also working on a caffeinated stuffing that will keep the family alert during those long Thanksgiving dinners. And we've come up with a maple syrup/coffee combination that'll have you wolfing down waffles compulsively till lunchtime.

How about a caffeine patch, like the nicotine patch? We could caffeinate envelope glue, or the backs of postage stamps. How about installing pre-packaged coffee filters right in the shower head? Get your morning jolt and a shampoo at the same time!

Now, some might see this array of products as evidence of a conspiracy by coffeemakers to get America hooked on their product. If that's true, it's fine with me. It would lead directly to the next marketing phase: mass decaffeination.

Highly trained in deprogramming techniques, equipped with mini-vacuums that can detect and suck caffeine from any substance, our special uniformed agents would travel in two-person teams from door to door, rather like Mormons or UPS employees.

As the final stage of the decaffeination program, they would distribute sample packets of herbal tea among the desperate and jittery.

The beauty part? The first one's free.

JOHN TRAVOLTA'S BODY | 1983

I can't escape John Travolta's body. I'm waiting in the market express lane, with a six of malt liquor—and there's that shaved and oiled shape on the cover of hip journals, bourgeois scandal sheets, on the cover of everything but THE NEW YORK REVIEW OF BOOKS. All right, John Travolta looks good with no shirt on. But he's got a gravity guider, a bodybuilding system, indoor heated pool, sauna, jacuzzi, hot tub, clothes, a ruddy Swedish masseuse named Olga; he can afford to eat well, dress well, he's got the leisure time to stay in shape. In the world Travolta lives in, he can do anything, or have someone do it for him. That body on display is a body of knowledge on display. He's a living collaboration, a work of art, a sculpture, a movie star, a product selling itself. The knowledge implicit in creating that naked display could fill an encyclopedia. Like moths to the flame, knowledge is drawn to John Travolta's body. And that's just one image. And that's just the surface of what we know.

We can build H-bombs or read Sylvia Plath. We know the difference between a byte and a bit. We've got the perfect martini and people on the moon. We've got experts on contract bridge, nutrition, flashbulbs and Photostats, clothespins and wheels, statistics, logistics, minicams and sitcoms—we know too much for our own good and enough is enough. The last person to know everything was Leonardo da Vinci. Let's stop. Let's declare a moratorium on knowledge and experience. Let's stop accumulating and start assimilating.

I don't want to compare my pale skinny body to John Travolta's* as I sit shirtless before the TV waiting for the all-night movie to start. I don't want to remember the secret ingredients of fourteen brands of soap. Let's go totally generic. Generic is soothing to the eye and saves money. White boxes with the name of the product in plain type—soap, cigarettes, movie star. Let's stop getting sold a bill of goods. Let's learn what the technocrats and bureaucrats know, and let them learn from us—how to get up, how to get down. Let's take a vacation from learning until all of us know what some of us know. Ronald Reagan reading HIGH TIMES, John Travolta reading SCIENTIFIC AMERICAN. Let's work for a world of fit, well read Renaissance men and women. Put clothes back on the naked body of knowledge, clothes on the emperor. Let's make John Travolta put his shirt back on. Experts have been running numbers on us long enough. Let's get their number, and then move on.

*Happily, John Travolta now looks like every other middle-aged guy.

JOURNALS | 1982

They used to be called diaries, and only high school girls had them. They were little gold-trimmed books kept under tiny lock and key. Some sixteen year old girl would curl up in her pink flannels with her tiny gold pen, turn her radio softly to Top 40 and pen her inmost thoughts, thoughts of dates and quarterbacks. Then, around 1971, schoolteachers found out what these girls were up to in the night, and they got the bright idea to make the girls write these inmost thoughts for grades.

Teachers said this helped students organize their thoughts, but I say it's just one more step on that American road where public and private lives are one and the same. Not brave enough to admit that Ralph Waldo Emerson and Walt Whitman were (contrary to popular belief) incredibly dull writers better left to gather dust on the shelf, English teachers tried to pry some "relevance" from these fogies, to apply these outmoded writers to a modern teenager's life. Not content to let the Beatles be good pop musicians, teachers insisted the Beatles were "poets," thus spoiling the fun for everybody. And, not content to let kids think or not think as they please, they forced these kids to have private thoughts, forced kids to view their own lives as if they were television programs, subject to grades, ratings, and cancellation by some jerk who barely squeaked through four years of college with a BS in education and a minor in psychology.

And what fruit has come in the '80s of these bad seeds: smug men and women in their late twenties who believe their opinions mean something. Self-satisfied calligraphers. Calligraphy was once the realm of ascetic monks illuminating holy manuscripts, now it's the realm of silly mystics and warmed-over hippies, anybody who can afford a pen. And what is written in this neat hand? Three-by-five index cards on the walls of laundromats: advertisements for psychic healers, Tai Chi babysitters, a nonsmoking single mother who wishes to share her fiat with a person who thinks the same way she does.

I sit in the laundromat, sipping my tepid malt liquor, folding my damp black T-shirts, watching the half-dozen Walkmans nod over hot limp clothes. I watch fine hands dip into journals, in the laundromats, in the sad cafes. Misspelled words and atrocious grammar, boundless clichés all stroll across the page in shapely lines. I watch them write these journals that will forever remain unread.

Who needs a neat hand in this age of answering machines and touch-tone dialing? Who needs a prose style? I know I'll never read another word by Anais Nin or Sylvia Plath. These people are losers, no matter what their relevance. I haven't written a letter since 1976.

What's the point? I've got postcards. I've got a phone. We're not trying to communicate, but advertise a lifestyle. We only talk to ourselves.

What we buy when we buy is not a product but a set of mental attitudes. There's the instant coffee that's supposed to make you feel like a character in a NEW YORKER story, divorced but still game, walking along a barren New England beach with an Irish setter. There's Paco Rabanne: "What is remembered is up to you." But we don't have any memories of our own. We're secretly disappointed that we have to wash our clothes every week. We're sad that the fog that surrounds us isn't as pearly and thick as the fog in CASABLANCA, that the boathouse we rented in Connecticut isn't as rustic as the boathouse in ARCHITECTURAL DIGEST. Our memories don't measure up to the vision on the box, and we're left with dusty bottles of foul-smelling aftershave. We're left with the dusty unlocked diaries of our adolescent thoughts. These thoughts used to mean something. Now they're just more empty words in a world that no longer needs them.*

Thanks to the mercurial rise of coffeehouses in urban centers, journals once again have an obscure cultural significance.

JURASSIC PARK | 1993

I recently examined the NEW YORK TIMES paperback bestseller list, to find four books by Michael Crichton in the top ten. Green with envy, I borrowed JURASSIC PARK to see if there was anything I could steal to create my own brand of fast paced technothriller. As I leafed quickly through the novel, visions of rave reviews and royalties danced in my head ("Shoales hits paydirt with NEANDERTHAL GARDEN". "NEANDERTHAL GARDEN is the roller-coaster page turner of the nineties!"). What was the secret of Crichton's enormous success? It sure wasn't the prose style, which contained many sentences like these: "Roberta Carter sighed, and stared out the window." "He gave a long sigh." "Grant sighed, and released his seat belt." "Hammond sighed." "Malcolm sighed."

When they weren't sighing, characters were whispering so velociraptors wouldn't hear them, or shouting at each other to watch out for velociraptors. The hero, as a sop to character development, had a dead wife, and caught more shuteye than other characters: "Grant closed his eyes, and slept." "He yawned, and closed his eyes again." "Grant lay back against the rubber gunwales, closed his eyes, and slept."

These were only brief lapses into lethargy, though. There was eventually action a' plenty; and the victims of prehistoric predators were quite vocal around it: "She was screaming." "No words, just a high-pitched scream." "Muldoon screamed at the top of his lungs as he ran..." "...[H]e opened his mouth to scream." "He shrieked, and slapped the animal away."

How did he handle the sticky problem of awe? Through a daring rhetorical mix of repetition and Christian spirituality: "'My God,'" Grant said. He was staring at the fax." "'Jesus,' somebody said." "'My God,' Ellie said softly.... 'My God,' Ellie said again." "'My God, think of it...'" "'Jesus Christ,' Ed Regis said, staring out the window.... 'Jesus Christ,' he said again." "'Jesus,' Muldoon said." "Jesus, that was the little girl!" "Gennaro slowed the car. 'Jesus.'" "'Wow!' Tim said."

When not being amazed by faxes, Crichton's characters aggressively pursued their fictional chores, which the author emphasized by bringing his protagonists full-bodied into the action, using their first and last names: "Mike Bowman whistled cheerfully as he drove the Land Rover..." "Dizzy with tension, John Arnold threw open the door to the maintenance shed and stepped into the darkness inside." "Tim Murphy could see at once that something was wrong." "Dennis Nedry yawned." "John Hammond sat down heavily in the damp earth of the hillside and tried to catch his breath," an expanded version of an earlier sentence in the book: "Hammond sighed, and sat down heavily." My personal favorite, for its fully observed slice of life, poetically expressed, is: "Ellie Sattler brushed a strand of blond hair back from her face and turned her attention to the acid baths."

Interspersed between breathless escapes and devourings were long interludes—virtual lectures by the author and his fictional stand-in, doomed Ian Malcolm. Through them, the novel was presented as a cautionary tale, a dark warning about Western science (called "thintelligence" by Malcolm), using chaos theory to back up the startling thesis that cloning dinosaurs is a bad idea. In between the good parts, I read of "computer-assisted sonic tomography," of

"Hamachi-Hood automated gene sequencers," of the "Loy antibody extraction technique." Crichton had a worse technology jones than Tom Clancy! The relentless urge to share information included this factoid, "As you know, zoos are extremely popular," and even a plaintive prose-poem: "'What do you know about velociraptor,' Grant asked Tim. He was making conversation." Still I closed the book, buying it totally, grateful for a thrilling yet educational experience. Dinosaur clones? Just say no.

But could I use any of this in my own stabs at best-sellerdom. I'd just read a novel about the unpredictability of large systems. But isn't a novel itself a large system? What if, I thought with a sudden chill, the novel itself is predictable? Dizzy with greed, Ian Shoales sighed, stretched and stared tensely at the blinking cursor of his word processor: "I'an Sholzz adjusted the cliché sequencer on his Atomic Scribbler," he clacked, "sighed, and stared up at the thin blinking moon of Cyberspace." He grinned, and whispered, "Thanks, Mr. Wizard." He might not know much about science, but he sure knew pulp fiction when he saw it.

I'm sorry, but there are no selections marked "K" at this time. Please try again later.

L

LASSIE 1994

They're either setting O.J. up, or he's getting away with murder. Not that it matters. The flesh-eating strep is probably going to get us all anyway. Or some comet aimed at Jupiter will miss it, and make a crater fifty miles wide on our own blue watery orb, bringing darkness for months, withering all life forms. Cockroaches will inherit the earth. And killer bees.

But let's not think about that. There is cause for hope. After all, it is Lassie's fiftieth anniversary. A brand new Lassie movie is in the theatres. I don't mind admitting that I tear up a little every time I even see an image of Lassie. And every time I hear anybody say, "Lassie, what is it girl?"—well, I'm bawling like a newborn babe.

It's true. This hard-bitten iconoclast skeptic is a sucker for a dog movie, especially if it stars Lassie. I've followed all the adventures of this mutant collie with the white blaze. I've sweat bullets with Donald Crisp and Roddy McDowell, waiting for Lassie to come home. I've watched her fight Nazis with Peter Lawford, and work through combat fatigue with Liz Taylor. I watched her outlast Tommy Rettig and Jon Provost, Cloris Leachman and June Lockhart. I followed her through the tangled landscape of syndication, where she ended her television days troubleshooting wilderness problems with faceless forest rangers. She put baby birds back in their nest; she saved toddler raccoons from forest fires; she put makeshift splints on the broken legs of wide-eyed does. Smokey the Bear has nothing on this pup. She is a princess, a paradigm of selfless nobility, the Elvis of dogs.*

Now she's back. I can't wait to see the new Lassie, even if it was produced by Lorne Michaels of Saturday Night Live fame. I'm sure this means that the boy Lassie must help will be one of these whiny media adolescents with floppy hair, rollerblades, and a jones for MTV. It means the soundtrack will be filled with Sonic Youth and Red Hot Chili Peppers, as an aural inducement for young consumers who ordinarily wouldn't be caught dead in a dog movie. As usual, Hollywood will mix blatant sentimentality with flagrant product placement, and hope something sticks.

Despite all that, I have to go. Don't I owe it to Lassie? Look at all she's done for us! A baby trapped on a mountain ledge by a cougar? Lassie's teeth are bared, and she's ready to take it down. Some old prospector's been snakebit? Suck out the poison, Lassie! Good girl! Rabid skunks are descending on the orphanage? The cub scouts are trapped in the ravine? Baby Jessica's in the well?** Lassie, what is it girl?

What if Lassie had been there that night in Brentwood, instead of that pathetic Akita? She would have taken the alleged perpetrator down before a blow was struck. She would have kneeled on his chest, barked him his rights, and kept him at bay until the proper authorities arrived. Lassie knows the early symptoms of flesh-eating strep, and can recommend both competent physicians and efficient HMOs. Why place our trust in astronomers? Lassie can see comets coming from light years away. She'll lead us to safety, if we only put our trust in her. Cockroaches and killer bees live in fear of Lassie.

I want to live in Lassie's world, a world where families are dutiful and loving, and children are perfect. You don't even need family values in Lassie World, you don't even need faith. Lassie doesn't ask that you believe in her. Just call her, and she will come. She will come.

I confess everything! I want to ride back to the farm from Capital City with Gramps. I want a beautiful fine woman by my side, a handsome son in the back seat, and the finest dog in the world riding shotgun. I'm ready, Lassie. I'm ready for the rural lifestyle. They do have cable in the country, don't they? I don't want to miss those Lassie reruns. Can you get me a deal on installation? Good girl!

*See "elvitude."
**The fireman who rescued Baby Jessica committed suicide in 1995.

LIBEL 1984

When I was in high school the principal threatened me with a libel suit. He wouldn't relax the dress code, so I called him a fascist in the high school paper. I don't know why he got so upset. When I called my parents fascists all they did was kick me out of the house.

I asked the senior class president and yearbook editor, a blond jerk with unnaturally white teeth—I think he'd had them capped in grade school—to defend me in court. I figured he was destined for a career in law and mine would be a landmark case. He was mildly interested until his father told him he'd kick him out of the house if he had anything more to do with me. It was just as well. There just wasn't room for two to sleep in my '63 VW—and besides, the VW would have been the legal fee.

It all worked out for the best, however. The principal dropped the suit, I got a haircut, and my folks let me come home, but it just goes to show you, the life of a gadfly on the body politic isn't all beer and skittles. Sticks and stones might break the bones, but it's the printed word that brings in the lawyers.

Which makes me wonder: what is honor in the modern world? When you say "That insults me," does it really mean, "My lawyers think I have a good case"? Does prestige come with a legal retainer? Can a blush be used as evidence? Is a legal staff a prerequisite to a damaged reputation?

It seems to me a damaged reputation is purely a rich man's burden, once avenged with duels. Now, I enjoy the image of General Westmoreland and the 60 Minutes gang taking measured paces with pistols at dawn, but those dueling days are gone, and the days when the word had cutting power are gone too.

Take the bizarre case of Falwell versus Flynt. God knows, I don't hold Reverend Falwell as a role model (though he certainly has a reputation to uphold), but how can anything said by Mr. Flynt possibly affect that reputation? How seriously can you take HUSTLER'S opinion on anything? Take the NATIONAL ENQUIRER. Suing them is like calling a spade a spade. You're not fooling anybody or changing anything, you're only translating your own embarrassment into a court settlement, and it's lawyers who get the blood from the stone of libel suits.

We have a superstitious fear of the printed word, of its power to harm us, so we draw a magic circle of legal briefs around it. Or we raise a mountain of red tape to stop the avalanche of information; ratings systems and the FCC tell us who can see what; books are burned, banned, ignored by critics, albums smashed, tapes erased, lawsuits filed. Psychologists and bureaucrats bury simple words in a mountain of jargon, a mountain of lies and truth, information and disinformation.

And what is information but something to be used by those who have it against those who don't? The networks give it out to win a ratings battle; the CIA keeps it in the national interest; the KGB distorts it in the national interest; advertisers select it so we will buy their products; we collect it to spread gossip about our friends; we smear it on our enemies; we use it as blackmail; we stick it to those we hate; for every Shakespeare play there's an enemies list. One of the reasons Dante wrote the INFERNO was to put his enemies in the fires of Hell. That's probably the main reason I write. Vengeance. Envy. Money.

All of this just goes to show I'm glad I'm not in high school anymore. I'm too old, for one thing; and I don't have a lawyer, for another. And it shows that those who say the pen is mightier than the sword are liars. Ask yourself: would you rather be called nasty names in the newspaper or pierced with a sharp instrument? I say, "No contest." I don't care what you call me, I've called myself worse. Compared to the real problems of the world, humiliation is a minor and temporary inconvenience. Only now, in these self-indulgent times, is personal embarrassment elevated to tragedy. That's my opinion. If you don't like it, sue me.

LITERACY 1994

Warning! The following contains references to polls and/or surveys.
Reader discretion is advised.

According to a new Department of Education study, nearly half of Americans are illiterate. This is probably alarming. Irwin Kirsch, the project director, told NEWSWEEK, "This test revealed that many people can read in the technical sense that they can decode the words, but they lack the strategies and skills needed to use the information."

Well, wait a minute. If I decode these words properly, what they really seem to mean is, "People can read, they just can't follow instructions."

Sure enough, sample documents I've seen from the test include a pay stub, a social security card, a bank deposit slip, and a bus schedule. Perhaps we shouldn't be so alarmed after all. This isn't a literacy test, it's a *job application*!

Once again, our nation's educators have stripped away any semblance of fun from reading. Once again, America is warned that reading for pleasure is a one-way ticket to Palookaville. We must master fine print and boilerplate if we're going to get ahead in life. Reading is a grim chore, analogous to scrubbing toilets.

If we can't read, I believe the fault lies not with us, but our reading material. I read **THE BRIDGES OF MADISON COUNTY** in about an hour, and had time left over to get an innuendo update on Michael Jackson, absorb the thoughtful media coverage of the Burt/Loni affair, and still had a second left over to ponder the value of literacy at all. Yet I still can't program my VCR. Despite days spent squinting at the VCR manual, I remain ignorant of what "VHS" stands for. I don't know the difference between APR and FICA. What makes a PG-13 movie that much less suitable for children than PG? I couldn't tell you. I can deconstruct a text as well as the next guy, but I couldn't wade through a cereal box disclaimer to save my life. Am I being disenfranchised by this study? Would this be cause for hope or despair?

My sensitive feelings aside, I'd say the bureaucrats have definitely found America's Achilles heel. It's hard to argue with those who say we have severely diminished comprehension skills. Even the most powerful among us can't cope with normal life. Remember President Bush's awe when confronted with a supermarket scanner? How many movie stars would recognize a bus schedule if they saw one? Could Ross Perot find the expiration date on a half-off coupon?

Of course, the powerful don't need to understand anything. That's why they have lawyers, to explain (for example) what a "wholly-owned subsidiary" is in terms even a CEO could understand. But lawyers don't need to understand anything either! Why have an attention span, when you can have a staff? As a matter of hard fact, all anybody needs to understand in America today is the interoffice memo. Memos and e-mail are the literary forms of the nineties. Master them, kids, and you'll go far.

I once knew two boys who had, according to the proper authorities, severe learning disabilities. Yet they could both name every Star Trek episode, in order, and offer a detailed summary of each plot. They had devoured the entire paperback line of Star Trek books. They had constructed intricate models of Federation and Klingon starships, so they obviously could follow instructions.

Oh, they'll probably grow up lacking the strategies and skills needed to respond appropriately to a sign like, "Don't even think of parking here," (which is, if you should find yourself thinking of parking there, to turn yourself in immediately.) They'll probably go ahead and buy a car anyway, never realizing that actual mileage will vary.

Here's the question, America: Do we want our kids growing up to be chipper obsessive Trekkies, or dreary anal retentives who can breeze through a freezer warranty with 100% comprehension? It's a grim choice, America, but it seems to be all ours.

LITTLE PEOPLE | 1983

Except for ROAD WARRIOR, which I've seen twelve times, I usually don't go to Australian movies. If I see the preview for an Australian movie, I feel like I've already seen the movie. But I went to see THE YEAR OF LIVING DANGEROUSLY, because (like UNDER FIRE, a great movie) it showed journalists in a state of confusion. I love to see confused journalists anywhere, but that's not what I want to talk about.

I want to talk about Linda Hunt's Oscar. She did a great job, and deserves any award that comes her way, but her role in LIVING DANGEROUSLY was the same role given to so-called "dwarves and midgets" since the beginning of literature. This role is, near as I can put it, the tortured conscience of man. It was the same role Michael Dunne played in SHIP OF FOOLS, only he was the life force of pre-WWII Europe, or Oscar in THE TIN DRUM representing the stunted heart of WWII Germany.

Writers from Edgar Allen Poe to Carson McCullers have used little people as stand-ins for the "little guy." Or they're used for comic effect, or to make Ricardo Montalban look taller. Or they're a symbol of decadence on rock videos, cute and magical in WIZARD OF OZ, they're a stand-in for aliens in E.T. In POLTERGEIST and DON'T LOOK NOW, they were psychic and psychotic respectively.

Little people are used as a symbol for some kind of oogieboogie connection to the collective unconscious. Well, I guess being a symbol isn't a bad job as far as it goes (though personally I thought allegories went out of literary style in the late Middle Ages, excepting certain TWILIGHT ZONE episodes), but if I were a little person and an actor, I'd want more out of my career than symbolizing the sick soul of modern man on one hand, or making a hunk of STAR WARS tin move on the other hand. Little people lead lives like the taller rest of us, they have kids, they work downtown—how about it, Hollywood? Why not cast little people as people? It's not too much to ask. If you want a symbol of decadence and alienation, why not use Dustin Hoffman? He'd probably like the challenge and be grateful for the change of pace.*

*In the excellent independent feature, "LIVING IN OBLIVION", the dwarf refuses to be part of a dream sequence, angrily insisting that dwarves are not and have never been part of anybody's nightmare.

LONG DISTANCE 1995

A few years back telephone companies used the softest of sells to persuade us to use their services. Commercials featured wistful little piano filigrees and a deep-voiced announcer on the brink of tears. We watched Grandpa pick up a receiver to hear the first gurgles of his offspring's offspring, a young lover coo "I wuv oo"s to a long distance other, a suburban housewife with an exotic accent make contact with Mutti and Poppa back in the Olde Country. It was a tribute to the Reagan years really.

Today it's all about money. Telephone companies have developed incredibly byzantine long distance savings programs. Every phone bill I get has some boldface reminder of how much money I save each time I spend money.

As corporate lies go, I prefer the fiction that every time I make a long distance call I'm putting a nickel in my piggy bank to the fiction that, by their very being, telephones are electronic conductors of intimacy, but still, why the change?

The Information Revolution bears much of the blame. When network television ruled the airwaves, advertisers could be assured that millions of people were watching at any given moment. A warm 'n' fuzzy approach works best with a critical mass of humanity; the smaller the audience, the more embarrassing it becomes (as anyone who's been seen talking baby talk to a loved one can attest).

Now cable television has exploded, not to mention the Internet, talk radio, and John Grisham novels. When a network show is rated Number One today, only a few hundred people are watching it, tops, and most of them are doing something else—writing an angry letter to Congress, seething over imagined slights, making bombs.

These are not warm 'n' fuzzy times. We're fragmented, bitter, and about to be laid off. If people do come together in the 90's, it's either to join a cult, or accuse others of being in one.

Telephone companies are no exception. Faced with a shrinking and difficult-to-reach buying public, they have turned to telemarketing with a vengeance. In their zeal to attract consumers one by one, they've come to resemble strange cults themselves.

Every time I switch long distance services (which I do every time one bribes me with a rebate), I get panicked calls from their rivals. "Why have you abandoned us?" the service representative sobs into the phone. "Who can we kill to get you back?" Oddly, I get even more calls from the service I've chosen: "Thankyouthankyouthankyou," the rep utters breathlessly. "Please hold the line for my supervisor who wishes to thank you personally as well."

I'd be flattered by the attention, except they always want the names and numbers of my friends and relatives, supposedly so I can put a nickel in my piggy bank every time I call them, but really so marketing zealots can pester them at odd hours.

Why the desperation? What are they afraid of? Are we going to throw our telephones away and live in caves, communicating only with smoke signals? To keep us happy with our phones, phone companies offer ever more outlandish and nonsensical services, the latest being Caller ID, a box installed with your phone that lets you see the number of the person trying to call you. The trouble with Caller ID is that those who don't want the service can have their number blocked.

So the only numbers you'd ever see displayed on your Caller ID box would be, oh, sales representatives for example. Hm. On second thought, sign me up. Please don't call and thank me though. I won't be answering any more.

MACAULAY CULKIN | 1993

Macaulay Culkin, the charmless young person who shot mysteriously to superstardom with two appalling HOME ALONE movies, tried to "stretch" by playing a murderous bad seed in THE GOOD SON.

A sister, a cousin, a dog, and even Mom herself were targets for the precocious pre-teen psycho. Some critics were worried that "Mac" (as the media cozily call him) was playing too much against type. It was feared that his legions of fans will attend the movie, hoping for a good-natured PG-rated sadistic romp, and instead find a grim R-rated sadistic romp.

"When's he going to say, 'Yessss!'" terrified young ones wondered. "When's he going to do his trademark hands-on-the-side-of-the-face scream?" Moviegoers left the theatre reeling, the thin fabric of their reality torn. "Mac: What Happened?" group therapy sessions sprouted up all over the country. There was a sudden surge of troubled experts on OPRAH! Senate subcommittees took off in motorcades to Hollywood, blue noses in the air, blue pencils ready to strike.

Well, let's calm down. After all, besides being America's newest sweetheart, Macaulay Culkin* is quite the little cinematic sociopath already. He displayed alarming glee when he bounced bricks off heads, scalded men with hot irons, or threw them down flights of stairs. Oh sure, he befriended a crusty grandpa and a homeless pigeon lady in the course of his rampages, but if they'd entered his house without knocking, he'd have hurled them through a second story window without even opening it first. The moviemakers were probably trying to put a wacky cartoon gloss on the mayhem, but the combination of Tom n' Jerry violence, formulaic sentimentality, and basic crudity made the HOME ALONE movies a curdled entertainment stew at best.

But does that mean awful movies should be regulated? No. I don't care if it's Jesse Helms or Carol Mosley-Braun; neither should be allowed to peer over producers' shoulders with helpful suggestions. Public sector micromanagement of images is a bad idea, especially when mingled with competing ideologies. "That desensitizes young people to violence!" or "That condones a homosexual lifestyle!" are inappropriate responses when having a pop culture experience. A simple "Yuck!" or "Wow!" is sufficient. Federal intervention can't eliminate mediocrity, it can only create a smoother level of banality. Even if we do remove the nuts from the rancid chunky peanut butter we call pop culture, will we really improve the taste?

MADONNA | 1990

Warning! The following contains references to polls and/or surveys.
Reader discretion advised.

DICK TRACY has finally been shoved in our moviegoing faces, in what may be the twilight of Warren Beatty's career, and another false dawn of Madonna's. Moviewise, Madonna's had bad luck at everything but publicity. Maybe it's because she seems like a gal who spends her days bleaching her hair and developing her pallor and career, and her nights racing down the middle of Sunset Boulevard in a merry widow and torn fishnet stockings. This behavior is fine for music videos, but a little thin for a feature-length motion picture.

Last spring SPY magazine commissioned an opinion poll for its snotty television special. Being somewhat snotty myself, I watched the darn thing, which informed me that sixty percent of American men would not have sex with Madonna even if she asked them.

I realize the poll was intended to be a joke, but still—sixty percent? Even if she asked? I'll admit that it's difficult to imagine a social situation in which Madonna would ask a non-celebrity layman for sex. She probably has her own washer and drier, so it's a safe bet you won't run into her at the laundromat. She takes limos, so she won't be ripping your shirt off at the bus stop. She doesn't punch a clock, so you can't spurn her advances at the copy machine. The BYOB football parties you attend are definitely not her social milieu, so you're definitely out of luck there too.

And what does sex with Madonna entail, exactly? What do you do with a woman like that? Massage her ego? Paint her toenails while she makes a few important phone calls? Is the sex act preceded by megadoses of vitamins and a low-impact aerobics workout? Is her entourage present during the physical encounter, or are they dismissed from the suite? If they're dismissed, do they stand around in the hall complaining?

Madonna herself is mildly terrifying. Her hair frightens me, I admit it. And her clothing—what there is of it—has many sharp angles, which might cause injury in an embrace. Even if those fears are overcome, what's to stop her from comparing you unfavorably to other lovers she's had, having you removed from her presence, beaten to a pulp and thrown into a dumpster? Nothing.

Still, if I were alone in my dank flat, watching a tape of EVIL DEAD II, cracking a cold one and dreaming of popcorn, and I heard the whisper of a knock at my door, and then, when I had put on a clean shirt to answer it, I were to find Madonna, of all people, smiling sadly and whispering in a weary little voice, " Hey Ian, how about it?"—I tell you folks, I'd pause that tape in a New York minute.

All right, call me a victim/perpetrator of a patriarchal sexist oppressor culture but golly, a fella's gotta daydream about something while he's waiting in line to see DICK TRACY. Who knows? Madonna might be in that line. One thing might lead to another. Fools dream. At least forty percent of them do.

MADONNA 2 | 1994

I told Madonna, I said, "Look, when you do Letterman don't offer Dave your panties. I've offered my underwear to talk show hosts before. Believe me, they don't appreciate the gesture."

"But you're, like, a guy," she protested.

"That's not the point," I said. "And lose the cigar. It's bad enough when you see a man swagger around like a robber baron with hip pretensions, puffing on a stogie big as a pool cue. But a woman?"

"That's just sexist," she said.

"Only two people in the world know how to smoke a cigar, my grandfather and Fidel Castro. My grandfather's dead and Fidel's outmoded. Think about it."

"I'm gonna talk about an unusual way to prevent athlete's foot, and say what I really think about nose picking. I'm going to sit on a top ten list, and kind of flirt with him in a really stupid and annoying way."

"You're making a big mistake, Maddy" I warned.

"It's just kicky fun," she whined. "I don't care what you say. I'm gonna use the eff word a lot, and never ever leave."

"Fine," I said. "But you're heading into Michael Jackson world, babe, Neverland, Palookaville. You'll never see SEX come out in paperback. You're kissing your movie career good-bye."

"What movie career?" she sneered, and hung up on me.

She wouldn't listen. And look what happened.

I have heard that during a commercial break on her LATE SHOW appearance, major CBS executives appeared on the set, wearing three piece suits and wielding crowbars. As the television audience cheered, they pried her from her seat and lifted her over their heads to dump her unceremoniously on the busy streets of Manhattan. Oh, did I mention that Dan Rather was there too? "You'll never work in this town again," he's rumored to have told her. Connie Chung (she was there as well I think) kicked Madonna in the ankle, leaving a bruise. Memos have been handed down to the staff of 60 MINUTES. "Get Madonna," is all they say.

All across America, teenage girls are throwing their Madonna CDs on chamber of commerce sponsored bonfires. Her former dancers have formed a support group. Camille Paglia has returned Madonna's promotional materials with big red X marks slashed across them, and was last seen writing fan letters to certain loud Seattle-based girl groups.

I like to think that Letterman himself was above all this. I like to think that after the Material Girl had been swept away from his program, and the studio cleared, he sat alone at his desk in the darkness, staring at Madonna's underwear mournfully and wondering, "Why? Why, Madonna, why?" Perhaps I'm just an idealist.

And Madonna? I got a collect call right after the show from someone calling herself "Your contrite dominatrix," but I refused the charges. I knew it was her, but enough is enough.

Still I pity her. She's out there somewhere, I know, wandering the streets of Manhattan, tears glistening on her alabaster cheeks, as the door of every hot new club closes in her face. She stumbles in the gutter, and no hand will help her. When she goes shopping, clerks no longer offer fawning deference, but the usual bored contempt reserved for the rest of us. I think of Anne Baxter in ALL ABOUT EVE,

Patty Duke in VALLEY OF THE DOLLS. "Madonna who?" New York sniffs. We may never know the answer.

How ironic. She first made her mark in downtown Manhattan, now she ends her career mauled in midtown. But hey, that's New York. New York will make you and break you. Ask you out, break your heart.

I don't know much, but I know it's a lonely town (particularly if you're the only surfer boy around). I know the Bronx is up, and the Battery's down. I'll take Manhattan, sure. I want to be a part of it, New York, that is, New York. But every so often, like Madonna, we need to face the bitter truth. New York can be the coldest place on earth. Especially if you're not wearing any underwear.

MAGIC | 1993

In '93, Magic Johnson was forced to retire a second time from professional basketball. Why? Well, he got a cut on his arm during a game. He has AIDS, you know.

I'm not a sports fan, but I caught a videotape of the crucial moment on PRIMETIME LIVE. There was Magic Johnson watching the game from the sidelines as a sports doctor applied a cotton swab to his arm. The camera pulled in to locate the scratch, but it was so teeny, it couldn't even find it. It was just a nick, a little gash, one might even call it an *owie*.

But there we were, Magic Johnson, interviewer, a play-by-play man, color man, camera crews, basketball teams, networks, millions of viewers, an insidious little virus, all collaborating in a vast complicated manner to create a viewing experience that not only helped Magic's playing career self-destruct, but also served as promotion for his autobiography, which he didn't really write.

MEN | 1995

Warning! The following contains references to statistics.
Reader discretion advised.

I guess I've always known, in my heart of hearts, that the male of the species is essentially worthless. Some new research now suggests that, worse than useless, he's actually in the way.

Zoologist Dr. Rosemary J. Redfield has taken recent findings on mutation rates in sperm cells, incorporated them into a computer model, and concluded that the rate of human sperm mutation may be at least six times greater than in a woman's eggs. And this is in a young male. The mutation rate increases with age.

If this is true, any woman who feels a primal maternal urge may soon choose to mate with a lithe callow unemployed youth rather than a successful silver-haired corporate executive. This may decrease the risk of a dip into the gene pool, but what will it do to our capitalist system?

On the bright side, capitalism could soon provide women with ways to fertilize or clone themselves, like snails and lizards. Not very sexy, I know, but the mating dance as such does seem to lead to potential genetic calamity. That's in addition to the usual heartache, dysfunction, and James Ivory movies.

So the question is, "Is there a place for The Guy in the asexual world of tomorrow?" I've been racking my brains trying to figure out what on earth males are good for. There's not much, frankly.

—Grunting encouragement, shouting hoarsely, and drinking heavily at professional sporting events. Women could train small animals to do these simple tasks.

—The creation and development of complicated handshakes. I just know women could come up with their own, if they put their minds to it.

—Spitting and scratching in public places. These would almost certainly be phased out, if women were left alone in the world, along with movable toilet seats, high heels, bulimia, necktie pins, and any game that requires inflatable shoes or "winning."

—The formation of rock and roll bands. True, there are some women rockers, but I would suggest they are as yet statistically insignificant. I would even venture to predict that rock and roll, being primarily a hormonal display by young men for young women, will also gradually disappear.

—Defending the perimeter. Before the present depletion of the testosterone layer, it had been the traditional job of the guy to defend the perimeter. Once women are alone, the concept of a "perimeter" will become increasingly quaint. Without men around, what the hell do women have to defend themselves against?

—In this same vein, various important elements of civilization almost certainly were introduced by men, including the interoffice memo, the uniform, the concept of "athletic foot-wear," superheroes, and of course, sports trivia. Interoffice memos will flourish, but the rest will go the way of the dodo.

—We have men to thank for the invention of, if not time itself, then at least the minute and second hands of watches. Impatience, in general, is a male realm. How many times have you see a woman pacing restlessly, looking at her wristwatch? I'll bet you could count them on the fingers of one hand. (Counting things on one hand, by the way, ticking off points in a debate, and measuring things by comparing them to football fields are all testosterone-driven activities. Or so studies indicate.)

—Men are the definite pioneers in the development of impenetrable professional jargon (not to mention the incorporation of data into computer models), though women are starting to make inroads in this all-important field.

In conclusion then, in a world without men, say farewell to cigars, chugalug contests, hearty guffaws, and long anecdotes designed to make the teller seem more important than he is. There will be jokes, of course, but without men nobody will remember exactly how they go. Porches, gardens, tea, moderation, chats, and long leisurely dinners will become the rule not the exception. Restful color schemes will become the order of the day.

All in all, I have to admit it sounds pretty good. Wish I could be there. Unfortunately, someone needs to stay behind and watch for invaders. I know you women won't be bothered to do it.*

*The foregoing generated an alarming amount of anonymous phone calls, informing me that I was not getting with the program re: the empowering of white men.

MISSION: INAPPROPRIATE | 1996

I'm one of several million who shelled out a chunk of their disposable income to attend the recent blockbuster, MISSION: IM-POSSIBLE. (If you haven't yet seen the movie, stop reading now; I will be revealing its major plot twist— be warned!!!)

The flick has much to recommend it. For instance, you'll recall that in the late lamented television series, there was always the threat that "the secretary" would "disavow" knowledge of their actions should any of the Impossiblers be caught or killed.

I always wondered two things: (A) Who was this secretary? An overly powerful administrative assistant, or shadowy cabinet member? (B) What happens when you get disavowed? Nobody ever get disavowed on the teevee show, not in any rerun that I ever saw.

Well the movie reveals the process at last! (Though who "the secretary" is remains a mystery.) The mysterious feds for whom Tom Cruise works disavow him early in the movie, forcing him to blow up an aquarium with chewing gum. In desperation, he must then hire scab Impossible Missionaries to break into the Pentagon to steal a computer disc, which contains something or other. This theft in turn causes the mysterious feds to frame Tom Cruise's mom and dad for drug-smuggling.

So there you have it. Disavowal is a cross between excommunication and extortion. It's good to have that detail cleared up.

Also, the movie takes place in actual European locations. The teevee show, though it supposedly sent the team to either grim vaguely Eastern European police states or grim vaguely Caribbean police states, they all looked pretty much the same— drab buildings on a studio's back lot, to be precise. More mysteriously, the petty despots of these Backlotslovakias all spoke English with the same guttural accent. "We" was always "vee," "have" was "haff," "if' was "eef," and "luff" was just a trick. Many were the tyrants' hearts broken by Barbara Bain.

In the movie, the foreigners were all French and spoke English with genuine French accents. I'm glad they spent the extra money for this slice of realism (though luff in the movie remained an illusion).

But the movie does make a severe error in judgment. It makes Jim "Good Morning Mr. Phelps" Phelps the arch-villain of the piece.

I won't go into the shadow this slur casts on righteous fictitious covert organizations everywhere. But did any of the monsters in Hollywood take the feelings of Peter (TV's Jim Phelps) Graves into account? The guy should be enjoying the fruits of his semi-retirement, hosting A&E's BIOGRAPHY, and resting on his laurels. Instead, his laurels are ashes.

Look at his accomplishments.

—He's Jim (TV's Matt Dillon) Arness' brother.

—He played Bobby Diamond's foster father on FURY.

—He was the German spy in STALAG 17.

—He was the pilot who kept asking the kid if he liked gladiator movies in AIRPLANE.

—And, of course, he was Jim Phelps on the incorruptible MISSION: IMPOSSIBLE.

These are enough accomplishments for two lifetimes. But now Peter Graves huddles angrily in his compound, a bitter broken man. Jim Phelps betray his team? That's like saying Fox Mulder is behind alien abductions, Mary Richards is a conniving backstabber, and Eddie Haskell is a nice kid.

These damn movie people think they can trash any value they please, and get away with it. I think Peter Graves should assemble The Team for one last mission and teach these movie weasels a thing or two.

Being masters of disguise, they could easily pose as Tom Cruise and his "people." Then they could approach studio execs offering to do the MISSION: IMPOSSIBLE sequel for scale. Simultaneously, they could approach Tom Cruise and offer him five gazillion dollars for the sequel, plus points.

The ensuing lawsuits should tie up everybody for years.

In the meantime Peter Graves and Barbara Bain can spend their golden years in Backlotslovakia, wiretapping Nazis, disguising themselves as corrupt prime ministers and their mistresses, and proving to the world that luff can conquer all after all.

That's what I'd do, if I were Jim Phelps.

MOHICANS | 1992

In the new film version of LAST OF THE MOHICANS the hero's name has been changed from Natty Bumppo to Nathaniel Poe. The new monicker does have panache, but does it capture the untamed spirit of the man my English teachers called Hawkeye, Pathfinder, Deerslayer? Well, probably not, but the book didn't either. If you've ever read James Fenimore Cooper, you'll recall that his prose style is as stiff as dried leggings. His books achieve a turgidity matched only by Silas Marner. I have a hunch that the Leatherstocking saga and SILAS MARNER, taken together, form the primary cause of both rising dropout rates and teenage illiteracy.

Director Michael Mann, creator of MIAMI VICE, is probably responsible for this name change, as well as giving old Leatherstocking Madeleine Stowe as a love interest. The original frontiersman was a mite skittish around womenfolk, preferring to hunker over pemmican in the solitude of the wilds. Who'd want to see a movie about that? Two hours of a gaunt antisocial stoic gnawing jerky, squinting at the horizon, and absently plucking ticks off his buckskins? Not in the nineties. Not with Lyme Disease. Today's wild man owes more to Rob't Bly than Dan'l Boone. Today's wilderness is only a site for weekend seminars; rassling grizzlies is discouraged.

So Natty becomes Nathaniel, a non-smoking hardbody who wears sensible all-natural clothing, is emotionally available, and can peg an elk with a tomahawk at forty paces. If this New Age bumpkin catches on, he could become a kind of pre-colonial James Bond. THE LAST OF THE MOHICANS could be the first in a series.

This new wrinkle in popular culture would mark a return to some old themes, however. The Cold War is over, and with it the need to battle despised Soviet spy networks; we can go back to a centuries-old Western tradition: despising the French. We can dust off those coonskin caps. And we'll see sequels, part of a tradition as old as Oedipus and Colonus: NEXT OF THE LAST OF THE MOHICANS, NEXT OF THE LAST OF THE MOHICANS II, SON OF THE LAST OF THE MOHICANS, FIRST OF THE MOHICANS (a prequel), and MO' HICANS.

Just as our man Flint, Matt Helm, Maxwell Smart and the girl from U.N.C.L.E. clung like remoras to the shark of James Bond, there will be low-budget ripoffs trailing in Nathaniel's wake: MOE OF THE MOHAWKS, LASS OF THE PEMMICANS, THE PENULTIMATE APACHE, and SAVE THE LAST DANCE WITH WOLVES FOR ME.

Leather jerkins and Mohawk haircuts will appear among white collar workers, who will start to commute by flatboat. Many will take up the banjo. There will be a renewed interest in Stephen Foster and Gary Cooper. No back yard will be complete without a smokehouse, and hardy families will host barbecues during full-blown blizzards. Madonna's next album will be called A WINSOME COMELY LASS. She too will take up the banjo. Spittoons will be installed in singles bars, as laconic men pass the jug and eye the modest womenfolk along the walls. The standard pickup line, "Hey, how you doin'?" will be replaced by "Wal, this chile's seen a heap o' purty gals, ma'am, but you-all'd mortify a passle o'poseys, I swan." The proper response will be to lower one's eyes and blush prettily.

It won't all be flagons of grog and butter churns, though. This cultural phenomenon will generate controversy. As more and more people discharge flintlocks at pigeons, emergency rooms will fill up with neo-pioneers plugged by stray musketballs. AmerInds, disgusted with the resurgence of the "noble savage," will make their own movie, LAST OF THE STUPID WHITE PEOPLE, with Jim "Hi Vern" Varney. Horrified vegetarians will open deer parks all over the country, run by volunteers wearing simple uniforms stitched together from twigs and dried berries. Women will complain that their menfolk come home smelling like wet fur. Shakers will gain many converts. We'll get purely fed up with eating squab every night.

The fad will peak in '95, when the network series, MONONGAHELA MORALS SQUAD doesn't last the season. Things will then gradually get back to normal. Banjos will pop up at garage sales, pigeons will waddle out of hiding, and Madonna will release her new album, MO' SEX. But that's a lot of moons from now, hoss. Best keep your powder dry.*

*The Mohicans fad failed to catch fire. So I'm not Faith Popcorn. So sue me.

MORONS | 1994

A few weeks ago I took a meeting, as we say in California, with a producer for a network weekly news magazine which shall remain nameless. My fantasy was to become a regular commentator on the show, the new Andy Rooney America's been secretly desiring. I'd make fun of toothpaste and kooky hair products well into the 21st Century and take home a five figure check for my efforts. My hopes were cruelly dashed. You know what that guy said to me? "Keep in mind," he said, "that our audience is mainly morons."

Maybe it's just me, but I don't think a news producer should think of his viewers as "morons." If you're trying to explain the intricacies of Whitewater, for example, or even the Olympic legal committee's attitude on kneecapping, you should assume that your viewers have if not some prior knowledge at least a willingness to learn.

But finally I wondered, what if he's right? Maybe we are a nation of imbeciles. If there are pockets of individuals out there with a hunger for sentences that don't contain the word "suck" maybe they're demographically insignificant. Do we know anything anymore? Somebody must still know something.

Somebody, for example, knows why the caged bird sings. Somebody saw what you did. Somebody knows who you are. Somebody knows what boys like. Somebody knows what girls want. Somebody must know what makes things tick. Somebody must still know the difference between shinola and a hole in the ground. At least one person must know why Clint Eastwood's partners always die, or who Milli Vanilli really was.

Who was telling the truth? Anita Hill? Clarence Thomas? Somebody knows who killed the Kennedys and Martin Luther King. There must be thousands convinced that they know the secrets of the pyramids, the origins of life. Who knows where Elvis* is, or Coke's secret ingredient? What really happened to the Lindbergh baby, Judge Crater and Amelia Earhart? What is David Brock really up to? Somewhere on the information highway answers can be had. But I'm not really worried about the dumbing down of America, only how it will affect me careerwise. After all, I'm supposed to be a wise man. Or a wise guy. Take your pick. I don't know much, but I know this much. I know which one you'll choose.

*Elvis was a very popular singer for many years. See "Elvitide."

MULTICULTURALISM 1994

What's this multiculturalism flap all about? On the one hand a bunch of old white guys are concerned that kids today are no longer forced to read the books the old white guys were forced to read when they were kids. For some reason, they think this is alarming.

On the other hand, many today believe that the choice of books they read in their literature classes could have a magical healing effect on the lifestyles of emerging Third World nations.

And there's more to it than that. Everybody's enraged, for one thing. Conservatives are enraged that family values aren't nurtured on today's campuses (as if they ever were!). Old-fashioned virtues like responsibility, fortitude, and temperance, and prudence are the victims of situational ethics and creeping humanism—the psychic serial killers of the cultural id. That's why conservatives are so hot on prayer in school, poems that rhyme, and stories that have a moral.

And kids today, those lovable neo-Stalinist trendsetters, are even more enraged than conservatives (if that's possible). They're angry about date rape, ecology, racism, and "inappropriate behavior," among other things.

Luckily, kids today confine their rage largely to school, where they force insensitive professors and fellow students into therapy and counseling programs. Occasionally, some book spills out of one, usually focused on "gender issues," but for the most part their off-campus activities seem confined to pamphlets and letters to the editor.

Off-campus, old white guys are winning the so-called culture wars hands down. Over the past few years, they've spewed out scads of bestsellers, most recently Harold Bloom's THE WESTERN CANON and James Finn Garner's POLITICALLY CORRECT BEDTIME STORIES. There were IN DEFENSE OF ELITISM, ILLIBERAL EDUCATION, DISUNITING OF AMERICA, CULTURE OF COMPLAINT, DICTATORSHIP OF VIRTUE, THE CULTURE WARS—and many more, all dedicated one way or another to the proposition that our cultural traditions are being trashed by humorless snotnoses.

But if humorless snotnoses are such a leech on society, where are their bestsellers? Maybe the P.C. geezers don't have the influence the old white geezers think they have. Maybe both groups are indulging in wishful thinking. There's nothing like having an enemy to make yourself feel important.

It seems to me the true culture of this country is being pitched to thugs, morons, and suckers for a con. And that's the way we like it. Most Americans, when they feel rage, don't have the urge to write an angry bestseller, or even an angry letter to the editor. No, I think I speak for most Americans when I say that when I feel rage, I have the urge to punch somebody's face in.

Of course, I don't. I'm too old, weak, and cowardly. That's why I'm a writer.

Yes, we must all work through our rage issues. We must celebrate our differences. That's why I've prepared this helpful chart...

POP CULTURE PRODUCES:	ART PRODUCES:	MULTICULTURAL ARTIFACT PRODUCES:
spine-tingling fear	fear and trembling	vague anxiety
guilty pleasure	aesthetic bliss	guilt
warm gushy feeling	awe and pity	purging of patriarchal values
indulging of vicarious revenge fantasies	catharsis	rooting out insensitivities
sexual arousal	fainting with longing and desire	gender-bending
NAUSEA in response to really gross part	**NAUSEA** as one realizes the full tragedy of the human condition	**NAUSEA** as one realizes the full extent of one's false consciousness
TYPICAL CONSUMER IS CALLED: a consumer	**TYPICAL CONSUMER IS CALLED:** an intellectual	**TYPICAL CONSUMER IS CALLED:** a victim
TYPICAL HERO beefy guy with unusual accent who blows up stuff	**TYPICAL HERO** anguished aristocrat who winds up killing himself	**TYPICAL HERO** there are no heroes.
PURPOSE OF POP CULTURE: give more bang for the buck	**PURPOSE OF ART:** art is its own reward	**PURPOSE OF MULTICULTURAL ARTIFACTS:** to nurture cultural diversity
SAMPLE QUOTE: "I'm takin' you off the street!"	**SAMPLE QUOTE:** "To be, or not to be; that is the question."	**SAMPLE QUOTE:** "The grid of patriarchal assumptions reveals a slavish devotion to phallocentric ideas, which makes a discourse that further marginalizes the already disenfranchised."
HUMOR: "When Arnold blew that guy's kneecap off, I about shit."	**HUMOR:** "Rex Harrison uttering a Nöel Coward bon mot can always make me chuckle appreciatively."	**HUMOR:** "That's not funny."

I urge you to clip this helpful chart and keep it near. It will help you navigate the treacherous waters of modern culture. Failing that, you can rip it to pieces in a fit of rage. Beats punching somebody's face in.

N

NARROWCASTING | 1993

Recently, while making my way to the mall, an empty tank forced me to stop for gas. As I stood squeezing fuel into my vehicle, idly watching numbers on the pump turn over, and lazily inhaling exhaust fumes, I thought I heard something. Yes, just under the roar of traffic, the clatter of the passing trolleys, and the shouts of my fellow travelers, I heard a tinny orchestra, and a sultry woman's voice. What was she saying with such sexy enthusiasm? I could barely make it out: "Welcome to the 19th Avenue BP!"

I noticed tiny speakers above the gasoline pumps, from which this friendly voice repeated its pre-fab greeting. Apparently, an actress had been paid good money to make a taped address to the station's customers. Looking around me, I didn't notice anybody else paying the least bit of attention to it. Sure, my hearing is unnaturally acute, the result of years of goofing off at temp jobs and listening anxiously for the steps of a supervisor, yet even I had to strain to hear the voice. So: to whom is this message addressed? What was its intent?

I assume this bold PR decision was made at the corporate level. This means that some poor actress spent weeks in front of a microphone, saying, "Welcome to the Washington Avenue BP! Welcome to the Lincoln Place BP!" Welcome to the Main Street BP! *etc.*," until each BP self-serve around the globe was represented, and her voice was hoarse and ragged!

To what end? Does British Petroleum really want us to stick around, and enjoy its hospitality? Maybe it's just me, but when I'm fumbling with a gas cap, in front of a line of scowling tourists, hearing a cheerful woman's voice say, "Welcome!" still doesn't make me want to pull up a stool and start whittling.

No, I want to get my gas and get out. Isn't that what BP wants, as well? Wouldn't BP be better served by, say, knocking a penny or two off the price per gallon of their fine product?

I swear, I'll never understand capitalism.

Maybe there's some subliminal audio manipulation going on that's beyond my ken. When you enter the upscale toy shop of FAO

Schwarz, for example, your ears are assaulted with a chorus of boys and girls singing a repetitive ditty, not unlike "It's a Small World After All!" called "Welcome to the World of Toys (I assume, since this phrase is repeated to the point of no return, and beyond)!"

I heard this song dozens of times during the brief period I was in the store. During the course of a working day, it must be heard thousands of times by employees. I asked a clerk, "Doesn't this drive you crazy?" Looking up at me with glazed eyes, she said, "What?" If this song is annoying to patrons, and shunted to the back brain of FAO Schwarz employees, then denied, what then is its purpose?

At Toys R Us, customers are treated to random tunes by Bonnie Raitt and John Denver. In between songs a deejay informs us we are listening to "WTRU: the official radio station of the world's biggest toy store!" However, the tape's magnificence is frequently undercut by some employee on the public address system requesting the presence of another employee in the action figure aisle. Throw in a screaming four year old, and a snarling mother dragging her reluctant offspring away from the troll display, and frankly, you don't have an ambiance conducive to appreciation of lite rock. Again: point?

Why aren't consumers allowed to buy in silence? Would we linger too long at the pump or stuffed animals rack, and send profits into a tailspin? Would silence create too reverent an environment, in which we would shop on tiptoe, in whispers? Why are we subjected to hearty voices that we neither requested nor desired? What is being accomplished?

I can only conclude this is some kind of social engineering, programming designed specifically to create a nervous shopper, an obligated shopper, one who buys something anxiously, then gets out. Are social engineers trying to discourage the demographically inappropriate from purchasing items? Is this the subliminal message: "Welcome to the 19th Avenue BP! But not you, Mr. Shoales. Please leave immediately. Thank you! Welcome to the World of Toys! Now get out!"

NATIONAL TASTE 1983

It's probably official. I saw it on television, in a commercial for one of America's soft drinks. There was a close-up of Coca Cola and a smooth voiceover saying, "If America had an official taste, this would be it." This is an entirely new concept in advertising and patriotism. The Eagle is our national emblem; our national taste is Coke. But what about the other senses? What's the national smell? I nominate popcorn, ladies and gentlemen. National touch would be the telephone—as in "Reach Out and Touch Someone." (Americans don't need intimacy, just communication.) National sight: rock videos. National sound: annoying electronic pings.

According to the media, America is a healthy young person, white and thirty, laughing on the beach, grabbing the gusto, turning it loose, dancing the night away, working hard, playing hard—feeling good about itself. And if this young white person on television feels good, America feels good. As this young white person goes, so goes the nation. It's America in Sensurround and Dolby. We've got a foreign policy, we've got an official taste. We've got senators and lawyers, diet sodas, and wars in small countries. We've got everything we need to quench our thirsts and fill our stomachs.

So why do the soft drinks we drink—no caffeine, no sugar, no calories—taste like tap water laced with acid bubbles? If our body is becoming America, and America is becoming our body, where's the doctor? What if America gets the flu? Where will America go to the hospital? Does America have medical coverage?

I don't know. I only know that if my body is becoming the body politic, and if my physical senses are linked with the fate of the nation, I'd better start taking better care of myself. No more soda pop. No more malt liquor. I certainly wouldn't recommend malt liquor as the national taste. God no.

NEO-STAND-UP | 1993

All through the eighties late night television had a different slick white dude on every channel, standing in front of a brick wall making jokes about airplane food and recent immigrants. Then the nineties hit. Comedy clubs, like factories everywhere, closed their doors, forcing comics to move to Mexico, where they tell tired airplane food jokes for sub-minimum wages.

The system worked fine for awhile. TV loved stand-up comedy. Get a camera, a few ambitious comics, a brick wall (of course), a two-dollar budget and BA-BING—you had yourself a program. Comics loved the system too, both for the paltry checks and the free publicity for their live performances.

But viewers eventually realized that the same act that cost ten bucks and a two drink minimum at the Chuckle Factory was available in their living room for free. Then they figured out that nine out of ten of these comics weren't funny, and America turned to reality-based cop shows, infomercials, and encore presentations for its insomniac entertainment needs.

Some comics bucked the trend by turning their acts into "solo performance pieces." It's easy to do.

Just cut half the jokes, replace them with heartwarming anecdotes, move from a club to a theatre, and triple the ticket price. Before you know it, you'll have a development deal with a major network to create a warm situation comedy about a newly widowed father trying to raise three kids by himself.

Or you can write a book. Howard Stern's "memoirs," PRIVATE PARTS entered the NEW YORK TIMES bestseller list at number one, bumping SEINLANGUAGE by Jerry Seinfeld (another comic!) down to number two. Maybe I shouldn't be too alarmed. I've been told that Seinfeld's book contains many fine jokes about the lighter side of household objects. It was thoughtful of him to write these down for posterity. Where's the harm? It really doesn't affect sales of the classics, does it? People still read them.

Howard Stern may not be among them, however. At the time I first wrote this, he told NEWSWEEK Magazine that he'd only read three books in his life.

What were they, I wonder? CURIOUS GEORGE? THE STORY OF O? JOKES FOR THE JOHN? This could be a fun new party game. What three books would you take to a desert island, if you were Howard Stern?

As a semi-successful comedian/author myself, I'll confess to a certain amount of bitterness, rancor, sour grapes, envy, and even loathing. I know that the publishing industry (Hollywood East) is always on the lookout for a blockbuster. But this seems like a long way to go for it: "Wow!" says the publishing world excitedly. "A shock jock who hates books wants to write one! Sign him up!"

I should say that Stern's booklike object has candor to burn. In the excerpt I read he said of his wife's miscarriage, "Every slob on welfare has kids, why can't I?" At once a plaintive cry of anguish and searing social criticism, this sentence reveals a side of Howard Stern America's never seen before. Not in cold print anyway.

But again, I'm being unfair. In the first place, Jerry Seinfeld is no longer just a "comic." He's TV's "SEINFELD." If that doesn't deserve a book deal, nothing does. And Howard Stern was never a comic at all. He's a "radio personality," a vague term used to describe any egotist whose demand for attention is so powerful that listeners even more anxious than he allow themselves to be sucked into the vortex of his need. These are called "fans." They display a cultlike devotion to his every utterance. Ten thousand people showed up for Howard Stern's Manhattan booksigning!

The last time I had a booksigning, eight people showed up. One of them told me he didn't have much money; did I have any used copies? Another presented me with a copy he said he'd "liberated" from the local library. So much for the Ian Shoales cult. Let that be a lesson to you. If you're going to develop a cult following, make sure it has a disposable income.

NEO-STARVATION | 1994

We do a lot of things wrong in America, but when we hold a walk-a-thon for quadriplegics, we don't usually demand their participation. Unless tax dollars are involved, we never require contributions to a charity fund from those for whom it's intended. We don't make victims of a disease contribute to their own demise. (Well, we might subsidize tobacco growers, but that's not quite the same thing.)

Attitudes are changing though. The powers-that-be have decided that it's time for those lazybones in Zaire to walk back home to Rwanda. Never mind that they're starving and dying. The deep thinkers in charge of this operation apparently figure that a fifty mile trek will weed the shirkers from the truly cholera-ridden. Those that survive the little hike will get food and shelter for a reward.

Spokespeople for this idea from Hell shrug off criticism of it. It's just another one of those "tough choices" we're always whining about. What else can be done? There are too many people to feed, and most of them are going to die anyway. Why not speed the process along with a little old-fashioned social Darwinism? If all that are left at the end of the trek are death march crossing guards and media observers, fine. They can afford to buy their own lunch. The whole venture could even turn a profit.

We don't give strobe lights to epileptics, or sugar to diabetics. Should we make the starving power-walk to their food? The notion is bizarre, but I guess it's an idea, like "compassion fatigue," whose time has come. Once I would have said the starvation consultants in charge didn't quite get the concept. Now I think they get it more than I do. They're taking America's can-do pragmatism to its logical extreme. Take Barbra Streisand's recent act of generosity. She sold tickets to her concerts to charities at face value; they in turn scalped the tickets, and pocketed the difference. That's philanthropy in the nineties, kids. It's a mighty long way from the soup line.

But what do I know? If I put my palm out and asked for a quarter, I'd be shunned and feared as a glad-handing lazy drug addict. If I put my palm out and asked for a billion dollars for research, I'd be showered with quarters. It's not even considered begging, if the sum of money asked for is large enough.

However, we must make sure that any money raised never goes to the cause for which it was intended. It must all go to staff, fund-raising strategies, three color brochures, to lobbyists.

If Johnny needs a new kidney, Mom and Dad aren't going to be given the bucks to go buy one. They must sweat for it. They have to form their own charity, appear on local television to appeal to the community at large, organize volunteers to go door to door holding out donation cans decorated with Polaroids of little Johnny, and pray that the pennies collected will add up to the price of a new organ by the time Johnny's gives out. If it works to the best, the media will feed us the human interest story, and we'll all feel warm and fuzzy. If it doesn't work, well, tomorrow's another newsday, isn't it?

The moral? Tough love is the answer to everything. We'll never fix the homeless problem by putting the homeless in homes. That's wimpy socialism! We're not going to fix it by making them build their own homes, either. That's simplistic! No, we must make the homeless build an office building for those who are working on the homeless problem. If the media are there for the groundbreaking, we could raise millions! That's what I'd do, if I had to make some tough choices.

Welfare reform! Reduce the cycle of dependency! Make the sick work for a cure! Weed out the surviving truly needy. Force them to pay interest on any charity we grudgingly bestow upon them. In other words, down for ten pushups, buster, or you'll get no painkiller from me.

O.J. | 1994

Like the rest of America, when it comes to the consideration of the O.J. Simpson spectacle, I'm drowning in a sea of useless emotions. It was bizarre all right: handsome wealthy endangered people, white Bronco, helicopters, cell phones, cheerleading drunks jamming the freeway with handmade signs, and a vicious double murder kept discreetly offstage, to spare our addled feelings.

I only saw bits and pieces of the dramatic anticlimax, the suicide-free arrest. I was working at the time, rehearsing a play actually, and only saw segments when we took a break. I'd go to the corner store to find young men watching the slow Bronco and talking in fast Spanish. When we finally stopped rehearsing, sweaty and tired, we turned on the eleven o'clock news. Various reporters were as shocked and incredulous as their formats would allow. We made weary wisecracks about lawyers, cops, and media, then went home to sleep.

Being rather isolated in my underpaid work situation, I had no idea of the impact this event had on our country. The next day everybody was talking about it. A strange exhilaration filled the air. An old woman in a drug store turned to me in line. "Did you watch that Simpsons?" she asked excitedly.

Appalled experts began to rise to the occasion. Perhaps this event will call attention to spousal abuse, they suggested. Is there a connection between professional sports and violence, they wondered? And actors? Aren't they a problem as well?

Being an occasional actor myself, I certainly have never considered myself a role model, whatever that means. On the other hand, I've never blamed a loved one for my own shortcomings. I've never beaten up a lover, or stabbed one to death with an entrenching tool. The way things are going, maybe that will earn me a statue in the town square, if the town square hasn't been torn down to make a mini-mall.

Is this saga some kind of metaphor? Are we seeing the death throes of family values, romantic love, glory and fame? When communication breaks down completely, when we suddenly realize that the words coming from our mouths are not the words we wanted to say, will we all reach for the gun, the blunt instrument, the remote control?

Knee-deep in divorce and dysfunction, will we watch the tube in horrified desperation? Will we eye our spousal units in fear?

How isolated have we become from each other? It's one thing for Mr. Simpson's sportscasting colleagues and friends to be shocked by these events, but do the rest of us have a right to any kind of emotion at all? O.J. was well-liked. What does that mean? I've never watched a game of pro football in my life, and only knew the man from commercials and movies. I guess I liked the guy too, but that only means he had a familiar face. I knew who he was when I saw him and he didn't give me the creeps. Is this "likeability?" Is it a virtue? Is it something that can be stripped from you, like dignity, a medal, or a job?

If he remains likable in the face of the demonizing process now in progress, and it's proven that he committed this brutal crime, how will it affect national opinions on the death penalty? Nowadays, we want to give the chair to every intruder, every illiterate bum whose rage is matched only by his lack of imagination. The execution process is very hot right now, but so far it's only been applied to lowlife trash who murder store clerks.

Sure, odds are good that likeble O. J., if found guilty, will only be put away for life. But if the state does go for broke, and exercises its vengeance option, will we put our money where our mouth is? This isn't some tattooed schmuck with no cash flow, this is O.J. How will we feel about killing a likable guy? Will we have the heart to juice the Juice? Will the execution be televised? Stay tuned. I know that you will.*

*Say, what happened with that trial, anyway?

OLD JOBS | 1996

Now that Timothy Leary, demon/imp/guru/con-man, has passed on, where will we turn for scoundrels? Sure, we have the Reverend Al Sharpton, but he's a poor substitute, if you ask me. Somehow I can't see the Reverend Al tripping his brains out, cavorting in a field of daisies with blissed-out hippies.

In the good old days, America was full of snake oil salesmen. The streets teemed with quick-talking "reverends," "doctors," and "professors." We had pamphlets, quack cures, dimwit ideologies, get-rich-quick schemes, and Three-Card Monte variations coming out our ears.

We still have initial public offerings, conspiracy theory videos, Internet UFO newsgroups, 900 numbers, and New Age Physics, but things are not the same. The wacky is now the mainstream. We have become a nation of bitter suckers, with not one but dozens born every minute.

Still, I look at our culture the way I look at a carnival midway. The worthless prizes may change— from stuffed Teenage Mutant Ninja Turtles and Barney the Purple Dinosaurs, to the Mighty Morphin' Power Rangers— but the games remain the same rigged attractions they always were. The wizened carnies of summer may be replaced in the society-at-large by Powerbook-wielding marketing types, but those games too remain the same.

The latest scam seems to be "downsizing." We're supposed to believe that corporations must now shrink, like hemorrhoids, in order to sit comfortably on the new economy.

There's been much discussion about what to do with downsized workers. Republicans and Democrats agree that what the economy needs is new jobs.

What new jobs? Well, outside of the interactive media field, there actually aren't that many. And even workers in the world's Silicon Gulches are just doing digital versions of old jobs— they're artists, engineers, writers, and musicians working together to build an edifice. Software is created the same way the Mafia once built casinos. Oh sure, there's the Internet, but every day that seems more and more like an infinite version of the Yellow Pages.

Near as I can tell, the only truly new jobs are that of trend-spotter, post-structuralist literary critic, right wing talk show host, and fund-raising consultant for non-profit corporations. What special training is needed for these professions? None, other than the mastery of a specialized vocabulary.

The literary critic must learn to use the word "hermeneutics" in casual conversation, and the right wing talk show host the phrase, "Our first amendment rights have been abrogated!"

Both trend-spotter and fund-raising consultant must be able to say, "I'll have my staff model that, and I'll get back to you," in an aggressive yet perky fashion. Other than that, these jobs are a piece of cake.

No, whether you're aiming to become a programmer, Internet provider, or wait-person, you just don't need retraining.

You only need to know these simple phrases: (1) "No problem." (or "No prob," or "No prah-blay-moh.") (2) "You got it." (3) "Have a nice day." (Or "Have a good one.") (4) "Take care." (5) "Let's touch base." (6) "Working on it." (7) "Room for cream?" (Or "Fries/Pie with that?") (8) "That's a software problem." (9) "That's a hardware problem." (10) "We don't have small. Just medium."

If you plan to enter middle— or upper— management, of course, it's a little different. You'll need to pepper your speech with nuggets like "new paradigms," "corporate culture," "vision," "excellence," "market share," and "leadership." Nothing new there.

And why are we so concerned about "newness" anyway? Pop culture is dizzily recycling the fifties, sixties, and seventies. Yesterday's premature anti-fascists are today's disoriented film stars. Yesterday's shrink is today's Internet addiction recovery program counselor. Perhaps the entire economy needs to go retro. Instead of worrying about new jobs, maybe we should bring back some old jobs.

It's too late to revive pin boys, smithies, and boot blacks, but lounge singers have made a comeback— Tony Bennett has become the hip elder statesman of MTV. We can't bring back cowboys, but what about The Singing Cowboy? I recommend a national talent hunt to find the Roy Rogers for the Millennium. America's on the verge of losing its precious ability to yodel!

Here's some other professionals America may be ready to embrace once more:

Waitresses in all-night diners who have dyed red hair and call you either "Buddy," "Honey," or "Sugar."

Ventriloquists.

Dirigible pilots (and blimpmakers).

Elevator operators.

Hat check girls (and haberdashers, of course).

Cabbies. I'm talking about real cabbies now— who chew unlit cigars, wear porkpie hats, and great you with "Where to, Mac?"

Cynical reporters, not the whiny babies we have today.

Real strippers, not the buff pseudo-feminists we have today.

Blaxploitation stars. Who will be the Jim Brown of tomorrow? The farmer.

I'm getting my resume together myself. I'm pretty sure that my gadfly position is about to phased-out; I just don't annoy a large enough database to be effective.

So I'm looking to become either a lumberjack, a scribe, or the charismatic leader of a drug-addled cult. If I can't find an opening there, I either want Howard Stern's job, or Camille Paglia's— if I can just figure out what it is exactly that they do.

OVEREXPOSED | 1984

When the Jacksons put on their shades and plug in their amps this summer, they'll have to book entire states to contain the crowds, who will show Michael Jackson the kind of wholehearted devotion usually reserved for popes or a visitor from another planet. One could say that this kind of intense devotion to a frail young man verges on mass hysteria. Like the Kennedy clan, Elvis or John DeLorean, Michael Jackson is one of those media figures about whom we can never hear too much. We even devour stories about his glove, as if it were the magical totem of a saint. Understandably perhaps, Michael Jackson is the most nervous superstar we've ever had. If it's lonely at the top, like they say, his solitude is raised to a pitch not audible to the human ear. He hides in his room, afraid, say the stories. He rattles around in his limo with nothing to keep him company but old cartoons on the tape player. He's a monk, a hermit in the desert of fame.

We're meant to believe that the burden of the spotlight is almost too much for his fragile mortal frame to bear. He's supposed to be like some albino fish in a cave, drawn to the light but hurt by it, some beautiful shy creature that only comes alive in the spotlight, a creature who needs special clothing and sunglasses to keep from withering away. What we're supposed to feel for Michael Jackson, in other words, is not admiration, but pity. We're actually supposed to feel sorry for the guy!

Well, that much fame dropping on a person is almost pagan, and maybe we should stop paying attention before the poor guy cracks, like a doll of bone china clutched too hard by greedy grasping children. If he is, in effect, the twentieth century equivalent of a human sacrifice, if he's suffering for our pleasure, let's remove the source of his pain. Maybe it's right that he should be overexposed at last, like a bubblegum card dropped on the sidewalk to fade in the sun. Maybe we should turn the lights off for a while and give Michael Jackson a break. I'll put a rumor to rest now and get that ball rolling. In case you were wondering, I am the father of Billie Jean's child. It's off my chest at last, and I'm glad I said it here.*

Michael Jackson has, of course, since retired from show business.

PBS | 1992

This spring, conservatives threw out another non-issue to clutter further this murky election year. They want to get rid of public broadcasting because it betrays a "liberal bias." Talk about your code words! When conservatives talk about liberal bias and the Corporation for Public Broadcasting, I don't think they mean those pseudo-Edwardian mysteries imported from England, or documentaries about kangaroos giving birth. I don't even think they mean FRONTLINE (who watches that?). No, they're talking about Bill Moyers.

The guy is annoying. He's a one man middlebrow philosophy machine. Thanks to his unrelentingly thoughtful packaging, Robert Bly is now a figure of fun and adulation across the country. Joseph Campbell books gather dust on coffee tables from coast to coast. On the other hand, what's wrong with that? Why shouldn't fuzzy thinking one-worlders get the programming they enjoy? They're the ones who pledge, aren't they?

But the point is moot. The argument over funding among our eminently sensible legislators has quickly focused on, of all things, SESAME STREET. Those pro-Sesame Street (let's call them hard-core left-wing terrorists) argued, uncharacteristically, that the show has become an American tradition and, what's more, pays for itself. The anti's (let's call them fascist demagogues) argued, disingenuously, that the show should be yanked because very few poor people watch it. I don't know when conservatives started caring about the viewing habits of the poor, but apparently, in their view, SESAME STREET is another failed welfare program.

On this highly important controversy, I'm of two minds. Snuffleupagus (true spelling unknown) for example, represents everything I hate personally about public television. I suspect he's supposed to be cute, but he looks and sounds like a small shaggy mammoth with adenoids, or perhaps a gerbil with elephantiasis. As another mark against him, he's best friend to Big Bird. When they play together they're like walruses on Prozac.

Recently there was an attempt, on the part of the PC imagineers who put together SESAME STREET, to make Snuffy a role model for children of divorced parents. So they wrote in a divorce. I understand there was a moving scene of Snuffy alone in his room, weeping and throwing his toys about. It sounds like a pre-teen-mutant-mammoth homage to Orson Welles' tantrum in CITIZEN KANE. But the scene only proved puzzling to the focus group of toddlers for whom they screened it, and the whole Snuffy-as-victim-of-divorce model was dropped.

Smart move, I say. Are we so far gone that kids from broken homes need a television program to tell them how to cope? How much do we want to know about the anguish of puppets anyway? If Oscar the Grouch lives in filth, should he get cholera? Of course not! And Bert can't leave Ernie, the poor guy would be devastated. Let The Count count blessings, not agonies! If I wouldn't mind seeing Big Bird revealed as a serial killer, that's just a personal sick fantasy. ("The whole Street's in shock," said Bob, local resident. "Who knew? He was so quiet, so polite.") No public funds need be involved.

But I do approve of Bert & Ernie (what is their relationship by the way?), Oscar the Grouch, and Grover. For them alone, I say keep the show on the air. There's certainly not much in the private sector for kids. There remains no finer show than the old Warner Brothers cartoons, which had no instructional value whatever. Bugs Bunny didn't even have personal problems! What a role model! TINY TOONS ADVENTURES is just a pale rip-off of that old Bugs energy, an animated illustration of a corporate idea of anarchy. Instead of being hip, the Tiny Toons pander to hipness. They turn presexuality into a lifestyle, where you can simultaneously mock and wallow in the trash of pop culture. In the context of the WAYNE'S WORLD which America is rapidly becoming, what's wrong with letting old Snuffy get a few public bucks? We've got to spend it on something besides cops, jails, and missiles, don't we? Think about it. And give my Big Bird idea some thought while you're at it. (Sesame Street-person The Count was an eyewitness: "Big Bird killed one! Two! Three! Ha! Ha! Four!")

PENNIES | 1993

"Find a penny, pick it up," goes the old saw, "and all the day you'll have good luck." Why, that old saw isn't worth a red cent. I've been picking up pennies all the days for years, and my luck hasn't changed, unless you think being knee-deep in pennies is lucky. As a kid, I could have exchanged this hoard for a lifetime's supply of kisses, suckers, and gum. I could have bought enough penny nails to build a treehouse, and used that old saw to cut the timber. In today's economy, a gallon of pennies and a dime won't even buy me a cup of coffee. I've tried, believe me, and lugging an industrial size mayonnaise jar full of change to coffee house after coffee house is no picnic.

And take wishing wells. Americans have always had a mysterious compulsion to toss coins into standing bodies of water. Well, the layer of pennies in public fountains is not only deeper than it used to be, a growing silvery gleam of nickels, dimes, and quarters can be seen amidst the glow of underwater copper. Even our wishes face inflation! Before you know it we'll be throwing dollar bills into stagnant pools, where they'll float on the surface, like dead lily pads.

Pennies today may be as numberless as pebbles on a beach, but they're just jetsam tossed up as the sea crashes against the boulders of leading economic indicators. Enter any corner store. You'll find mounds of pennies by the cash register, with a handmade sign urging us to leave one, pick one up... Consumer and merchant can no longer tolerate the penny-ante business of penny dispersion. Why dig in a cash register or pocket for loose change when there's a common pool in which we both can dip?

This sudden proliferation of pennies doesn't indicate an embarrassment of riches, but actual personal embarrassment, like having lice, mice, or roaches. Even as pennies pop up everywhere, their status as legal currency has never been lower. And the country is taking steps to exterminate all cents. Some stores now program checkout scanners to "round up" totals, turning pennies into a nickel, seven cents into a dime, the intention being to make merchant's bookkeeping easier and the consumer's pocket lighter.

It looks like the penny's days are numbered. The last time it rained pennies from heaven was the Great Depression. Ever since then, the rain has to be composed of thousand dollar bill droplets before we'll deign to sing in it. Small children, bright as a penny, would once recite a verse for Grandma and get a penny in return. Piggy banks bulged! Literacy rates soared! Today's children are shifty-eyed and stoop-shouldered. If they condescend to memorize a verse for Grandma, they won't settle for anything less than ten bucks. There are lawyers involved, contracts. Things are real ugly.

In these arrogant times, there's no room for the humble penny. Poor pennies are corroding with the homeless, out on the streets. Even beggars sneer at them. A pocket full of pennies is only a child's idea of wealth. When you're grown up, you want empty pockets. Empty pockets mean you're so rich you don't need to carry money. It just spoils the lines of your suit. You have a credit line. You have people to buy things for you.

The vulgar exchange of cash for a service or product is just not done in higher circles, or when it is, it's done discreetly. The finer restaurants, for example, always present their bills in a handsome leather folder, to disguise the fact that a transaction is taking place. One doesn't violate this discretion by cramming the folder full of pennies, does one? That would be like screaming in church.

And yet our self-esteem remains low. A thought's worth only a penny, an opinion two cents. How American—a thought is worth exactly half that of a thoughtless opinion. (When rounded-up, though, to be fair, both thought and opinion would be worth a nickel in today's dollars.) No longer penny wise, pounds make us even more foolish. The poorer we become, the more we want. We've pinched pennies into non-existence, as we drool over the fin, the sawbuck, the Grant. We're chumps, and broke to boot, yet too proud to be bothered with chump change.

PERFECT CITY 1983

If this were a perfect world we'd have at least one perfect city. The perfect city would look a bit like Fritz Lang's METROPOLIS, without the worker problems and without the electronic music. In the perfect city, big band jazz would be broadcast nightly on the streets, which would be paved with bricks and lined with elm and maple trees.

The only dogs allowed would be African basenjis, which cannot bark and would be trained to curb themselves. All cars would float on silent cushions of air. All the cops would ride horses. There are no pigeons and no statues.

In the perfect city, automatic tellers would spew cash at random every half hour or so, the concerts would all be free, all be reggae music, and never be crowded. Drinks are half price, and it is always early autumn in the perfect city.

In the perfect city, Woody Allen would be funny again, Steven Spielberg would take a vacation, and there would be a Kurosawa festival once a month. Westerns would make a comeback, and theater seats would be six bucks tops. Critics would be wise, enthusiastic and fair, and so with the artists of the city. No art after 1900 would be displayed in the museums. Admission to museums would be free, and large groups of children would stay well away until I had left the building. I would never be put on hold in the perfect city.

In the perfect city, all parties would be "by invitation only," and guests would receive cash prizes when they went through the door. I would be invited to all these parties, and no matter how rude I became, I would never be asked to leave.

In the perfect city there would be a twenty-four hour French restaurant but all the entrees would be under five bucks. The waiters would be named "Mac" and the waitresses would all call you "Honey."

In the perfect city, clothing would be well cut, sharp, swell and inexpensive. People would roam the streets in formal eveningwear. In the perfect city, I would have a nickname like "Spats" or "Captain Danger." Every newsboy, flower seller, and cabbie would know my name; even the muggers would know my name. The mayor would call me for advice, my quips would be legendary in the society columns, the library would be well stocked, and superheroes and heroines would drift lazily among the skyscraper peaks, seeking out wrongdo-ers everywhere.

The shower in my apartment would be hot and powerful, and all my neighbors would work nights. Women would laugh at my jokes, and men wouldn't tell them. Guitars would stay in tune. I would have many friends, and they would not ask me for money. They would all have jobs, and their jobs would be good. I would have my own news program, in which I would bring bad news to the perfect city, but nobody would mind, because everybody would know I had a bad attitude anyway.

Women would stay with me longer than two months, or if they left they'd at least leave their record collections, which would include all recordings by the Ramones. And they'd leave me a record player. And some money.

All transportation is free, including tickets out of town. And down those mean streets a man would go, who was not himself afraid, and that would be me, the oldest pro on the block. Ian "Captain Danger" Shoales. In the perfect city.

POSERS | 1991

The two hunky hairstyles the world called Milli Vanili might have shocked some ethics-burdened fans with the news that they were not, in fact, Milli Vanilli, but posers. But most people knew that Milli Vanilli were posers, even before the deception. This means they were, in fact, posing as posers. Not even genuine posers, they were poser *poseurs.* How post-modern can you get?

What's the big deal anyway? The Monkees did the same thing as Milli Vanilli, and we used to think they were cool, or at least blameless.

POST-MODERN | 1993

Browsing through a NEW YORKER recently, I came across a listing for a new exhibit in Manhattan: "An entertaining and provocative eighteen hole miniature golf course, in which each hole has been designed by a different contemporary artist." The course includes the obligatory Elvis hole, in which you try to knock the ball into a cup called "Las Vegas: Hole of Fate"—a hole which has you try to run your ball past a "larger-than-life inflatable clown, who wears a hat called Censorama, and looks suspiciously like Jesse Helms," and, of course, the AIDS commentary hole: "...you putt a ball...through a replica of the White House made of neon tubes and AZT and Zovirax bottles." Golf balls are inscribed with Jenny Holzer aphorisms ("Absolute submission can be a form of freedom"). You can rent a putter for five dollars, or look for nothing. The installation is called "Putt-Modernism."

Sure, it sounds like urban fun. But does Manhattan really need an ironic miniature golf course? I'll bet it doesn't even have an attitude-free miniature golf course. When you're the only My-T-Tee in town, you probably shouldn't get too high brow. Give that art crowd an inch, and the next thing you know, they'll be piping rock videos into bowling alleys.

This is not to say that art and miniature golf are incompatible. I once saw a truly baffling sculpture at a course near the Wisconsin Dells: it could have been a pre-Columbian fertility goddess or Paul Bunyan. But this ambiguity didn't matter. The only thing that mattered was timing your swing to get that ball past the genderbending statue's ax. With miniature golf, making art must take second place to making par. I hate to sound like Jesse Helms, but there are such things as miniature golf values. They must not be mocked.

If you're looking for places to create site-specific art, there are other more value-free environments to consider. A laundromat, for example. Do a performance piece there in which the audience brings dirty clothes (and quarters), and the actors actually clean them as they perform. The piece would be in two acts of course (Wash and Dry). How about parking lots? A friend of mine once sought funding for what he called a "car alarm symphony." At a prearranged signal, people scattered all over Los Angeles would whack parked cars, creating a cacophony of sirens, a unique commentary on the urban milieu.

Or take motel rooms. I have in my possession a little paper napkin, with the motel chain logo at the top, followed by the phrase, "For Our Guests," in flowery writing, and a list of helpful instructions: "Use this towel to clean your—Shoes! Luggage! Eyeglasses! Auto windshields! Razor! Make-up! Just about anything! Take it along!"

Those who feel the post-modern compulsion to mock the obvious, could begin with this (complimentary) paper towel. If you're a Jenny Holzer fan (and who isn't?), commission her to confound weary businesspersons with ominous slogans as they bend over their shoes: "The job market can absorb cutbacks," "A certain amount of brain damage is tolerable," "Take your room key with you."

Unfortunately for art, unnecessary instructions are post-modern already. If you put arrows and a label in the waistband of trousers that say, "Insert legs here," you're either post-modern or adhering to federal regulations. But there are other options. Artists could invade nature itself with their little ironies. Put labels on pointy sticks, "Warning: Do Not Poke In Eye!" On dirt: "If this substance comes in contact with skin, wash affected area in soapy water."

There are all kinds of areas post-modernism could impact (and probably will), but again, real life is a tough competitor. Just the other day, I saw a commercial with a woman saying, "I want my children to grow up in a healthy environment." For sheer inanity, that statement is hard to beat. Jenny Holzer herself couldn't have said it better.

PROZAC | 1993

When I was a teenager I was deeply frightened by Rod McKuen's LISTEN TO THE WARM. Every time I saw it displayed in a bookstore I gave a little yelp of terror. It seemed by its very title to command readers to hear something not only intangible but auditorially inappropriate.

Appearing as it did at the height of the sixties, this book must have seduced hundreds of gullible young people into cocking their heads at the sun, burrowing their heads in the sand, even placing their ears directly on hot plates. Gradually, of course, America learned that drugs and bad poetry just don't mix. The nation turned away from LSD and STANYAN STREET AND OTHER SORROWS, to embrace Valium and HOW TO BE YOUR OWN BEST FRIEND, and finally to consume the prescription drugs and Robert Fulghum booklets we enjoy today. I wish I could believe we're better off.

However, the popularity of a recent book called LISTENING TO PROZAC, written by some shrink or other, has me worried once again about the state of America's mental health. Recent studies reveal that almost half of America can't read. Apparently the other half is so depressed by what it reads that it's turned a book about a pep pill into a bestseller! People are forking over twenty bucks just to bone up on an anti-depressant! It's—well, it's depressing. It almost makes me want to take a Prozac. Is that the author's hidden agenda?

Again, I haven't read LISTENING TO PROZAC (I'm scared, I admit it), but, again, even the title conjures the image of a room full of desperate depressed people holding capsules to their ears, gazing off into the middle distance with an air of anxious anticipation. If they listen, what will Prozac say: "Hi, my name is Prozac! I'll be your mood elevator for the next four to six hours?" Maybe there's a little string to pull to hear canned phrases, like "Come on, slugger! Let's see that happy face!" "Boy, I feel great!" "Hi! Eat me!"

Perhaps Prozac is in fact a sentient being. If so, how would we know we're really hearing Prozac, and not just a prerecorded message? Does Prozac have E-mail? Can one fax Prozac?

I suppose that this "listening" is meant metaphorically. Prozac "speaks" to a grumpy anxious America in the same way THE WAY THINGS OUGHT TO BE speaks to the liberal-blaming dittohead, or THE BRIDGES OF MADISON COUNTY speaks to the bored housewife with low self-esteem who wants to have a mad week of passion with Robert Redford. (This latter book, by a strange coincidence, also indulges in some minor sense displacement. In one scene, speaking of dinner, the hero Robert Kincaid says to Francesca Johnson, "It already smells good... It smells... quiet." I haven't gleaned THE WAY THINGS OUGHT TO BE for sensory hallucinations, but if Rush Limbaugh's next book is called something like SMELL MY MIND, I'd say it's proof that America has a serious problem.)

Noisy smells, loud caplets, boisterous warms—are we, as a nation, hallucinating? If we are, has the warm affected our hearing because we take too many prescriptions drugs, or are we taking prescription drugs because the warm is keeping us up past our bedtime with blaring hip-hop and crude animal rhythms? Did Rod McKuen unleash a fierce beast (or noisy warm, I suppose) of the collective unconscious?

Call it a paranoid fantasy, but that's my hunch. Watch out for sequels America! POKING THE PROZAC, STARING AT THE PROZAC, TASTING THE PROZAC—all are hideous possibilities. HAVE YOU HUGGED YOUR PROZAC TODAY? HAPPINESS IS A WARM PROZAC! JONATHAN LIVINGSTON PROZAC! PROZAC LOVE STORY! LISTEN TO THE WARM PROZAC! The mind boggles. Pills used to be tough to swallow, now they go down easy as THE PROZAC OF MADISON COUNTY. As Ann Landers used to say, "Wake up and smell the coffee!" She didn't say, "Smell the Prozac." Yet in the nineties, alas, SMELLING THE PROZAC may be our olfactory-impaired civilization's last gasp.

PUFFALUMPABILITY 1986

Warning: Poll!

The Fortune 500, Nobel Prize Winners, the annual ESQUIRE list of attractive yuppies under forty who've actually done something, the roll call of the United States Senate—well, I just found another list I'll never be on. Check this out, from USA TODAY, Oct. 30, 1986:

Bill Cosby is No. 1 in "Puffalumpability"—lovability and huggability—says a Fisher Price poll of 1000 USA Moms. Cosby rates an 8/31 Puffalumpability Quotient on a ten point scale to beat out Michael J. Fox (7.18),

Tom Selleck (7.06), and Kenny Rogers (6.48). Top Gunner Tom Cruise was at the bottom of the twenty man list with a 3.28.

Okay, I can live without puffalumpability. My P.Q. is nonexistent; I accept that. Millions of Americans are not puffalumpabilious at all, and I am not ashamed to join their ranks. After all, what's the alternative?

If I had a P.Q. of 10 I'd have a thousand USA Moms loving me and hugging me everywhere I went. I'd have to hire bodyguards (P.Q. 0.00) to keep the USA Moms away from me. They'd camp outside my hotel, just waiting for a chance to hug me. Their homelives, husbands, and children would suffer. I don't want that responsibility. I don't envy Bill Cosby the heavy puffalumpability burden he and he alone must bear.

But who are the puffalumpabilitators? What are the precise components of puffalumpability? Lovability and huggability, sure, but how are these measured on a scale of 1 to 10. If 10 is perfect, what does that mean? Could this be a form of "hug addiction?" Once the 1000 USA Moms get their love-starved hands around the perfect P.Q.er, would they never stop hugging? Would the P.Q. police have to pry them apart with crowbars?

If Cosby gets an 8.31, where does that fraction come from? Does it mean that the 1000 USA Moms only want to hug him for a second? Does it mean that, while there is something definitely huggable and lovable about him, there is an indefinable something that is slightly off-putting?

Do the Moms want him around the house so they can hug him between loads of laundry? What if the Moms are working Moms?

When will they find the time to hug him? Where will he find the time? He's a busy guy, you know. And the prospect of being hugged and loved by a 1000 USA Moms might be frightening to him.

I don't know. All I'm saying is that I question the process here. It's not as precise as it could be. Science demands rigor, an open mind, and arms held out "so big." Not to mention a 1000 USA Moms with empty arms and time on their hands. These days that's hard to find.

We are experiencing difficulties with "Q" entries. Please stand by.

-R-

RAVE 1994

Always alert to consumer trends, I've been tracking the so-called "Rave" scene. "Raves" are all-night dance parties attended by alarmingly fit young people who gulp down smart drug smoothies and Ecstasy, a kind of LSD-lite. Aha! In the 60's we had acid tests; in the 90's we'll have acid quizzes. Groovy! Then there are the great efforts made by computer wizards to create Virtual Reality, an alternative universe which we can enter at the flip of a switch. Think of that! Soon you'll have a personalized in-your-face adult theme park, summoned into being by pale fuzzy hackers! Bummer! I mean, far out!

Finally there's been a flurry of articles about Terence "Timothy-Leary-for-the-nineties" McKenna. He has a new book out, with a title designed to challenge those of us with permanent short term memory loss, THE ARCHAIC REVIVAL: SPECULATIONS ON PSYCHEDELIC MUSHROOMS, THE AMAZON, VIRTUAL REALITY, UFOS, EVOLUTION, SHAMANISM, THE REBIRTH OF THE GODDESS, AND THE END OF HISTORY. Trippy!

In every feature I've read about the guy, the authors weren't content with mere puffery. No, the authors, all forty-ish white guys, took the opportunity to ingest DMT and share their experiences with us. I swear, I haven't heard so much about walls of insect faces, alien dimensions, and H. P. Lovecraft since campus security hauled my roommate away back in 1971.

But why DMT? Why now? Well, a DMT trip only lasts twenty minutes. Aha! No wonder! It's time-efficient! A fortysomething journalist can glimpse the hidden face of God on his lunch hour, grab a sandwich, and still have time to interview Kim Basinger. Whoa! Dig it! Gear! Fab!

So now the trend becomes clear. We are about to enter a new era of fearless pychic discovery, as our schedule permits. We will pierce cyberspace and reclaim paradise, if we can find a sitter.

I know that famed trend-spotter Faith Popcorn has predicted that America will be "cocooning" in the 90's ("cocooning" being consultantese for "staying at home"). Other marketing types have insisted that we're experiencing "neo-traditionalism" (family values as filtered through Ralph Lauren). These terms don't go far enough. I'd like suggest that we're entering the age of neo-acid-traditionalist pupating. It's a mouthful, I know, but see if I'm wrong. Watch for the following:

—New designer drugs obtained, by appointment only, from psycho-pharmaceutical consultants specially trained to help you find the hallucination that's right for you.

—Psychedelics in the workspace. Art directors and copy-writers will add spice to brainstorming sessions with mindblowing drugs. This will lead to such catchy slogans as, "If Coke is the real thing, what is reality?" and "Pepsi: Another Sweet Brown Liquid." But when copywriters start to insist that carbonated beverages stop competing and live together in harmony, the powers-that-be will throw flower power out the window, and everybody will go back to coffee.

—Men will spend days shaving. Women will spend weeks painting their toenails red. Couples will throw their televisions out the window, to spend their leisure time staring at the wallpaper, and giggling mysteriously.

—Actor Mickey Rourke will give up show business to form a tripmaster/babysitter service. For a modest fee, his firm will feed the kids, talk you down, then tuck everybody in.

—Power paisley.

—Delusional world views will become fun again. There will be no more negative-energy speculations like "Who killed the Kennedys?" or "Was there an October Surprise or what?" No, we'll devote our energies to Elvis-spotting, and spinning cheery fantasies about Lemurian elves frolicking in The Lost Empire of Mu with Atlanteans.

—President Shirley MacLaine. Why not! And for vice president? Dan Quayle. Yes, once we all get tuned in to the unique Dan Quayle energy, we'll realize that he wasn't a fool, he was operating under an alien belief system.

Once we surrender our egos, it will all became clear. We
are all Murphy Brown! We are our own fathers!

By 2001, this whole fad will blow over. We will discover a big black
slab (or monolith) on the moon, and it will tell us to just grow up.
Mickey Rourke will wash his hair, and Dan Quayle will become a semi-
pro golfer. This period will be known as neo-caffeinationism, but
that's another trend for another time. And what is time, really? *

Once again, as far as spotting a trend, I was way off base, and I apologize.

RIGHTWING POSTER BOY | 1995

I must grudgingly admire the self-importance conservatives can
muster. They rival the Chicago Seven in their inflated sense of self-
worth. They natter on constantly about the forces trying to stop their
message from being heard (as if there's any other message being
heard out there in AM radioland). They truly believe there's a sinister
cabal of Marxist/Leninist gender studies professors whose influence
on the culture at large can only be countered by dittoheads. In their
view, the Blame-the-Victim mentality in America has obscured the
fate of the true victims in America: white men.

I've been racking my brain trying to figure out what white men
these white men are talking about. In today's cultural climate this
would be a handy thing to know. I think I've finally figured out. The
ultimate conservative poster boy is: Michael Douglas.

In movie after movie, he plays the ultimate victim. He's successful,
but he could fail at any moment (WALL STREET, DISCLOSURE).
Insane feminists are trying to destroy him (FATAL ATTRACTION,
BASIC INSTINCT, DISCLOSURE). Vicious Japanese are trying to
destroy him (BLACK RAIN). Los Angeles is trying to destroy him
(FALLING DOWN).

Our modern rebel is a middle-level executive whose two-car
garage is being threatened by barbarian encroachments. The only
thing standing between Michael Douglas and utter ruin, near as I can
tell, is the motion picture industry. Yes, it looks like even the
Hollywood hotbed of liberalism has made a contract with America.

ROBERT REDFORD | 1986

Have you ever noticed, as Andy Rooney likes to say, that the more famous movie stars get, the less they have to do? The SATURDAY NIGHT LIVE gang got famous by churning out comedy one night a week. Now Bill Murray or Eddie Murphy make a movie once every two years.

Well, I don't know if you can call BEVERLY HILLS COP or GHOSTBUSTERS movies exactly. They're more like test results. An audience wasn't even needed to validate these movies. Personally, I only went to them to fulfill the market projections. As a moviegoing experience, GHOSTBUSTERS was sort of like voting. It was thrilling to be part of the process, but my presence wasn't really necessary. I was just another lump of dirt in the landslide.

But I digress. Take Robert Redford. His last movie, THE NATURAL, made baseball seem like a mystical fuzzy experience, which it may well be, but I don't know if we needed a movie to prove it. His latest movie, OUT OF AFRICA, makes Africa seems like a long baseball game.

Meryl Streep, his co-star, pulls another foreign accent out of her actress bag—where does she find all these accents? But Robert Redford, the Perry Como of the silver screen, has never been more relaxed. He plays an Englishman so relaxed he doesn't even talk British. Well, you and I always knew that if you awakened a foreigner in the middle of the night he'd talk normal. Robert Redford has now made a movie proving this.

But he doesn't need to work hard. Sidney Pollack, the director of OUT OF AFRICA, told NEWSDAY, "Bob is a close-up actor. He has real screen savvy. Most actors on screen do way too much." Apparently you just give the guy a comfy chair, turn on the cameras, and watch the magic happen.

Ivan Reitman, the director of Redford's new movie, LEGAL EAGLES, says, "The most amazing thing I ever saw was him walking in for his makeup test." Lest you think Mr. Reitman is too easily amazed, he says later in this interview, "The light goes into his body and shines out." Now that's something. With most people, when light goes into their body, it just stays there. The associate producer of

LEGAL EAGLES had the final word on Robert Redford, "The man is a work of art."

Put together what these fellow professionals said about Redford and what do you have? A lazy masterpiece who glows in the dark. With a specimen like that, why do you need screenplays or directors? Or film, for that matter?

They should start a church or a museum, and put him on display. You'd save a bundle on crews and writers. Americans would come by the truckload to stand and gawk. Maybe we'd finally solve the enigma that is Robert Redford.

ROGER RABBIT? 1988

WHO FRAMED ROGER RABBIT? had a lot of things going for it. It brought back frame-by-frame animation, and it breathed new life into the true spirit of animation—anarchy, chaos, and pointless violence, psychology be damned. It gave us Toon Town, a great little suburb, and gave a great part to Bob Hoskins; any movie with Bob Hoskins (except COTTON CLUB) is worth the price of admission. It even had Christopher Lloyd as the villain.

That said, I must drop a grand piano on the bunny's head, and say WHO FRAMED ROGER RABBIT? may just be the ultimate in yuppie self-indulgence.

Now obviously Spielberg and company had the best of intentions making this movie, but that's exactly the problem. These guys just don't have a light touch. They're great at making blimps, but water balloons are beyond them. And isn't that the subject of this movie? Water balloons? Old cartoons?

I used to watch cartoons as a kid, 3:30 weekdays on a black and white television, and they were old even then. When I see those familiar characters pumped up on a 70 mm screen, what I miss is charm.

As a professional pundit, I owe more to Bugs than Mencken, attitude-wise, but is the effort to recapture that spirit worth 40 million bucks? You gotta have a delicate touch with cartoon characters— they're like quarks or lightning bugs, they're *short subjects*—you glimpse them on the fly; they're something you see on your way to the main feature, figments of pop culture's peripheral vision.

When a movie makes them the center of attention, as big as a building in Dolby sound, the movie seems less than what it was intended (an homage to the wacky icons of our youth), and more like the action of spoiled rich kids who never grew up, and have no real life outside of movies, who have nothing at all, really, except oodles of income.

And the movie seemed like something else: a slick corporate decision. I hate to break it to you, but Bugs Bunny died back in the sixties when Warner Brothers shut down the animation department, realizing, in that charming way corporations have, that cartoons weren't making them any money.

So what this WHO FRAMED ROGER RABBIT is, is one last wring of that cartoon money wringer. It does no honor to Bugs and the gang, it entombs them. It's a 40 million dollar wake. It was hard enough defending pop culture from my parents when I was a kid. How will American culture survive its defenders?

ROLLING STONE | 1985

Ever since ROLLING STONE rejected my generous offer to review records for them in 1972, I've been looking for ways to get back. Now, by golly, I think I've found it. No, I won't attack the movie PERFECT.*
Making the most useless movie ever made is a special accomplishment, not to be sneezed at. But check this out.

There was a special insert in a recent ADVERTISING AGE, placed by ROLLING STONE to attract advertisers. When you opened this brochure, you saw two facing pages. On the left was a picture of a hippie with the caption, PERCEPTION; on the right a picture of what looked like a kid whose father is putting him through med school, with the caption, REALITY.

The brochure went on in this vein—hippie van, PERCEPTION, really sharp car, REALITY; loose change, PERCEPTION, credit cards, REALITY. The sales pitch wound up with a picture of George McGovern (PERCEPTION) and a picture of Ronald Reagan (REALITY). The copy read, "If you think ROLLING STONE readers are taking left turns when the rest of the world is taking rights, consider who they voted for in the last election. The winner."

I had never seen voting considered as shopping before. There was nothing in the copy about Ronald Reagan being the best man for the job, only that he won, and that ROLLING STONE readers followed the pack. The election was treated like a trendy event. If you voted for Reagan you got to get into the disco and the fine cocaine, but if you didn't you were left out on the street with all the guys who get their clothes from Penney's.

Finally, on the back of this little brochure were two quotations. ALL YOU NEED IS LOVE, The Beatles, 1967, and WHAT'S LOVE GOT TO DO WITH IT? Tina Turner, 1985. See, you might have needed love when you were in high school, but up here in the real world, all you need is ROLLING STONE.

ROLLING STONE always did have an inflated sense of its own worth. Fifteen years ago, the only ROLLING STONE reader I knew was the kind of guy who got nervous if you touched his records without wearing the special gloves. He didn't have a record player, he had a component system.

ROLLING STONE: hip to what's happening, and shaping the opinion of a hip America, PERCEPTION. What's the reality? Move stars and musicians out to plug their new products inhabit a gossip-filled tabloid run by total cynics afraid of passion, quality, and commitment, and filled with contempt for anything but their own self-image.

Sure, that description fits me to a tee; they should have taken me when they had the chance. Here's my attitude: if ROLLING STONE wants to harbor the delusion that it was once capable of considering something outside its own world view, it's a harmless delusion. Many of us need self-delusion just to get out of bed in the morning. But at least I don't consider getting out of bed a cultural achievement. It ain't heavy, it's ROLLING STONE.

PERFECT starred John Travolta.

ROMANCE | 1991

Last week I tried to catch THE RUSH LIMBAUGH SHOW, but fifteen minutes into it, my then-girlfriend huffed into the room, put her fist through the radio, and said in a harsh quaking voice, "How can you listen to that right wing creep?" I said, "He gets more dough from one self-satisfied little talk show than I've made in a lifetime of rancor. He's made bonehead smugness pay off big! There's gotta be a way to make it work for me."

But she wasn't listening. She was off on a rant about the patriarchal power structure, maintained by white men like Rush Limbaugh, who keep people of color from empowerment—

"Hold it," I said. "'People of color?' Isn't that like saying, 'colored people?'"

"Don't be so seventies," she said. "'People of color' is more inclusive: not just African-Americans, but AmerInds, indigenous third world cultures—"

"No people of white?"

"You're being negative," she observed shrewdly.

"I haven't had my coffee of morning yet," I reminded her.

"Get out," she said between teeth of clenchhood. Sadly, I put on my shoes of brown, shirt of pink, pants of black, and left that flat of pain.

Sure, it's a grim picture. But I can help you avoid the pitfalls of my miserable lifestyle. Yes, you, genderless reader! I can help you hack out a paradise of love in the jungle of political correctness we call the nineties. How? By following the rules of PC Romance.

Fellas, on that first date, if she buries her nose in your neck and starts sniffing loudly, don't be alarmed. She's just making sure you don't smoke or use a personal fragrance. Caution! Only womyn may initiate sniffing. For myn to sniff womyn without consent is a violation of female personal space, and is very rude. Guys, if you wish to sniff, ask first! You would both be wise, however, to prolong the sniffing process, thus avoiding speech, which always leads to trouble. If a scent other than a natural body aroma should happen to be sniffed, it is proper form either to (a) recoil in disgust and hiss, or (b) regard the offender with compassion, then turn, shaking the head, and slowly walk away.

If you smoke, give up the habit four to six weeks before your first date. Throw away your English Leather, fellas, and gals—ditch that Obsession. Bathe only in recycled water. Instead of washcloths and soap, why not try the more politically acceptable loufas and raw aloe leaves? Ideally, you should show up for your rendezvous, bleeding slightly from your raw pores, and smelling like a rain forest. If you are a rain forest, read no further. You will have no problem finding PC romance in the 90's.

Spend several hours before the date itself drawing up a contract that spells out who pays for what. Include everything in the budget—movie, music, meal, busfare home and/or condom(s). Caution, again! Any intense act of physical intimacy—even safe sex—is a leading co-dependence indicator. If left unchecked, co-dependence can lead to denial, cycles of abuse, and a surplus of radio psychologists. Severe physical intimacy may be a Trojan Horse for the truly PC, best left outside the gates.

On the "date" itself (the technical PC term, by the way, is Voluntary Personal Growth/Mutual Individuation Process/Syndrome), avoid movies and eating altogether, unless a Thai food/Woody Allen combination is available. Anything else might generate un-PC "controversy" in your personal "speech." Why not spend your "date" recycling together? Or invite that potential significant other to view your pamphlet collection? Offer to share your videotapes of the complete Oliver North testimony. That'll heat you both up! If you want to take a crack at intimacy, try a tape of Alice Walker reading from her own work, two sets of headphones, a jug of Evian, and enough Orville Redenbacher to feed an army.

If you must speak, avoid bashing Japanese corporations, "the homeless," Israel, Palestine, and Spike Lee. These subjects tend to raise the voices of the PC, and we must remain calm! Bashing of American corporations, Reagan, Bush, Jesse Helms, and Bill "William" Bennett, however, is not only compulsory, but soothing. You may allow yourself a Dan Quayle joke, but only if it's old and not funny. Watch the jokes about Marilyn Quayle, Madonna, Nancy "I Coulda Been Susan Hayward" Reagan, and Barbara Bush, though. After all, even in the corridors of power, they're still just plain old womyn whom denial has made precious. All in all, for either gender and every sexual preference, it's a good rule of thumb to say nothing at all, and appear concerned. I'll bet it works for Rush Limbaugh, and, frankly, as my Mom would say, "He's no prize."

RULES FOR ROCKERS 1996

On October 21, Blind Melon singer Shannon Hoon, 28, was found dead of what the media always call an "apparent drug overdose," in the band's tour bus.

Rock stars have been overdosing for years now, not to mention getting arrested for indecent exposure, trashing hotel rooms, disdaining hairbrushes, and only shaving every three days. You'd think they'd learn.

There's probably nothing we can do to stop brash young musicians from sneering at all authority, and wearing tight shiny clothing not always appropriate to their physique.

Besides, attrition will take its toll on most teen heartthrob wannabes before any real damage is done. A drummer's girlfriend will force him to choose between the band and her; a bass player's dad will decide that he needs the garage to store his power saw collection, thus eliminating his son's rehearsal space, and ending his rock career forever; some sullen longhairs will even come to realize that driving twelve hours to a gig, only to be screamed at by a hostile crowd who throw full pitchers of beer at their heads, is not as much fun as it was cracked up to be.

Still, despite the best efforts of girlfriends and the free market, there are some rock-and-rollers who actually do "make it." This leads to a whole other series of problems.

For instance, a young rocker could make millions from "Armageddon Twist," but that's the only hit he'll ever have. He'll end his days a bitter old man, eking out a living lip-synching his ancient ditty at county fair Golden Oldies revivals.

Others can go from hip to ridiculous in an eye blink! One day our rocker causes teenage girls to swoon with his hoarse vocalizations, and the next day some latenight comic points out the amusing similarities between the star's hoarse vocalizations and Elmer Fudd's. The next thing you know our superstar's albums are going for a dollar fifty-nine in the cutout bin at the corner drugstore, and he's riding that long black train to Palookaville.

Rock fame is no picnic. Critics call your second album a "major disappointment." Sales plummet. Your once-sexy pout is now perceived as silly. You add a second guitar to the mix, and your fickle fans accuse you of selling out, then abandon you in droves. You marry a supermodel more famous than you, causing severe loss of self-esteem. You spend more time on a tour bus than in a studio, and start to like it! The arrogance, rudeness, and self-indulgence that made you successful destroy you.

We need to help those few who actually get a recording contract survive long to do an "unplugged" CD. We've got to help them live long enough to save the rain forest, marry that film star, buy that mansion in the south of France, get knighted, and take up golf. If we put our minds to it, we can make sure that all of today's screamers can grow up to be semi-respected Frank Sinatras.

Kids, you need to follow these simple rules:

Drugwise, stick to ibuprofen, decaf lattes, and pale pilsners. Never deviate! Wear earplugs and protective headgear at all times. Keep it simple, and stick to it. Bo Diddley had a beat named after him, and it wasn't 5/4. 'Nuff said.

If your stomach is not a flat slab, please leave your shirt on while performing. Wherever possible, take limos. Pick your band's name carefully. (STRAWBERRY ALARM CLOCK, for example, has not aged well.)

If your girlfriend asks you to choose between her and her music, sell your instruments immediately— especially if you're a drummer. If you do make it, be sure to buy Dad a new garage. Not only will he appreciate it, but if your second album is a major disappointment (as it probably will be), you'll have a place to go.

Finally, go easy on the supermodels, don't forget to tune, and remember: a tiny bit of dry ice and lasers goes a long way. Ditto with tattoos.

RUSSIA IS AMERICA | 1996

Boris Yeltsin's rival for the Russian presidency, the Communist Gennady Zyuganov, has been running around telling potential voters that the United States was to blame for the collapse of the Soviet Union.

Hooray for our side, huh? President Reagan knew what he was doing after all, right? Well, not quite. Zyuganov says that President John F. Kennedy did it.

According to the San Francisco Chronicle, Zyuganov claims that "the Soviet breakup occurred as a direct result of a secret 'new war' Kennedy started after the 1962 Cuban missile crisis. Under Kennedy's orders, the United States took control of the Soviet mass media and used it to sow dissension—including nationalist and religious separatism, and disrespect for the elderly—that led to the collapse."

Doesn't that sound like what's going on in the United States today? Some want to build a wall between America and the rest of the world—there's nationalist separatism in a nutshell. Others are setting up quasi-religious enclaves in Wyoming, Idaho, and Montana—religious separatism! And if trying to eliminate social security isn't disrespect for the elderly I don't know what is.

But I'm still confused. If we undermined Russia back in the sixties, who are this so-called "we?" I thought we were supposed to believe that the United States' media are run by a left-leaning cabal. Did we stage a top-secret journalist exchange in the sixties? Did we swap our right-wing reporters for their left-wing reporters, to try to cause the collapse of both Communist and democratic ways of life?

If so, who is behind this conspiracy? What is to be gained?

Let's examine this further.

In his day, President Kennedy was considered a liberal. Nowadays this means "socialist." No true socialist would strive to bring about the collapse of socialism. Therefore John Kennedy must have been a covert Republican.

If this is true, however, what does that make Republicans? Back in the sixties, hippies warned us to mistrust authority. Today, it is Republicans who warn us that authority is not to be trusted. But Republicans, unlike hippies, are themselves authority figures. By telling Americans to trust them when they say not to trust them, they undermine their status as authority figures, thus driving themselves to the fringes of culture where their extreme opinions would (paradoxically) gain more credence. Don't you get it? Republicans are undercover hippies! They're all wearing tie-dyed tee-shirts under their blue suits!

Look at the militia movement. Militias all settle in armed compounds. Could these compounds be virtual hippie collectives, with guns? Maybe the militia do not allow federal agents on their property because they are trying to conceal the fact that they are actually organic gardeners. They spend their free time not on target practice but playing Frisbee and learning the chords to "Uncle John's Band."

Here's a horrifying thought. What if we aren't America at all, but Russia in disguise? And what if Russia is actually America? Yes, the giant corporate mergers of the last few years were not capitalist movements, but socialist. When the time is ripe, these materialist giants will reveal that they aren't corporations, but revamped socialist multinational collectives, in which shareholders, not workers, own the means of production.

And Russia? It is fast going down the road to laissez faire capitalism at its most emblematic— the black market. Russia will soon be a free marketplace ruled by gangsters, pirates, and corrupt officials.

So Boris Yeltsin is actually a Communist, Zyuganov a democrat, Gingrich is Jerry Garcia's evil twin, and Clinton really didn't inhale after all. Who's behind all this? Well, the Mafia of course, the CIA, and the Illuminati. But who was the mastermind?

Surprisingly, it wasn't John Kennedy, but Jackie! Her demise was faked, you know. The entire latter half of the twentieth century was just a fiendish plot to drive up the value of her personal possessions. She's secretly living off her auction profits in a sumptuous underground mansion in Bethesda, Maryland with Aristotle Onassis' clone. I think Howard Hughes, Amelia Earhart, and Jimmy Hoffa are in on it too. I don't know what they're up to down there, but it can't be any good.

SCANDALIZED | 1984

Miss America naked. Oh boy, another scandal. As we get more and more sophisticated, and more and more lawyers, paradoxically we get easier and easier to shock. It used to take a movie star found on the yacht with an under-age girl, or a public official caught in the wading pool with an exotic dancer. Now James Watt trying to remove his foot from his mouth, or a lovely black woman revealing her body for photographers gets the same gasp of breath as the resignation of a president. What happened to scandals?

Joan Rivers at the Emmys, remember that? Vanessa Redgrave or Marlon Brando at the Oscars. Mountains out of molehills. Marlon Brando is a real molehill. All our celebrities are molehills. There hasn't been a decent flap in this country since the Vicki Morgan sex tapes.

Admit it. You haven't watched the Miss America Pageant since they canned Bert Parks. And you haven't picked up a PENTHOUSE since they rejected your letter about that interesting experience you had with that stewardess in a New York Toll Plaza in 1981. I'm not going to plug in my TV again, or shell out a couple of bucks to Bob Guccione, the Caligula of girlie magazines. This isn't a scandal at all. There weren't any kickbacks or break-ins—just a black woman who took off her clothes for money. If she made an error in judgment, it's a mistake that might make her a stronger person.

What can they do to her? The Miss America crown is a badge of wholesomeness. Can she have wholesomeness stripped from her, like badges from a disgraced official? Will they take away her swimsuit and dorky high heels? Or conversely, will Bob Guccione become the new Bert Parks, with his light meter and gold chain, trying to persuade Miss Congeniality to remove a few things in the back seat of his gold Rolls Royce? I doubt it, but then again, in a nation where a PLAYBOY can have a philosophy and Larry Flynt can run for President, anything is possible.

I think it will blow over in a couple weeks. It won't even get a -gate or -scam attached to the end of it, like a big-league scandal. It's barely worthy of the NATIONAL ENQUIRER, in whose pages lawsuits are as common as weight-loss programs. Scandals are on the downswing. Nobody wants to tell a whopper, just point to a little molehill. There are too many lawyers. Litigation has led to a failure of the imagination.

Miss America meets PENTHOUSE. It's a media collision between two false images of the American woman, and bland images to boot. The bland lead the bland in this country. We're supposed to think it's tragic that Miss America got sexy. A black woman got to be just as bland as the rest of white America, and she threw it away. But I think it's for the best. Vanessa Williams will be naked in the spotlight for a moment, then put on her clothes and go on with her life. Take it from me, Vanessa. America's better off. Miss America has a body now. And PENTHOUSE will sell a lot of magazines. That's the bland truth.*

* Ms. Williams seems to have weathered the storm alright.

SCHOOL PRAYER | 1984

The issue of prayer in school gets trotted out every couple of years by dim-witted conservatives who don't have anything important to worry about. I won't presume to speak for God, whose ears no doubt glow when they hear the heartfelt mutterings of red-cheeked boys and girls. And I can't quarrel with the Norman Rockwell images conjured up by school prayer. I happen to like Norman Rockwell. He painted a world nobody ever lived in, but he was good at painting it.

But let's talk about kids. Let's be honest, folks. Where I grew up, it was hard enough to drum up enthusiasm for the Pledge of Allegiance. Like all public displays of affection, the Pledge of Allegiance always embarrassed me. I'm embarrassed by most group activities—including protest marches, conventions, singalongs, chanting, parades, you name it. And what value does a prepackaged pledge have anyway? Kids didn't write it. The teacher made us stand up and say words that kids wouldn't use in a million years. We didn't know the history of the American flag, we couldn't vote. What does "republic" mean to an eight year old kid? An eight year old kid understands comic books and skateboards. But "one nation, indivisible"? Forget the strained syntax, what's indivisible? Isn't one already indivisible? What does mathematics have to do with patriotic duty?

The idea behind school prayer is that kids would have a choice. The kids who don't want to pray won't have to. So what will they do, sit and doodle while the devout bow their heads? Will they get an extra ten minutes of recess? In "one nation, indivisible," this sounds divisive to me. The kids praying will envy the kids playing, and the kids playing will call the praying kids square. The underpaid teachers will have to keep track of this along with everything else. It can only lead to religious persecution, and isn't this what America was founded to escape?

It's a free country, folks, and if you have an atheist eight-year-old— an incongruous thought in itself, like a fish with wheels—that's the price you pay for liberty.

If adults want to nip the godless menace in the bud, that's fine with me, but fight the godless menace in the privacy of your own home. School is for finger painting, multiplication tables, and making friends. Pray at home, pray in church. But fight the good fight on your own time; leave the kids out of it. The only thing they'll pray for anyway is better grades and a longer recess. Believe me, I've been there.

SCHOOL PRAYER 2 | 1994

Well, okay, say we do allow it. What if the teacher should happen to overhear this student's prayer: "Please don't let Miss Norgaard find out I'm an illegal alien?"

If Miss Norgaard turns the child in to the FBI, does her act separate church and state, or bring them together?

Or, what if an angel should appear and, on its Own Authority, grant the praying tyke citizenship there on the spot? Such an act could never be admissible in a court of law. Religious displays, after all, have no place on public property. Miracles are not permitted in the public education process.

Prayer in school is a lame idea. It can only end badly: plagues, fires, locusts... I say, render unto Miss Norgaard the things which are Miss Norgaard's, and unto God that which are God's.

What about orphanages though? Whose things are they, God's or Miss Norgaard's?

In the public debate so far, it's hard to tell. In their endorsement of molding tanks to alter the pathological behavior of the offspring of the poor, both Newt Gingrich and the insistently intelligent George Will made reference to BOYS TOWN, a 1938 movie about a delinquent who's morally turned around by Father Flanagan, the founder of Boy's Town.

Sure, I'm looking forward to the remake of BOYS TOWN (retitled as the more gender-appropriate PERSONVILLE, due out next Christmas I suspect.) The wayward youth will now be a "gangsta." Tupac Shakur, if he makes parole (otherwise Snoop Doggy Dogg reprising Mickey Rooney's role), will be redeemed by Mister Norgaard, a troubled social scientist with a dream (Robert De Niro totally replacing Spencer Tracy in our hearts and minds; I can even see an Oscar or two in the horizon). This movie will make America feel good about itself for weeks.

Unfortunately for the Republican utopia however, Father Flanagan is no more. Mickey Rooney would undoubtedly jump at the chance to head BOYS TOWN 2000, but he'd be a rather eccentric public servant, I'd think. I don't know much, but I know that pop culture and public policy make volatile companions.

Even if we could assemble a bunch of surrogate parent/civil servants who possess the minimum of the compassion/ability levels required by law to turn this darn welfare state around, and produce a significant number of responsible young people who drink sensibly and don't experience safe sex until married, well, you know what will happen won't you?

Ten years from now, talk radio America will squint only at those whom this wonderful system failed, and whine, "My Johnny doesn't even have a pony! This little motherless child wants cinnamon on his gruel! They're coddling these pre-teen criminals! At our expense! I can't afford house payments!"

Frankly, folks, our sympathy level is pretty close to zero. In America, the request, "Please sir, more," will always be met by "Maybe, kid. First, fill out these forms."

What about the private sector? Why don't we unfetter the free marketplace, so they can deal with orphans in a truly capitalist environment? Couldn't some enterprising entrepeneur come up with

PARENTS (patent pending), providing low cost authority figure/ androids to those who desire them? These could be made available to poverty-stricken dysfunctional families through special lotteries, (Or coupons! Poor people virtually worship coupons!) Think of the public relations value!

Despite everything, this problem is best left to the private sector, in my opinion. Government management of orphanges can only lead to a whole new generation of disgruntled postal employees, even a revival of miserable singer/songwriter/would-be poets. I don't know if the culture could stand it.

In last week's NEWSWEEK, George Will dismissed Hillary Clinton's criticism of this idea as an indication of her "tendentiousness (if this is a sin, my friends, George Will is twice-damned)," and says the notion of orphanages is being considered by "serious people." Good grief, don't conservatives know any humorous people? Believe me, they'll be necessary in the absurd times ahead.

SENSELESS | 1990

The other day, on a parked car, I saw this bumpersticker: "This vehicle protected by Smith & Wesson three days a week. Guess which three." I'm a sucker for a belligerent riddle, so I stopped to figure it out. Okay, on which three days out of seven does the owner hunch in a nearby bush, finger on the trigger, itching for a perpetrator to blow away? Well, what does he do on the other four days? Work? Doubtful. What kind of job only goes four days a week? Perhaps he has a second car that Smith & Wesson protects the rest of the week. But if this "second car theory" is correct, when does the guy sleep? No matter how you slice it, this proud gun and car owner is spreading himself awfully thin.

There are many thin riddles in America today, and I just don't have the answers. Senseless violence itself, for example—how do we stop it? Thanks to nonstop television viewing, I can pretty much pinpoint the sources of today's senseless violence: disturbed fans, disgruntled postal employees, disenfranchised youth, Beirut, the IRA, aimless drifters, Peruvian Maoists, drug cartels, small Balkan countries, all-night convenience stores, dysfunctional families, and the LAPD.

That's the who of violence, but not even a maestro of senseless violence like Stephen "Whoops, I wrote another one!" King can give us a how or why. He throws zombie pets, sinister clowns, and pre-adolescent sexuality into the stone soup of his oeuvre, but it's not a meal improved by the delicate spices of social responsibility and literary finesse. In that regard, bless his potboiling heart, his books are extremely lifelike. As a matter of fact, speaking of life imitating over-written books, I read recently that one of Mr. King's fans is suing him, saying that he/she was the model for the disturbed fan in Mr. King's MISERY. Frankly, I didn't know psychos could be libelled, but I guess they have feelings too: "I felt personally violated by Mr. King's novel. The kidnapping of writers, the smashing of legs with a blunt instrument—it was me. By the time I finished the book, I barely had the strength to smother the neighbor's puppy. Consequently, I seek financial compensation for my mental anguish. I'm naked, vulnerable, and receiving messages from the CIA in the fillings of my teeth."

I say, let's put some common sense in this senselessness! Mr. King was merely exploiting The Disturbed Fan, our newest cultural phenomenon. Would we have fewer Disturbed Fans, and novels about them, if we had stricter gun control? Perhaps. But we mustn't forget what guns have contributed to American culture, like venison, the NRA, and belligerent bumperstickers. The Disturbed Fan could also be an argument for stricter pop culture control. Ban controversial works. Or put a potential audience through a psychological screening process, a questionaire perhaps: "When I see Jodie Foster in a movie, I feel like (a) buying popcorn, (b) a motherless child, (c) there's an angry puppy in my stomach, (d) going to the CIA for a root canal."

If we'd had this test in the sixties, Charles Manson would have been barred from buying Beatles records, and "Helter Skelter" would've been nipped in the bud! Of course, some people today would just as soon block Beatles records themselves, so they won't give psychos funny ideas. But I say, "When the Beatles are outlawed, only outlaws will have Beatles!"

Let's put violence in perspective. Remember: one person's rugged individual is another person's wacko. The American West itself was first explored by misanthropic loners, and they're still considered role models, mountain men. A hundred years ago, most violent crimes were committed by disappointed office seekers. You might say The

Disappointed Office Seeker was the Disturbed Fan of the 19th Century. Yet nobody at the time suggested that the public sector was the root cause of violence. If most Republicans today urge an end to big government, it's a century late and a dollar short. Even the tiniest government won't bring back James Garfield.

So what's the answer? I don't know. I did take a stab at the bumpersticker brainteaser, though. I scratched, "Monday, Wednesday, and Friday?" on the hood of the car with my Swiss Army Knife, and went on my way. Nobody shot me, so maybe I got it right.

SEXIEST 1987

Who is the sexiest man alive? In 1986, it was Mark Harmon, star of ST. ELSEWHERE and beer commericals, the guy who gave Bruce Willis a run for his money on MOONLIGHTING. I remember seeing his picture on the cover of PEOPLE Magazine and thinking, "Nice work, if you can get it." One minute he's walking along photogenically, sipping beer from a paper bag, and the next thing you know, POW! He's the sexist man alive.

Sure, I wonder about the selection process. How do you find the sexist man alive? I'm sure they didn't sort through every man alive before they discovered Harmon's inherent sexiness. The staff of PEOPLE Magazine didn't parachute into the jungles of Brazil to see if there's a man there who might possibly be sexier than Mark Harmon. They probably didn't even consider Red Chinese or Serbs. My hunch is they leafed through a TV guide until they found a picture of Mark Harmon and said, "There he is. There's our guy, the sexiest man alive."

But I kept my mouth closed. Until this year.

In 1987, PEOPLE selected LA LAW's Harry Hamlin as the Sexiest Man Alive.

So what happened to Mark Harmon? Harry Hamlin was alive in '86, why wasn't he the sexiest then? Was he just that much less sexy than Mark Harmon, but something happened in the latter half of the year to give him the edge of sexiness he needed to put him over the top?

Can there be two sexiest men alive? I doubt it.

The global village isn't big enough for the both of them. I think pistols at dawn ought to put the issue to rest once and for all. Can you see the headlines? SEXIEST MAN ALIVE KILLS SEXIEST MAN ALIVE IN DUEL. With any luck, they'd kill each other.

SICK JOKES | 1985

Against my better judgment I went to see a movie everybody's talking about, STRANGER THAN PARADISE. I thought it was an hour too long and looked like every French movie I saw twenty years ago, but the very American shaggy dog, mildly sick twist at the end got me thinking about the nature of jokes. Many movies and books are just extended sick jokes. LOVE STORY springs to mind, when Ryan O'Neal pushes aside the IV tubes to share a tender moment with Ali MacGraw. I remember vividly that the scene in VALLEY OF THE DOLLS in which Patty Duke tries to sing a duet with a brain damaged pop singer had me screaming so hysterically I had to be escorted to the lobby by two burly ushers and forbidden to see a movie in that theater again unless I signed a written statement that I would control my emotions. Of course that was merely bad taste, but even a great work of art like LOLITA is a sick joke, and Americans love sick jokes.

You know what I'm talking about. The joke you heard by the photocopy machine about Vanessa Williams? The joke about Claudine Longet that had you groaning in your coffee? Mommy mommy jokes, Little Willy jokes, Idi Amin jokes, Hitler-and-Holocaust jokes, jokes about Ethiopia, famine, disease, plague, death, the suffering of innocent people, Anne Frank jokes, Helen Keller jokes. You've heard them. You've told them.

When I was a boy we played a boys' game called "Which Would Be Worse?" Would you rather be blind or deaf? Would you rather lose an arm or a leg? Would you rather be staked on the ground and have bamboo grow through you or staked on a beach in a swarm of hungry crabs? Would you rather have bamboo splints put under your fingernails or be rolled down a hill in a barrel full of nails?"

Of course, the "Which Would Be Worse?" game was the direct result of too many James Bond novels, but it goes to show that the human heart has many chambers and the world is a cruel place. Maybe the sick joke isn't so much a cynical response to cruel events, as a frightened response to our own knowledge of these events. The sick joke posits a world even worse than the one we live in, and if we can laugh at that, or even just say, "Eeyew," and go back to work, well maybe there's no harm in it, so long as we keep the moral juices flowing and the CARE packages in the mail.

Despite the fact that we shell out hard-earned money to gawk at pictures of dead movie stars in a book like HOLLYWOOD BABYLON, or use pictures of fetuses, bludgeoned baby seals, or starving children to bolster respective ideologies in the same way an advertiser uses copy points to push a product, I still hope moral outrage is a pure emotional condition, and not the creepy residue of disturbing images displayed for our consumption.

But I have to admit I don't like sick jokes much, and if they are a problem, I've got a solution: the bland joke. The bland joke is designed to replace the ethnic joke, the sick joke, the joke of reduction. If the Lutherans don't mind, I thought I'd make them the subject of a series of jokes. Try these around the water cooler:

> Why did the Lutheran cross the road?
> *To check with his insurance agent about automobile coverage.*

> How many Lutherans does it take to screw in a light bulb?
> *One.*

> How many Lutherans can fit in a Volkswagen?
> *Four comfortably. Five, if one is a child.*

You get the idea. I think they're inoffensive, but if any Lutherans object, how about a bland limerick?

> *I went to the movies and then*
> *I took the bus homeward again.*
> *I took a short nap*
> *With my hands in my lap,*
> *And got off at my stop around ten.*

Come on, let's get that oral tradition back on its feet. I've got the ball rolling, now it's up to you. Which would be worse? Would you rather be mildly amused by a bland joke or say "Eeyew" so hard you spill hot coffee all over yourself? The choice, America, is yours.

SNACKS | 1994

For those of us who abhor the sound of the human voice until nine a.m. at the very least, listening to the radio or turning on a chipper yet cozy teevee morning show is not a viable means to ease the way into the waking world.

But the printed word has its pitfalls. The other morning, waiting for my coffee water to boil, after a glance at some meager newspaper headline ("Clintons Turned Profit Despite Left-leaning Principles! Nation Shocked!"), I was forced to turn my attention to the back of my cereal box. This got my heart pounding faster than any caffeinated beverage.

It read, "A Great Nighttime Mix. The Tonight Show with Jay Leno is a great mix of music, superstar interviews and comedy.... It's the perfect recipe for laid-back, late night entertainment. And for the perfect snack, time after time, it's the Kellogg's Original Crispix Mix. For snack time, party time, or any time, enjoy the great tasting mix of Crispix cereal, pretzels, nuts and spices. It's the greatest snack of all time!"

I was shocked to learn that the former THE TONIGHT SHOW was now officially THE TONIGHT SHOW WITH JAY LENO. (What will happen when Leno retires? THE TONIGHT SHOW WITH JAY LENO WITH HOWARD STERN?)

Despite this valuable piece of information, this was still the kind of boilerplate advertising copy that always makes me ponder the value of capitalism. It depressed me to think that some poor hack had actually been paid to write this down. Not only that, the copy probably had to be approved by various vice presidents, perhaps even by Jay Leno himself.

And for what? To sell you a product you'd already purchased. You're sitting there eating the stuff, aren't you, trying to wake up and face the day? Then the hysterical and somewhat desperate tone of the last line finally drove truth home to my caffeine hungry brain. "The greatest snack of all time?" Think of it! Erasmus and Luther and Homer and Goebbels didn't have a snack as great as this. Darwin and Freud went down in flames, never dreaming that a snack like this was possible.

Obviously, this snack breakthrough wasn't just a scheme to corner the breakfast cereal market, but the late night cereal market as well. I hadn't even known there was such a thing! The copy was designed to make you think that if you poured a bunch of cashews into a bowl with Crispix, your enjoyment of film clips on THE TONIGHT SHOW WITH JAY LENO would be heightened geometrically.

Okay, but if you're up til all hours devouring party mix and watching Winona and Jay banter, how in the hell are you going to get up in the morning and be alert enough to read the back of the cereal box in the first place?

It's enough to make you take up donuts.

Just as the kettle whistled, I noticed under the cereal box picture of Jay Leno (always referred to as "lantern-jawed"—I think it's a federal law) the stern disclaimer, "No Celebrity Endorsement Implied." Did Kellogg's pay him money to put his picture on a box for no reason?

I'd do the job for half what they're paying old Lantern Jaw. I'd throw in my endorsement gratis. Just pay me what he pays in taxes, you can photograph me swimming naked in Crispix. While we're at it, I'd host THE TONIGHT SHOW WITH JAY LENO for scale. That's still good pay, as far as I'm concerned, and I'll bet I wouldn't have to get to work until after nine.

If it means not reading cereal boxes in the morning, I wouldn't mind being the star of a show called THE TONIGHT SHOW WITH JAY LENO WITH IAN SHOALES. And when I retire, if the show's called THE TONIGHT SHOW WITH JAY LENO WITH IAN SHOALES WITH DENIS LEARY, I have no legal objection. Not as long as I get to sleep in.

Coffee sales will plummet, of course, but the way I see it, that's one of the tradeoffs you make in an Information Revolution.*

*The Information Revolution is what we're experiencing right now.

SOPHISTICATION 1984

There are some among us who yearn for the sophistication of an earlier age—William Powell and Myrna Loy knocking back highballs high over art-deco Manhattan. Naturally that ultrasophistication went hand in hand with severe alcohol abuse. Hard drinking was once thought charming, a mark of high intelligence and style. Nobody opposed the sophistication of drinking but Eliot Ness and Carrie Nation.

If you didn't drink in those days, you were some kind of sentimental sap—a poor mother in rags singing "Daddy Come Home" outside the saloon on a Friday night. But the main concept, unique to the time, was to drink vast quantities of alcohol and not show it. This was called "holding your liquor." Hemingway, Hammett and Fitzgerald were supposed to drink with the left hand, knock out elegant prose with the right, and spend their spare time armwrestling and sneering at one another's prose style. Drinking was heroic. The hangover was a badge of courage.

Alcohol is unhip now, unless it's white wine and light beer. Grab the gusto, but don't get drunk. Things are different, but not that different. For all our talk of alcoholism as a disease, it's still considered a character flaw at worst and sort of cute, like Dudley Moore in ARTHUR. And you don't see sophisticated society dames in their seal furs singing "Daddy Come Home" to their three-martini-lunch stockbroker husbands. No, today we have the discreet clinics that can afford to advertise on television, help that is just a phone call away. Oh sure, they say the phone call is hard to make, but all you really need is a major credit card, and the staff of experts will leap into that alcohol problem, solve it, and then run the ten miles home.

Today the hip thing to do is get high on your body. Running huge distances is supposed to provide a feeling of euphoria and elation. There are entire magazines devoted to running, which the runner pores over for types of shoes, in the same way a sophisticate sniffs through a wine list. Only in rich America can severely monklike behavior turn into self-indulgence.

If drinking was once considered the mark of a great soul and good conversation—ghost stories over brandy, Cole Porter over cocktails, romance over fine wine—now nondrinking is transformed into a mark of virtue. We used to drink and not act drunk, now we try to get drunk by not drinking.

The function of exercise used to be to make the body fit for battles and chores. Now we get fit to get high. And as far as drinking problems go, if credit cards and touch-tone phones are necessary adjuncts to will power, I'd say we're still a nation of drunks and over-the-hill jocks. Our running shoes are a pathetic badge of mortality. You can't outrun the grim reaper, folks, or drink him under the table either.

SPORT | 1990

Ask a professional man how he wants to spend his next vacation, and chances are he'll say, "I dunno. Bang on a drum in a tick-laden backwoods with a bunch of guys, shriek in a sweat lodge, swap chants with Robert Bly maybe. You?" The enthusiasm once brought to boardroom takeovers has now turned inwards. Today's mild-mannered David Banner* is tired of repression; he wants to jump in the poison oak and release the Hulk inside. Aging boomer boys are knocking at the door of their psyches to ask plaintively, "Hello in there? Anybody home?"

According to a NEWSWEEK cover story last June on the so-called "men's movement," most retreats forbid men from talking about sports, politics, cars, and careers. I'd fit it right in, no problem. I don't have a job. I don't know anything about cars. My opinions on politics are so eccentric they leave most men speechless anyway. As for sports—well, I've heard that Jose Canseco is a jerk, but what team he embarrasses or what position he plays, I couldn't tell you. He's a jock with a handgun. That's all I need to know.

So yes, I'm willing to raise my mytho-poetic consciousness in a sauna with my peers, if they don't mind talking about old Gloria Grahame movies while we develop our thick veil of perspiration, or which voices Paul Frees did on ROCKY & BULLWINKLE. In return, I'll urinate on trees, throw entire telephone poles on roaring fires, chug brews, laugh lustily, try to remember the words to Beatles songs, and whimper about old girlfriends. That's what guys do in the woods, I accept that. But if I'm expected to whang a bongo and weep for the lack of Daddy in my life, I don't know, folks, I might take my chances *mano a mano* with Jose.

As a child, I spent many happy hours inventing ways to avoid mowing the lawn. I'm proud to say I gave Dad the best alibis of my life. Don't I owe the Spirit of Deep Masculinity that same respect? I'm man enough to admit I'm a bit of a weasel. When I ask myself, "What is a man?" my deepest self must whine back, "That's too hard. Can't we make it a true or false question?" In other words, how bendable are the rules?

The ban on sports talk, for example. If I bring up kickboxing in the course of a crash dive into the subrational, how could my shaman/drummer/therapist object? I doubt if kickboxing is even a sport. I don't know what the hell it is, frankly, except it's inspired a major motion picture and sequel. This puts kickboxing a jump ahead of tennis, which only inspired one motion picture that I know of, PLAYERS, one of the few movies in history that audiences actually crossed town to avoid. This might not tell us anything about manliness, but it might get a conversational ball rolling.

Many American men enjoy watching trucks with really big tires roll over cars in large dusty arenas. If Trucks-With-Really-Big-Tires are neither sport nor car, can we talk about them? How iffy are Frisbee, croquet, female mudwrestling, or the ski trips of John Sununu? When we're tired of talking, can we fish? Can we shoot .22's at "No Trespassing" signs? Do we deflate our Reeboks when entering the hogan? Most important: who's bringing the keg?

Again, I'm not saying I want to, but as I rub sage into the tense muscles of a brother and incant Native-American power poems, can the topic of professional wrestling be broached? When I was a boy, pro wrestling was only attended by wiry old ladies with dyed red hair and a thirst for blood. Today, it's a growth industry, definitely manly, with perks for its stars like action figures and starring roles in bad movies. It's no sport, so why not bring it up? Does Robert Bly have an action figure? Think about it.

We could market this Man thing, really bring it home to mainstream America, if we lighten up on the restrictions. Make it a kind of a Bohemian Grove for wusses. Merchandise a special Wild Man® Spandex outfit, get a fashion spread in ESQUIRE. But no girls, okay (except on Women's Night), okay? All right. Put her there, bro. Us guys got to stick together.

David Banner is The Hulk's alter ego. On television he was played by the late Bill Bixby. Thanks for asking.

STUPID | 1993

On a recent Christmas, the cockles of the nation's heart were warmed by the story of the young father who trudged through miles of snow to get help for his wife and baby, shivering in a cave in the wilderness. For months after their rescue, they were media darlings, the front page, the top of the hour. Producers waved checks with many zeroes. Thanks to modern media, one family's frostbite was transformed into a nest egg.

But I wonder, when their harrowing adventure shows up on the tube, supposedly "fact-based" (which is to truth what astroturf is to grass), how will the producers handle the scene in which the young couple first got themselves lost. If I recall correctly, they were driving to visit relatives, when a blizzard grew so severe that the freeway closed. Yes, even the superhighway, with its gas stations, food, shelter, snowplows, and proper authorities, had been shut down in the face of the worst storm in years. And yet, instead of going back home, as anyone possessing the sense God gave a goose would do, this young couple goes down an unpopulated country road, to end up stranded miles from warmth. Where I grew up, these people would have been considered lucky to be alive. Will TOO STUPID TO LIVE be the title of their movie of the week? Doubt it. Not if they want to attract star quality to the project.

SUBURBAN MAFIA | 1994

Last year in the American Midwest, a high school principal hired a hit man to kill his ex-wife, because she was trying to expose his having seduced her then-underage son, his stepson.

You with me so far?

The hit man (a 19 year old friend of her son's), instead of killing the ex-wife, told her he'd gladly kill her ex-husband instead for the low price. She agreed, and they drove to a K-Mart, where (according to the LA TIMES), "he picked out a deer knife, a sharpener, gloves and a carton of cigarettes."

The three were soon arrested, nipping their shopping/killing spree in the bud. But apparently the mobbing up of suburbia has become yet another Alarming Trend.

The LA TIMES noted: a teen in Chicago asked around in class for someone to kill her Mom and Dad because they'd grounded her; an alleged Florida child molester was indicted for hiring an undercover cop to kill the toddler who dropped the dime on him; Malcolm X's daughter is accused of hiring an FBI stoolie to off Louis Farrakhan. And remember the Texas case? A typical suburban Mom wanted to murder her daughter's high school cheerleading rival?

What does it all mean? The influence of the Mob is waning in America; perhaps gangland activities need to surface somewhere else. Maybe along with an inner child, each of us has an inner mobster. If the inner child doesn't get what it wants, it feels the need to blow away those responsible.

In the golden days of the Mafia, the reasons for killing people did seem more sensible. If you stole their stolen money, say, or muscled in on their racket, whacking you made good business sense. Call me old-fashioned, but I don't think that a K-Mart is the proper milieu for a vendetta.

Maybe for the bargain-conscious middle class, it's the sheer affordability of a hit that makes it so attractive. In my first example, the kid was willing to ice either party for 2500 bucks. That's pretty reasonable! I could max out a credit card and have somebody waxed myself! The guy next door, for example, who's always blocking my driveway with his second car—but don't get me started.

Where will this lead?

Some language will have to change, obviously. When we embark on a suburban-style execution, we can't growl to our victim that he's "going for a little ride." Suburbanites live in their cars, after all, they don't die in them. I suggest we nudge the victim in the ribs, and ask politely if he'd "like a little barbecue."

It's also time to bid farewell to the so-called "cement overshoes," and offer a "drywall overcoat" instead. This might even give a boost to the troubled building contractors industry.

After we "make a hit" (or "touch base," as I propose we call it), let's not say that our victim "sleeps with the fishes," but rather, he "naps on the patio."

In the future, do we "make people an offer they can't refuse?" No. We offer to let them "borrow the lawnmower."

Elmdale USA should branch out of the simple art of murder into the more sophisticated gangland activities of extortion, illegal gambling and drug smuggling. (I don't know what the equivalent will be: veiled threats over the backyard fence, unauthorized Thursday night poker games, and counterfeit Sudafed?)

But before we do that, we need a godfather. Since these are the 90's, and suburban murders seem to be leisure activities shared by couples, I believe that godfathers should be replaced by "godparents." As a gesture of respect, applicants for their favors should refer to them as "Bud" and "Missy."

There's going to be no shortage of bloodthirsty bourgeoisie, I predict, folks who look just like you and me. They'll launder money, do the laundry, even pop a cold one with you. But if you're ever standing around the Weber in your flip-flops, and Bud's flipping burgers, and Missy's making the rounds with the lemonade pitcher, whatever you do, don't make fun of their special sauce.

Many have mocked it. Many nap on the patio.

SUPERMODELS 1994

When it comes to fashion models and magazine ads, the anorexic look has been part of the package so long it no longer shocks me. Back in the sixties, though, I was a real bleeding heart. I'd airmail sandwiches to Twiggy. If we'd had it then, I would have used Fed Ex to overnight canned goods to Penelope Tree.

Now I'm hardened, callous. When I leaf through a two year old VOGUE in my dentist's waiting room, and see some half-starved waif lounging half-naked on a chaise, I just yawn and stifle the urge to buy a personal fragrance system, like everybody else.

That's why I was a bit taken aback when I first saw Guess Jeans' new ad, a photograph of four models who seem to be harvesting rice.

Unless you consider pouting, sucking in one's cheeks, or the wearing of scanty overpriced clothing a physical activity, it's highly unusual to see models actually doing anything. Yet there they were, complete with big rubber boots and scythes, slogging and sweating through a damp paddy. Glamorous!

These models were also a bit more full-bodied and mature than the bulimic pre-teens I'd grown accustomed to seeing. They were actually buxom, one might even say as differently-breasted as Jayne Mansfield. They looked like they were all named Lola.

How does this ad sell jeans? None of the models were wearing any. They were wearing halter tops and short shorts.

(In itself, this isn't so strange. These days it's bad form for clothing or perfume commercials to show their products at all. Television ads for Obsession even seem to suggest that their cologne will make you brood, take your shirt off and write bad poetry. Yet the stuff sells like hotcakes!)

Maybe jeanmakers were trying to push a harvest line of clothing on rice farmers, but this seems like a dubious marketing strategy. Do they even have malls in Viet Nam?

Well sure, there are farmhands with access to major shopping centers. I haven't done an independent poll, but I've met a couple. One was a large man named Sven, and the other a rangy tobacco chewer called Slim. I don't know if they ever shopped for halter tops, but I know if they ever split a nail during their chores, they didn't whine about it. I don't see much of a demographic there.

Were the target customers those consumers who resemble starlets from the late fifties and happen to be employed as farmhands? I don't see much of a demographic there either.

But maybe I should keep an open mind. There's no reason, besides lack of a disposable income, that a farm worker can't be as chic as an account executive.

And we are living in a downsized economy. There may be a subculture of working class supermodels that I know nothing about. Full-figured models, who don't get as much work as their painfully thin colleagues, may be forced to supplement their income through backbreaking labor.

Was this ad intended as some kind of documentary evidence, a shocking expose of the kind of working conditions bosomy fashion victims are exposed to every day?

Maybe it's even more sinister than that. There might not be busty supermodels toiling away in coal mines or doing drywall construction, but think about this:

We consumers buy stonewashed jeans by the boxcar, but do we ever wonder who scrubs the jeans with stones before they get to the store? When we first put those pre-ripped jeans on our bodies, do we ever stop to wonder who did the pre-ripping? We'll pay more for these tattered pants than we would for ones we could tear to shreds and smash with rocks ourselves, for nothing!

Maybe the women weren't harvesting rice at all. Maybe blue jeans were under that water, and these poor women were slicing them up with their scythes, stomping them with stone-filled boots, getting them ready for the market, all at sub-minimum wages. Maybe jeanmakers are just rubbing our noses in it and laughing. I urge readers to write Congress immediately. Lolas of the world, unite! You have nothing to lose but your chains!

SUPREME COURT UNPLUGGED | 1993

Ever since World War II, pop culture has made subtle inroads into the uptight corridors of Washington, DC. Harry Truman used to tinkle the ivories. Even Richard Nixon, a man born with lead in his pants, would pound the 88's from time to time. Not only did he say, "Sock it to me?" on Rowan & Martin's Laugh In, he allowed himself to be photographed with Elvis Presley. Before he was elected, John Kennedy spent some time in Vegas with Sinatra's Rat Pack, back when Vegas was truly a palace of gilded sin, not the Disney World for grown-ups it's become today.

When the late great Lee Atwater rocked the house at President Bush's inaugural celebration, I thought, "At last. That vast untapped Beltway soul is about to be unleashed like a healing river on a grateful America!" No such luck. Lee Atwater's R&B record stiffed, Vice President Quayle started nattering about family values, President Bush started whining about draft-dodgers, hip-hop became young America's music of choice, and Bill Clinton found himself President. President Clinton himself is rumored to do a dynamite Elvis impression, but ever wary of our increasingly grumpy media, he's kept it to himself so far. (Maybe he amuses Chelsea with it. I don't know.)

But there is suddenly new hope. The Supreme Court has recorded all open sessions since 1955, on tapes stored at the National Archives, where a political science professor from UC San Diego found them, and decided that they deserved a wider audience than just legal scholars. As a result, the Wireless Catalogue (a profit organ of non-profit radio) now offers MAY IT PLEASE THE COURT, six ninety minute cassettes consisting of excerpts from arguments concerning twenty-three key cases, including Roe vs. Wade (so my sources tell me). Wow. Talk about your picks to click. Too bad it's not available on CD. Too bad it costs seventy-five bucks.

The Supreme Court itself is of two minds about this (maybe even of nine minds, I haven't followed their response that closely). The judicial branch is concerned, apparently, with issues of propriety. What if this thing catches on? If young people start to "dig" the hot sounds of argument and rebuttal from the highest court in the land, where will it end? Posters of justices may adorn dorm rooms. Teens may adopt black robes in homage to their heroes. William Rehnquist could become "Ringo" to a generation that's never even heard of the Beatles.

We could have a media orgy:

> —Feature articles in teen mags, "David Souter: The Shy One," "Sandy's Shopping Do's and Don'ts." "Ruth Ginsburg's Bad Hair Day," "Tony Scalia: America's Grumpy Sweetheart."

> —Clarence Thomas agrees to pose for Cosmopolitan Magazine, the profits from which go to the Heritage Foundation.

> —William Rehnquist, getting in the spirit of the millennium, releases a dance mix of his greatest decisions, and tours behind it with Tupac Shakur.

> —Anthony Kennedy gets his left ear pierced, and takes up rollerblading.

I don't see this as a bad thing. If this tape catches on, we could reach back in history to put new life into some old tapes. Put a world beat behind the Nixon tapes and we could have something the young people could really get behind. Think of the new career a Hal Holbrook could have with "Lincoln: Unplugged." John Malkovich could rake in some big bucks with a one-man show, "Ike: The Dark Side."

And think of all the video potential! Newt Gingrich, who has logged more time on C-Span than any living human, could put out a videocassette, "Spanning the Years: Newt's Best Bites." "Address the Tee with Gerald Ford" could make millions—it has for him. "I Yield the Floor to my Extinguished Colleague: Senate Bloopers" is a sure-fire late night television seller.

As for me, I'll wait for Ronald Reagan's "Dutch Does Dennis Day," beautiful spoken renditions of Irish ballads. Failing that, I'd settle for "Al and Bill: The Righteous Brothers." Reagan doing "Oh Danny Boy?" Clinton and Gore doing "You've Lost That Loving Feeling?" As Randee of the Redwoods used to say, "Either way is fine with me." This is truly a bi-partisan issue.

SURVIVORS | 1982

A survivor used to be a guy who didn't die when his plane crashed. A wavy-haired reporter in a three piece suit would cram an imposing microphone into the survivor's face to ask a rude question guaranteed to trigger massive weeping from the survivor and massive channel switching from the rest of us, who'd rather watch THREE'S COMPANY reruns than the anguish of some poor sap we've never even met. But the guy who doesn't die doesn't qualify as a survivor in the '80s. He's just more food for the hungry mouth of telecommunications. The survivor ain't in the hospital anymore—no, a survivor in the '80s is a guy with two hit series under his belt.

In the '80s the TV entertainer has a life so special and intense that a mere consumer can only be allowed brief hallucinatory glimpses of it. On the back pages of PEOPLE Magazine some third-rate actor says, "I'm a survivor." You realize with shock that he's only talking about the hard time he's had adjusting to fame, as though fame were some sort of dread disease that only the lucky few survive. Survival means self-pity transformed by egotism into something awesomely creepy.

Here's the survivor: some bland actor, the hot new star of LOTSA CARS ON THE PRAIRIE, replaces another bland actor, who was fired mid-season over a contract dispute. In the TV GUIDE interview there are discreet references to divorce, drugs, hassles with agents and fellow stars. It's not an easy road, he implies, but everything's better now, thanks to the special love of a special woman, invariably described as a "terrific" lady. Terrific is the survivor's favorite adjective, used to describe with equal enthusiasm people, food and emotional states. Just by studying the obviously staged photograph of this mediocre human being, surrounded by his special lady, his special poodles, his special shoes, all cavorting in the overheated pool—you can tell that this is one actor ready to join the ranks of the truly famous.

The truly famous are a terrific group of people. They get to write autobiographies or have them written, they get to put both feet in their mouths on talk shows, making ill-advised comments on controversial issues they know absolutely nothing about. The truly famous are the true survivors.

Shelley Winters is a survivor. Stewart Granger is not. Liza with-a-Z survived. Tiny Tim couldn't cut the mustard. Erik Estrada is a survivor. Bruce Jenner is not. Suzanne Somers ain't gonna make it, but Lynda Carter will. It remains to be seen whether the gals on Charlie's Angels—even the smart one—will survive. The ultimate survivor is Orson Welles, who is remembered less as a filmmaker today than as an amateur magician and drinker of dry table wines.

So how does a survivor die? Death is doing the guest spot on MAGNUM P.I. for scale. If you need the exposure, you're dead. Death is selling the second Porsche. Death is landing a cameo appearance as the third victim in a drive-in horror movie. Death is waiting by the drained pool for the calls that never come. Last year's officer on CHiPs parks cars for a living while millions of dolls bearing his likeness sell like hotcakes in shopping malls throughout the land. You're living out the zombie half-life of the once famous, caressing your clippings, your videotapes as you sip your Margarita alone. You've run out of prime time. Your special lady has left you for this year's model. You're off the air, pal, and nobody remembers your name.

* Re: Erik Estrada: I was sadly mistaken.

SWEAT 1987

The most important rule in America today, according to the deodorant commercial, is "Never let 'em see you sweat." If you must sweat, in other words, do it in the dark.

Those damp little patches have become another symbolic gesture, proof that the working class is truly disappearing. What does sweat mean? It means you work hard. In most professions, the appearance of hard work is to be avoided. Hard work is low class. Sweating conjures images of steel mills, coal mines, factories, anxiety—in today's hip service economy, sweat could indicate that you actually spend your time doing something. Makes you shudder doesn't it? Makes you sweat.

In some professions the appearance of not sweating must actually make you work up a sweat. Those bikinied babes in the Spuds McKenzie spots, for example. They're out there rollerblading in the heat, under those hot television lights, with this lethargic dog that could become vicious at any moment. What do they do when the first tell-tale drop begins to trickle down that shapely ribcage? They can't make for the shade, no, that would actually cause sweating. They're probably not paid enough to have their sweat glands surgically removed. My hunch is that they employ bronzed and brawny grips, just off camera, equipped with little towelettes, who sponge off the tiny hints of dampness between takes. Who sponges off the grips, you ask? I don't know.

I'm exaggerating, of course. There are still some professions where it's okay to sweat. Professional wrestling, singing in rock bands, acting in Sam Shepard plays—these come immediately to mind. But sweating in those jobs doesn't necessarily mean that you are working hard, only that you look like you're working hard. Sweating is the brand of authenticity, kind of like a trademark. So if you're acting in a Sam Shepard play, and the audience starts throwing you salt tablets and Gatorade, you can be reasonably sure of a Tony nomination.

Sweating and not sweating are two sides of the same coin. You either sweat to make it look like you're sweating, or you look like you're not sweating so people will think you're sweating. Sweat has either become a formula, like Classic Coke, or a secret ingredient, like the formula for Classic Coke.

So there's another pop culture riddle unraveled. Now if I can just figure out the appeal of Spuds McKenzie, I'd have it made in the shade. What's fun, exactly, about that dog? Where is the precise location of the fun? Does the dog drink beer? Does the dog buy beer? Every time I think about it, I break out in a cold sweat. Where nobody can see me of course.

T

TEENAGERS | 1983

You don't normally think of Alexander the Great as a teenager, but the fact is he conquered the world at an age when most of us were still trying to find a summer job. Think of the epic lads and lasses through history: Heloise and Abelard, Romeo and Juliet, Mozart, Rimbaud, Shelley, Keats, Laura Ingalls Wilder. They were young, tragic, romantic—they were pioneers. Two hundred years ago it was tuberculosis that carried away the young. Tuberculosis, a disease much admired by the Romantics, was analogous to the car accident of the 1950s. It was the tragic flaw of flaming youth, proof that you were larger than life. You lived fast, died young and left a beautiful corpse.

Teenagers once had the good sense to die young, like Sal Mineo in REBEL WITHOUT A CAUSE. He was too sensitive for the world. If they didn't die young, at least they saved the world from space aliens, like Steve McQueen in THE BLOB; or they actually became monsters (young Michael Landon in I WAS A TEENAGE WEREWOLF) which is about as misunderstood as youth can get. In the '70s modern teens found even more creative ways to die, at the hands of murdering psychopaths in movies like HALLOWEEN and FRIDAY THE 13th. It was all part of an ancient Western tradition.

But now it's come to an end. In movies like PORKY'S and ANIMAL HOUSE, the Dustin Hoffman figure of the '60s is not merely confused, he's emotionally retarded. In movie after movie, young teenage boys are just seeking brief glimpses of a young woman's undraped female bosom, the sight of which sends the teenage boy into a leering lust so intense that he actually faints, or at least falls down.

Even stranger, the teenage girls take their shirts off at every given opportunity. Why? Where's the thrill? They take off their shirts— BAM! The boyfriend faints dead away. Whose idea of a sexual relationship is this? It's not promiscuity and it's not repression either. It's something different—a side effect of the sexual revolution.

I blame the Republicans, who were so afraid a teacher or parent might let a kid in on the secrets of procreation, that a woman's body has once again attained the kind of mythical dimensions that it had in Greek myths, wherein a mortal glimpsing the goddess bathing in the sacred grove would be struck blind. It's the woman's body as Medusa's head.

All right, there's no war right now for the young man of today, but there is something wrong when the only rite of passage available to the young American male is through the turnstiles of these incredibly stupid movies. It's just a milk gland, kids, come on, get it together.

TELEVISION VIOLENCE 1984

I have to admit I pretty much stopped watching network television when ROCKFORD FILES went off the air. But from what I've read, psychologists and worried Moms have a point: network TV is too violent. Network TV promotes a world view at odds with reality. Sure. Tell me something new.

It's true, our founding fathers didn't exactly have television in mind when they wrote the Bill of Rights. They didn't have it back then, you know; if they had, they probably would have done the Bill of Rights as a video, or more probably surrendered to the British then and there. The British have conquered us now anyway, at least on MTV. Duran Duran has succeeded where King George failed.

On the other hand, I hate to have to point this out, but nobody forced us to buy TV sets. One of the sacred freedoms in this country is the God-given right not to buy something. I know, you're saying, "We have them now, we're stuck with them." And you're probably also right when you imply that every violent crime in this country is the fault either of the television industry or of education. Guns don't kill people, television kills people.

And since we do possess the God-given right to possess handguns (I'm sure it's in the Bible somewhere), and the subsequent God-given right to gun each other down in stupid domestic squabbles, and since registration of handguns is the first step toward confiscation, which leads, of course, to Nazism, Communism, and the end of the known universe—I would say the time has come to do something about television. What other choice do we have?

I recommend, first of all, a battery of psychiatric evaluation tests for each and every would-be TV purchaser. Try this sample question:

When you see a rerun of CHARLIE'S ANGELS, do you:

    a. Drool.
    b. Switch the channel.
    c. Harbor vague thoughts about remodeling
       the living room.
    d. Have a sudden desire to get off the couch
       and kill all living creatures with a chainsaw.

I realize a crafty psycho might answer "a" to throw you off the scent, so the test would have to be organized by experts. Remember: if every psychotic in this country has Remote Capability, only moral chaos can follow.

If we can't get the psychology together, at least get an IQ test. An IQ of over 100 gets you a black-and-white, over 120 you get color, over 130 if you want cable or VCR. This is absolutely necessary. Otherwise we'll have to outlaw television. When TV is outlawed, only outlaws will have TV.

And people who can't tell the difference between their television screens and their lives deserves everything that happens to them.

TEMP | 1984

Along the way to my present success I've had to work for a living, usually at "temp work," as it's called in professional circles. I have moved furniture, filed, typed, answered phones, and I probably have the world's record for getting fired. This is because I'd show up at work unshaven, wearing sunglasses and not wearing socks. I figured, "I'm not an executive, who's gonna care?" Well, after my third temp job in a week, I finally took Mom's long distance advice, got a beige seersucker three piece for five bucks at Goodwill. It fit me like a glove, and I wore it to my next temp job. But when the permanent employees saw me approach the water cooler, they all scattered. Nobody would come near me. Finally a little bald guy worked up the courage to ask me who I was. He had me pegged as some corporate honcho checking up on worker efficiency, I guess, because when I told him I was a temp worker, a look of relief passed over his face. Then he replaced that look with one of utter disregard. By noon, all employee fear of me had vanished. So the next day my suit vanished to be replaced by blue jeans, and the next day my job vanished to be replaced by poverty...

But if you're an artist of any kind, it means you're going to have to get the kind of job you get till you get to do what you want to do. So let me give you some advice about the tempworker scene.

- Never drink beer at your desk. Supervisors don't like it.

- Permanent employees probably won't appreciate your Joe Cocker impression.

- If you're moving furniture, don't move a desk if somebody's sitting at it.

- Never call corporate executives by their first name, or ask them if they want to play a couple of holes on Saturday.

- Don't try to find Pac Man on the personal computer unless you're invited by your supervisor. Never ask the supervisor for a date.

- If you're answering the company phone, say "Hello," not "Yeah, what do ya want?"

- I know temp work can get dull, but never rearrange the filing system without permission.

- Don't rewrite business letters in blank verse.

- If you're supposed to show up at work on Tuesday, don't come in on Wednesday.

I know this is basic stuff, but don't draw faces with whiteout on the desk; don't make jewelry out of the paper clips; don't compose melodies on the touch-tone phone; don't ask to borrow the Selectric overnight—remember always, you're just a ghost in the working world.

Somebody will eventually publish the 1,500 page rock and roll novel gathering dust in your sock drawer. Your ship will come in, and then you'll have temps of your own. And they better not call you by your first name.

TERMINATOR 2 | 1991

T2 ends with a nice robot, after destroying the nasty, being melted down in a pot of molten steel; we, the audience, are expected to get teary-eyed about it. You'd have thought this cyborg was Old Yeller!

Don't get me wrong. I love movies about robots from the future who blow up moving vehicles in present-day Los Angeles. (In my opinion, L.A. traffic patterns might be improved by a berserk automaton or two.) But if the original Terminator was a relentless bucket of bolts that blew up anything in its field of vision, the sequel's metallic superdude can barely muster the pluck to put a bullet in a lousy kneecap. Oh sure, Termy eventually kneecaps the entire LAPD, but you can tell his heart isn't in it. Besides, I've seen the robotlike Daryl Gates on television; he's rendering the LAPD immobile, without machine guns, without semiautomatic grenade launchers, just by being him.

TIRED WIRED | 1996

In the April issue of INTERNET UNDERGROUND, musician Todd Rundgren says he is "the poster boy for interactivity." In that guise I suppose, he describes the World Wide Web as being "like a strip mall." Expanding on this image, he continues, "It's like riding along a Dallas freeway where there's nothing but fucking billboards."

At first I thought: he's just jealous because he doesn't have a cute web site. But then I read the cover story of April WIRED; boy, did it give me second thoughts.

It's an in-depth profile by Pamela McCorduck of Sherry Turkle, "cyberspace explorer and professor of the sociology of science at MIT," author of LIFE ON THE SCREEN. Turkle's thesis, based on the theories of the major French dude Jacques Lacan, seems to be that the notion of Self has become outmoded (upgraded?) in the computer age. She offers the computer itself, or networking anyway, as the very model of postmodernism.

Oh, okay, what is meant by postmodernism? McCorduck explains, "Modernist birthday parties had cakes, candles, presents, and games; the main game at postmodern birthday parties is watching and commenting on the videos just shot...." All video, no cake: that's postmodernism!

And what differentiates Lacan from, say, Freud is that he "presented himself as analyst and analysand simultaneously, often declining to distinguish between material and its interpretation."

So when aging boy wonder Todd Rundgren looks out from his poster at the World Wide Web billboards, he is both doer and watcher, commentator and comment, container and thing contained, cruiser and cruised, clicked and clicker, dragger and dropped.... I get it! Getting it is modern, confusion is postmodern!

I'd thought postmodernism had bit the dust around 1989, much like camp did in the 60's, but now the Web has given it new life. Thanks to e-mail, we can still ponder (as Turkle puts it) "the precedence of surface over depth, of simulation over the real, of play over seriousness." Or, as McCorduck puts it, "In the culture of simulation, we aren't alone with the self but with many others— some of whom are our own avatars."

So post-modernism is a slow ideological spin that allows each of us (and avatars too!) to justify not having an attention span. Get a handful of adjectives, like "permeable," "liminal," or "decentered," add a double latte, and you can amuse your various selves for hours, looking for cultural echoes on BAYWATCH, or simply skimming in-depth articles in WIRED.

Here's more: "People use the Internet as 'a significant social laboratory for experimenting with the constructions and reconstructions of self that characterize postmodern life. In its virtual reality, we consciously construct ourselves,' Turkle writes. Players in a MUD are authors too, hundreds of them at a time. 'When each player can create many characters and participate in many games, the self is not only decentered but multiplied without limit.'"

See, back when you played RISK or MONOPOLY on a rainy Saturday, you were just pretending to take over the world; when you role play on the Internet, you actually are taking over the world, one decenter at a time. As a result when you play solitaire now, you aren't just trying vainly to amuse yourself, you are creating a self to be amused. And when you play poker, well... try to find a poker game in Las Vegas today, just try. See what I'm saying?

Turkle continues, "'The goal of healthy personality development is not... to become a unitary core, it's to have a flexible ability to negotiate the many— cycle through multiple identities.'" So not only do I have to read WIRED to keep up with what's going down, I have to create in myself the kind of reader who gives a flying fuck. It's not easy.

Nothing is easy. Even agreeing to do the interview with Ms. McCorduck, Ms. Turkle had to wonder, "'am I going to be the authoress, am I going to be the mom, the colleague?'" I know where she's coming from. Just the other night, I was working on this column, watching POLITICALLY INCORRECT, popping popcorn, drinking a cold beverage, and arguing with my girlfriend on the telephone, all at the same time. I was very anxious, until I suddenly realized that I was multi-tasking, and found a measure of peace, just before my girlfriend hung up on me.

What can be done? Fortunately, Turkle tells us, "'We have only one body, and for the foreseeable future will only have one body.'" What a relief! And she concludes, "'We stipulate several selves, but they attach to that immune system called Me.'"

So, what did the immune system called Ian get from this profile? Well, we play solitaire differently than we play poker. We can yell at the dog but never the boss. The emperor can be naked and well-dressed at the same time, depending on which avatar we use to look at him. We can't be in two places at once, but a boy can be on a poster and look at a web site. And an inflated sense of self-importance is very important in these postmodern times; a dinky little self would just get lost in the billboards.

THAT DOG'S GONNA DIE | 1985

Let's talk movies, let's talk cinematic experience. Jimmy Stewart's pal, usually Walter Brennan, gets wasted by Dan Duryea, forcing Jimmy to dust off the Colts and go to town. In THE WILD BUNCH, General Mapache killed Angel, and the Wild Bunch killed everything in sight. Give the hero a friend, a dog, a girlfriend, a little handicapped boy with learning disabilities; then kill the dog, and the hero's ready for battle. Good suffers, then Good is redeemed in combat. This is what I call the That-Dog's-Gonna-Die school of screenwriting.

James Bond's first girlfriend (Shirley Eaton in GOLDFINGER) is always killed bv the villain. Innocent children drop like flies in Billy Jack movies. Even in THE LAST PICTURE SHOW, as soon as the retarded boy began to sweep the streets I knew he was a goner. Screenwriters love to kill off harmless creatures for the sake of the plot line. Finding the scapegoat is half the fun. THE ROAD WARRIOR: The bad guys killed the warrior's dog, and warrior killed the bad guys. BLUE THUNDER: Bad guys killed Roy Scheider's pal, Roy killed the bad guys.

I thought I had RETURN OF THE JEDI figured out. Skywalker was going to get wasted in a sacrifice play, so Han would get the girl and the rebels would get the galaxy. Bye-bye Luke. That dog's gonna die. But RETURN OF THE JEDI wasn't even true to its own clichés. The only thing that died were robots and muppets, and you can fix robots, they don't even count.

If you haven't seen RETURN OF THE JEDI, I'm sorry if I ruined an incredibly dull experience for you, but it ruined my whole That-Dog's-Gonna-Die theory of screenwriting. Not only that, but Darth Vader unmasked looked exactly like Uncle Fester on THE ADDAMS FAMILY. I don't know what that means, but if that's all the dark side of the force can come up with, we sure live in a bland universe. You might as well let the dog live.

TIME ZONES | 1982

I live on the West Coast and nothing annoys me more than getting a phone call at seven in the morning from some friend or agent in New York, wanting to borrow something or clinch some deal. I always hang up the phone feeling ripped off, and no wonder: it's three hours later there. New Yorkers have had their coffee and their danish, they've read USA TODAY and the TIMES. They're on top of the world, and they've had a couple of hours to sort things out.

And when I finally hop out of bed at two o'clock and call East to take back everything I said in the stupor of half-sleep, New Yorkers are gone for the day. They're out having cocktails, wearing tuxedoes, tangling with muggers, sampling the rich Manhattan nightlife. Time zones were created by the power elite of New York City to keep themselves as the cultural center of America. We don't need time zones.

Time is a fiction created by the government to make sure that trains and airplanes run on time. Time is a fiction created to sell digital watches. We have time only because businessmen want to go home sometime. The farmer doesn't need time. The sun comes up, and the farmer gets up; the sun goes down, and the farmer goes to bed. And for me, the opposite is true.

Time measurement, like the dictionary or telephone, is part of a conspiracy to make our lives more complicated in the guise of making our lives easier. Dictionaries were invented by stuffed shirts on a power trip, to tell us how and why a word should be used. I resent that. I resent telephones; an obnoxious loud noise tells us there's somebody on the line we wouldn't give the time of day to if we were standing face to face. And I hate time—take time, make time, get there on time, I don't have the time.

But what can I do against this tyranny? I can move to New York or unplug the phone. I can play the Eastern establishment's power game or smash my alarm. New York is cold, expensive, and I hate to fly. So bye bye Timex. See you later touch-tone. I'm going back to bed.

TOADS | 1994

Last week, elite narcotics forces in Northern California arrested a man in Calaveras County, with plans to prosecute him for—well, I guess I'm not sure what the charges are, really.

Okay, there's illegal toad possession, one. He supposedly had kidnapped four Colorado River toads (whom he had named Hans, Franz, Peter and Brian). The authorities seized all four—as of March 1, it is a misdemeanor to possess one. (There's talk of organizing a toads-for-toys swap, to get these things off the street, but so far it's come to nothing.)

Two: the toxin this toad secretes, bufotenine, is listed as a controlled substance with the Califorrnia Department of Justice. If licked, bufotenine can kill a household pet. (Why a household pet would lick a toad is another question.)

It turns out that our alleged perpetrator stands accused of squeezing the venom from toad glands ("like a pimple," according to San Francisco Chronicle reporter Dan Reed's account), drying it, and smoking it to achieve a brief trip, which, he described to the police, as like hearing "...electrons jumping orbitally in his molecules."

The toad toker seemed to be more of a psychedelic experimenter than drug-crazed felon. Still I suppose it was proper for the majesty of the law to come down on the dude. This could have led to harder stuff, snorting salamanders, bull-frogs, rattlesnakes... Before you know it, he'd be buying duck-billed platypuses on the black market, and robbing gas stations to support his habit.

Some questions remain, however.

Why did the state of California list bufotenine as a controlled substance in the first place? As a citizen of the Golden State, I am daily made painfully aware that we don't have the money to fix potholes, schools, or any other infrastructure perk we used to take for granted. And yet the state managed to fund some research, somewhere, giving it the necessary legal clout to prevent us from ingesting toad secretions.

I guess I'm relieved. But doesn't it seem rather like creating a crime from whole cloth, then inventing a criminal to justify the expense? Was this whole thing was a state-induced hallucination? Maybe the Department of Justice was on toads at the time.

In the 90s, America is ready to put everybody in jail, for anything. We're ready to implement the "Three strikes you're out" policy, designed to put scores of over-the-hill criminals into overcrowded federal pens, which (since we don't want to pay taxes to enlarge them) would have to release the criminals who haven't committed that "third crime" yet.

Plus there's our war on drugs. Toadsuckers, or their equivalent, all across America are doing time because of harsh new laws. Who's being displaced?

And who's being hurt by our perp's behavior? Last I heard, Arizona doesn't want the toads back. Authorities are looking for an interested aquarium, hopefully, one without a record.

So what's the problem? If there is such a thing as a victimless crime, this would certainly fit the bill. If the guy wants to suck toads in the privacy of his home, I say let him. And if the toads want to form a support group, I'm in favor of that too.

TONYA/NANCY | 1993

As a member of the insignificant minority who wished the Winter Olympics would just go away, I watched none of it, and only absorbed the Tonya/Nancy saga through the print media.

Oh, I know the gist of the story. One figure skater, a hardboiled product of a broken home, may or not have played a part in the physical assault on a second, America's sudden sweetheart. Both were catapulted, as a result, to unnatural levels of fame. Was Tonya given short shrift or too much slack? Was Nancy good or just goody-goody? Pundits vary.

But now the epic tale is behind us, joining other brief blips on the screen of human history. I think I've isolated its significance, and its ultimate meaning. Our fascination with Tonya and Nancy is nothing less than the yearning for our own psychic dualities to be merged.

Hey, no laughing out there! I'm serious!

See if these helpful comparisons don't strike a chord: TONYA is to NANCY as...

Freud is to Jung, as bowling is to golf, Joan Crawford to Katherine Hepburn, Nixon to Kennedy, beer to lite beer, macaroni to spaghetti, Fox to PBS, cigars to cigarettes, or cigarettes to nonsmoking.

Tonya is to Nancy as a doughnut to a bagel, white wine to red, teevee to movies, domestic violence to divorce, a dirt road to the information superhighway, a Chevy to a Volvo, John Belushi to Chevy Chase, a wink to a nod, an angry shout to a muffled sob, an all-beef hot dog to a turkey frank, a convenience store to a clothing store, or Tommy Lee Jones to Rickie Lee Jones (though that might be stretching it).

It's AM to FM, Irving Berlin to Cole Porter, cheeseburger to cottage cheese, United States to Canada, K-Mart to Target, Vegas to Disney World, Africa to South America, malt liquor to ale, seven and seven to margarita, dim piano bar to karaoke bar, World War I to World War II, crack to cocaine.

Tonya might be addiction, and Nancy habit, but if Tonya is habit, Nancy is cold turkey. If Tonya is cold turkey, Nancy is a twelve step program, but if Tonya is a twelve step program, then Nancy has always been a teetotaler. If Tonya has always been a teetotaler, Nancy is an addict currently working on her memoirs at the Betty Ford Center. If Tonya is the Betty Ford Center, then Nancy is a health care professional.

If Tonya were Arsenio, Nancy would be Letterman. Yet if Tonya were Letterman, then Nancy would be Leno, and if Tonya were Leno, Nancy would be Ted Koppel.

Irresistible force, the immovable object. Space, time, yard sale, estate sale, wink, nod. Yet who is the blind horse? We're talking rayon and silk here, felony and misdemeanor, passionate affair and guilt-ridden adultery, Jean-Claude Van Damme and Arnold Schwarzenegger, Lewis and Martin, Kansas and Oz, House and Senate, lust and desire, desire and love, losing and winning (relatively).

We're looking at gaps as small as the difference between MCGYVER and STAR TREK, or MISSION: IMPOSSIBLE and STAR TREK: THE NEXT GENERATION. The Nancy within likes any title with a colon in it, yet it's the Tonya inside who rejoices at sequels!

We can be either one at any moment. Feel like ordering a pizza? You're indulging your Tonya. Some Thai food might hit the spot? That's Nancy talking.

And what of the Jacksons? Interest in the Jackson family is certainly Tonya-esque. Yet if LaToya is Tonya, then Nancy is Michael, if Tonya is Michael, then Nancy is the Jackson Family, and if Tonya is the Jackson Family, Nancy is the Jackson Five. Which is Partridge Family, which Brady Bunch?

We will never be content, and will continue to be fascinated by tiny spectacles, until we learn to marry the Tonya and Nancy inside. In real terms, if a drummer were to marry a bass player, the union could be exquisite in its *Tonyanciness*. Even more so if a the girlfriend of a roadie married a backup singer, if a mercenary loved an ideologue, a Sunni a Shiite. Alas, we have trouble now telling which is which.

So many of us despair before we've even begun. There's no blame in this. After all, if Tommy Lee Jones did marry Rickie Lee Jones, she'd still be Rickie Lee Jones, even if she kept her maiden name. Think about it.

TOPLESS 1994

Talk Show America has been keeping itself occupied lately with a unique controversy: topless subway women. Topless subway women haven't showed up on Geraldo yet, and they don't have a lobby, but they have summoned enough clout in Manhattan to make their behavior legal, if it isn't disruptive. Toplessness is now officially tolerated on New York City's rapid transit system.

I guess I'm out of touch. I hadn't even realized that bare-breasted women underground were a big enough problem that public policy needed to be formulated. Of course now I only take cabs when I frequent the Big Apple, but I seem to recall New York's subway system as a noisy, overheated, overcrowded, seething mass of unhappy humanity, reeking of sweat, urine, ancient dirt, and electricity. It wasn't, in other words, a beach in the south of France.

Maybe it's just me, but I associate topless women with foreign film festivals. Don't starlets at Cannes loosen their halters at the drop of a hat, in the hope that Italian photographers will capture their likeness for tawdry European publications, thus earning themselves a paycheck and giving the starlets little tiny increments of publicity? Are there a lot of sullen French starlets in string bikini bottoms hanging on straps aboard the IRT? Somehow I can't picture it. One might emerge topless from a limo to make a splash at a hip Manhattan nitery, but striking a cheesecake pose as the doors open on the Times Square Shuttle just doesn't have the same impact, PR-wise. How many Italian photographers commute by train anyway?

Even if they did commute by train, if you're a starlet trying to bring yourself to the attention of stocky men in open-throated shirts, chests glittering with gold chains, hoping to land the coveted part of Victim # 2 in MAFIA BRAIN ZOMBIES III: A NEW BEGINNING, you'd probably want a cleaner more sunsplashed environment in which to display your assets. I know for a fact that nasty little deposits of grime collect in the folds of one's skin within seconds after exposure to Manhattan's rich atmosphere. Are you sure that's what you want a casting director to see?

So I think we can safely rule out the Miou-Mious of tomorrow as the culprits in this New York crime wave. Who else takes their shirts off? If we can believe Abby and Ann, many housewives do their housework in the nude. It seems unlikely they'd transfer this practice to public transportation, however. Strippers, of course, disrobe for a living. But what would be their percentage in giving away peeks for free?

Perhaps there's a mighty race of Amazons who have claimed the subway tunnels as their fiefdom. As I said, I haven't ridden the subways in a while, but there could very well be a fierce tribe of women down there, upper torsos oiled and shining, who ululate at each stop and lay about them with broadswords. This would certainly explain the willingness of authorities to tolerate their toplessness: fear, pure and simple.

More likely, I'll bet there aren't any topless subway women in New York, any more than there are alligators in the sewers. But Manhattan, as Rush Limbaugh has taught us, is a liberal hotbed. Just because a thing doesn't exist is no reason to persecute it. Manhattan, our nation's cultural leader, has once again boldly gone where no metroplex has gone before.

Mark my words, nude commuting will become the next New York trend. The trend will spread to the rest of the country. Skinnydipping will make carpooling attractive. This will lead to clothing optional mini-malls, and on to the workspace itself: topless receptionists, CEOs naked as a jaybird except for their power ties, and nudist number crunchers in cubicles fully equipped with one-way mirrors.

This can only lead to the death of the fashion industry. It will, however, make sleazy Italian photographers fabulously wealthy. We'll see them everywhere, naked but bristling with strategically placed Nikons. As for the rest of us, we'll all find employment as victims in **MAFIA BRAIN ZOMBIES V**. It's not much a future, I'll admit, but hey, at least it's a living.

UNABOMBER 1995

The Unabomber has been very patient, and now it's paying off with big ratings, Not only does he have the nation living in fear, he's got the NEW YORK TIMES and the WASHINGTON POST in a state of moral anguish.

He sent them his fifty-six page manifesto, and told them he wouldn't kill anybody if they published it within three months. Ever since the offer, the powers that be at the TIMES and POST have been pacing their offices and dithering: do we publish this maniac's ravings or not? (Didn't we used to call this extortion? Ethical dilemmas just aren't what they used to be.)

Then PENTHOUSE magazine offered to print his manifesto, and put a major monkey wrench in the works. The Unabomber has literary pretensions, you see, but he's picky: he considers PENTHOUSE a tawdry publication; if his manifesto is printed there, and nowhere else, he feels compelled to kill one person to make up for it. (The mathematics of his decision are mysterious to me: one dead per centerfold? Is that how he figures it?)

PENTHOUSE is certainly a pillar of journalism; I only read it for the articles myself. While the TIMES and POST stand around brooding like Hamlet, Bob Guccione has offered to give the Unabomber "a page every month, indefinitely," on condition that he not kill anybody.

As a writer, this offer fills me with envy. I haven't killed anybody in my life, and don't plan on killing anybody in the immediate future. If I signed an affidavit to that effect, could I get a page too?

Probably not. I just don't have the Unabomber's strong sense of moral purpose. If you're going to blow up people, it has to be for a darn good reason. The Oklahoma City bomber, for example, apparently didn't like paying taxes. So he registered his objections to the Internal Revenue Service by blowing up helpless civil servants in Oklahoma. I guess that's just simple logic.

The Unabomber doesn't like computers, so he blows up college professors. He probably put it best when he said, "If we had never done anything violent and had submitted the present writings to a publisher, they probably would not have been accepted.... In order to get our message before the public... we had to kill people." Mark Twain never faced this problem, but hey, this is the end of the 20th Century where homicide and literacy go hand in hand.

Can I make a compromise? If I just wound somebody slightly, could I get an agent to return my calls?

UNEXPLAINED | 1985

These are modern times, the New Age, the Computer Age, the Age of New Technology, but the old mysteries still surround us. Think of all the stories—the tales of UFO's, of the Bermuda Triangle, of psychics and poltergeists, of exorcists and terrorists ....

The blind albino alligators in the sewers of New York; the woman in Texas who never washed her beehive do, so a spider made its nest in it; the poodle that exploded in the microwave ....

The ghosts: phantom hitchhikers; phantom truckdrivers; the ghost of Paul McCartney on Abbey Road....

The homicidal maniacs: the killer's hook in the handle of the door; the boyfriend's body thumping gently on the roof of the car; the frat pledge found on the mansion roof after the initiation, his hair white, his eyes insane, tapping the roof with a bloody hammer...

The sinister conspiracy that killed the Kennedys; the babysitter's discovery that the killer was in the house with her.

All the old teenage werewolves and Frankenstein monsters have grown into '80s adults. Think of the scary images thrown at us—the Jolly Green Giant, Mr. Clean, Man from Glad, the Welchkins, E.T., Muppets, the Alien, the Thing, Care Bears, Cabbage Patch Dolls, even Betty Crocker and her mysterious bland omnipotence in the American kitchen.

Think of the tiny destructions of video games: apocalypse and rejuvenation for a quarter. Think of the power of coins: the images of dead presidents engraved on rare metals; the seeing eye of the pyramid on the dollar.

And think of real terror: punk's power to shock and society's power to turn shock into glamour; Edie Sedgwick, Andy Warhol, Sid

Vicious, Jayne Mansfield, Charles Manson; society's misfits and monsters. Think of Christ's face on a taco, Elvis glimpsed in a vision, falling hunks of Skylab, radioactive Russian satellites; think of Baby Fae, think of the Heart Men...

We've got the bomb for good now. The old black magic is still afoot, in our dreams and deeds, the gods and demons are not dead. And the Bogey Man'll get you—if you don't watch out.

VAMPIRES 1992

As common household pests, I believe vampires pose less of a problem than, say, spiders. I might be more sanguine in my attitude, I admit, if faced with a vampire infestation. After all, to debug a flat, you only need one bug sprayer. To remove the undead, you need a fleet of exterminators—exorcists, eccentric professors, stake-makers, stalwart young men with pure hearts... Try to find a stalwart pure-heart in the Yellow Pages. One who makes housecalls? Forget about it.

So why are vampires so popular? America's had more movies about Vlad the Impaler's unholy progeny than Romania itself, movies that seem to appeal to both men and women. For a woman, I guess, the idea that royalty (The Count) would want to sup from her democratic American veins is thrilling and flattering. Then there's the exciting option of joining the vampire team. Think of that! Normal American janes hanging out with old money decadents in large gloomy castles at languid all-night Eurotrash parties! Vampires never diet, never job hunt. They don't need roommates, day care, or healthy relationships. They just swoop down on the object of their desire, suck it dry, and move on. Throw in some hollow-eyed disciples to address them reverently as "Mistress of the Night," and you can see why so many American women say, "Wow! There's a unique career move!"

And men? We're problem solvers. We identify with the stalwart heroes, bulging with vampire destroying instruments: stakes, garlic, crosses, mirrors, holy water, etc. Guys always covet a fine set of tools. And don't forget, vampire slaying is a day job. It's not like destroying an alien in the dark bowels of a smelly spaceship. You don't have to shell out big bucks for silver bullets, and stay up late on full moon nights, as you must to bag a werewolf. Your sleep isn't disturbed, the way it is when you grapple with Freddy Krueger. You just stroll into the crypt, noon-ish, pop open that coffin, give a whack or two with the mallet, and knock off for lunch.

But if Dracula is an interface between boy and girl movies, what are boy and girl movies themselves? As a rule of thumb, women get pleasure out of seeing people eat on screen. Put the diners in fabulous outfits from another era, and you've got yourself a Masterpiece Theatre miniseries. (Come to think of it, even Dracula could be seen as a drama about food preparation.) Men, on the other hand, enjoy movies about unshaven undercover cops exchanging semi-automatic weapons fire with psychopaths in mob-owned bowling alleys.

Break it down this way. An elegantly dressed Edwardian couple having a picnic in a meadow is a girl movie. Two rumpled cops eating tacos as they track a space alien in an abandoned subway is a boy movie. Motes of dust playing in a stream of sunlight? Women. Beefy men in overcoats striding through swirls of smog? Men.

Sample dialogue includes, "I love you," "I love him," "I love her," and "I don't know what love is any more," for gals, and "I'm taking you off the street," "You're a dead man," "Ow," and "I'm bleeding heavily!" for the fellas.

Locations? A warehouse, parking ramp, desert highway, casino, jungle, and post-apocalyptic wasteland are generic boy movie locales. For women, a kitchen, babbling brook, meadow, fabulous country estate, and *fin de siecle* Vienna are among the locations of choice.

Women can tolerate a horror movie about battling an ancient evil, if the ancient evil has really nice clothing. Guys, however, prefer an ancient evil that is scaly and drips green fluid. Again, Dracula moves from fop to slavering beast at the snap of a finger. Hence, more cross-gender appeal.

The ultimate boy movie of 1992? RESERVOIR DOGS, about a gang of men dying in a warehouse. The ultimate girl movie? ENCHANTED APRIL, about a gang of women lying around an Italian seaside villa. If the reservoir dogs had opened their hearts instead of opening fire, they might have had more intergender appeal. And if that villa had contained a scaly predator, more men might have made reservations. But the real questions remain: If Dracula can't see himself in a mirror, how does he dress so well? If people don't like garlic on a pizza, are they undead? If vampires only come out at night, do they ever go bowling?

VEGAS | 1994

On the front page of the paper the other day, I saw a picture of Tonya Harding leaving a fast food outlet with a couple of soft drinks. What a scoop! Stop the presses!

A guy with a video camera was in the shot behind her, taking pictures of both her and the guy taking the photograph of her. Think of it. There are thousands of well-paid imagemakers being paid to do nothing but follow Tonya and Nancy around, taking pictures of them drinking sodas. This truly is a Golden Age of Telecommunication.

On the other hand, sleazy media coverage of the Tonya/Nancy brouhaha has lifted figure skating to even greater Olympian heights. Sure, it's always been popular, in a way ballet could never hope to be. It's not elitist, for one thing. When ice shows come to town, most of us can still afford to see them. There's something stirring about figure skating, watching ordinary people become extraordinary through their own efforts and our eager attention. And you don't have to rent a tuxedo to watch them.

Their brave innocence often brings them fame. Too bad fame these days is fueled by public relations. Heroes used to have poets to sing them into history. Now history's just another damn information warehouse, and odes have been replaced by press releases. I have obtained some official CBS Olympic figure skater profiles, never mind how. They make disturbing reading.

First of all, the profiles make no pretense of being objective. They're often as catty as an old-fashioned gossip column. Of Marie-Pierre Leray, the anonymous correspondent states: "...unfortunately for Leray, marks are given for technical ability and not beauty, and recently Leray's has been anything but beautiful... the gangly Leray appears not to have grown into her body..." Ouch! That's gotta hurt!

There are also surreal lapses in knowledge. The profile of Katarina Witt states that the music she uses for her free skate is "'Where Have All the Flowers Gone?,' an anti-war song made famous by the late Marlene Dietrich during World War II." When was that? After she starred in "Gone With the Wind?" (If it didn't happen, maybe it should have. I rather like the image of Marlene Dietrich singing "Where Have All the Flowers Gone?" in a bombed-out Berlin cabaret.)

But what does it matter anyway? The world is getting stranger every day. The Olympics descend into a explosion of flashbulbs, misinformation, and screaming tabloid headlines, reminding me of nothing so much as Vegas in the fifties: showgirls, thugs, cynical reporters! Meanwhile Vegas, ironically, has become a G-rated theme park.

Oh, it's still bizarre. Stephen Drucker in the NEW YORK TIMES recently profiled the new Las Vegas. At the Luxor, shaped like a pyramid (sphinx included free!), he walked into a hotel bar to find a woman in a blonde Cleopatra wig playing "Send in the Clowns" on a harp. Casinos meet Egypt meets Renaissance music meets Sondheim? Shouldn't we have laws forbidding this sort of cultural smorgasbord?

In the larger America, images of ice skaters getting a cold one can have us slavering. Yet in Vegas, nobody blinks an eye at the most outlandish things you can imagine. A casino that features a sea battle in its lagoon six times a day? A hotel shaped like a giant lion? Big deal.

Vegas even offers gambling lite: video arcades for the kiddies. No longer the haven for the Rat Pack, the mob, and chain-smoking Americans out for a quick divorce, no more gumsnapping chorines, hookers, and high rollers named Slim, Vegas is now family fun.

Yet if we placed Cleopatra singing Sondheim on ice, we could have another free skate competitor. Would that subject her to vicious character smears and death threats? Vegas gets wholesome; figure skating goes underground. Skaters get an offer they can't refuse, while gamblers skip down a yellow brick road with Toto. What is reality?

Bugsy Siegel must be rolling in his grave. Not to mention Sonja Henie. Remember her? She made "Blowing in the Wind" a hit back in 1956? But don't get me started.

VICE-PRESIDENT 1984

I've never been able to understand exactly what it is that a vice president does. I've seen vice presidents on television, wearing headdresses, eating exotic local foods at social functions, even going to funerals that the President can't attend. The Vice President's job seems to be to display absolute loyalty to the President, making the

Vice President (or Veep) the only person in politics with a constituency of one. Not exactly a dynamic job, sort of like (on the surface of things) a Victorian housewife. But for some reason, men have always held this position.

What a President does is obvious. He (or, someday perhaps, she) provides a focus for the nation, a living metaphor of the inner workings of the government. Face it. We watch the government on TV and one person (the President) is a lot easier to look at on that tiny screen than a bunch of Congressmen standing around in a lump. The President is the government, a walking talking bundle of jokes, homely metaphors, lively comparisons, tortured syntax, tough talk and a positive attitude.

The Veep is a support system for the President's image. The requirements for Veep have traditionally been strong white teeth, pulsating male rhetoric, a firm handshake, a slight but vigorous nodding of the head whenever the Prez makes a telling point, and hearty male laughter whenever the President tells a joke.

My question is: Can a woman laugh at a man's joke? Is a woman capable of that forced, hearty, throw-back-the-headband-roar laugh that America seems to love in a politician?

On the bright side, a woman would be great at fireside chats, a woman Veep could keep the First Lady company on those lonely White House nights. And maybe the President will learn how to bake an apple pie, maybe the White House will become a place where the coffee cups are never empty, the doors are never locked, a place where jokes are never laughed at, unless they're funny.

VR | 1991

A hot new medium, Virtual Reality (VR to insiders), premiered in March at the San Francisco Cyberthon festival. VR lets you seem to move through 3-D electronic environments, using a special glove and goggles. According to reports from the VILLAGE VOICE and ESQUIRE, Virtual Reality is a lot like this reality, only fuzzier. Fuzzy realist Timothy Leary was there to bless the psychedelic technology, and Terence McKenna, the ethnobotanist scholar of natural hallucinogens, whose stirring defense of VR was quoted in ESQUIRE, "Our world is networked together using small mouth noises, which are speech, or symbols for small mouth noises. This is not a wide band of communication, this small mouth-noise thing."

It's not often that you find such an eloquent piece of rhetoric. It proves its own point so elegantly! But the implications are, as we pundits say, disturbing. Does it mean that small mouth noise things will be replaced by non-verbal digital dioramas? Well, last time I checked, a hit of acid still costs under five bucks. Since a VR unit goes for three hundred thousand bucks, I don't think it'll become the drug of choice at Grateful Dead concerts any time soon. The damn thing probably wouldn't even fit in the bus.

Still, there are disturbing signs of the waning of small mouth noises. Pauline Kael, acerbic Athena, goddess of gall, the only movie critic I've ever read who actually seemed to enjoy movies, has retired. Thus endeth an era. Today's movies don't really respond to the small mouth noise thing of critical analysis. For example, when I first saw PRETTY WOMAN, I felt like I'd already seen it ten times. Maybe it was the enthusiastic oblivion to which it consigned any sense: "Julia Roberts is a Hollywood hooker." Why not? "Richard Gere, the richest guy in the world, doesn't know where Beverly Hills is." Sure. "The richest guy in the world drives his own car." Pass the popcorn!

Personally, if I was the richest guy in the world, I'd tell my driver, "Bruno, take me to Beverly Hills, get me a hooker that looks like Julia Roberts, and make it snappy." But there's no movie in that scenario, now is there? Just tiny little mouth noises. Take SILENCE OF THE LAMBS. Wasn't that just a NIGHTMARE ON ELM STREET for grad students? Wasn't Jodie Foster just a hipper version of every other movie gal who barges into the dark room where the monster is? Why doesn't she wait for sanctions to work? Or call for air support?

Speaking of mouth noises we were awash for weeks in appalled reviews of YOU'LL NEVER EAT LUNCH IN THIS TOWN AGAIN, a weasel-eye view of weasels, by former cokehead Julia Phillips. In its pages, apparently, she trashed every person she ever met, in a style designed to drive former friends away from the printed word and into the comforting arms of a VR unit. Will they then go to Betty Ford to kick a VR habit? And what then? Write their own nasty bestsellers? Create a nasty VR scenario about their nasty VR experiences? I don't know. I hardly have a brain cell left to boggle.

As more proof of its fear of prose, Hollywood announced that it would no longer shoot movies in the literary bastion of Manhattan. So what's Woody Allen going to do now? Move to Toronto to deliver his glum one-liners about death? Is this the real reason why the inveterate Pauline Kael retired? Maybe she just couldn't go on making small mouth noises in a world where a movie like NEW JACK CITY can cause riots. Riots! Over a movie with Judd Nelson in it! What is reality?

I know I have a fantasy: I'm the richest guy in the world, see. I'm driving my car down Broadway, and I see a young and sexy Pauline Kael busily ripping the feathers off Kevin Costner's head. Smitten, I shout, "Excuse me, ma'am? How do I get to Carnegie Hall?" She turns and says, "You won't find it in Canada, bub. I know that much." Okay, it's not much of a movie idea, but what do you expect from a pathetic mouth-noise-thing maker like me? Hands-on sex with a hologram of Julia Roberts? I don't think so.

WACO 1993

Before it went up in flames, homeowners seeing that compound in Waco must have felt not just pangs, but surges of envy. After all, the besieged middle class is stuck in Rancho Del Mar Vista Acres, alone with their 1040's and drooping property values, protected only by dinky little "Armed Response" signs on the lawn—and there were the Branch Davidians with their own arsenal! Armed federal agents couldn't even get in, much less thieves. Now *that's* home security.

If David Koresh had any business sense, he'd have phased himself out of the prophecy business and become a developer. He could have employed his church's cult status and bunker mentality to promote the compound as the ultimate gated community. (He wouldn't even have had to change the name of his group. Branch Davidian sounds like a plausible name for a real estate firm: "Rancho Apocalypse Condos from 300,000! Call David Koresh at Branch Davidian!")

There were disadvantages, certainly. In order to live there, I gather you had to surrender your will to an evil messiah. Most successful housing developments don't have evil messiahs. On the other hand, many housing developments no longer have a tax base to maintain schools, sewers, garbage disposal, or a police force. Maybe submission to the Antichrist is a necessary evil if you're in the market for a safe, secure, affordable starter home.

At Rancho Apocalypse, there's no need for overweight security guards, not when your community has its own machine gun. Except for maintenance and ammunition, a machine gun is a one-time expense. You'd have to fire it yourself, but this needn't be perceived as a cumbersome chore. Occupants could see it as community service, like membership in an old-fashioned volunteer fire brigade.

A cluster of condos bristling with weaponry is your guarantee that solicitors of every stripe will steer clear of Rancho Apocalypse. Rancho Apocalypse even has its own satellite dish, so you can fire on cable installers at will. Fun! True, armed rival sects may invade from time to time, but this must be put it in perspective. If you live in a trailer park you put up with tornados, don't you? If you live in a Manhattan co-op you must step over the homeless, undo fourteen locks to enter a postage stamp-sized cockroach infested hovel, and then bribe the Mafia just to get your toilet fixed, no? All in all, occasional firefights with rival cults is a small price to pay for a luxurious millennial lifestyle.

For those who enjoy shopping by phone, admittedly, it will be difficult to lure UPS to your door, unless a demilitarized package delivery zone can be mutually agreed upon. Even this inconvenience can work to your advantage. All you need is a zoning permit and a municipal tax break to break ground for the Four Horsemen Mall. A few well-placed threats can work wonders with an intransigent bureau-cracy—from groundbreaking to one-stop shopping convenience be-hind barbed wire and substandard concrete could take as little as six months.

Obviously, Koresh and his followers blew it big time. But it's not too late for the rest of us. Only zoning and gun laws stand between us and the community of tomorrow.

WAXING POETIC | 1984

If I have any regrets about my life—and with my personality I'd better— it would probably be the lack of an elegant prose style. If there were any takers I might give my soul to produce a stately flow of prose like Nabokov or John Cheever. I had a prose style in college, but the plain truth is, I needed a prose style then, to cover up my ignorance of the subject at hand. The real world doesn't need a prose style, all the real world wants is copy, material, product.

We've lost a lot over the years. Remember when movies weren't rated? Before we had G, PG, R and X, people actually used to read reviews and make up their own minds about a movie. Now there's just a glance at the ad. If it's G or X, kids won't be caught dead at them. I suppose the ratings system was developed so people wouldn't waste time finding out what a movie's about, but if people are that short of time, they shouldn't waste it at the movies anyway. Movie ratings are just one more stupid system to keep people from thinking. And what happened to Cub Scouts? When I was a kid, we made little sewing baskets for Mom out of popsicle sticks, nowadays kids just want to see Tom Cruise with his shirt off, and Mom's left alone with Dad, wishing Clark Gable was still alive.

There's so much we lose as the years go by. We lose buttons in the morning, socks in the laundry, pens, books and records to our so-called friends, phone numbers in the other pants, we lose our hearts to our lovers, our lovers to our friends, our friends to the changing times. If you own a ten-speed bike, it will get stolen. Same with your car stereo system. We lose our jobs, our faith in humanity, our wallets, and watches, youth, memory and minds. Some things we're glad to lose, like the Mr. Microphone we got for Christmas and the hideous tie. QUINCY's off the air, thank God, and Dial-A-Porn's days are numbered.

But we still have situation comedies with social implications. We still have psychoanalysis, flourescent lights, and quadraplex movie theaters. And whither Greenic stickum caps? Whither the 10-cent comic book? Whither Audie Murphy and Randolph Scott? Whither the girl with red hair who sat in front of me in my seventh grade geography class? My Mom still has the paperweight with the picture of me in my Cub Scout uniform, slightly smeared with plaster of paris, but I never made it past my bear badge. Microwaves are getting bigger. Soon all the telephones will be shaped like cartoon animals. Soon smoking will be a capital crime. And the golden years are gone, gone like the snows of yesteryear. Mm. That's good writing.

WEDDINGS | 1984

I just broke up with what was, by my count, my twenty-third girlfriend. I was low on money, down in spirits, and down on my luck when—in the debris she left behind—I found a wedding invitation.

She had known the couple, not me, but I RSVP'd anyway, much to the chagrin of the bride and groom. I slept through the vows—I hate watching people make a public promise: if you can keep it you're bragging, and if you can't, why tell the world about it? At the reception, however, my stomach full of free food and cheap bar scotch, sitting at a table in the rear of the Howard Johnson's multipurpose room, a large table filled with undesirable relatives and me, I listened to the band and thought back on all the weddings I've seen through the years.

The Polish weddings, where the official drink was Seven & Seven and the only thing to eat was great hunks of bloody roast beef, where stiff-necked old couples danced with bodies as nimble as their faces were frozen; the Jewish wedding, where the glass was smashed under the heel; the hippie wedding, where red balloons flew up, and the dog bit the minister from the Universal Life Church; the Catholic wedding, where the best man had too much to drink and put grape Fizzies in the Holy Water.

In courtrooms, hotels, warehouses, parks, backyards, churches, underwater, in the sky—vows and rings are exchanged, flowers are thrown, bulbs flash. We see the forced good humor of the father of the bride, who fingers his checkbook and hopes the liquor will last long enough for everybody to pass out or go home. We hear the airy platitudes of Kahlil Gibran or the stern sexism of Saint Paul, the tuxedoed musicians who can make the most bizarre musical transitions you can imagine—from ""Havah Nagilah to ""Maniac to Michael Jackson to Prince. They can play anything you request, but every tune will sound like a polka.

As I sat and listened to "I Wanna Be Sedated" by the Ramones (my request), I thought about romance. I remembered girlfriend number three. Like all teenage boys in the '60s, I played the guitar, and like all teenage girls, girlfriend number three had a voice as sweet as Joni Mitchell's. We were invited to a friend's wedding to sing "Bridge Over Troubled Water" and "White Bird." I expected a little money out of the deal—after all, I'd learned two new chords—but the only payment I got was an English Leather grooming set, even though I had a struggling beard at the time and the only soap I used was Dr. Bronner's.

Like the saps we were, girlfriend three and I got high on cheap champagne and made our own wedding plans. A month later of course, she ran off with a bass player named Rocky, I traded my guitar for a battered Underwood typewriter that couldn't make capital letters, and I started on my long career of cultural commentary.

So. Twenty girlfriends later, I watched two families join and dance, watched the dark groom and pale bride kissing under the spinning lights, and I thought of those scary words, "Till Death Do Us Part," and all the weddings ripped by divorce.

Maybe the true wedding dance is done by lawyers to the rhythms of prenuptial agreements, and maybe I'm just married to irony, but I know that love is more than a score in a tennis game. I might be a curmudgeon, but I miss that old guitar and the battered Underwood. I even miss girlfriend three. When my mother told me girlfriend three had married a real estate salesman and moved to Ohio, my cold heart jumped a bit, sure. But to tell you the truth, today I can't remember her name.

WELTANSCHAUUNG 1994

When I was a boy, the other kids dreamed of being firemen or drug dealers.

Me, I dreamed of typing up strong opinions, adding a byline, and slapping them into a newspaper. Now that I've grown to be an actual syndicated columnist, sometimes I have to pinch myself to make sure I'm awake.

Other times, however, I curse my destiny. Topics come along that seem tailor-made for scorn, and I find I have no opinion about them at all. There was a recent story in USA TODAY, for instance, that Alan Dershowitz, gadfly lawyer, was furious with Sean Penn, gadfly actor. He believed Penn stole his hairstyle for the sleazy lawyer he played in CARLITO'S WAY, on purpose.

The concept of haircut plagiarism is ripe for satire! Why couldn't I do it?

Last year, US NEWS AND WORLD REPORT's John Leo called a controversial art show at New York's Whitney Museum, "agitprop." He wrote, "...it's about replacing the center (mainstream America and its values) with the margin (the race and gender ideologues and their allies)." He wrote, "Two large paintings—of Hansel and Gretel, and Santa Claus with small children—are surrounded with smaller ominous pictures of danger and abuse. A guide said chirpily: 'These story boards show that underneath "normal" family life, a lot of sinister things are going on, a lot of child abuse and evil.'"

I won't bring Santa into this, but did John Leo, speaking for the mainstream, think that the Hansel and Gretel story wasn't about child abuse and evil? Were the "race and gender ideologues" so thick they'd just found out it was? Stepmother with cooperation of Dad abandons children in woods, where they're found by witch who plans to eat them? Yoo hoo? Hello in there?

Fortunately, whenever I'm stumped, baffled, or buffaloed, I have help. My life could have taken a wrong turn years ago and I'd have ended up with cronies, cohorts, and co-conspirators; but instead, as a syndicated guy, I have colleagues, esteemed ones.

Always on the lookout for guidance I read an essay the other day by esteemed colleague William Safire, quoting our late (esteemed) colleague, Joseph Alsop, who had told Safire, "Nothing is more contemptible than a columnist without a Weltanschauung."

Did I have this problem? I patted my pockets and roamed my dismal flat. I had a CD player and a word processor, but my Weltanschauung was nowhere to be found. Had I ever had one? If I had had I given it to the Goodwill by mistake? To face the contempt of Joseph Alsop beyond the grave over something as measly as a missing Weltanschauung! The shame.

What the hell is a Weltanschauung anyway? It apparently involves having a strong opinion about Russia. Call me contemptible but I don't have one opinion about Russia. Even if I did, those in the position to do something about Russia will do whatever they do without consulting me. I'll even bet that whatever they do about Russia will have no actual effect on Russia. Does Russia itself have a Weltanschauung? They had a rather nasty one for sixty years or so. Are they now taking a Weltanschauung vacation? I just don't know. What does Strobe Talbott think?

I'm anschauungless on so many important issues. What do I think of Charles Manson suddenly becoming an icon? Guns 'n' Roses' Axl Rose, another icon for those who don't expect too much, included a Manson song on the band's latest CD. As a result, the media expressed concern that turning Manson into a folk hero is sending the "wrong message" to society. Is it?

Manson came to LA in the first place to become a recording artist. If he'd landed a contract back in the sixties, he might have become the next Dylan, embarrassing himself on Grammy ceremonies even as I write, instead of the inhuman hillbilly America fears and/or idolizes today.

And if he makes a buck from a song, so what? He's not profiting from crime, is he? Isn't that a meaningful step towards rehabilitation?

What's he going to spend the money on anyway? A Weltanschauung? He's probably already got one. That's probably what got him in trouble in the first place.

Maybe I should put things in perspective. Ask Boris Yeltsin about Manson, he'd probably just say, "Charlie who?" Maybe that's what a good Weltanschauung is all about.

WHAT I LIKE | 1983

I know you people out there are mighty grateful to me for setting you straight on issues of cultural importance, and I'd like to thank you in turn for all the letters I get.

All right, it's just one letter, a thankful letter from Maryland, who likes my incisive comments but thinks I spend too much time on sarcasm and not enough on constructive criticism. This kind soul is worried about my emotional health and recommends, among other things, that I read the **FINDHORN GARDEN BOOK** and take up horseback riding.

In response, let me say that I enjoy sarcasm, but I don't enjoy horses or gardens. Horses and gardens are large and lumpy, and you have to go outside to appreciate them. I don't go outside until the sun's set, that's the way I am. It's my responsibility to say "No" in a world that says "Yes" to every lame idea that comes down the pike. It's my destiny and my joy to tear down without building up.

But to make you feel better (I feel fine), let me share with you a few of the things I actually like about the modern world.

I like strong beer. I like animated cartoons—not those Oscar-winning political allegories from Hungary, but real cartoons with fuzzy animals trying to kill each other in cute ways. I like computers and answering machines; I like any machine I can turn off. I like novels by Elmore Leonard and Thomas Pynchon. I like good sex if it doesn't last too long. I enjoy playing video games with other people's quarters. Like most Americans, I enjoy being afraid of Cuba. It's a harmless fear that makes America feel better and Cuba too. Cuba gets an inflated sense of national worth from the weight of our paranoia. I like getting large checks in the mail, especially if I've done nothing to earn them. I like the aroma of popcorn and women who like to hear me talk. I like to laugh at dogs. I like to call toll-free numbers and chat with the operators. I like phones that ring instead of chirp, clocks that have a face, Audie Murphy Westerns, duck á l'orange and onion rings, old movies on television, and every tenth video on MTV.

Reggae music, Motown and the songs of Randy Newman are an undiluted pleasure. I like the way rock singers pronounce the word baby—Bay-Buh. Bay-Buh. It never fails to amuse me. These are a few of my favorite things—about all of my favorite things. Make me feel real loose like a long-necked goose and—ooh bay buh—that's what I like.

WHITE LIES | 1983

White lies help us get through life. We hear white lies at work and play, we tell white lies for pleasure and convenience. We use white lies the way a carpenter uses a hammer: Mr. Shoales is on another line. He's away from his desk right now.

Your check's in the mail. Easy to install. Only takes a minute. A child could do it. This won't hurt a bit. Trust me.

Be glad to do it, no problem. Slices, dices, in seconds. Actual mileage may vary. It followed me home, can I keep it? I mailed it a month ago. I'm working late at the office tonight. This is my real phone number. I forgot to turn on the machine.

I think of you as a friend. She's just a friend. I need time, time to think, time to be myself.

White lies are an umbrella in the stormy weather of unrelenting truth:

Beauty is only skin deep. It matches your eyes. She has an interesting personality. You have an interesting face. Your poem is the best poem I've ever read. It was—interesting. I had a wonderful time. It was the best time I've ever had. I'll call you. I love foreign movies. Let's have lunch. We'll do it again sometime.

White lies are Band-Aids on the gaping wound of the morality gap: I didn't know you sang so well. You don't act like a Capricorn. Diamonds are a girl's best friend.

Money isn't everything. You're a gem, a jewel, you're irreplaceable. We don't need a contract. If we don't like it we can quit. We can stop any time. We can take it or leave it. Trust me.

White lies give us an excuse to do what we're going to do anyway: This is just a neighborhood watch. This is just a border patrol. We don't use these weapons, we just have them. This is just national security. These aren't troops, they're advisers. I'm sorry. I didn't mean it.

The end justifies the means. Just little white lies. They help us get through life.

WILLIAM BENNETT | 1991

When I read that William Bennett was being considered to head the NEA, I thought, "Looky here! Another idea from Hell!" My friends, bitter art paupers all, had similar reactions. "Just say no to art," snorted Raoul derisively. "William Bennett, art czar," sniffed Debbie.

My friends are lucky. Twelve years of venom dripped on their heads from the peaks of the public sector have left most art paupers too weak to seethe. They can only mutter at their day jobs, and dream of an America where taxpayers may not support art exactly, but at least don't begrudge the federal pennies (roughly 69 cents per year, per taxpayer) thrown its way.

But William Bennett has dreams of his own. True, he's failed at his duties in the past, but that only makes him the perfect conservative appointee. As Secretary of Education, he flew from school to school sneering at teaching methods and slashing budgets like the Tooth Fairy gone bad. As drug czar, he resigned and declared the drug war won, at just about the same time the American public was sick of hearing about it. Now, as our schools disintegrate and crack makes pretty sparkles in the streets, he turns his basilisk gaze on the arts.

I don't know what he thinks art is, but I'll just bet he knows what he doesn't like. I imagine, if appointed, he'll gather his SWAT team, then raid galleries at random, leading sculptors and performance artists away in cuffs. "Look at this!" he'll say in disgust to the eager media, as he holds up some abstract lump of clay. "A six year old could do better!" And, as we've seen, he won't fund six year olds either. What a jerk!

But I exaggerate. He might not even become art czar. Besides, if President Bush is bent on dismantling the NEA to give himself a few ratings points over Pat Buchanan, it doesn't really matter which incompetent sanctimonious opportunist blowhard he puts in charge. And maybe those who say the state shouldn't fund art are right. Maybe we need *laissez faire* performance artists; maybe rage-filled feminist diatribes should compete in the open marketplace. Maybe art should be less *avant garde*, and more like, say, professional football.

But this would present a paradox. Artists committed to free market capitalism, those artists who by conservative logic truly deserve NEA money, would be bound on principle to refuse it, wouldn't they? Sure they would.

We could try a lottery system. Lucky artless citizens, chosen at random, would get a ten thousand dollar grant and a box of crayons. We could fund cheerleading chants, dinner theatre, decoupage—that would give taxpayers the culture they deserve!

How about the neglected art forms? Let's set up a "light bulb riddle" development fund! How many conservatives does it take to screw in a light bulb? (Three. One to screw the bulb, one to blame liberals for the bulb that burned out, and one to hold a press conference to point out that only a turn to the right can make the bulb work again.) How many liberals does it take to screw in a light bulb? (That number will be determined once the committee has examined the impact of bulb-changing on the environment.)

We could fund limericks!

> There was an appointee named Bennett
> Who held a conservative tenet,
> Which was this: "No on drugs,
> Educators are slugs,
> So are artists—I'm running for senate!"

Come to think of it, we haven't had a state-sponsored sonnet in a long time either—

A BUREAUCRAT IN LOVE

> When, as to the file cabinets I go,
> For forms that make our process viable,
> My supervisor tells me, "Take it slow.
> Action may only leave us liable,"

I pause. I nod. These words strike me as right.
We claim we'll square every caller's whim,
Yet hang fire under harsh fluorescent light.
Complainant's chance for redress? None to slim.
Call the toll-free number from our brochure!
In a maze of optics, there are trapped groans
Of victims, the dissatisfied unsure.
I watch lights blink on untouched touch-tone phones.
My boss crumples a query. Ah, cruel eyes!
This windowless hot room is paradise!

How about it, feds? Make you a deal. If you don't make me fill out a grant application, I'll let you have all of the above for a dollar. If that's not cost effective art, I'll eat Jesse Helms' hat.

X, Y, Z

These letters are currently unavailable.

Index

E

F

I

J

L

M